Red Spirit Woman

Kathleen Medina

Dedication

For the power in all women, and the men that support them.

Contents

Acknowledgements...1

Preface 3

Chapter One 5

Chapter Two..9

Chapter Three...19

Chapter Four..29

Chapter Five...39

Chapter Six...47

Chapter Seven..63

Chapter Eight..75

Chapter Nine..97

Chapter ten...105

Chapter Eleven...119

Chapter twelve...125

Chapter Thirteen...143

Chapter Fourteen 157

Chapter Fifteen 177

Chapter Sixteen 191

Chapter Seventeen 197

Chapter Eighteen 217

Chapter Nineteen 249

Chapter Twenty 263

Chapter Twenty One 277

Chapter Twenty Two 283

Chapter Twenty Three 299

Chapter Twenty Four 311

Chapter Twenty Five 323

Chapter Twenty Six 325

Chapter Twenty Seven 331

Chapter Twenty Eight 343

Epilogue 359

About The Author 361

ACKNOWLEDGEMENTS

I'm so grateful for all the people that have contributed to this novel. This book went through numerous iterations over 13 years.

First and foremost, I thank Cari Cohen for her steadfast support and friendship. Barbara Roth for her tenuous midwifery and early edits to bring the heart of the story out. I thank Andre for our relationship and the years together. Jacqueline Kaplan for her early reads.

I wish to thank Andrea Kayne for her indomitable enthusiasm—especially through the tough times. I thank all the friends and clients who traveled with me to the Magdalene sites.

I thank Margaret Starbird for her pioneering work—a huge inspiration.

Thank you to the amazing editor Chandika Devi and our numerous conversations regarding truth in fiction.

Special thanks to Jessie Jury for the copy edits, masterful work on all the final details, and holding my hand as I entered the world of social media.

Finally, I wish to express my sincerest gratitude to all the people (and spirits!) who kept Magdalene's history alive. Bless you all.

PREFACE

This book is a work of fiction. However, the narrative regarding the history and legacy of Mary Magdalene are based on years researching academic texts, gnostic gospels, Kabbalah, poring through documents and ancient writings, books by reputable authors, and many moons on the ground in Provence, Languedoc, Chartres and Paris. There is a plethora of documentation, art, intact burial sites dating to the first century that some may say ironically, has been preserved within Catholic Churches.

For those interested in a bibliography and more relevant information go to redspiritwoman.com.

CHAPTER ONE

K atie closed her eyes and was lulled into a half sleep by the low roar of the jet engines. She pulled the blanket up to her chin and leaned into the little pillow. She hadn't flown in a few years, and other than a couple of trips to Mexico, she'd never been out of the States. Her slim frame fit easily into the seat and she was able to rest her feet on top of her knapsack, tucked under the seat in front of her. Looking out the little window, Katie watched as the seemingly endless expanse of Atlantic Ocean faded into twilight. She rested her forehead on the glass as the darkening light reflected her big dark eyes and pale skin.

As Katie thought back over the events of the last week, her life felt like a dream or a movie. She was spending nearly the last of her money on an impulsive trip to France to visit an aunt she hadn't seen in ten years. Katie had reached out to Ariel in desperation when the events of the last few months had hit a crescendo and she didn't know where to turn.

She felt like she'd been swimming against the current for a long time. No matter how hard she tried to navigate forward, she found herself going in circles. Lately, it was worse; she had the sensation of being pulled downward, as if she were being sucked into a whirlpool. She'd emailed Ariel after finding some papers that Ariel had given her tucked into a journal.

5

Katie didn't know her father's younger sister that well. She'd only seen her a few times since her dad died. But she'd always felt a connection to her and looked forward to her visits. Ariel was different from anyone else in the family—she was an astrologer and world traveler and had most recently been living in France with a man Katie had not met. In fact, the last time Katie had seen Ariel at all was on her eighteenth birthday. Ariel happened to be in town and one afternoon when Katie's mom was out getting her hair done, she had surprised her niece with an astrological reading of her birth chart.

The two spent a couple of hours sitting at the kitchen counter as Ariel explained the complex diagram. Her birth chart, a large circle divided into twelve sections full of glyphs and crisscrossing lines, was accompanied by pages of written explanations. Katie had recently uncovered the pages folded inside an old journal. She pulled the pages out of her knapsack and unfolded them, the creases worn from having read them so many times, and especially over the past week. "Sun in Scorpio, Moon in Libra, Rising Sign Aries" was written at the top in Ariel's slanted handwriting. Then came the notes:

You need to find a way to be independent and exercise your own will in the world. You have an intrinsic detective's mind and can investigate, seeking out deeper meanings and underlying motives. Be careful of misguided choices in romance—your passionate nature can lead to impulsiveness (both good and bad!). You need to find your own way in the world but will always seek comfort in relationships even when it is to your detriment. You are here to pioneer something important, which will bring you a lot of fulfillment and success.

Katie never told her mother about that afternoon with Ariel or the chart. Her WASPy mother wasn't exactly religious, but she definitely disapproved of Ariel's profession; in fact, it seemed like she was a little bit embarrassed by her mystical, metaphysical sister-in-law. But Katie was always drawn toward Ariel's strange world. She remembered thinking Sunday school teachings were magical stories and would come up with a six-year-old's version of deep theological questions, which Ariel always seemed to enjoy exploring with her.

This was not the case with Katie's mother. Trying to reckon with the idea of how Jesus helped people, she had once asked, "If I were being chased by a lion, would Jesus reach down and pick me up so the lion wouldn't eat me?" Her mother had just rolled her eyes. "These stories are just to learn about right and wrong. They're not fairytales," she explained. Soon after she pulled both Katie and her brother out of Sunday school. From then on, religion meant visiting the local Lutheran church on Christmas and Easter. Katie's dad didn't interfere; his family had been non-practicing Jews, and he stayed quiet on spiritual matters.

As an adult, Katie had lost interest in spiritual exploration, but she sensed some kind of divine providence was at work when Ariel responded to her email right away and invited her to France. Katie bought the ticket right then before she could think about it too much. She decided not to tell her mom until she was at the airport. Even then, she had just sent a quick email before shutting off her phone. She knew her mother wouldn't approve; a last-minute ticket to France certainly wasn't in her budget.

Katie couldn't explain to her mother how desperate she was for guidance. Ariel had always seemed to follow her own spirit and trust herself—both things that Katie didn't know how to do. She knew her mother would first belittle Katie's decision, and then turn around and make it all about herself. She would explain how hard it was to raise two kids alone after their dad died and decry Ariel's inability to understand real responsibility. So instead, Katie made sure her mother didn't find out until or at least couldn't respond until she was somewhere over the Atlantic Ocean.

The flight attendant came by with the cart, and she carefully folded the pages of her birth chart to put them away. Katie was initially reluctant to eat, but when she discovered that food and drinks were actually included on an international flight, she got a glass of red wine and chose the ravioli dinner. She closed the little window shade, and with the dim lights and blanket and pillow, it felt rather cozy. Katie turned on the screen in front of her, and a list of available movies popped up. She sipped the wine and relaxed as she watched her movie, embracing the state of suspended animation that flying between continents affords. It felt like a few hours nestled between the past and the future.

CHAPTER TWO

When the plane landed in Paris, Katie woke with the realization that it was time to abandon her little cocoon. She sleepily followed the flow of passengers through the bright corridors of the airport to customs and immigration. She didn't understand the official's accent at first, so when he asked her how long she'd be in France she replied, "Um, I'm visiting my aunt." He looked at her, smirked, and stamped her passport. Katie followed the symbol for baggage claim and found her oversized duffel on the carousel. She hoisted the duffel onto her back and looked around for a sign indicating the train station. Somehow, she had forgotten the signs would be in French in France and experienced the shuddering sensation of being way outside her comfort zone.

Katie saw the *Toilettes* sign and chose the door with a picture of a dress. "*Femmes*," she read. That was a start; she was a *femme*. Katie squeezed herself and her duffel into a stall. Then, relieved, she went to the sink and splashed some cool water on her face. She ran her fingers through her limp hair and put on some lip gloss. Then she found a vending machine that had bottled water, but when she reached into her wallet, she realized she only had dollars.

Oh my God, she thought, I'm really not in Kansas anymore. She wondered momentarily if she was the most ill-prepared traveler in the airport that day. But she found an ATM and withdrew a couple hundred euros from her credit card. She tried not to think about the dwindling balance and concentrated instead on feeding the five-euro bill into the vending machine. The bottle dropped down along with a two-euro coin. Then she found an information booth. Luckily, the attendant spoke English and instructed her on how to get to the train station.

Katie navigated her way through the internal passageway from the airport to the train station and waited in the central lobby until the information for her train scrolled across the departure screen. She found the track and, after some confusion about the cars and the numbering system, she found where she was supposed to sit. Katie put the duffel on the rack by the sliding door and sank into her window seat.

As the train pulled away from the station, she watched the outskirts of Paris give way to open countryside. Every time they passed by a village, she was amazed at the clusters of stone houses with blue or gray shutters and planter boxes full of colorful geraniums. It was late spring and the trees shone with bright green leaves. Acres of grain whizzed by, and the fields were dotted with red poppies. After years of living in Brooklyn, it looked like a landscape from a fairytale.

She dozed as the train rumbled beneath her. But she couldn't fully rest; she was nervous that she'd miss her stop. Finally the train slowed. "I think this is it," Katie whispered to herself as they approached a good-sized town—another medieval wonder with arched bridges crossing a river. She searched for the name of the town as they pulled into the station, craning her neck to see the approaching sign. *Avignon*. She had a buzzy feeling that was part lack of sleep and part adrenalin. She stood up and walked slowly, holding the back of the seats for support as she made her way to the luggage rack. She pulled down the duffel and rested it in front of her until the train stopped. Then she opened the sliding exit door and moved with the other passengers leaving the train.

Katie followed the crowd as they walked down the platform and into a large open area. There were cafés and small shops. She realized how hungry she was but didn't want to be late. In Ariel's last email, she wrote that her neighbor would be running morning errands in town and would be picking Katie up from the train station. She stepped through the wide glass doors and looked up and down the street as cars drove slowly past. After a few minutes of hopeful glances to passing vehicles, Katie sat down on a stone bench. She looked at all the unbelievably stylish people around her and suddenly felt embarrassed about her faded jeans and flannel shirt—Brooklyn grunge didn't seem right in this setting. Women wore ballet flats and blouses or striped shirts with scarves around their necks. Katie looked down at her worn, clunky motorcycle boots. *My God*, she thought. Even the men were prettier than she was, in their brightly colored slim cut pants and leather shoes.

Katie pulled her cell phone from her knapsack and powered it up. She connected to the train station wifi to check her email. Maybe Ariel had sent her a message. Or maybe she couldn't pick her up for whatever reason. Maybe this was the stupidest thing she'd ever done. Katie could almost hear her mother across the ocean saying, "I told you so."

"*Allo!*" a woman's voice called out.

Katie looked up from her phone. An ancient-looking yellow truck was idling in the pickup lane. A petite middle-aged woman stood on the running board staring at Katie.

"*Kaytee?*" the woman asked.

Katie nodded as she stood up. The woman smiled at her and waved for Katie to come.

"*Je suis désolée*," the woman said.

Katie looked at her with a confused expression. The woman laughed as she pointed at her chest and said, "Sorry to be late. I'm the neighbor of Ariel."

Katie smiled and took a deep breath; she pulled her knapsack over her shoulder and picked up the duffel. The woman came and helped her with the bag. The back of the truck was full of plants, but the woman pushed around some pots and made space.

"*D'accord*," she said. "I am Elise."

Katie smiled. "I'm Katie," she said.

"*Oui*, good," Elise said. "I take you to your aunt."

Katie nodded. "Great," she said. "Thank you . . . ah, *merci*."

Katie got in the passenger side and put her knapsack between her feet. Elise got in and released the hand brake, then put the truck in gear. The windows were down and a fresh breeze came through the cab. Elise looked at Katie.

"I don't speak much English," Elise said.

Katie smiled. "It's okay," she said. "I don't speak any French."

"*C'est bon*, écoutons *de la musique*," Elise said.

Katie caught "*musique*" and gave her a thumbs up.

They left the station and drove through the outskirts of Avignon. Soon they were on a small freeway. It was late morning and the sun was already high in the sky. As they drove farther into the countryside, a range of mountains came into view, dominated by a large conical peak.

"*Les Dentelles,*" Elise said. "*Et Mont Ventoux.*"

Katie nodded.

Soon they exited the highway and came to a series of roundabouts. Katie watched the scenery change to acres of vineyards and orchards. Elise drove along narrow two-lane roads as Katie watched the signs proclaiming "*vin,*" "*fromage,*" and "*produits biologiques.*" She turned toward the foothills of the mountain and they came to a small village, deftly curving through the narrow streets flanked by three story stone buildings, all with large windows and blue/gray shutters. They passed a small plaza with poplar trees and benches surrounded by a couple cafés and bars.

Katie watched the scenery and kept thinking, *I'm in Provence.* She could hardly believe it.

Elise drove out of the village and turned onto an even smaller road, that curved around the foothills and opened to a vista of rolling vineyards and olive orchards. As they followed the winding road along the forested hillside, Elise pointed to a small chapel.

"Healing chapel," Elise said, "Special place." Katie looked up at the ancient looking chapel with a statue of Mother Mary on the roof as the road descended through the sun-dappled trees. Just past the chapel, they turned down a gravel driveway, the truck sputtering, as Elise downshifted and they rolled to a stop in a small parking area. A large stone house sat off to the right and a big barn-like building was to the left. In front of them was a sign that said, "*degustation*/wine tasting" with an arrow pointing to the building. Surrounding the immediate property were row after row of grapevines. Katie had never been to a vineyard before and wondered if they were all so idyllic. She took in the Provencal style house—large and airy, with French doors opening onto the garden and bright magenta bougainvillea growing up the side wall. A large old oak

13

tree stood at the edge of the garden and a small table and chairs had been carefully nestled underneath the canopy of leaves.

Katie opened the door and stepped out of the truck. Two dogs ran over to her, an affable black lab mix and an old tan Chihuahua who circled around her ankles, giving a low guttural growl.

"Okay, Chico, that's enough," Ariel said as she came around the back of the house and the Chihuahua became quiet. As she stepped into Katie's view, she saw that her aunt was much like she remembered—small in stature with a carefree style and loose curls framing her face. Her dark hair had turned salt and pepper, but her tan face was still youthful as she smiled broadly.

"You made it!" Ariel said as she crossed the garden and gave Katie a big hug.

Katie smiled. Elise went to the back of the truck and pulled out Katie's duffel and carried it to where Katie was standing. Elise leaned in and kissed Katie on both cheeks.

"*Profitez bien Kaytee!*" Elise said.

"Of course she's going to have fun," Ariel said. "*Merci beaucoup, Elise! À bientôt!*"

Katie smiled. "Thanks for the ride, Elise!"

It was only when Elise headed back up the driveway that Katie fully realized that she had finally arrived.

"Aunt Ariel, this is your place?" Katie asked. She looked at Ariel in awe.

"Yes," Ariel said. She laughed at Katie's expression. "Not what you were expecting?"

"Not at all," Katie said as she picked up her duffel and followed her aunt. "My mom said you lived in a little farmhouse in the middle of nowhere. She said you barely had cell phone coverage and probably didn't even have electricity."

"Your mother is as full of shit as ever, bless her heart," Ariel said. "She had no problem calling me on my cell early this morning."

Katie stiffened. Ariel saw Katie's reaction and waved her through the open French doors and into the living room. "Don't worry about your mother," Ariel told her, "I think you did the right thing by not telling her you were coming until it was too late for her to try and stop you!"

"Oh, God." Katie cringed. "What did she say?"

Ariel waved her hand dismissively. "The usual. So I told her I invited you out here to make a little promo video of the wine operation. We needed help and thought of you and you had graciously accepted my offer."

Katie sighed in relief as she caught the gleam in her aunt's eyes. She looked out the open doors taking in the stunning landscape that surrounded them. "Ariel, seriously, this is like something out of a movie."

"C'mon," Ariel said. "I'll show you your room and then we can sit outside on the patio. Have you eaten breakfast?"

Katie shook her head. "Nothing since dinner on the plane."

Ariel led Katie through the living room. Katie took in the terracotta floor tiles, two brightly colored sofas, and a comfy looking armchair arranged around a large fireplace. They climbed a narrow staircase that widened into a landing. Ariel opened the door to the right and Katie peered through. It was a cozy room with a steeply sloped ceiling. There was a queen bed against the wall with an antique picture of Madonna and child hanging above it. A chest of drawers sat against the opposite wall, and a small writing desk was situated under the large open window at the far end of the room.

"I thought you'd like this room," Ariel said. "It's the most spacious."

Katie nodded and smiled. "It's great, Aunt Ariel. Thank you."

She didn't know why, but she suddenly felt overwhelmed. She looked down and blinked quickly, feeling herself on the verge of tears. Ariel pretended not to notice and instead turned to go downstairs.

"The bathroom is on the other side of the landing," Ariel called over her shoulder. "I'll be downstairs putting some breakfast together, come down when you're ready." Her voice faded as she disappeared down the stairs.

Katie pulled herself together and sat on the edge of the bed. She leaned down and unzipped the duffel, pulled out her toiletries kit, and set it on the bed. Then she reached in for the padded bag with her video camera. She appreciated her aunt covering for her with the story about making a promo. Actually, she thought, maybe it was something she could offer to do. She reached up and straightened the picture of Madonna and child above the bed. There was something odd about it. The Mary wore a bright red robe and had a kind of mischievous grin that seemed to look right through her.

She rustled through her duffle bag and found a fresh t-shirt to put on. She changed and took her toiletries kit to the bathroom. It was a large bright room that faced the vineyard. Katie looked at herself in the mirror. Her hazel eyes looked darker than usual against her pale face. She ran her hands through her brown hair and pulled it into a ponytail. She was growing her bangs out and they were at the worst length, always hanging in front of her face. Katie pulled the bangs across her forehead in a side part and secured them with a large black bobby pin. She shrugged at her image in the mirror, thinking that bad hair was the least of her concerns.

CHAPTER THREE

She went downstairs to find Ariel humming as she prepared breakfast. Katie stood in the doorway of the kitchen. The sun came through a large window illuminating the yellow plaster walls. The doors opened onto a patio covered by a lattice of flowering vines. The black lab lay sprawled on the warm floor tiles, and Chico lay in his doggie bed, his big eyes following Ariel as she moved around the kitchen.

"It's so pretty here, Aunt Ariel," Katie said.

"It is a kind of paradise," Ariel said in a mock French accent. She put a bowl of fruit salad on a tray next to a basket of croissants. "Go ahead and grab the coffee," Ariel said, pointing to a large French press. "The milk is in that pitcher." Ariel stacked a couple plates and coffee mugs on the tray and carried it out to the wrought iron table under the latticework.

They sat down to a late breakfast. Katie took a few sips of the strong coffee and looked out over the grassy hillside that led to a swimming pool.

"I'm so curious how you ended up here," Katie gestured around her.

"Oh, that's a long story... Basically, my research on Mary Magdalene led me to France." Ariel said.

"Mary Magdalene?" Katie asked. "From the Bible? What does she have to do with France?"

"A lot, actually. She lived here for thirty years, wrote a gospel and inspired a movement that, if fully understood, could change history," Ariel said.

"Seriously?" Katie asked.

Ariel nodded, her face taut in frustration. "It's a project that really has me by the balls, so to speak. But I did not invite my niece for a visit to talk about my stuff. I want to hear about you. It seems like every time I was in New York over the years, I missed you."

Katie thought back on the few instances when she knew Ariel was traveling through, but she was always busy with school or working nights. And her mom usually waited until the last minute to tell Katie that her aunt was in town.

"But your mother keeps me up to date about you and your brother," Ariel said. Her tone was casual, but she was watching Katie closely. "He seems to be doing well," Ariel said. "I wasn't surprised he went into banking," Ariel said with a sly glance. "I recall he had a penchant for making high-interest loans when he was a kid."

Katie laughed. "He was terrible! If you needed something, he was always trying to make a deal. He would charge me interest to loan me a book!"

"Banker in the making," Ariel said. "He likes Chicago?"

"I think so," Katie said. "We don't talk that often. He's living a glitzy life—model girlfriend, high-rise apartment, makes good money."

Ariel nodded. "Well, I'm glad he's doing well," she said.

Katie turned her coffee mug in her hands.

"What's going on with your work?" Ariel asked. "You finished film school?"

"I finished my master's degree in filmmaking," Katie said. "And I've done some editing work. But I haven't really found the right fit for me."

"It's no small thing to get a degree in filmmaking," Ariel said. She looked at Katie pointedly with her eyebrows raised. "And I bet it wasn't cheap."

"No, it wasn't," Katie said. "I got a partial scholarship and a student loan, which at this rate I'll be paying off until I'm fifty. It was a good program; really fast-paced, and I learned a lot, and my shorts were well received. But since I graduated, I've creatively kind of hit a wall. I haven't had a project move forward yet. I've been waiting tables to make money until I can figure out what to do next."

Ariel nodded. "Your mother told me you split with your husband."

Katie took a deep breath and smiled wanly. "Yeah, it's been a good year."

"Well, you got married really young," Ariel said. "It's hard to know who's right for us when we are still trying to figure out who we are."

Katie nodded her head. "We're still friends, but we were never a real couple. We were more like roommates. I think our relationship helped us both to feel more secure. It's kind of hard to explain, but the last year or so, I felt like nothing in my life was really growing. I felt stuck, and Allen, my ex, *was* stuck. I wanted to leave New York, but he wanted to stay." Katie shrugged.

Ariel took a sip of coffee. "Where is it you wanted to go?"

"At the time, I thought I'd go to New Mexico. It has a good film industry, lots of productions and jobs, and I really like the West. Al and I took several camping trips there. But I didn't feel quite ready to make such a big move on my own, so after we split up, I stayed in Brooklyn and got a studio apartment. And you know, Mom's close by in Connecticut, and I kind of fell for someone at the restaurant I work at." Katie looked up at Ariel, trying to gauge whether she should continue or not. Her mom didn't know anything about her manager, and she didn't want her to find out.

Ariel waited for Katie to continue. "And . . ."

Katie took a deep breath and sat back in her chair. "And honestly, I don't really know what I'm doing, Aunt Ariel."

"Time to drop the 'aunt,'" Ariel smiled.

Katie fidgeted in her chair. She wanted to tell her story and get Ariel's advice but suddenly felt a wave of trepidation. She'd learned not to expose too much about her personal life; when she had done so in the past, others seemed to become uncomfortable. So it had become easier to hold things in. But she'd come all the way to France because something in her had told her to seek out Ariel. That her aunt was someone she could trust and would understand her and probably not judge her.

Ariel seemed to read her thoughts; she leaned forward and looked at Katie intently.

"You know, I've made my living counseling people using astrology, numerology, the tarot, clairvoyance. My clients are mostly women, and I've heard every kind of story you can imagine," Ariel said. "Just so you know, whatever you want to share with me is strictly confidential. You won't get any judgment from me, and I'd be happy to help any way I can."

Katie smiled nervously. She picked up her mug but it was empty.

"While I make us some fresh coffee," Ariel said, standing up, "why don't you tell me about this guy you fell for."

Katie followed her into the kitchen. Katie leaned against the butcher block table while Ariel filled the kettle with water.

"Well, I decided to take a break from the editing job I had," Katie said. "Which, honestly, I hated. Sitting in a dark editing booth all day working on mindless content from a reality TV show wasn't for me. So I got a serving job at this restaurant in my neighborhood. I figured I could make ends meet and have time to focus on my own film projects, find something that really inspired me and that could get funded. The serving job turned out to be kind of fun, a lot of the people I worked with were creative types, too. And then I fell for my manager. He's tall with dark curly hair, and he's funny and good looking in that sexy, black Irish kind of way. Do you know what I mean?" Katie asked. She realized she was talking fast. The caffeine must have kicked in.

Ariel looked up at the ceiling. "Oh yeah, I know *exactly* what you mean," she said. Then she motioned for Katie to carry on.

"Well, he was really sweet and flirtatious. We worked together a lot. I found out he and his wife were separated, but I didn't know the details. A group of us started going out to hear music after work. My husband was never very social, so I was happy to be out of the apartment and, you know, engaging in life again.

"One night I covered a dinner shift for a coworker. After closing, he stayed late and had a few drinks with me. We'd been doing this dance for months. I've probably watched too many rom/coms because I thought we were moving on to the next act."

"And?" Ariel asked when Katie stopped talking.

"Well, we had this amazing night together. The chemistry was off the charts. I went home floating, planning for the next time we'd be together. But for weeks, we'd make plans, then he'd cancel at the last minute. I finally found out from a coworker that he and his wife got back together. He didn't even tell me that was a possibility. We just returned to an awkward professional relationship. Then he cut my hours to part-time."

"When did all this happen?" Ariel asked as she carried the fresh coffee out to the patio.

"Over the last couple of months," Katie said. "The cutting my hours bit happened two weeks ago."

Ariel whistled, "Okay."

They sat back down under the lattice. The chihuahua, Chico, got out of his dog bed, stretched, and then went to stand next to Ariel's chair. She picked him up and put him on her lap.

"Let me see if I've got this straight," Ariel said as she petted Chico's head. "You quit a job you hated—the editing job—got the waitressing job with the intention of working on your own projects. But found yourself taking time to have some fun, got rid of a dullard husband, and had a short affair with an opportunistic Irishman. Is that about right?" Ariel asked.

Katie cocked her head, nodding with a pained expression on her face.

"How old are you now?" Ariel asked.

"Twenty-eight," Katie said. "I'll be twenty-nine next November." She held her breath, bracing herself for what her aunt might say next.

"Perfect," Ariel said, clapping her hands together. "You're right on track. It's your Saturn return!"

Katie looked at her aunt. It wasn't the reaction she was expecting. "Aunt Ariel," Katie said and before she could continue, Ariel coughed. "I mean, *Ariel*," Katie said, "What the hell is a Saturn return?"

"It takes Saturn 29.2 years to orbit the sun. So typically, between the ages of twenty-eight and thirty, people pass through a phase of life called a 'Saturn return.' Saturn returns to the place it was at your birth. And Saturn represents structure, focus, your foundation. Are you in the right place at the right time? Set up to move yourself in the right direction? For a young person, it's the first major check-in to see if you're following your soul's path. If not, you'll know it. If you're on the right track, Saturn will back you up and you'll be able to stabilize and grow. If not, what isn't working will become worse until you change course."

"But that's what I've been trying to do, Ariel," Katie said. "I've been trying to create a foundation for myself—first marrying Allen, then getting my master's so I could get a more secure job. But it hasn't worked. I seem to quit everything I build. Or it quits me."

"You're quitting because it isn't part of your soul's path," Ariel said slowly. "Listen, I understand where you're at and what you've been trying to do. And I think you need to give yourself more credit for how much you've accomplished already. You're much further ahead than I was at your age." Ariel smiled. "You have advanced degrees and a first marriage under your belt and you're not even thirty!"

The way Ariel put it made Katie laugh. Then she looked at Ariel, "I don't want to pry Ariel, but what were you doing when you were my age?"

"Hey, you're not prying," Ariel said. She looked off to the left side, a place people seem to look when thinking about the past. "Hmm. Let's see. When I was twenty-eight, I'd been living in Hawaii for a few years, had become a massage therapist and was really into all things metaphysical. I did tarot and astrology charts for friends, but I wanted to do it for a living; though it was my real passion, I didn't know how to make it happen." Ariel thought for a couple moments, and then a smile crossed her face. "When I hit the exact Saturn return, I had an opportunity to travel to Australia with a friend. It was a brilliant adventure. But for me it was more than a trip; I really felt like I belonged there. I know it's a cliché, but the land called to me. And when I came back home to Hawaii, I couldn't shake the feeling."

"So what did you do?" Katie asked. "You said the Saturn thing pushes you to be on the right track. Was Australia the right track?"

"It was, because the impossible became possible. I wrote a letter to the owner of the guest house in the beach town on the outskirts of Sydney we'd stayed in. I noticed she'd had foreigners working for her. She wrote me back within weeks—this was before email—and offered me a work exchange job. I could have room and board in exchange for cooking and cleaning at the guest house. This bolstered my confidence, so I applied for a long-term visa at the Australian Embassy in Honolulu. I was shocked to receive a four-year visa two days later in the mail! These visas were very hard to come by. Within a month, my plans were set. And right after my twenty-ninth birthday, I left for Australia."

"Seriously? It all came together that fast?" Katie asked. "And did you find a way to do your readings? In Australia?"

Ariel nodded. "I did," she said. "I got my start at a local café owned by an American woman. I set up a sandwich board in front of the café: 'Tarot readings: $10.00 for ten minutes.' The first night I did six readings, which I considered a big success. The second night I did twenty! Within a few months, I had weekly positions at two metaphysical shops, and I was hired a lot for private parties and corporate gigs and media events, and I even did several television spots."

"No shit, Ariel, it started just like that," Katie said as she snapped her fingers.

Ariel looked at Katie and nodded. "Yeah, it was a dream realized. For four years I succeeded, doing the work I loved, had fabulous friends, lived in one of the best cities in the world, and traveled extensively."

Ariel smiled as she relived her past.

Katie loved Ariel's story. It gave her a lift, a sense of magical possibilities. But it was Ariel's story, and *she* had always been magical.

"But Ariel, I'm not like you, I can't just make a big leap like that. I need to do things step by step," Katie said. "I feel like I need to build my base first, find my tribe, find love before I can really launch."

Ariel shook her head. "Katie, it's exactly the opposite. You need to trust your intuition and follow yourself. That's what the Saturn return is trying to help you do. What about your New Mexico idea? That feels right to me. You know, I lived there for a while—the film production scene is really vibrant, my neighbor worked in the industry and she always had a job."

"Really?" Katie asked. She felt a momentary flush of excitement, but it was quickly replaced by fear. This feeling happened when she started to expect or hope for too much. The anxiety would rear up so she'd back down.

Ariel watched Katie's face. "Listen, I've been there. These choices can be really scary," she said. "And they don't often seem rational. Who moves to a foreign country to start a tarot business?" Ariel winked at Katie. "But I'm telling you, sticking to the status quo or playing it safe is often the most dangerous thing we do. And believe me, I haven't always followed my intuition. I've been stuck and scared plenty of times."

Katie held her coffee mug between her hands. She looked at Ariel, who seemed so carefree and at ease. It was hard to believe she would have ever struggled with trusting and acting on her intuition.

"Ariel, why did you leave Australia? It sounds like it was perfect for you," Katie asked.

"Well, I only had a four-year visa, so I had to go. Believe me, I wasn't happy about it," Ariel looked off into the distance. "But I also remember knowing that I needed to return to the States. I didn't know why exactly, but it turned out I needed to come back before the next chapter could unfold. And I sensed that I would meet my man in the States," Ariel said.

"And you did. That's where you met Henri?" Katie asked.

Ariel nodded, laughing a bit. "Eventually yes. But it wasn't a straight line. I had quite the journey of self-discovery first."

"So..." Katie prompted.

"So what?" Ariel asked, smiling mischievously.

"So, what happened when you returned?" Katie said.

Ariel looked off into the distance. "Well, it's a bit of a saga. But maybe there's value in relaying some of that time—if anything it provides a cautionary tale of what happens when we succumb to fear and get stuck."

Katie still found it hard to believe Ariel had ever been stuck.

CHAPTER FOUR

ARIEL

Okay, I think this is a good place to start. After I left Australia, I ended up in Washington State. I'd been gone from the mainland US for ten years—six in Hawaii and four in Australia. I didn't want to return to Hawaii. It was too small and isolated for me after years in Sydney. So I landed in Seattle where my friend Marsha lived with her husband. We'd met in Hawaii and stayed in touch through the years. She knew I was essentially starting over and offered their little studio apartment over the garage until I could get myself organized and figure out what to do next.

I showed up having no idea what was happening in my life; I was at a crossroads, kind of like you are now. So Marsha insisted I see this guy named Thundercloud. She took me to Pike Place Market and we walked through the maze of food stalls and kiosks to a Tibetan shop. The familiar scent of Nag Champa incense filled my senses. In the back corner of the store, surrounded by a sea of books on Tibetan Buddhism, sat Thundercloud, the Native American seer who Marsha swore by.

Thundercloud glanced up at me with his penetrating eyes and nodded toward the empty chair at his table. He handed me a well-worn deck of cards to shuffle. They were divination cards that he'd designed himself using Native American symbolism. As I moved the cards through my hands, I prayed for guidance. I honestly didn't know where to go or what to do next. A big chapter of my life had just come to an end without the next one in sight. I needed direction and, frankly, some inspiration. I set the deck down in front of Thundercloud. He then laid a number of cards out on the table and took a few moments to study them before speaking.

"You're in a place in your life where the main theme is relationship. Maybe you thought you were at this place before, but you weren't. Now you will be learning how to be yourself in an intimate relationship." Thundercloud looked up at me and squinted. "There are two ways this could go. If you trust your intuition, you will go where you can thrive, and you'll meet the one you're ultimately destined for. But this will probably be too big of a jump for you. The second scenario is that you will find someone you're more comfortable with. You'll learn more about yourself and your relationship, but that relationship will reach its end and you'll move on and then meet the right one. It depends on you. You have a strong intuition, so when it tells you where to go, like 'Go to Tucson,' go to Tucson. Don't question things too much or you'll get in your own way. Good luck."

I left feeling much better, thinking maybe that was the reason I found myself back in the US starting over: true love was here. I ended up staying in Seattle for a few months. I worked temp jobs and saved money and bought a Jeep. It was bright red with a soft tan top, it came bare bones, no backseat or air conditioning. I named her Tita, which in Hawaii was slang for a strong, tough girl. I knew it was time to move on. Seattle wasn't right for me, and no amount of late night talks with Marsha poring over a map of the US was going to reveal my future home. I just needed to hit the road and find it.

I packed my few belongings into the Jeep and drove to the East Coast. On the way I stopped at places I'd never been: Yellowstone Park, Wounded Knee, Niagara Falls. Often I would drive at night, listening to music as the landscape seemed to float by. When I arrived in Connecticut, I visited with family—including your dad!—most of whom I hadn't seen in over a decade. It was nice to see everyone, but I couldn't shake the fish-out-of-water feeling. I still believed I could set up my intuitive work and thrive like I'd done in Sydney if I could just find the right *place*. And the only place that I really had any connections was in the Northeast.

So I got a job as a live-in nanny in New York City which covered all my expenses and freed my weekends and some evenings to look for places to do my magic. But I just hit dead-ends. I took some writing courses in the evenings and made a few friends. But soon, a deep restlessness stirred in me and after six months I knew I had to hit the road again. Logic said to stay in the Northeast and keep trying to find my way, but intuition said keep moving. I decided to head south and find some tourist destination on the beach. I figured I could get a job and do readings on the side. I'd never been south of New Jersey, so I packed up the Jeep and headed down the map.

After a day and a half on the road, I stopped at a beach campground in Kitty Hawk, North Carolina. It felt liberating to pitch my tent by the dunes in the fresh salt air after six months in the city. One evening I drove to Jockey's Ridge State Park to watch the sunset and saw signs for a hang-gliding school. I'd always wanted to hang-glide, so I signed up for a class and the next morning had my first flights on the dunes. Two days later I had a job with the hang-gliding company and a rental unit for the summer.

I enjoyed that summer. I didn't worry about how I was going to set up my intuitive business or where my long-term home would be. I stopped mourning my good life back in Sydney and just had fun. I bonded with Dermot, one of the guys I worked with, and started hanging out with him in the evenings. Eventually, it became more than that. I spent easy summer days working outdoors at the flight park helping with the hang-gliding operation and eventually soloed as a hang-glider pilot.

For the first time since I'd been back in the States I felt... at ease. And I didn't want to get back on the road, I wanted a home. So I stayed in North Carolina after the summer hang-gliding season and got a job at the local airport. I worked the evening shift running out on the tarmac to park and fuel airplanes. Things got more serious with Dermot and I moved into his house. We eventually got married in the Smoky Mountains, no ceremony, just the two of us under the winter sky.

In the early days I'd tried to set up and do readings. I'd gotten an opportunity to set up a table at a nearby pub. But I found myself spending more time dealing with drunken men who'd rather try to pick me up than have their cards read. At one point, I found a coffee house open to the idea, but during my first afternoon a woman made a scene claiming I was doing the work of the devil. The owner felt bad but asked me to pack up and leave. So I figured my reading days were over. Maybe it was enough to just have a home, a husband and some normalcy.

And for a couple of years, it worked. Dermot was happy; he was living his dream, hang-gliding on the weekends and running the flight park during the season. He'd found a woman who hang-glided and worked at the airport and was happy to drive the support vehicle for his long-distance flights. And I was. For a while, I almost forgot I'd had a completely different life before—a rather magical, globetrotting life.

Then I started to get depressed. I'd quit flying after a couple of mishaps replaced exhilaration with fear. I guess I could have worked through it, as I'm no stranger to fear, but I just wasn't that interested anymore. I hadn't found any kind of community or friends outside the hang-gliding world, so quitting isolated me even more. During quiet moments at the airport, I began to search online for places where I could offer readings again. One night I stumbled upon Rancho Encantada, this big wellness center in Tucson, Arizona. They had a metaphysical department with people doing tarot, numerology, clairvoyant readings and astrology. They had been open for over thirty years and always had an astrologer on staff.

As I investigated Tucson further, I realized there were a number of large spas and another world class wellness center. I felt an excitement I'd not felt for quite a while. My intuition said, "Bulls eye!" So I printed out pages of information to bring home for Dermot. That's when I remembered Thundercloud's words from several years earlier: "When your intuition tells you 'go to Tucson' go to Tucson!" I'd thought he was just using Tucson as an example! Oh my God, what if it was literal?

It was only then that I remembered what else he had said. He had suggested I had two possibilities with men: finding the right one immediately, or a "comfortable relationship" first. I was pretty sure I knew which one Dermot was. As I drove home, I thought about a way I could pitch going west to Dermot. He'd told me he'd always wanted to go out west to fly the giant thermals over the desert. We could go check it out, just take a trip before the summer season started. I could send out resumes to the various centers and we could see if we liked it there. We were young, we were free, we should be out exploring the possibilities! When I got home from work, I pitched the idea, but it didn't go over well.

We rarely argued in our relationship. But everything came out that night. He told me he had been disappointed in me since I'd stopped flying and become so listless. I told him I was tired of only having my existence validated when it was aligned with him and his life. I argued that I at least wanted to try to do my work again, to find a way to thrive in my own right. He argued that he hadn't coerced me; I had *chosen* to stay there with him in North Carolina. And he was right.

The marriage ended as easily as it had begun. I left with not much more than I'd arrived with two years earlier. All my personal belongings fit in four large Rubbermaid containers. I drove away thinking about everything Thundercloud had said about the "comfortable first relationship."

I made it to Tucson in five days. I had rented a furnished apartment before I left North Carolina, so I was able to move right in. I'd also submitted resumes and had an interview lined up at one of the spas. But it didn't go well. I'd had so much success in Sydney that I assumed I would pick up where I left off, but the manager was clearly not impressed with my presentation. I didn't hear from Rancho Encantada or the other spas either.

I was rapidly running out of savings and living off my credit cards. I looked into renewing my massage license, but it was from Hawaii and wouldn't transfer. I was unable to go back into massage unless I repeated my training and sat for the Arizona state test. I searched for any job I had a remote chance of getting, but the timing was terrible. It was 2009; the economy was in free fall and millions of people were scrambling to find work.

Frantically searching the internet and newspapers for anything, I came across an ad from a truck driving company: "Need drivers. Will pay to train." I thought I could do that. Back in Hawaii I'd put myself through massage school by driving for a shuttle company. So I enrolled in the training program. It had been only four months since I left Dermot and our life in North Carolina. But it felt like another life. I had been sure I was doing the right thing; my intuition had been so clear. But I'd gotten it wrong. Maybe someday I would find my way back to my work. But for now I just focused on what was right before me, consoling myself with the fact that I could look at it as an adventure, I would be a renegade chick on the open road—one who could at least pay her bills.

It was midnight into the second week of my trucking externship. Derek, my trainer, lay asleep behind me as I drove through a mountain pass in southern Utah. He was younger than I expected him to be and, different as we were, we had formed a surprising sort of friendship. After he picked me up from the Greyhound bus station in Las Vegas, we had begun a deep conversation that wove its way through the nearly two weeks we'd been driving together—pausing only when one of us was asleep in the bunks behind our seats. I enjoyed telling him about my life and my past; Derek was interested in all of it. Looking back on it I can see that reliving better days wasn't only a distraction from the exhausting hours in the truck, it also helped me remember more magical times, lifting me out of the recent struggles.

I shifted down through the gears to ride out the descents. I could feel the thirty tons of cargo pushing against me. The empty road unraveled stark in the pale moonlight. I had been struggling to learn the ropes, driving half the night, sleeping in the upper bunk when I could. We drove around the clock, taking turns, stopping only for fuel or to load and unload. I tried to focus just on the road ahead and not think about how I was feeling. If I let myself feel I wouldn't be able to get through the remaining weeks.

I took a deep breath and reached for the radio. Then, a shadow crossed my peripheral vision. I looked up to see two large deer running across the interstate. I panicked and hit the brakes—exactly what we're taught not to do. The trailer fishtailed. Suddenly terrified, I let off the brakes. The first deer made it to the other side but the second stopped right in my path. Time slowed down, the tractor trailer seemed to float, and the deer stared, its eyes penetrating into the cab. I knew I couldn't swerve, otherwise we could flip over. The deer never turned away; our eyes were locked as the forty tons of metal smashed through its body. The horrible impact reverberated as the wheels crushed it. I couldn't breathe. I had a death grip on the wheel, my eyes locked forward.

The impact woke Derek. He came up behind me and put a hand on my shoulder as he sat down in the passenger seat. He rubbed his beard and disheveled hair. "You did the right thing. I know it's horrible," he said groggily. "But you did the right thing." I couldn't take my eyes off the highway, but I nodded slightly. My focus stayed fixed on the road, my heart pumping, barely breathing, trying to ride out the wave of sick emotion.

Derek pointed up ahead. "Look, there's a rest area. Time to take a break."

I nodded and downshifted, taking the exit to the rest area. Letting the engine idle, I turned off the ignition. I grabbed my knapsack, climbed down out of the cab and headed straight for the rest room. I couldn't really feel my body; I seemed to be kind of hovering over my head. I went to the sink and washed my hands, running water over my wrists. I splashed water on my face and through my hair.

I went outside and found a picnic table under some large pine trees. I sat down and pulled some Native Spirit tobacco from a pouch in my knapsack and rolled a smoke. As I lit it, I prayed for help—guidance, direction, anything. I'd tried truck driving out of desperation, but it was all too much. I couldn't keep going but I couldn't see any other options. I felt both trapped and abandoned.

"Why have you abandoned me?" I asked, looking up at the dome of stars overhead.

"Why have you abandoned yourself?" I heard a voice say.

For a moment, I was stunned. I hadn't expected a reply! And didn't know if it was my own intuition or an angel or God, but I was pissed at all of the above.

"What the hell?" I responded. I'd been doing what I thought I *had* to do. I struck out on my own to find my life again. And trusted my intuition—but obviously my inner guidance system is broken. No wonder I can't find work as an intuitive! I sobbed into my sweater, then began crying in earnest. The tears released the fear and frustration that had been trapped in my body for weeks.

All cried out, I looked up at the night sky, something I hadn't seen in days, and felt a momentary sense of spaciousness and clarity. Not only was I on the wrong path, I sensed I was at a critical juncture in my life. My reality was stark and clear like the moonlight on the empty highway. Both my choices were scary: either stay on the wrong path or jump into an abyss of total uncertainty. What could I do back in Tucson? I was out of ideas and money. I thought I'd tried everything. I'd given up even thinking I could make a living doing my intuitive work. The days of great success in Australia, using my gifts and thriving because of that, seemed a distant memory from another life.

I went back to the truck. Derek was dozing in the lower bunk. He sat up sleepily. "Better?" he asked.

I nodded. "Derek, I'm sorry, I need to get off the truck."

He grimaced. As crazy as it sounds, it was company policy to leave a person where they were if they quit the externship. We were being paid for our externships and getting off the truck was breaking the employment contract. But Derek wasn't going to leave me at a rest area in the middle of the night in the mountains of southern Utah. And I wasn't going to drive anymore.

"Okay," he said. "I'll take you to St. George, it's only fifty miles off our route. The company will never know and there must be a Greyhound bus station there."

I pulled out my cell phone and called Greyhound. There wasn't a bus station in St. George but they had a pickup point at a McDonald's in town en route to Las Vegas. As Derek drove, I packed up my stuff from the upper bunk. We arrived at the McDonald's around 1:00 AM. Derek helped me offload my gear. We stood looking at each other awkwardly.

"This isn't because of you, Derek," I said. "Being with you these last couple weeks has been great, but..."

"Look," he interrupted. "I think you're doing the right thing Ariel."

"You do?" I asked.

"Yeah. Hey, are you going to be okay here?" he asked, tilting his head at the deserted McDonald's parking lot.

I nodded, managing a grin.

"Put in a good word for me with the spirits, okay?" Derek said as he turned to walk back to the semi.

I smiled and nodded, suddenly feeling very alone.

CHAPTER FIVE

"Whoa, Ariel," Katie said. "You were a truck driver? That's badass!"

Ariel smiled broadly. "Well, I *almost* was!"

"So what happened? You went back to Tucson?" Katie asked.

Ariel shifted in her chair.

"Yeah, I got to the Las Vegas bus terminal and tried not to panic as I waited for my bus to Tucson. I was living off the dregs of my credit cards; I didn't know how I was going to pay the rent when I got home. As I sat there, I kept getting this image in my mind of the Little Match Girl, scared and alone, not knowing how to navigate a hostile world."

"What do you mean?" Katie was confused by Ariel's reference.

Ariel cocked her head. "You don't know the Little Match Girl story?"

Katie shook her head.

"Ah," Ariel said. "It's an old Hans Christian Andersen story. Strangely, that fairy tale helped me find a way to move forward out of the paralyzing fear I felt."

"Like how?" Katie asked.

"Because I decided to rewrite it," Ariel said. "I'll explain. The original story goes something like this: An impoverished little girl is alone in a village square trying to sell the only commodity she has—her matchsticks. But no one is buying her matches, and it is growing dark and cold in the bitter snow. She walks down an alley to peer inside a house glowing with golden light. Inside is a warm hearth, a table laden with delicious-looking food, a family gathered together. She dreams of joining the happy scene as she stands shivering outside in the frigid night. The little girl lights her matches one by one to eke out a little light and heat. Then her grandmother comes. She embraces the little match girl and together, they depart to a new world. This story has kind of haunted me since I was a little and I first heard it."

"But I thought you said her grandmother finds her and takes care of her," Katie said.

"No, the match girl dies of exposure, alone, unable to reach what she longs for," Ariel said. "Her grandmother was a spirit who came for her after she froze to death. It's a very scary story! Basically saying that the little girl—alone, impoverished, vulnerable—could never survive against such odds. There was a frightening sense of inevitability in her story that made me very uncomfortable sitting on the floor of the Las Vegas bus terminal broke and alone."

"Okay, I get your point," Katie said. "But you said somehow it helped you."

Ariel nodded. "I got this intuition to rewrite the story. It sounds weird but I felt like if I could rewrite the story and create a better ending, I could rewrite my own story. And maybe have a better ending!"

"So how did you change it?" Katie leaned forward in her chair.

"I broke the Little Match Girl's challenge down into steps. The first step would be for the little girl to accept the harsh fact that because no one in the village is buying her matchsticks, and it is getting dark, she needs to do something besides stand in the snow and gaze dreamily into somebody else's warm house. She doesn't have much, but she does have matches, she can start a fire and stay warm. This shift—the little girl realizing what she has, meager as it is, can save her—was instrumental. From that change in perspective I began my alternative version of the tale.

"Before darkness descends and the little girl is too cold to move, she goes into the forest. She collects twigs and branches into a small pile and with one of her matchsticks she lights a campfire. Then she collects larger branches and builds a simple lean-to. She gathers more wood and stacks it to dry by the crackling fire.

"The next morning the girl goes back to the village and sells little bundles of the firewood she has dried. The village people eagerly buy the firewood because they don't like going into the forest themselves. So my girl makes some money to buy food and provisions for herself. She repeats this daily, and soon she has a warm coat and some fleece-lined boots. She begins to experience the world as a safe place that provides for her. She realizes she's not alone in the forest. The wolves watch out for her, the beaver leaves his wood trimmings that help her insulate her shelter. Birds drop off feathers for her bed. The fir trees knit together to create a green canopy protecting her camp.

"The Little Match Girl gains confidence and strength of spirit. She has found what she needs: warmth, shelter, companionship. And one night as she is drinking bark tea and staring into the starry sky, the spirit of her grandmother comes to her. Not to take the little girl to another world, but to show her secrets about this one, teaching her ancient magic that only wise old crones know. With the guidance of her grandmother, she grows into a strong young woman, and her life becomes a wonder exceeding all her wildest hopes and dreams."

"Yeah!" Katie said, clapping. "That is an awesome revision, Ariel. I love it!"

Ariel stood up and took a bow. "Thank you, my dear." She sat back down smiling.

"So what happened when you got back to Tucson?" Katie asked, eager to hear a good ending to Ariel's story.

"To borrow from another fairy tale: when lost in the woods, follow the breadcrumbs, and one step will lead to another. I thought about my revised Little Match Girl story. And every day I asked myself how I could best use my assets. If being an intuitive was my best asset, I would focus on that. I went to the metaphysical bookstore in town. They were hiring for the holiday season and I got the job. It was low-paying, but they would let me do readings on the side. This kept me going and I got through Christmas.

"I kept getting a nagging intuition to drop by Rancho Encantada, the wellness center I had first seen online when I was still in North Carolina. I had sent them an application months before but had never heard back and hadn't followed up. When I went in they told me they'd actually been looking for a numerologist for some months and they'd never received my online application! I left them a resume and got a call back, an interview and was hired by the end of the month."

"What?" Katie asked. "Just like that?"

"Yeah," Ariel said, nodding. "Just like that. I ended up where I was meant to be, I just took a few detours. But my intuition was right all along. If I had just followed up with Rancho Encantada when I arrived in Tucson, I would have had the job in the metaphysical department right away. Numerology wasn't common, and I'd studied and used it for years. So I was able to put a program together quickly. You know, I could have saved myself months of fear and stress. But then again, I wouldn't have learned how to drive a semi," Ariel said with a glint in her eyes.

Katie laughed as she watched her aunt's animated expression. "I guess I still don't get why you seemed to lose your mojo when you came back to the US."

Ariel tilted her head as she considered the question. "When I was overseas, I felt a kind of freedom. It was as if I had risen above the gravity of old fears and doubts and I was able to soar. When I was with Dermot, I was essentially sharing his life and was in a kind of bubble. But it was a temporary respite because I wasn't really living *my* life. In hindsight, and even back then to some degree, I knew I needed to return to face some demons, to change my narrative from the inside out. Otherwise, the old stories would keep running in the background—of feeling abandoned and alone in a harsh world—the Little Match Girl. That was the stark reality I came to while sitting on the floor of the Las Vegas bus terminal! And believe it or not, the simple exercise of rewriting the Little Match Girl story from one of desolation to one of empowerment shifted something in my psyche. Then all I needed to do was follow GPS."

"GPS?" Katie asked. "Did you guys even have GPS then?"

"The original GPS," Ariel winked. "Goddess Positioning System."

Katie laughed,

"Seriously," Ariel said. "It's the ultimate guidance system, and you access it by your intuition."

"C'mon Ariel," Katie said. "If that's true, what happens if you don't follow it?"

"Did you hear my story? It re-routes you!" Ariel said. "Just like the GPS in your phone, it will keep rerouting you until you reach your destination." Ariel smiled and said, "You have arrived," in a robotic tone.

Katie laughed. "Okay, I get the metaphor."

"Katie, it's not a metaphor! Where do you think they got GPS from?" Ariel said, her eyes sparkling.

"C'mon Ariel!" Katie laughed. "You're telling me that there is some kind of universal guidance system that anyone can tap into by using their intuition?"

"That is exactly what I'm telling you," Ariel said, giving Katie an exaggerated haughty look.

"Okay, say that's true. How come nobody knows about it?" Katie asked. "Or uses it?"

Ariel paused before answering Katie's question. "Were you ever taught how to use your intuition? By your parents or in school or by your religion?"

Katie shook her head. "No."

"So if most people, education systems and religions don't teach us how to use our intuition, or that it's even a real natural part of us, how would anyone know they had the app and could connect into the big GPS?"

"They wouldn't," Katie said, getting Ariel's point. "So is this Goddess Positioning System like what's called 'feminine intuition'?"

"Bingo," Ariel said. "And it can be developed, just like any other part of us. We all have the app, we just need to use it."

"So in some way you're saying we have no choice, there is a destination and we'll eventually reach it," Katie said.

"We have free will, so we can go any direction we want. But if we want to follow our spirit's path and not just go around in circles and keep hitting dead ends, it's a good idea to align our will with our intuition," Ariel said.

"Okay," Katie said, "*that* I hear."

"Good," Ariel said, smiling. "I'm thirsty after all that, how about some lemonade—homemade?"

"That sounds good," Katie said. She was lost in thought, feeling a bit scrambled.

Ariel collected their cups and brought the coffee tray back to the kitchen. Katie stood up and stretched. She walked over to the small stone fountain at the edge of the garden. A stream of water came through the stone façade of a lion's mouth into a mosaic-lined basin. Katie cupped her hands into the flow of water and then patted the water on her face. She could hear men's voices and what sounded like a big truck on the other side of the property.

Katie walked back to the patio. Ariel brought out a pitcher of lemonade and set it down on the patio table. She went back into the kitchen for a couple of glasses.

"You know, I was just thinking about my revision. Not only did it help me psychologically to break out of some old fear patterns, it was also prescient. I did meet Grandmother not long after I got my shit together," Ariel said, handing Katie a glass of lemonade.

"Your Grandmother? I thought she died before I was even born," Katie said.

"Not *my* grandmother, *the* Grandmother," Ariel said.

"Okay, you've completely lost me," Katie said.

Ariel waved her hands across her face. "Sorry Katie, I didn't mean to open up a whole other saga. We have two weeks together; we'll save that for another time."

"Yeah, I don't know how much my brain can take in right now. I think the jet lag is hitting me," Katie said. She drank down the whole glass of lemonade. "Wow, Ariel, I really think I need to take a nap."

Katie stood and picked up the half empty jug of lemonade and glasses from the patio table. Ariel followed Katie into the kitchen. "Don't worry about the dishes," Ariel said. "Go upstairs and have a good rest," Ariel said. "If you're not up by dinner time, I'll wake you."

"Thank you, Ariel. For, well, everything," Katie said, stifling another yawn.

"*Mon plaisir*," Ariel said. She nodded toward the stairs. "If you want to take a shower, the towels are in the bathroom closet. And *C* on the shower faucet is for *chaud*—hot. *F* is for *froid*—cold."

Katie walked up the steep terra cotta staircase slowly, her mind swimming with the somewhat bizarre concepts, Goddess Positioning Systems and Little Match Girls. As soon as she got up to her room she flopped diagonally across the bed, pulled the coverlet over her as she fell into a sound sleep.

CHAPTER SIX

Katie woke up feeling groggy; for a moment she wasn't exactly sure where she was. Then it came to her. I'm in Provence! She went to the bathroom and turned on the taps for a shower. It was just getting dark; the twilight cast the rows of vines in purplish tones. She stepped into the shower, letting the warm water wash away the travel, and felt her muscles soften. She felt more relaxed than she had in quite awhile, she thought as she got out of the shower and towel-dried her hair. There was a hotel-style bathrobe hanging on a hook in the door, she slipped into it to go back to her room and find some clothes.

When she stepped out into the darkened corridor, she noticed a light on at the end of the hallway. She realized there were two more guest rooms and another room with light streaming from the door, left ajar. Katie peeked in to find an office. There was a large wooden desk covered with papers facing the window. Along the back wall and the adjacent wall were rows of bookshelves. Katie realized it must be Ariel's office when she spotted two rows with titles all relating to Mary Magdalene. Katie saw what she at first thought was a set of leather-bound encyclopedias, but when looking closer she saw *The Zohar* engraved in each spine.

In the corner was a reading chair with a matching ottoman. On the seat of the chair a book was laying open face down. Katie picked it up so she could read the title, *The Woman with the Alabaster Jar: Mary Magdalen and the Holy Grail*. She thumbed through it. Eventually, Katie felt guilty about looking around Ariel's private space, so she backed out and left the door ajar like she'd found it.

Katie walked back to her room and found her favorite pair of worn jeans and a long-sleeved jersey shirt with a picture of a cat in oversized sunglasses on it. She slipped into her old Ugg boots. As she made her way down the darkened stairs, she heard Ariel's voice. From the one-way conversation she gathered her aunt was talking on the phone.

"No interest, then?" Ariel's voice dropped. "I understand that. They're looking for something or someone who can back it up, yes I've heard all this before."

Katie heard kitchen sounds—the oven door opening and closing, utensils clanking together. The other person on the phone must have been talking because Ariel was quiet for a few minutes. Katie tiptoed right up to the kitchen door. She heard her aunt take a deep breath.

"Okay, that's not a bad idea. You're right, it's a big conference and if I could find a fresh angle, it could get the attention of someone," Ariel said.

It was quiet again.

"That's less than two weeks! But the conference isn't until the fall," Ariel's voice rose excitedly. "Finding more compelling proof by then is basically impossible!"

After a pause, Katie could hear Ariel's voice soften.

"Okay," Ariel groaned. "Listen, it's a good idea, Georgia, and I know you're trying to help. I'm sure when you took me on you didn't think it would be two years and we're still trying."

"No, I won't give up," Ariel said, her voice softened. "Okay, I'll check their website and see what I can do."

Katie heard Ariel set the phone down on the counter.

"Well, boys," Ariel said. "Your mama just got some shitty news, but we're not going to think about that right now. Let's get you your dinner."

Katie heard Ariel open a cupboard, then the sound of kibble being poured into the metal bowls. She waited a few seconds and yawned loudly before walking through the kitchen door.

"Hey, you're up," Ariel said, smiling. "Good timing. I was just going to wake you. Dinner is almost ready."

"Wow, it smells great, Ariel," Katie said. "What did you make?"

"Spinach and ricotta lasagna," Ariel said. She touched the top of the lasagna tentatively. "From the Italian restaurant in the village. I have a whole stash in the freezer for the nights Henri is out. He's the cook in the family."

"Oh, Henri's not joining us?" Katie asked.

"No, he came home earlier hoping to meet you, but I didn't want to wake you up." Ariel turned and looked at Katie. "He's out with Vincent, the winemaker, for the evening. They needed to consult with the expert at his lab. There is some mysterious business going on with this red wine assemblage that Henri is keeping secret."

"Oh, okay," Katie said, not very successfully hiding her disappointment.

"Don't worry, he promised to join us for breakfast tomorrow, so you two will have a chance to meet," Ariel said.

Katie brightened, "Okay, good."

"Here, while I finish getting the salad together, you can set the table." Ariel pointed to the drawer with the silverware. "Napkins are in the drawer below. Since it's just the two of us, I thought we'd eat in here. It's cozier than the dining room."

Ariel placed the salad bowl on the table and then put two squares of the lasagna on plates and brought them over. She grabbed the bottle of wine and set it on the butcher block island next to them. Ariel popped a piece of carrot from the salad into her mouth.

"Get yourself a wine glass; the shelf is right behind you," Ariel said. "Rule number one of the vineyard: know where the wine glasses are!"

Katie smiled and got herself a glass and then poured herself some wine, then topped up Ariel's glass.

"*Santé*," Ariel said as she raised her glass.

"*Santé*," Katie repeated.

Both of them were hungry, and for a few minutes they ate in silence. Then Ariel got up and sliced a few pieces from a baguette on the counter. "Almost forgot the bread," she said. "*Mon Dieu!*"

"And *sacre bleu!*" Katie said.

Ariel laughed.

"I never really knew what that meant," Katie said. "Is it kind of like 'holy cow,'?"

"*Exactement*," Ariel said.

They finished dinner. For a few minutes they each seemed lost in their own thoughts as they digested the meal. Katie reached for the wine and poured a bit more into her glass.

"This is really good, Ariel," Katie said, taking a sip. "I don't know anything about wine, but even I can tell how much better this is than Two-Buck Chuck!"

Ariel sighed. "Ah, I do miss Trader Joe's," she said wistfully.

Katie took another sip of red wine, and then sat back in her chair.

"When I got up earlier, I saw a light on at the end of the hall," Katie said. "That must be your office."

"Yep," Ariel said.

"I have to confess to going in and looking at your bookshelves," Katie said.

Ariel waved a hand dismissively.

"Honestly, I never knew so many books were written about Mary Magdalene," Katie said.

Ariel nodded. "It's true, and they range from the sublime to the ridiculous."

"I looked at the book that was open on your chair," Katie asked. "There were pictures of tarot cards. Are they somehow related to the Magdalene history?"

Ariel nodded. "That author, Margaret Starbird, goes into great detail about the evidence of Mary Magdalene's role in early Christianity and what was known as 'the Grail heresy.' She found this evidence in medieval art, European history, and also the major arcana of the tarot."

"I didn't know tarot had been around that long, I thought it was a more recent, new age thing," Katie said.

"No, the oldest complete tarot deck is from the 14th century, discovered in France. And her thesis is the medieval images on the cards relay the story. It was a way for people to learn and hand down the 'heresy' under the guise of playing a card game. She wasn't coming at this from a metaphysical angle; she was a devout Catholic and scholar with a Master's degree in comparative literature. Her book, *The Woman with the Alabaster Jar*, was the pioneering work on the subject of Mary Magdalene as Jesus' bride and partner."

"This sounds like *Da Vinci Code* stuff," Katie said.

Ariel laughed. "This is *Da Vinci Code* stuff! Dan Brown made those ideas famous, but he certainly didn't invent them. In fact, he credited Margaret's work for the development of some of the ideas that went into his novel. Her book went into second print after *Da Vinci Code* came out, because his work really put Mary Magdalene on the map for many people. It was based on a whole lot of research and many readers went on to search out more information on Mary Magdalene and the gnostic gospels."

Katie had never read the book but she had enjoyed the movie. She vaguely remembered something about Mary Magdalene and some secrets the church was trying to hide, but she was fuzzy on the details. "What's the Grail heresy?" she asked.

"Heresy, in Christian theology, refers to anything that goes against the church's official account of their own history. But as we know, history is always recorded by the winners. There are many versions of each story, and the church isn't going to tell you what the voices they snuffed out were trying to say. So there's all this business about the Holy Grail, right? Some sort of important vessel carrying Jesus' blood, or life force?"

Katie nodded.

"Well, the Grail heresy is part of an alternate story of early Christianity that theorizes that Mary Magdalene *was* the Holy Grail, a vessel that had once held the holy blood of Christ. That she and Jesus had a child that she brought with her to France after Jesus' death and that his royal bloodline continued through the Merovingian monarchs of France."

"Whoa," Katie said slowly. "That's a big claim. Do you agree with it?"

"I'm not exactly sure. I think that Mary Magdalene did carry 'Holy Grail' with her to France. But I'm not talking about a baby; I'm neutral on the topic of whether or not Jesus and Magdalene were married or not—there is evidence to suggest both—and while it's pretty clear that a young girl arrived with Magdalene's party in France, I can't assume her parentage. What I believe, and I've got some pretty strong circumstantial evidence to prove it, is that the grail refers to the secret esoteric teachings that Jesus gave specifically to her. And after his death, she came to France, which was Roman Gaul at the time, and taught these sacred teachings for thirty years. This seeded an alternative, egalitarian Christian movement that somehow survived, despite brutal suppression at many points in history. And these teachings are resurfacing today."

Katie stared at her aunt wide eyed. "Really?"

"Yes, really," Ariel said, nodding. "That's what brought me here."

"You got this history from knowing the tarot?" Katie asked. She couldn't imagine how her aunt would even discover this information. She was also a little skeptical; if any of this were true, wouldn't she have heard about them?

53

"No, I found out about the tarot connection later. Sure, my knowledge of the tarot archetypes, numerology, astrology and all that, helped me understand the symbols and patterns of a larger story. But I first stumbled upon Magdalene history nearly twenty years earlier."

Then Ariel seemed to slip deep in thought as she sipped her wine.

Katie stood up to clear the dishes. She picked up the plates and utensils and brought them to the sink, looking out the window as she turned on the tap and waited for the water to get hot. Ariel came back to the present and pushed her chair back to face her niece.

"It really tested me, uncovering this information. It's still testing me today. And I'm not alone in that; everyone that gets deeply involved with the Magdalene history is tested in some way."

Katie looked at Ariel. "What do you mean tested, like a curse?"

Ariel grimaced. "No, not a curse. But they each have a battle to fight against darkness or loss. Like what Starbird describes in her memoir, *Goddess in the Gospels*. I haven't read it in a long time, but there is a section that is so powerful. I'm going to grab the book. I'll be right back."

Ariel left to go upstairs. Katie finished the dishes, stacking them next to the sink to dry. She wiped her hands on the dish cloth.

Ariel came back with a new burst of energy. "Why don't you pour us some more wine," she said.

Katie smiled and reached for the bottle pouring a bit more in each of their glasses. Ariel held the book up for Katie.

"I like the cover," Katie said, studying the picture of a dark-haired woman holding a chalice. "Is this the Holy Grail?" Katie asked.

Ariel nodded. "The woman and the cup. And the woman and the teachings. This book is about her personal journey. As she followed the clues and delved deeper into the investigation of Mary Magdalene, she found that the information was shaking her very foundation. She was a conservative Catholic, the daughter and wife of military men, and she didn't expect to discover a different narrative. Yet her research kept leading her further and further away from the structures she'd built her life around. She kept finding clues from the oldest known deck of tarot to the gematria in the New Testament."

"What's 'gematria'?" Katie asked.

"It's a type of numerology. In classical Greek, every letter has a number equivalent. In fact, letters were also used as numbers. So words were groupings of numbers. If you add up the letters with their number equivalents, there is symbolic meaning in the sums. Even Pythagoras believed that numbers could reveal the underlying energy that creates matter. 'The universe is built upon the power of numbers,' he said. In the New Testament, which was originally written in ancient Greek, certain words were coded with numeric meaning for those who knew gematria."

Ariel thumbed through the book until she came upon a folded paper tucked into the appendix. She pulled out the chart of the ancient Greek alphabet and the corresponding number combinations. Katie leaned over her shoulder and studied the chart.

Greek Alphabet for Gematria

A	B	G	D	E	digamma	Z	E	Th
A α	B β	Γ γ	Δ δ	E ε	ϝ	Z ζ	H η	Θ θ
1	2	3	4	5	6	7	8	9

I	K	L	M	N	Ks, X	O	P	qoppa
I ι	K κ	Λ λ	M μ	N ν	Ξ ξ	O o	Π π	ϙ
10	20	30	40	50	60	70	80	90

R	S	T	U	Ph, F	Ch	Ps	O	sampi
P ρ	Σ σ	T τ	Υ υ	Φ φ	X χ	Ψ ψ	Ω ω	ϡ
100	200	300	400	500	600	700	800	900
	ς							

"Certain number combinations were thought to be powerful. This system is used in the Hebrew Bible, too, in the Old Testament. Every Hebrew letter is also a number. There are twenty-two letters; 22 is a master number meaning 'builder of form.' When letters are put together to make a word, the sum of these letter/numbers is the numerical representation of that form. And 'coincidently,' there are 22 major arcana or trump cards in tarot."

"Margaret Starbird studied gematria and realized that the number for the Magdalene, in Greek, was 153. That is a significant number in the geometry of the ancient Greeks. It represented the *vesica piscis*, or the *mandorla*."

Ariel reached over and grabbed a piece of notepaper and a pen from the counter. She drew two intersecting circles. She pointed to the almond shape in the center. "That's a *vesica piscis*, Latin for 'the measure of the fish.' It is the feminine inner sanctum, or, ah, the matrix from which life comes."

Katie looked up at Ariel, "You mean it's like, um..."

"Yep," Ariel said, finishing Katie's sentence. "Vulva, pussy, yoni."

Katie's face flushed and she laughed at Ariel's ease with words; she could barely say "vagina" without feeling self-conscious.

Ariel smiled at Katie. "When you can name it, you can claim it."

Katie laughed again and waved her hands in front of her face. "Okay, okay," she said. "You told me you were going to read something from this book."

Ariel quickly thumbed through the dog-eared pages. "What happened is the more she discovered clues of a completely different history of the early church than what she was taught, the more unstable her foundation became, because she realized her spiritual understanding had been built on a framework of ancient cover-ups and misinformation. Information that nearly erased the women and the feminine aspects of deity from history. The ancient practices of gematria, the tarot as well as gnostic gospels that were purposely omitted from the Bible, included stories about Magdalene and women in the early days of Christianity. And she believed that Magdalene was the true partner of Jesus. And the fact that the church omitted that has had a devastating effect on Catholicism. Remove the feminine principles of care, nurture, love, exclude women, you get an imbalance. Now, during the time she was researching all this, the problems in the Catholic Church were coming out: large scale corruption at the Vatican bank, and the horrible sexual abuse of children by priests. Both of those things were happening before, but the general public didn't really know about them."

Ariel scanned a couple pages. "Okay, here it is. She says it better than I can."

"'The solid granite walls of my inner bastion were crumbling. Suddenly it was the dark night. Someone had lied! The 'kingdom' could not come; it was built on a gigantic and fatal flaw. God was wounded. The Grail had been lost, Eros was denied. The passionate woman—the Beloved—had been named Prostitute instead of Bride.'

"'Bleeding spear, bleeding cup; wounded male, wounded female; holy blood, holy grail... The symbols finally overwhelmed me. I was having a nervous breakdown.'"

"Whoa," Katie said.

"It's intense, isn't it?" Ariel said. "But she got her balance and went on to write the pioneering book on Magdalene. There's an authenticity to her life and work that isn't always found regarding this topic. And frankly I find her journey truly heroic."

Ariel kept reading to herself, drawn into the narrative.

"Umm, Ariel," Katie said, after a few moments of silence. "If I want to get a general overview of the Magdalene story, is this the best book to read?"

Ariel put the book down and got up and put the kettle on. "Hmm," she said. "I think the best book for you might be Tau Malachi's." She nodded, feeling more sure of her choice. "It's a more obscure text called *St. Mary Magdalene, the Gnostic Tradition of the Holy Bride*. Malachi created a compilation of the oral history and wisdom sayings passed down through a gnostic sect called the Sophian Tradition, which dates back to Magdalene's time in France." Ariel said. "I found it buried in a pile of used books in Tucson, and it turned out to be quite a find. There is virtually nothing written about her life before Christ. There are no records. This oral tradition was the first and only source I've come across, and there's deep wisdom in the stories. I think you will find it really interesting."

The kettle whistled. Ariel turned off the gas burner.

"How about some verveine tea?" Ariel asked. "It's a natural relaxant."

Katie nodded. "Sounds good." She stretched her arms and let out a big yawn.

"I think tea, book and a cozy bed are just what the doctor ordered," Ariel said.

"That sounds perfect," Katie said, smiling.

Ariel set a little white tea pot, cup and napkin on a small tray. "Here you are," she said as she handed the tray to Katie. "I'll go upstairs and find the book."

"Thanks, Ariel." Katie paused for a moment, looking at the tea tray. She felt an unfamiliar sensation. As she walked up the stairs and into her room, she realized she felt nurtured. Katie set the tray down on the nightstand, pushing the small lamp to one side. She fluffed up the pillows then stripped down to her underwear and t-shirt and got under the duvet. Then Ariel knocked on the partially open door.

"Come on in," Katie said.

Ariel stepped inside and set the book on the duvet next to Katie.

"Thanks Ariel, this looks interesting," Katie said, looking at the cover.

Ariel smiled. "You'll wake me for breakfast if I'm not up?" Katie asked. "I don't want to sleep all day again."

"Sure. I'll make sure you're up so you can meet Henri. Then you and I can make a plan for the day."

Katie smiled. "Sounds good."

Ariel winked as she stepped out of the room and closed the door behind her.

Katie poured herself a cup of tea and took a sip. It was mild with a fresh, herby scent. She picked up the book and studied the cover. A woman dressed in red robes held a small jar. She had a mysterious look in her eyes as she stood in the countryside with a snake at her feet. Katie opened the cover and read a few words. Tau Malachi wrote that his tradition referred to Mary as the red lady. Katie's skin prickled. She pulled up the duvet, the crisp cotton sheets felt cool on her bare legs.

Katie opened the book and was quickly drawn into the strange narrative. There was a description of the young Mary prone to divine visions and dreams of angels speaking to her. A mystical little girl born into a "normal" family, she didn't have anyone to talk to about her visions and learned to keep them to herself. She received a good education, as was the custom of a well-off Jewish family to guarantee her a good marriage match, considered the best option for a young woman at the time. With her beauty and status, her father was able to arrange a marriage to a wealthy Jewish merchant in Babylon. So Mary, her maid, and her dowry traveled by caravan to Babylon.

On the way, though, her caravan was besieged by bandits. The men in her party were killed and the women were raped. The leader took a special fancy to Mary, keeping her to himself until they reached Babylon.

Katie had to read the next part twice and it still didn't make any sense to her.

While Mary was being raped, a kind of deity named Lilith appeared. The book explained that it was part of the common thought at the time to have spirits enter people. Nowadays they would probably be thought of as archetypes or complexes. Lilith was Adam's first wife, whom he'd thrown out of Eden for being too independent, replacing her with Eve. Normally Lilith had no time for the children of Eve, but in Mary she saw something that fascinated her—a special light. And witnessing the evil and violence of the bandits, she empathized with Mary. So Lilith waited until the darkness of night and her spirit entered Mary Magdalene and all Lilith's power and brooding darkness entered with her.

It was both strange and weirdly compelling, Katie thought. Was Lilith some kind of demon? Of course she'd heard of Adam and Eve, but not Lilith.

The story continued to chronicle Mary's time in Babylon and how she went from slave to prostitute. This Lilith helped her to stay strong. She used her beauty and education to control her situation with men and finally attained the means to buy her freedom. Once independent, she began to amass her own wealth, running a brothel and taking in women who had suffered a similar fate.

Mary knew she could never go home; in the culture she was living in, what had happened to her would bring disgrace upon the family. But when word came that her father had died, she decided to make the trip back to Israel. This was the same time that Jesus was traveling around Galilee, gaining a reputation for being a great teacher and healer. When she returned, she met Jesus and they had an instant connection.

When Jesus banished the seven demons from Magdalene, he didn't banish Lilith. He took Mary as she was and in doing so, he helped to redeem Lilith. The history continued to illustrate Mary's healing and spiritual awakening with Jesus. He saw her innate spirit and mystical soul. He saw the woman who was his true companion—a person who could understand the depths of his teachings.

The author went on to explain more about Lilith. He said in the beginning, Eve and Lilith were joined together, making a complete woman, an archetype he called 'the Supernal Woman.' Adam was overwhelmed, so he got rid of Lilith and kept Eve, who—without Lilith—was the prototype of the submissive woman. Lilith was angry and became the classic woman scorned. Eve stuck around to have babies, which became all of humanity. When Eve and Lilith were reunited in Mary Magdalene, the full expression of womanhood was restored in her and she became a 'Supernal Woman'.

The narrative chronicled Magdalene's travel to southern France and her years there as a great spiritual teacher. The author mentioned that because Mary Magdalene was the one to carry the deeper message of Christ, which took hold in France, France was considered the new holy land. Katie's eyes kept closing so she finally put the book down. She turned off the light and lay back onto the pillows. As she drifted off, the strange and disquieting narrative followed her into sleep.

CHAPTER SEVEN

The next morning Ariel leaned against the kitchen counter and waited for the kettle to boil. It was early, but she was restless and finally decided to get up and work on the proposal to present at the conference on the gnostic gospels. She stared out over the vineyard, the rising sun casting a warm yellow glow across the young grape leaves. Her mind was on Mary Magdalene. Talking to Katie had stirred up Ariel's passion for her story and had also unleashed a torrent of old memories. Being a mystic, she believed everything happened for a reason, even though that reason was often hard to understand. The Magdalene story had pulled her in years ago and never let her go.

The kettle whistled. Ariel poured the hot water into the French press. She heated a little ceramic creamer of milk in the microwave and searched for her favorite mug in the cupboard. She put everything onto a tea tray. Chico came into the kitchen and looked at her sleepily.

"Good morning, *bonbon*," Ariel whispered as she leaned down and picked up Chico, giving him a kiss. She put him back down and picked up the tea tray; Chico lapped up some water from his dog bowl. "You want to come upstairs and work with Mommy?" Chico looked up, his eyes wide. He had cataracts and his golden hair had faded, but he was still her pup, with her since the early days in Tucson. Chico followed

Ariel upstairs and to her office. He lay down on the rug in front of her desk and went back to sleep.

Ariel sat down at her desk and poured herself a cup of coffee. She inhaled the earthy scent of the dark roast, poured in some warm milk then took a moment to savor the first sip. The first coffee of the day was always the best. She sat back in the desk chair and took a few minutes to try and collect her thoughts. She always worked best in free hand, so she took a few blank pages of printer paper and then started to write some ideas, but nothing was coming easily. She crumpled the page and tossed it in the basket. Then she thought to write a flow chart; sometimes making diagrams helped organize her thoughts. After another few minutes trying to force some inspiration, she grew frustrated. She needed to come up with a new angle on her research, something that might get the attention of an academic researcher or an academic press.

Ariel swiveled the chair around until she faced the wall of bookcases. She spotted *The Gospel of the Beloved Companion*. It had been a long time since she read it and she was drawn into the introduction. But it made her feel more frustrated instead of inspired. Here was the complete gospel of Mary Magdalene brought from Alexandria Egypt to the Languedoc during the middle part of the first century, only recently translated and published by Jehanne Quillan, a member of the Cathar community who'd had it since the first century. And hardly anybody knew about it!

Ariel put the book down and pulled a box from the bookcase that was full of loose papers and file folders. She quickly flipped through them until she found a red folder, searching her notes until she found what she was looking for. Ariel sat back and studied her drawing of the Tree of Life when she heard some noise downstairs. Henri must be up, she thought. She set the drawing back down on her desk and got up and stretched.

Chico looked up at her. "It's been a long, strange journey, hasn't it, buddy?" Ariel whispered. She took another sip of the now tepid coffee, then picked up the tray and took it with her downstairs.

Ariel was surprised to find Katie in the kitchen instead of Henri. "You're up already?"

"Yeah," Katie said as she let out a big yawn.

"I'll make some fresh coffee," Ariel said. "How did you sleep?"

Katie leaned against the breakfront. "Okay," she said. "I had weird dreams."

"Oh, yeah?" Ariel asked as she filled the kettle.

Before Katie could explain, Henri came through the backdoor and into the kitchen with a bag of fresh croissants. "Oh ho, the ladies are up early!" he exclaimed.

"Yes, my darling," Ariel said.

Henri turned toward Katie. "This must be the *neveu* I hear so much about," Henri said.

"Niece," Ariel corrected him. "Katie this is Henri, and right on time with the croissants, I must say!"

Henri set the bag of pastries down and leaned in to give Katie a kiss on the cheek. "In Provence, *c'est trois*," he said, giving her one more kiss on each cheek.

Katie blushed as she looked at Henri. He exuded masculine charm; his light brown hair was streaked with white and pulled into a little ponytail, his blue eyes smiled as he looked at her. Then Henri went to embrace Ariel. "How's the proposal going?"

"What proposal?" Ariel said. "That's how well it's going." Ariel shook her head, looking forlorn. "And Katie here had weird dreams."

"Yeah, I was reading about this Lilith last night," Katie said.

"Oh, that dark Lilith, she'll give you nightmares," Henri said.

Ariel rolled her eyes as she brought the fresh coffee to the kitchen table. "Not all aspects of the divine feminine are sweetness and light!" she said.

"Yes, *ma chérie*, we can see that," Henri said, winking at Katie.

Ariel smirked as she watched their interaction.

Katie wasn't sure why but there was a slight tension in the air. The three of them sat for a few moments, drinking their coffee and eating the warm pastry. She focused on her coffee cup, as if reading some great message in the swirling milk.

Henri cleared his throat. "The expansion on the cave should be finished by the end of the week. Then we'll be able to do the assemblage of the red wine."

"That's great, darling," Ariel said. "I'm glad it's progressing."

Henri paused then asked, "What do you ladies have planned for the day? Hang out by the pool?"

Ariel grimaced. Katie caught her aunt's expression and quickly said, "I'm not much of a sun-and-pool person."

"Maybe take your niece to the market at Isle sur la Sorgue," Henri suggested.

Katie waited to see her aunt's reaction to that suggestion. But Ariel seemed to be lost in thought.

Katie searched her mind for something to say. It was clear that Ariel was disturbed about her work. She thought about the previous night and how passionate Ariel had been. She looked up at Ariel sitting across the table. "You know what I'd really like to do, if possible, is visit one of these Mary Magdalene sites. Didn't you say she was buried not far from here?"

"Her basilica is about an hour and a half drive from here," Henri said.

"You up for a visit to Magdalene's crypt?" Ariel asked Katie.

"Sure!" Katie said with slightly more enthusiasm than she felt.

Ariel perked up a little.

"Well, if we're driving to St. Maximin we should go to her cavern as well. It's only another forty minutes' drive from the village. And it's magical." Ariel's face brightened.

"Watch out, Katie. My darling loves nothing more than all things Magdalene," Henri said, reaching out to squeeze Ariel's elbow. "Maybe you can ask your muse to give you some help with the proposal."

Ariel nodded, her face lightening. "That's not a bad idea, darling!"

Henri smiled as he stood up. "Okay, ladies. Looks like you have a plan, and I need to get to work. You have a big day. Will you be back for dinner?"

"Ah, if we get out of here in the next hour," Ariel said, looking at the clock on the wall. "Have lunch in the village before going to the cavern—maybe. I'll give you a call when we're leaving La Baume."

"*Bon*. Okay, drive safe," Henri said. He leaned down and gave Ariel a kiss. "*A toute suite* Katie. See you soon."

Katie smiled at Henri and gave a little wave. She was pleased to see Ariel feeling better.

"Little more coffee before we get ready to go?"

"Yes, please," Katie said. "You know, I didn't imagine Henri with a ponytail."

Ariel chuckled. "Yeah, he's gone a little bohemian since we moved here."

Ariel got up to put the kettle on. Katie sat back in the chair and stretched her legs.

"Want to tell me about the dream you had?" Ariel asked as she leaned against the kitchen counter waiting for the water to boil.

"Yeah," Katie said as she tried to recall the details of her strange dream.

"Well, I remember I was in some kind of underground room, like a cellar, and it was really damp. In fact, water was kind of leaking down the walls." Katie said. "I heard a noise behind me; I turned around and there was a woman, she was glowing with an eerie kind of light, not a bright clear light but sort of dark silvery gray. She reached out her hand to touch me and I stepped back against the wall. She was beautiful but creepy. And I didn't want her to touch me. That's when she said something like, 'You may not like me, but you need me.'" Katie looked up at Ariel. "Then I woke up."

"Hmm," Ariel said. "Was she more of a spirit, or did she remind you of someone you know?"

"Definitely spirit-like. And I had the sense she was very powerful." Katie said. "When I woke up, I thought it might be related to the story about Lilith in the book you gave me—like maybe it *was* Lilith."

"With dreams, in general you trust the first feeling you get. And it sounds like a Lilith visitation to me." Ariel said.

"I never knew Adam had a first wife," Katie said. "They don't teach that in Sunday school."

Ariel chuckled.

"Many people haven't heard of Lilith," Ariel said. "She was the primordial woman. Honored as an aspect of the Great Goddess in Babylon and Sumeria. She's mentioned in the Talmud, but as the patriarchal God Yahweh took over, she became associated with Satan and was demonized."

"I'm still not clear why she was kicked out and replaced by Eve," Katie said.

"Well, Adam and Lilith were created to be together. They were different—but equal," Ariel said. "She loved Adam, but she was also independent and adventurous and liked to do her own thing. After a while, Adam began to wish she'd be more attentive to him."

"So I guess it's like, one evening, when Lilith returned home after collecting some wild herbs, Adam confronts her." Ariel stood up and puffed out her chest and spoke in an exaggeratedly low voice. "'You know, Lilith, the Creator made me bigger and stronger than you. The more I think about this, I realize the Creator wants me to be the leader.'"

Ariel moved along the counter and changed her gestures to mimic Lilith. She cocked her head and looked where she had just been standing as Adam.

"'We are both made in the Creator's image, to be equal partners,' Ariel said, adjusting her voice to speak as Lilith, 'you *know* that, Adam.'

Ariel shifted again into Adam, looking about furtively, "Well, I think you're spending too much time in the forest, collecting herbs and I saw you talking to that big serpent the other day."

Ariel adjusted her stance and voice to Lilith. "You've been following me? What's gotten into you lately? Is this why you always want to be *on top*?" Ariel pumped her hips. Katie started laughing.

Ariel came back to the table. "Unfortunately, he continued to try and dominate Lilith, but she wouldn't let him. She grew more and more weary of him and stayed away even more, preferring the company of the wolves and lions. Adam sulked and complained to the Creator that he was lonely and he just wanted someone to share *his* life. The Creator felt sorry for Adam, so he gave him a secret utterance that Adam used to banish Lilith from the garden.

"Now that Lilith was out, the Creator made Eve from Adam's rib, so she would always be connected to him and not so independent. Eve was the submissive helpmate, caring and nurturing and tending to his needs and, over time, the needs of their kids.

"This created an imbalance because now the feminine archetype was split. Mother God was marginalized on the Earth, Lilith was exiled and Eve was missing her power. Adam's actions created disharmony, the garden was thrown into chaos, and it no longer reflected the sacred marriage of Mother/Father God.

"Each woman born from Eve was fractured and under the domination of only masculine power, also called the demiurge until the power of Mother God was restored on Earth. And that is through Lilith, a badass, herb-collecting, serpent-talking feminist!"

"Yeah, I get she was exiled, but it doesn't seem like she's trying to actually help Eve out," Katie said.

"Well, you need to understand that when exiled from the garden, Lilith grew bitter, angry, and jealous. Who was Adam to separate her from what was rightfully hers? As time went on, it's said that Lilith became associated with the devil. She was feared. She taunted the sons of Adam with raw sexuality. She was rumored to kill unborn children in the womb. She was dark, powerful, and unpredictable. But again, that is the patriarchal slant on the independent first wife in the image of the vanquished Mother God—history is written by the winners, as I said before. So they had to get rid of Mother God too, and eventually the stories of Her fell to the shadows of ancient history."

Katie was trying to get her head around what Ariel was saying. "Okay, so what you're telling me is, before Christianity, there was a Mother God."

"Well before Christianity—don't forget Christianity sprang from Judaism, the old Testament is the Jewish Bible." Ariel held up her hand with three fingers extended. "Judaism, Islam, and Christianity are patriarchal religions based on the notion of the Creator as only Father God. But scratch the surface of them all and you find vestiges of an ancient Mother God. In Christianity, particularly Catholicism, she has survived somewhat as Mother Mary."

"So Lilith is an aspect of the Goddess or Mother God too, but one that got lost?" Katie asked.

"Yes, exactly!" Ariel said. "Lilith was exiled from the garden, so she is an archetype of the bride in exile. Like the historic Mary Magdalene, Jesus' closest companion, and maybe his actual bride who received special teachings. She became enlightened but was vilified by the patriarchy. She was also independent. Like Lilith, Mary Magdalene has largely been relegated to the shadows—but she lives on, mysterious and powerful, just waiting for the right moment to re-emerge."

Katie nodded. Her thoughts went back to the connection with Mary Magdalene.

"The gnostic book you gave me said that Jesus saw Lilith, or dark strength, in Mary when he was healing her. But he didn't remove Lilith. It said Mary was a kind of whole woman because she had the light and dark feminine integrated." Katie said. "But that does make it sound like Lilith is some kind of demon and not an aspect of Mother God."

"Only from a certain perspective. If we follow this narrative, it seems to me if Jesus didn't banish Lilith, he must have thought she was valuable, important or necessary. Personally, I would trust his judgment," Ariel said, smiling. "He obviously saw the value of the dark feminine; he wasn't afraid of this aspect. And we know he was very unusual for that time for having many women followers and supporters. He was a first century feminist!"

Ariel took her cell phone out of her pocket and tapped a few keys. She enlarged something then passed her phone to Katie.

"Take a look at this, the picture says it all."

Katie took the phone and looked at the stone sculpture of the tree with Adam and Eve in the garden of Eden. But she noticed instead of a normal serpent tempting Eve, the snake had the head and torso of a beautiful woman.

"Huh," Katie said, not sure what to make of the image.

"In this sculpture, the serpent is Lilith. Lilith is giving Eve *knowledge*, symbolized by the apple, so she can wake up to who she is and restore balance to their relationship and the garden of Eden. I love this idea: that the wisdom and the power of the feminine are meant to be reintegrated. That eating the apple isn't a bad thing, but symbolic of awakening to our full potential, which of course the patriarchy blames for all the evils in the world. Tell you the truth, I'm not even sure Eve has digested the apple yet—I think this may be an ongoing story. Mother God is yet to be restored. It is up to the female to be integrated. She can't wait for Adam to come around to his senses."

Katie looked at her aunt in bewilderment. She wasn't sure about these stories—were they Jewish, Christian, pagan?

"Check this out," Ariel shrunk the image and Katie saw that the scene was carved under a large statue of Mother Mary holding Jesus. "This is from the west façade of Notre Dame de Paris. The most well-known Gothic cathedral in the world. The builders were definitely trying to say something here. I believe they were showing the importance of Lilith, as the serpent—not of evil, but as the ancient most powerful symbol of transformation."

"Wow," Katie said. "They have this Lilith story on Notre Dame?"

"That is just the beginning, my girl!" Ariel said excitedly. She looked at the clock on her phone.

"Oh man, we need to move if we are going to make it to the Magdalene's crypt and have time to hike to her cavern before it closes."

CHAPTER EIGHT

Nothing was just regular life stuff in Ariel's world. As they took the small lanes in her black Peugeot, Ariel would point out a hawk flying overhead and say a message was coming for them. While heading south on the A7 freeway, she pointed out signs on the trucks. The elephant insignia over the truck company logo with its trunk pointed up was a symbol of Lakshmi, a Hindu Goddess of prosperity. She chatted breezily about how signs and symbols were everywhere; the Universe was always guiding and interacting with us, but most people didn't see it. Katie wondered if her aunt was just trying to find meaning where there was none. It seemed the mundane aspects of life were something she just didn't want to accept.

After about an hour and a half on the road, Ariel signaled to exit off the freeway. She pointed ahead and to the right. There stood a great basilica on a mound, rising in the center of a good-sized village.

"There it is," Ariel said. "Mary Magdalene's Basilica, built over her crypt in 1295. It's the largest Gothic church in Provence." They drove around the outskirts of the town and found a parking spot. Katie got out of the car and slung the camera bag that doubled as her purse across her chest. Ariel locked the car and then slipped her arms into the straps of her red leather knapsack.

St. Maximin was a charming village full of stone houses of various pastel colors, all with the ubiquitous wooden shutters. They crossed a small central plaza marked by an obelisk then headed up a narrow cobblestone lane which led to the large open courtyard in front of the basilica.

Ariel stopped, pointing out a large plaque embedded in the center of the courtyard. The star-shaped memorial had etched lettering in the metallic surface which was quite faded. But Ariel translated the meaning from French for Katie.

"This is commemorating the rediscovery of Magdalene's crypt by Charles Anjou II in 1279. He was the Count of Provence amongst other royal titles, including King of Jerusalem. He built this basilica, the convent for the Dominican monks and nuns to care for the basilica, and the adjacent building for the town to use as a government center."

Katie listened and nodded.

"Okay, let's go inside. I'll show you some key points in the church then we'll go down to the crypt, okay?" Ariel asked.

"Sure," Katie said.

They walked into the towering basilica and Ariel led Katie around, pointing out the symbolism in the paintings and sculptures. They approached the choir as midday light streamed in, creating a feeling of lift in the otherwise heavy stone architecture. A sculpture rose up from behind the altar, and mirroring it, an enormous painting covered the whole back wall of the altar. Both the painting and the sculpture showed a reclining Magdalene in the cavern.

Ariel pointed to the intricate reliquary set at the base of the sculpture. "Some of her bones are in there," she whispered. Katie took out her camera and got some shots, managing to capture the light streaming in from above. They walked to the back of the church where there was a reliquary of St. Sidonius' skull. He was described as a close friend of Magdalene's who had also come from Palestine. Under the reliquary was a beautiful painting of Jesus in the tomb after his death surrounded by those close to him. Mary Magdalene was applying oils to his wounds.

"This is an important piece of evidence that points to Jesus and Magdalene as being married. In Jewish tradition, only the wife or mother could prepare the body for burial," Ariel whispered.

Katie looked at Ariel and mouthed, "Ohhh," knowingly.

They walked to the entrance of the crypt. Katie didn't spend a lot of time in churches, but she had to admit she could feel something as they stood at the top of the ancient stone steps that led underground. A middle-aged couple was just leaving as they descended, and for a few moments they had the crypt to themselves. She put her hands on the smooth stone walls, "This is from her time?" Katie whispered.

Ariel nodded.

Katie had never touched something two thousand years old; she was struck by the power of direct contact with history. Inside the crypt there were two large marble sarcophagi flanking the passageway. "Maximin and Sidonius," Ariel whispered, "friends of hers." They walked to the back of the crypt, where another marble sarcophagus lay behind a wall of plexiglass. "That's Magdalene's," Ariel whispered.

Above the sarcophagus and behind a wrought iron grate was a very ornate large gold reliquary with an angel on each side. Inside was a long bone and at the top in a spherical case was a skull.

"That's her head?" Katie asked. It was bizarre looking, like a kind of baroque space helmet.

Ariel nodded.

Katie watched Ariel take a moment in prayer, then both women left the crypt, climbing the steps to the entrance and stopping at a large metal table where candles were burning. Ariel dug in her bag and took out a couple euro coins.

"It's part of the ritual to light a candle and ask Magdalene for assistance," Ariel whispered.

Katie took the small red candle from her aunt. In the church she had gone to growing up, they didn't light candles to make prayers. They also didn't have reliquaries of saints, a practice Katie found rather macabre. What she knew was the no nonsense, White Anglo-Saxon Protestant religion of her mother's family. But she thought the ritual suited the feeling of the place, so she followed Ariel's lead.

Ariel lit her candle from another larger candle and put it in a holder. She closed her eyes and said a prayer. Katie followed suit. She hesitated, not really knowing what to pray for. So she closed her eyes and thought, *Magdalene, if you can hear me, if any of this is real, I could really use some clarity and direction. Ah, thanks, and amen.*

They made their way back to the entrance and Ariel showed Katie the intricate story boards illustrated the history century by century.

"Oh, one more thing," Ariel said, speaking in a low voice now that they were nearly out of the building, "check this out."

There was a gift shop. It was closed for lunch, but they could see through the grate pulled across the doorway. "See that large painting on the back wall," Ariel asked. "What do you see?"

"Well, looks like Jesus in the center, surrounded by men, probably the apostles..."

"Yeah, go ahead and count them, and tell me if you notice anything unusual," Ariel said.

Katie counted left to right, noticing a woman at the right side of the painting. She was youthful, pretty, seemed confident as she held an open book and smiled mischievously.

"Is that..." Katie asked

"Yup, the woman and her gospel." Ariel smiled.

"That is pretty cool, Ariel," Katie said, nodding as she took a couple of pictures through the grate.

"It is. Or, at least, I think so," Ariel replied. Then, she seemed to snap to attention. "How about some lunch?"

"Sounds good," Katie replied, still looking at the interesting painting. She couldn't believe all this was in a Catholic church.

Ariel and Katie sat at an outdoor café looking out across the courtyard to the basilica. They both ordered the salad special and a glass of white wine. At first Katie was shy about ordering wine with lunch, but Ariel explained that in France, it was part of the meal. They raised their glasses.

"*Santé*!" Ariel said.

"*Santé*!" Katie chimed.

When their salads arrived, Katie understood why her aunt had suggested them. The server brought a large plate with crisp butter lettuce placed artfully on the plate accompanied by rolls of prosciutto, little wedges of fresh cheese, narrow asparagus spears, ribbons of carrot and radish and a little ramekin of black olive tapenade. The waitress came back with a basket of fresh sliced baguette.

"Wow, this is gorgeous," Katie said. The plate was picture perfect.

"Salads are amazing in France," Ariel said between bites. "But you need to get them at lunch. Dinner time, they're rarely on the menu."

They ate their lunches companionably. When they were done, Ariel ordered them each a *noisette*, a shot of espresso with a little "nose" of foamed milk on top. Katie sat back in her chair and took in the people walking across the plaza. She saw that people took their time here, savoring their food or coffee, just enjoying being out in town.

As Katie took in the unobstructed view of the basilica, her thoughts turned to Magdalene's crypt.

"Ariel, how can we be sure that is her skull?" Katie asked. "And I don't understand why they have her bones scattered around. Wouldn't they want to keep her body in the sarcophagus?"

"All good questions," Ariel replied. "I'll answer the second one first: relics, especially bones, were sought after by the churches. If you had a relic, you could draw pilgrims and pilgrims brought money. But there's a deeper, more mystical reason the Catholics started doing this. Bones have energy; the person's DNA is captured there, so there is a feeling that being close to a saint's bones can help you. It's actually a rather shamanic belief. In the Jewish faith, people visit the burial sites of say King David or Rachel the matriarch just to be close to the energy. They believe that doing so helps them elevate their consciousness.

"Each saint, or realized being, has a certain personality and is known for certain attributes. The idea is to visit the sites of that saint when you need those attributes in your life. In the Catholic tradition, basilicas are reserved for important saints or figures, and they always have relics of that saint or are built over their tomb."

"Many of the saints get all split up so that more people can spend time with them. There's another bone and part of her forehead in Magdalene's cavern. And another bone in the church at Vezelay, in Burgundy. For some time, there was contention over whether the church in Vezelay was her final resting place, but most evidence points to St. Maximin. I think this place makes more sense since it's the region in which she and her compatriots arrived."

"Ah, what was the second question?" Ariel asked as she paid the bill.

"Umm, her skull," Katie said. "How do they really know if it's hers?"

"Well, of course we can't know for sure. But it was carbon-dated and it's a first century skull of a petite Palestinian woman in her fifties. So it corroborates with the local history passed down since the first century: from the earliest Christians, housed in the first Roman Catholic church built here in the 4th century, through the protection of the Cassianite monks, the Benedictines and then the Dominicans. Now the story is told to the public, as you saw in those large teaching boards near the entrance of the basilica. You'll see more of this story when we get to the cavern. Speaking of, we should head out," Ariel said. "Ready for the next adventure?"

Katie nodded her head. "Ready."

As they made their way back to the car Ariel described the general plan to Katie. "We have about a forty-minute drive to the La Baume Mountains. I'll show you the monastery at the base of the trail. There's a very interesting chapel there and then we'll hike up the mountain to the cavern. Takes about forty-five minutes."

Katie wasn't sure of the cavern's significance but decided to wait and see what unfolded when they arrived. She was happy to just be out in the beautiful Provencal countryside. She looked out over the landscape as they started to drive; a hike sounded great.

They drove in silence. Katie watched the scenery as they wound through the small roads on the outskirts of St. Maximin. The countryside opened up as they passed through vineyards and fields of wheat, then as they began to climb into the mountains, the road narrowed, winding through a forest of deciduous trees. At one point they pulled over at a lookout so Katie could take some photos of the vista. It was quite spectacular to see the rows of mountains and fields spread below.

"Almost there," Ariel said as Katie climbed back into the car.

Katie was glad; her stomach was starting to get queasy with all the tight turns. When they arrived at a T-juncture, they turned right and drove up to a little hamlet. Ariel parked under a tree near a large stone building.

"This is the monastery," Ariel said. She popped the trunk and grabbed two bottles of water. They walked to the entrance of the monastery and crossed through a couple of glass doors. "Pilgrims can stay here," Ariel whispered. She showed Katie the main floor; the walls were flanked with large storyboards illustrating the Magdalene history and the history of the place.

"The dining hall is over there. The monks serve simple food but there is always red, white and rosé wine on the table for dinner," Ariel said, winking.

Katie smiled. "Seriously?"

Ariel led them through another door to a dark empty chapel. Katie could still make out the large murals along the walls of the nave. "Mary

Magdalene?" she asked, pointing to the woman with long flowing red hair pictured in each of the scenes.

Ariel nodded. She walked around the corner and Katie heard a click as overhead lights went on. Katie took photos of the beautiful murals: Mary at the seashore preaching, Mary with what looked like Jesus outside a pagoda in what Katie guessed must be Palestine, Mary standing with an older man in the countryside. And, behind the altar, Mary being lifted by angels from the cavern in the mountainside.

"Come check out the stained glass," Ariel said. Katie looked up to the right. "That's Jesus' family. He's in the center, and that's his mother, Mary, and his father Joseph."

Katie snapped pictures of the richly colored panels.

"And on the left side of the altar, you have Magdalene's family—her brother Lazarus to the right and her sister Martha to the left."

Katie took more photos, then turned to Ariel. "Martha from the Bible is Mary's sister? I never knew that."

"Depends on who you ask, but it's a big part of the Provencal legend. It's repeated at all the interconnected sites that Lazarus, Martha and Mary were a family from Bethany, next to Jerusalem. They arrived here together and all went on to spread Jesus' message. They're all buried in this region and Catholic churches house their remains."

Katie looked at Ariel. "Wow, it's incredible. I mean, this would be a big deal if people knew about it." Katie gestured around her. "I mean in the outside world, beyond Provence."

Ariel nodded. "That's what I think, along with others like Margaret Starbird, who've discovered just how much evidence there is here to support this history."

Katie looked back up at the stained-glass panel. "What's that strange black creature with Martha?"

"It's called the Tarasque, a legendary beast that was preying on the people of the area. I believe it represents some kind of evil person or situation. Martha came up the Rhone River from where they all landed and she 'tamed the beast.' The people revered her for it, changing the name of the town to Tarascon. Martha is buried there in a beautiful church dedicated to her."

"Is the town near here?" Katie asked.

"Yeah, a couple hours from here. Like I said, all these places are within 100 miles of each other. Lazarus went to Marseille, he was the first 'bishop' there, that's why you always see him with a bishop's staff."

Katie looked at Lazarus and studied his staff. It had a kind of curlicue top. "Is he buried nearby too?"

"Yep, he's buried in a tomb under St. Victor Abbey in Marseille. However, his head is across the harbor in another cathedral."

"What is the thing about the skulls?" Katie said.

Ariel laughed.

"The skull represents wisdom," Ariel said. "Lazarus' head is in a beautiful reliquary at the back of the cathedral, but they usually don't even have the lights on back there. But again, the whole story is repeated in storyboards in each church for the public to see. I call it 'hidden in plain sight.' All these places, the history of these people, it's all right here in these old Catholic churches, but most people don't know about it."

Katie nodded, taking in what Ariel was saying. It was as if there were this whole other version of Christianity in France—a very old one, at that—that the rest of the religion were ignoring.

"Ready to hike up to the cavern?" Ariel asked.

"Yeah, I'm excited to see this place," Katie said.

"Good," Ariel smiled. "To me, it's ground zero of her story."

Ariel shut the lights off and the two women left the chapel. As they exited the main entrance, Katie saw a white-robed monk in the reception office look up at her. She smiled but his stern expression didn't change.

"Not very friendly for a pilgrimage place," Katie whispered.

"No," Ariel said, out of the corner of her mouth. "I think women are still not highly regarded in their liturgy, despite the images all over their church."

They walked out into the sunshine. It was starting to get warm so Katie took off her flannel shirt and tied it around her waist, happy she wore a camisole underneath.

"This is our last chance for a toilet," Ariel said, as she entered an open door near the corner of the building. Katie followed, surprised to find it "co-ed" with urinals against the back wall and a couple of stalls for women. Ariel dug into her knapsack and pulled out a pack of tissues.

"Always a good idea to carry your own TP for public toilets in France."

Katie took a couple tissues and gingerly opened a stall door. It wasn't too bad inside, but the door didn't lock so she wedged her camera bag on the floor against it. When she went to rinse her hands at the sink, she found no soap or paper towels but at least running water. She brushed her hands against her jeans. Ariel was already standing outside.

"Okay, ready for action," Katie said, smiling. She was feeling quite energized.

Ariel led them past an outdoor cafe next to the monastery. They crossed a large open meadow and Ariel pointed about midway up the mountain.

"There it is," Ariel said. "You see the stone facades? They look like houses carved right into the mountain."

Katie shielded her eyes against the sunlight. "Oh yeah, I see it," she said. "That isn't what I expected. There are buildings up there?"

"Well, the Dominicans created a space for six or eight of them to live in, and there is a little room for pilgrims to rest, too. Oh, and a little gift shop. You'll see." Ariel said.

When they reached the edge of the forest, there was a T in the trail. "This way is called the *Chemin des canapés*, which means couch in modern French, but back then it probably was the way for coaches. I always take this trail up. The other trail is called *Chemin des rois*, the road of the kings. So we go up in coach and come down in first class!" Ariel said smiling.

Katie laughed. They turned right and followed the trail which gradually started to climb. The forest was beautiful with old trees, ferns and large granite boulders. They fell into an easy rhythm, only stopping for a water break after twenty minutes of steeper terrain. Katie took a long drink.

She had been thinking about what Ariel said—how the Catholic Church seemed to be hiding the story in plain sight. "Ariel, I'm curious about what the Church says about the cavern. I understand the history around the crypt, but what actually happened in this cavern? Why is it a

Catholic pilgrimage site?"

"Well, the official story by the church is Magdalene, after arriving on the boat with the others, came to this cavern and lived for thirty years repenting for her sins. The angels brought her food and Maximin came to give her last rites, then she ascended to heaven."

"Hmm," Katie said. She looked at her aunt, waiting to see her expression.

"There is no need to comment," Ariel said. "Here's what I think—she traveled around Provence and Languedoc teaching and healing which left a powerful legacy of spirituality we can trace through the Cathars and other Gnostic Christians and would come for refuge to the cavern to meditate, maybe commune with Jesus. In the Gallo Roman era it was a cavern for Artemis worship. There's a freshwater spring at the back of the cavern. This is replicated across France: grotto, spring, divine feminine worship. Whether it is Magdalene, Mother Mary, Isis, Artemis, Cybele, etc.

"I'd say the Church, or an inner sanctum within the church wanted to preserve the history of Magdalene and the others here. But they didn't want to give her too much credit or status. So thirty years in a cave repenting was the best they could do!"

Katie shook her head. She was starting to see the magnitude of Magdalene's history and how much the Church controlled the narrative.

They kept walking, slowing their pace as the trail became steeper. At one point they took a sharp right turn onto a cobblestone path which gave way to stairs carved into the rock bed. There was a wooden gate at the top of the steps with a plaque to the left. Ariel pointed to the writing:

MONASTERE

CASSIANITES 415-1079

BENEDICTINES 1079-1295

DOMINICAINS

(FRERES PRECHEURS)

1295-1793

1840-

"The break was because of the French Revolution," Ariel whispered. Then she pointed to a sign of a monk with his finger over his mouth. "We need to be quiet; the monks don't like too much talking up here, unless it's them preaching."

Katie smiled and followed Ariel up the staircase until they reached the courtyard in front of the mouth of the cavern. They turned around to take in the view. The monastery and other buildings below looked tiny. Katie was surprised they'd climbed that high so quickly. She took photos of the facades carved into the rock face, then one of the mouth of the cavern. It was easy to see where cement had augmented the natural curves of the entrance.

Two large wooden doors opened onto the entrance. They walked up a few stairs and stepped inside, leaving sunlight for the dim interior. They stepped around the wooden pews which faced a large stone altar and turned around to look at the richly colored stained-glass panels. Each panel told a chapter of Mary Magdalene's life with Jesus: the anointing, with Martha in Bethany, at the cross. But as Ariel pointed out, there was also unusual symbolism. A red pyramid with seven snakes, a dragon, and in the lower corner of each panel was a strange emblem that Katie thought looked like a Freemason insignia.

"This artist, Pierre Petit, was a Compagnon, the French craftsmen's guild, similar to Freemasons,;" Ariel whispered. "Mary Magdalene is their patron saint, and the modern Compagnons make a yearly pilgrimage to the cavern."

Ariel pulled Katie to the aisle between the pews and pointed to the central stained-glass panel over the entrance. She leaned close to Katie and whispered, "This one says it all, in words and imagery. You have the Magdalene, the jar, the book, the skull—the symbols that are most frequently pictured with her. You also have the crown and a lit candle, symbolizing enlightenment."

Katie took a couple of photographs when she noticed words embedded in the glass. She couldn't make it out. "Is that Latin or French?"

"It's French. It says, 'Until the end of time, we will tell what she did'."

Katie got the chills. She turned to Ariel who stared into the luminous glass. There was such a look of reverence on her face, Katie stepped back to get a photo of Ariel looking up into the light. She then wandered farther back into the interior of the cavern, surprised how big it actually was. She stopped in front of a gilded reliquary embedded in the stone. It looked like a leg bone inside.

Ariel came up behind her and whispered, "I'm going to light a few candles and say some prayers. Have a look around. I'll meet you at the back pew when you're done."

Katie nodded. The damp cool cavern air was chilly, so she untied her shirt from around her waist and put it back on. She watched Ariel buy some long, white, tapered candles and go to the very back of the cavern where there was a large marble sculpture of Magdalene in the clouds.

Katie walked along the periphery and found a staircase carved in the rock. She realized there was another floor to the cavern. She went down, taking care not to slip on the damp stone. When she reached the bottom earthen floor, she noticed a deep pool of water and wondered if that was where the spring was. To the right of the staircase was a door, probably to the monk's house. On the other side, a nicely dressed woman prayed in front of a stone carving of Mary. The woman was murmuring and weeping. Katie didn't want to disturb her so stayed back by the stairs. After a few moments the woman placed a pair of knit baby slippers at the foot of the statue, bowed her head, touched the statue then turned to leave.

Katie felt awkward and gave the woman a little nod, but the distraught woman didn't look up at her. She walked over to the altar in front of the statue and tried to read the plaque, but the only words she caught were, "Lost Innocents" with an outline of a mother and baby next to it. It seemed like some sort of shrine.

A breeze came through the damp open space and blew out the two votive candles that had been burning. Katie got the chills as she looked around her, and the stone walls seemed to close in. She reached out to steady herself and felt a trickle of water on the cold stone. *Oh my God, this is like my dream,* she thought. She felt really uncomfortable and quickly turned back to the staircase, tripping as her foot missed the first step. Katie grabbed the stone banister with both hands to steady herself as she hurried up to the main floor.

She took a deep breath, relieved to be around other people quietly moving around the cavern. Her heart was beating rapidly. She put her hand on her chest to calm herself. Then, she saw Ariel standing by the entrance in front of a statue of an angel. She walked over toward her aunt.

"Who is this?" Katie asked, taking in the very masculine angel, adorned in a suit of armor and plunging a long sword into the neck of a dragon.

"Archangel Michael. He's a protector of the divine feminine." Ariel said. "You often see a statue of him at a shrine dedicated to women."

Katie stared at the statue blankly. She still felt a little strange, but her heartbeat was returning to normal.

Ariel paused, and then asked, "You have a chance to look around?"

Katie nodded.

"Ready to get some spring water and head out?" Ariel asked.

"Do you get the water downstairs?" Katie asked quickly.

"No, the tap is at the back of the cavern," Ariel said. She gave Katie a rather strange look.

"Oh, okay, good," Katie said.

They walked around behind the large altar to a dark area of sloped rock. There was a small spigot that Katie would have never noticed if Ariel hadn't led them there. Ariel crouched down and filled her water bottle. Then held out her hand for Katie's bottle. She filled Katie's and handed it back to her. "Try it," Ariel said. "The water is really good, almost sweet."

Katie took a big drink, and found it was true, the water was sweet. She took another sip. They walked back past the relic and the staircase. Katie touched Ariel's arm and motioned with her head toward the shrine below.

"Ariel, what is that place?"

Ariel looked at her a moment before answering the question. "It's called the Consolation Way. A shrine to the babies never born."

When they got to the entrance, Katie took one last look around. She had to admit, this place had what she could only describe as a powerful spiritual energy. It was both potent and unsettling.

By the time they got to the car at the base of the mountain, both women were tired. They drove the two hours back to the vineyard listening to Ariel's modern Sanskrit music. It was melodic and calming and soon Katie was asleep, her head resting on the makeshift pillow she made with her bag. Ariel seemed content with her own thoughts as she drove along the freeway. They arrived home as the setting sun disappeared behind the foothills. Henri's car was gone. When they went to the kitchen, there was a note—he'd gone to the neighbor's house for dinner.

"We have a cold roast chicken in the fridge," Ariel said. "How does that sound?"

"Sounds good," Katie said. She was more tired than hungry.

"I have some taboule and lentils, too. We can piece together a decent meal."

Katie went upstairs and put her camera bag on the desk, then went to wash up in the guest bathroom.

Ariel gathered the food from the fridge and set out everything on the kitchen table. She put serving spoons in the salads and grabbed a couple plates and forks. Katie came down the stairs.

"Wine tonight for you?" Ariel asked. "I think I'm just going to have some sparkling water with lemon."

"Sparkling water for me, too," Katie said as she sat down. She felt a growing unease and didn't want to fuel her restless emotions with anymore alcohol.

As they ate, Katie could feel Ariel watching her. She kept her gaze on her food. Finally, Ariel sat back. She took a long sip of her water.

"So, what did you think of the Magdalene sites?" Ariel asked.

Katie finished chewing a bite of the roast chicken. She thought about the events of the day. "You know, I found the history of the crypt really interesting. How the monks protected her identity and history. How that Count kind of rediscovered her sarcophagus, then built the basilica and the monastery to protect it."

Ariel nodded.

Katie took a forkful of taboule. "This is really good," she said.

"And the cavern?" Ariel prompted. "Did you feel anything there? It seemed like you had some kind of experience."

Katie finished eating and took a drink of sparkling water to wash away any parsley she might have in her teeth.

"I did feel a kind of energy there. Maybe I can best describe it as a place of power. Also, I really liked the stained glass. I mean with the symbolism and the insignia on the bottom of each—is it the compass and the square? I found all that intriguing," Katie didn't want to talk about the Consolation Way and what she had felt down there, so she moved the conversation back to Ariel and something she'd been wondering about since she'd gotten to France.

"Ariel, I've been wondering. How did you even find out about the cavern and Magdalene's history here? I mean, it's amazing that her legend and the history seems so strong in these places, but nobody knows about it. How did you hear about it?" Katie asked and then settled back to finish her chicken.

"Hmm," Ariel said. "The short answer is, strangely enough, I found out about Mary Magdalene and her cavern when I was in India many years ago."

Katie was surprised. "India?" she asked.

Ariel smiled. "Yup. I met this Buddhist monk while I was in India, and he told me his monastery in France was built near the cavern where Mary Magdalene meditated and they considered her a holy woman, a bodhisattva."

Ariel took a sip of water. "Needless to say, I was pretty surprised to hear about this. And as he told me more about her history and reputation, it just struck something deep inside me. I vowed right then that one day I would find her cavern and discover her story."

"Wow," Katie said, shaking her head. "Some seriously wild stuff happens in your life."

Ariel grinned and pointed up. "GPS!"

"You've almost convinced me," Katie said, laughing. "So you started your research after you found out about the cavern?"

"Oh no, it was maybe ten years later when I started," Ariel said. She pushed back her chair, "How about some tea?"

"Sure," Katie said.

Ariel got up from the table and filled the kettle. She rinsed out a teapot and dropped a couple bags of herbal tea in it. Katie watched her aunt move around the kitchen; her actions were quick and efficient.

"So," Katie began. "Did something happen to bring you back to the Magdalene story after all that time?"

Ariel smiled mysteriously. "Yeah, you could say that."

"Well, are you going to fill me in?" Katie prompted.

Ariel poured the boiling water in the teapot and set it on the table with two mugs.

"When I drank ayahuasca with the Achuar tribe in the Amazon, I met the spirit of the divine feminine, whom they call The Grandmother. And *she* told me to move forward with the Magdalene research."

"What!" Katie exclaimed. "You drank ayahuasca?" Suddenly she didn't know why she was surprised.

"Yes, ma'am," Ariel said, smiling broadly. "And that night in the jungle changed my life."

"Okay," Katie said. "I definitely want to hear this story!"

Ariel smiled. "I'd be happy to tell you the whole story, but another time. We've had a big day and you must be tired. I don't want you to get over-loaded."

But Katie felt recharged. And she wanted to lose herself in Ariel's adventures.

"Actually, I've totally got a second wind." Katie said. "And it's only the middle of the afternoon New York time, so I'm good to go."

Ariel took a sip of tea. "You really want to hear this now?" she asked.

"Yeah!" Katie said.

"Alright, but let's take this into the living room. And I'm going to get something a little stronger to drink." Ariel got up and went to the pantry. She reached up to the top shelf and pulled out a bottle of Jameson's Irish whiskey. "Want a nip?" Ariel asked.

"No, I'm good with the tea," Katie smiled.

Her aunt took a small blue glass from the breakfront and grabbed her tobacco pouch, bringing the Jameson's with her.

"C'mon," Ariel said. "Let's get comfy for some story time."

Katie picked up the teapot and the mugs and followed Ariel into the spacious living room. Ariel lit several candles clustered together on the coffee table, then sat in a stuffed chair next to the fireplace. She rolled a thin cigarette. Katie sat down on a sofa and watched as her aunt lit the cigarette then blew the smoke into the fireplace. She took a sip of whiskey, then settled back and put her feet on the coffee table between them.

"Alright," Ariel said, as she took a puff. "I'm thinking about where to start. How about looking for love."

CHAPTER NINE

ARIEL

My life in Tucson was humming along nicely after a solid year of positive changes. I was enjoying my work and colleagues at Rancho Encantada. My numerology work was attracting interest and I continued to research the topic for lectures. I'd also finally regained financial stability—in fact, I was making more money than I'd ever made in my life! I spent days off hiking in the mountains with Chico. But something stirred inside me; I began to grow restless in my personal life. I longed for love—to experience a deeper connection with someone.

To celebrate the New Year, my friend Devra and I went to a Native American powwow in Tucson. The grounds of the municipal park were dotted with turquoise jewelry stands, arts and crafts vendors, and fry bread kiosks. Tucked among the tents was a full-sized teepee. A homemade sign read "Medicine man, free blessings." Devra and I looked at each other and got in line for a blessing.

I stepped inside the Chiricahua Apache's teepee. A large friendly man greeted me and in a soft melodic voice asked, "What needs healing?"

"I have so many blessings," I told him. "My work is good. I finally have some financial stability. I'm healthy. I feel good in general. But..." I choked up. "I can't seem to find love."

The medicine man held up his hand to quiet me. He began chanting in his native language. He lit a bundle of sage and, using a large feather, smudged me with the smoke. He picked up a bowl-shaped shell filled with herbs and tossed some onto the small fire in the center of the tee-pee. Praying the whole time, the medicine man took something from a leather pouch around his neck, leaned down, and rubbed a viscous substance on the soles of my shoes. He fanned the sage smoke over me again. A thin gray film rose up from my shoes and out the opening of the teepee. He set his feather down. Something caught my eye in the air above us. I looked up and saw a vision of white doves circling up and out of the teepee. I looked back at the medicine man.

He smiled and nodded. "It's a good sign," he said. "You'll find him soon."

"Thank you," I said. I stood up to walk out.

The medicine man pulled a business card from his wallet. "Call me when you do," he said, handing me his card. "I do weddings."

After our blessings by the medicine man, Devra and I stopped to get some fry bread and tea. We found some space at a picnic table and nodded a "hello" to the others seated at the table. A ruggedly handsome man with a mane of white hair watched me as I drank my tea. "Are you enjoying the powwow?" he asked.

I nodded and smiled. He had an amazingly deep, resonant voice.

"I like your pendant. Did you buy it here?" The man nodded toward my copper pendant of the Virgin de Guadalupe, which hung from a string of turquoise beads.

"No, I bought it in Mexico," I replied.

"I love that representation of the divine feminine," he said. "She really speaks to the indigenous people."

I smiled, nodding.

He reached out his hand. "I'm Ed," the man said.

"Ariel," I said, shaking his calloused hand. "This is my friend Devra."

As Ed reached across the table to shake Devra's hand, I noticed two large tattoos on his forearms. One was a dragon, the other a phoenix. I asked him about their symbolism. He explained their meaning and told us he was Cherokee, a priest of a certain lineage called red fire.

"We're from the tribe of Abraham," Devra said. I chuckled. "Ariel here is a Levite."

Ed gave us a funny look. Devra finished her fry bread and said she wanted to go check out the jewelry stand. Devra looked at me knowingly as she said goodbye to Ed. I took a couple bites of my fry bread.

Ed and I talked for a while. He invited me to a full-moon ceremony that his group was holding in a couple of weeks. He said there would be some Cherokee teachings, then a potluck by the campfire. We exchanged phone numbers and Ed drew me a map. I was flattered to be included in a Native American ceremony.

I found Devra looking over a table of turquoise earrings. "What do you think?" she asked, holding a pair up to her face.

"I like those," I said.

"Ed was certainly taken with you," Devra said, smiling.

"Really?" I asked, then realized her meaning. "No, it's not like that. He's a priest, a spiritual teacher."

Devra snorted.

A couple of weeks later I drove an hour into the desert and found the ceremony site just after sunset. There was a bonfire, chants, and some teachings. Afterward we ate. The group was quiet as Ed explained to me that he was the leader of his lineage. He'd been taught practices and carried sacred stories handed down for five thousand years and taught to him by his grandmother. Then Ed asked me about myself. He seemed especially curious about my work as an intuitive. I left late that night feeling rather drained and exhausted.

Ed called me a few days later and asked if I wanted to visit his compound. He wanted to share some teachings with me. So on my next day off, I drove out to his property, which was even further out in the desert than the ceremonial site had been. I was happy to have a Jeep as I navigated the rough terrain. As I approached the end of the road, Ed stepped into a turnaround near a large rock outcropping. He led me through mesquite trees and cacti to a round house made of sun dried clay. There were two women seated at a picnic table drinking coffee. As Ed introduced them, I shook hands with an older woman named Shirley and a woman about my age, Trudi.

Trudi left for work shortly after I arrived. Ed and I sat down at the picnic table under a tarpaulin and Shirley brought out some coffee. Ed rolled a cigarette and then said he had asked me to the compound because he felt that I had the capacity to understand his teachings. He wanted me to study with him and presented me with a golden eagle feather, an offering to indicate my acceptance to his lineage. I was surprised by the gesture. We'd only just met and yet he seemed to have a lot of confidence in me. I was flattered and accepted the feather.

Ed explained the red fire lineage had a tradition that a priest needed to teach seven women, and his female partner, the red woman, needed to teach seven men. As he spoke, I began to wonder what "teach" meant. I didn't say much; I needed time to process what he was saying. He then suggested we go for a hike to the site of some nearby ruins. After hours of sitting at the picnic table, it felt good to walk in the desert. We came upon a circular stone structure without a roof. He suggested I sit inside and meditate while he waited nearby. I looked inside, checked for rattle-snakes, and then sat down and took some deep breaths.

I couldn't get my mind to quiet down, though. I had too many questions. Did Ed really think I could be the woman in the prophecy? This whole situation seemed over the top. There was something very seductive about Ed. He was charming and attentive. I had met him minutes after a medicine man had promised that my love was on his way. Yet something didn't feel right. After a few minutes, I heard Ed shuffling around and realized my mind had wandered for quite a while. I took a couple of breaths and left the ruin.

"Well?" he asked. "Did you pick anything up?"

He meant intuitively, about the ruins. I shook my head. "No, I found it difficult to quiet my mind. And honestly, I was a little nervous about snakes."

"Ahh," he said, looking at me with a searching expression. "You don't like snakes?"

"No, I'm terrified of them!" I said. "I've seen a couple rattlers when I've been hiking but always at a distance, thank God."

"You know, snakes are very powerful medicine. Especially in dreams," Ed said. "If you ever have a dream about a snake and it wants to bite you, let it. The snake is giving you the most potent medicine there is—wisdom."

When we got back Shirley met us with some water. I saw Ed cock his head slightly, signaling to her somehow. He went to the roundhouse as Shirley motioned for me to sit down at the picnic table. Then she handed me a little bundle of dried grasses tied with red yarn. She explained it was a talisman she'd made for protection, something all the women in their lineage carried. Shirley invited me to a sweat lodge ceremony they were planning for the full moon. It was for women only, although Ed would be facilitating. Normally it was the kind of thing I would have jumped at but there was something about the situation that felt off. I told her I would check my schedule when I returned home and thanked her for the invitation.

I drank down the glass of water and stood up to leave. Shirley came over and gave me a hug. As if on cue, Ed emerged from their house and walked me to my Jeep. He leaned in the window, a little too closely. I shifted in my seat. He then proceeded to tell me if I ever got into trouble and needed a place to stay, I could bunk with them. It was such a strange thing to say that I could only smile awkwardly as I put the Jeep into reverse. I glanced up in the rearview mirror, but he was already gone. Driving away, I did not think I'd be coming back; the whole situation felt really creepy.

Ed called a few more times but I always politely declined his invitations. Eventually he stopped and I forgot about the whole episode. I figured he was just a harmless man, living rather eccentrically, who was just more afflicted by his own self-importance than anything else.

Not long after, I was contacted by a woman who received my name through somebody at Rancho Encantada. Sue and a friend came to my apartment for numerology sessions. Afterward we chatted for a few minutes over a cup of tea. Sue had just gotten back from Ecuador where she was a volunteer guide. She led trips twice a year with an organization called Pachamama. They brought small groups to villages in the Andes and also to the Amazon where they could directly experience the indigenous culture's way of life.

I told Sue I was interested in going on the journey and asked her to contact me when the next trip was scheduled. A few weeks later Sue called with the dates of the next trip. It turned out to be perfect timing; the next trip was taking place right over my birthday. I signed on and as part of the preparation phase there were a couple group phone calls designed to inform all the participants about the journey.

During the first call, Sue explained we'd be spending four days in the heart of the Amazon with the Achuar tribe. She explained the Achuar were a dreaming culture. They gathered together in their villages every morning to discuss the messages in their dreams. They also used the plant medicine ayahuasca. The dream state ayahuasca gave them offered information that could help with healing or tell them how to protect themselves and their land. They believed the spirit of the medicine, reverentially known as Grandmother, could help westerners change what they called "their dream of destruction of the Earth." Thus, the organization Pachamama was formed, and started taking groups into the rainforest. Those that came could partake in the medicine if they chose.

At first, I wasn't sure if I'd be taking ayahuasca, but the whole dreaming culture piece was very interesting to me. I've always had very clear dreams and over the years some have turned out to be rather prophetic. By that point in my life, I'd already come to the conclusion that one could access a parallel reality while dreaming.

Sue took questions from the group and then told us that the Achuar often contacted people before they arrived in the dreamtime. She suggested we pay attention to our dreams in the weeks leading up to the trip. And sure enough, I had a whopper of a dream not long after the call—one in which I'd been quite lucid, and which blurred the lines between dreaming and waking life more than I knew was possible.

I was walking through the Amazon rainforest when I came upon a huge red and yellow snake. I turned to run the other direction only to find it now floating in mid-air in front of me. I've had an intense lifelong fear of snakes; in dreams, they've chased me, hiss-talked at me, come out of my legs. I've run from them, chopped their heads off and levitated to get away, but they always returned.

Suddenly I recalled Ed's advice about snake dreams. And realized I was at a crossroads. This was an opportunity to surrender and let the snake bite me.

As the giant serpent moved wavelike in front of me, I held out my left hand. It slowly bit into the fleshy part of the outer palm. It was such a slow deliberate movement it didn't really hurt, but as the venom began to course into my hand and travel up my arm, I grew very uncomfortable. The pressure kept building. I began to squirm. It was taking too long and was starting to feel entirely too real! Just when I didn't think I could take the pressure of the fluid anymore, my consciousness began to rise up until I found myself awake.

CHAPTER TEN

The final weeks leading up to the Ecuador trip seemed to fly by. I was busy with preparations and packing and when the day to leave approached I was very excited. I had a couple of flight connections to reach the capital city, Quito, but the travel went smoothly. It had been a few years since I'd left the United States and I felt an almost indescribable joy when the immigration agent stamped my passport and said, "*Bienvenidos.*"

The group gathered in Quito. The next morning the journey officially started as we boarded a bus with our Ecuadoran guide, Julio. Julio was ruggedly handsome, with thick curly hair tied back in a ponytail and large expressive eyes. He introduced himself then said he was first taking us north to a small village in the Andes near the town of Otavalo. Nestled along a lake between two volcanoes, Otavalo is known for its textiles, weavers, and artisans, and also its healers. Otavalo Lake was believed to contain the spiritual forces of the volcanoes: Imbabura, the Grandfather, and Cotopaxi, the Grandmother. The shamans born in this vicinity were unusually powerful. We were there to see one of them, Don Estaban, a renowned seer.

A short, wiry man with a weathered, intelligent face, Don Esteban stood at the door and greeted each of us as we entered a large dimly lit room. I saw a large wooden table near the entrance covered with power objects: stones, feathers, bones, and a bundle of dried tobacco leaves. Plastic patio chairs lined the walls, and we each found one and sat down. There were three other Andean people in the room: two women dressed traditionally in long full skirts and white ruffled blouses, and a younger man in shaman attire with a woven belt and feather headdress.

The women handed each of us an unlit white candle and we were instructed to rub it all over our bodies. We looked at each other while awkwardly moving the candle across arms, legs, backs, and torsos. Then one by one we were called to the shaman's table to sit with Don Esteban. When it was my turn, I approached the table and handed the shaman my candle. He lit it and placed the candle in a holder. He stared into the flame and began to speak in Quechua. I found myself drawn into a kind of spell as I watched him.

The shaman's son translated his father's words from Quechua to Spanish, and then Julio translated them from Spanish to English. Sue sat next to Julio and transcribed the message.

You have a spirit that is capable of many expressions. Your spirit is looking for love—you haven't had real love and it is coming soon, possibly by the end of this trip. The obstacles have been cleared, and a good man with a good spirit is coming. Your spirit desires to lift herself up and advance herself. Find new ways to educate yourself, find new ways to understand yourself. You carry sacred capacities—creative expressions, art, writing, all very good. When you open up in new ways, your spirit will find deeper wisdom, more meaningful expressions. Work will come to you. Many opportunities will come to you out of exploring new ways. You are here to do big things and it will happen. Your spirit desires new energies, marriage, and a home you will love dearly.

106

I stared at Don Esteban, dumbfounded. My turn was over but I couldn't seem to get up from the table. He smiled slightly and nodded toward the room. Finally I got up and walked back to my seat, trying to digest the experience.

When everyone in the room had received their message from Don Esteban, the men left the room. Sue explained that we were going to have a *limpia*, a ritual cleansing and we needed to undress. Eventually ten of us, women of all ages and shapes and sizes, stood naked in a line in the center of the darkened room. The Andean women said some prayers in their native tongue and we were smudged with a pungent smoke.

Sue told us to close our eyes. I felt a light spray of liquid across my face and smelled grain alcohol. Then there was a hot blast of air. I opened my eyes slightly as a stream of fire was being blown toward me. My God, these people weren't playing around, I thought as I felt my skin tingle from the heat. I quickly closed my eyes. After the smoke and fire, we opened our eyes and watched as the Andean ladies circled each of us with an egg. Sue explained that the egg would capture any negative energy in our aura and contain it. We were then swatted with a bundle of tobacco leaves. Then the women rubbed each of our heads with handfuls of rose petals. We were told not to brush off the rose petals.

Each of us was handed a woolen Andean cap to put over our damp, rose-matted hair. Sue said we needed to keep the hats on for twenty-four hours without bathing, because they held in the cleansing energies that we had just received. Smelling of tobacco, grain alcohol, and roses, I happily got dressed and trundled out with the rest of the group into the fresh air. It had rained while we were inside and now everything sparkled. The land looked cleansed too. In high spirits, I wondered how it could get any better than this—and it was only day one!

After a few incredible days spent with the Andean people of the Highlands, we traveled by bus to the edge of the rainforest. We would now be traveling into the Amazon for the next part of our journey. The area we were going was only accessible by plane. I climbed into the back of the small Cessna, the tail of which was loaded with supplies for the Achuar. As we took off and made a broad turn, all I could see was a sea of green. We flew about an hour over the landscape of forest and winding rivers before landing on a dirt strip cut out of the forest surrounded by round thatched huts.

We were greeted by some shy villagers who smiled and nodded to us as we waited for the other two planes carrying the rest of the group to land. Barefoot children playing soccer nearby stopped and eyed us with curiosity. A young man with shoulder length dark hair and black markings on each cheek approached us. Julio met him and pulled him into a bear hug before introducing him as Ronaldo, our Achuar guide. Ronaldo nodded a greeting then led us to a riverbank at the edge of the airstrip.

The scene felt like something out of a National Geographic documentary. Two long thin wooden motorized canoes waited for us. The men took our gear and piled it in the back then helped us down the steep bank and into the canoes. As we set off, the river opened up and the sounds of birds and insects permeated the air. The dense forest on each side was teeming with life. I saw little wiry monkeys jumping across tree limbs. We traveled the waterways until we came to a floating wooden dock, then we disembarked and walked along narrow wooden walkways until reaching the camp. The collection of simple bungalows would be our base for the next few days as we journeyed to various Achuar villages to experience the dreaming culture.

At lunch in the open-air dining hall, Sue explained that we were being given a diet of lighter fare without meat or salt and we were asked not to drink alcohol for the next three days to prepare for the big medicine ceremony. There had been a lot of talk about "the medicine" in the last few days. We learned that ayahuasca is a vine that, when mixed with another indigenous plant called *chacruna*, is brewed into a tea to make the plant medicine. Sometimes called the "vine of death," it has been used by the indigenous people of Central and South America for thousands of years. Partakers had visions after drinking the medicine and many people have had profound spiritual awakenings.

Some people in our group had experienced the medicine before. We heard stories of incessant vomiting and diarrhea, and visions of blood-soaked hills covered in skulls. Another reported being swallowed whole by a giant snake. I purposely did not do any research on the medicine before the trip. I was nervous enough about what I may encounter in an altered state of consciousness. I didn't want to know too much and be scared off.

The next day we awoke at 2:30 AM. An air of excitement permeated the atmosphere as we traveled downriver by canoe. We weren't going to drink ayahuasca yet. It was customary for the Achuar to arise before dawn, drink a different medicinal tea, go outside and purge the contents of their stomachs, and then gather in the shaman's house to discuss their dreams. It was still dark as we stepped out of the canoes and were led to a simple open-air structure with a thatched roof and low wooden walls. In the center of the hut sat the shaman Raphael, an older man with a thick swath of silver streaked dark hair and hawk-like eyes. His wife served us small wooden bowls of the highly caffeinated tea, which tasted a bit like artichokes. We were instructed to drink two bowls each.

One by one, everyone had to leave to go outside and vomit. Each person then described a recent dream they'd had. Our two translators then relayed the dreams, English to Spanish, then Spanish to Achuar to be interpreted. When it was my turn, I described the snake dream I'd had after I'd signed on for the trip the month before.

I'd already told Sue about the dream the previous evening. She told me from her perspective snakes represented transformation, so the fact that I willingly offered up my hand after running from snakes my whole life was very positive. She believed this dream signaled the beginning of profound healing. And I believed it was true; since I'd had the dream, I'd felt happier and more relaxed. So as I sat with the group in the shaman's hut, I fully expected a glowing positive interpretation. After all, weren't big snakes powerful South American motifs?

As I explained offering up my hand, I watched as the shaman's countenance darkened. He scratched his chin taking his time to gather his thoughts, finally conveying his message to Julio, who shifted uneasily on the wooden bench as he listened.

"Well?" I whispered.

Julio looked at me. "I just want to say I don't really agree with this interpretation. I think it's a very cultural perspective." He paused.

"What is it?" I asked, suddenly feeling apprehensive.

"He said that you've been bitten by a bad shaman and you're in danger. He says if you lived in their village, you would have to stay inside the hut until you had a better dream."

"What?" I whispered to Julio. It certainly was not the interpretation I'd been expecting.

As we traveled the river back to our camp a dark foreboding came over me. I grew increasingly anxious about drinking the medicine the following evening. *Was* I in danger? I wondered. Maybe I was too sensitive to use a psychotropic, I thought. Rumors had been circulating about participants dying on the medicine and having to have their spirits retrieved by the shaman to be brought back to life.

I took a late morning nap and had a dream about being chased by a man with no face. I woke up soaked in sweat. I felt that no matter what I did, fear would always hound me. Just like my lifetime of snake dreams, always running or battling some sinister force, I would never be free of it. Old fears catapulted over me and I felt sick with unease. I got up and took a cold shower then decided to go to the dock and have a smoke. I found Julio sitting there and asked if I could sit with him.

We each rolled a smoke and stared out over the river. I told him I was becoming nervous about the ayahuasca. I had decided to drink it, but after that morning I was unsure. I felt very uneasy about shamans after hearing I'd been bitten by a bad one!

Julio insisted that the "bad shaman" was not Raphael, who would be conducting the medicine ceremony. He then told me his interpretation of my dream, which was very similar to Sue's. He said maybe the "bad shaman" idea was something more archetypal; some deep primordial fear that had kept me running—and something I needed to confront.

I nodded, "Maybe," I said. But I had a foreboding sense this "bad shaman" scenario wasn't over yet.

"And snakes are very powerful animal totems," Julio said. "Their venom, if it doesn't kill you, becomes your strongest medicine."

"Great," I said, groaning.

Julio said he couldn't tell me what to do, but he did share his feelings about his first meeting with Grandmother. He said it had irrevocably altered him for the better. As he described his experience, I sensed a preternatural spirit emanating from him. When I looked into Julio's eyes, I could feel a powerful loving presence within them. Fears aside, I knew I would drink the medicine.

It was dusk when our group approached the longhouse and the atmosphere was somber. A single white candle created a small circle of light around Raphael. His eyes were closed as he prayed over the medicine. We entered silently and sat down on the benches surrounding him. I happened to be seated closest to him, so I was the first person to be given the medicine. I sipped the little cupful of thick muddy liquid. Contrary to what I'd heard, it didn't taste bad; it reminded me of blackstrap molasses. The medicine was given to everyone, and by the time the last person drank, I was already in an altered state. I felt dizzy and not quite in control, so I closed my eyes and took some deep breaths. I did my light meditation, bringing a column of white light down around me and into the earth.

After a few moments the dizziness subsided and I found myself alone inside a giant kapok tree, the sacred tree of the Achuar. I sat on a bench made of tree roots. Above me was a canopy of green leaves that created a great cathedral ceiling. Ahead of me was a natural altar bathed in golden light. As I looked toward the altar, an incredible vision descended. There appeared before me a magnificent woman bathed in brilliant kaleidoscopic light. She wore a glowing cobalt blue robe and a gold crown studded with precious stones. Surrounding her were bands of green, magenta, yellow, and crimson. Incredibly colored birds and flowers, vines, and curling patterns of light danced around her.

"I am the Soul of the World," the woman said. Bells and wind chimes rang as she spoke.

I sat staring up at her, hunched forward, my mouth agape. This was much more than anything I'd imagined! As I gazed up at her, a long, thick silver vine slowly descended in front of me like a giant corkscrew. Somehow, I knew to reach out and grab it. It was cool and sturdy, so I stepped on a spiral curl of the metal vine and held on as it slowly lifted me up through the kapok tree cathedral.

Someone whispered my name. I opened my eyes. Julio was leaning down in front of me. He smiled and then took my elbow to help me stand up. As I rose, I realized that my point of reference was askew. My visual center seemed to be about three feet over my head! I felt like I was walking on stilts. I teetered back and forth as Julio helped me to the center of the room. He pointed to a little bench in front of the shaman. But from my vantage point, it looked like such a long way down to sit on that little bench! I didn't think I would land on it.

Julio helped me as I slowly crouched, touching the wood of the bench to steady myself. Once settled, shaman Raphael began chanting in his native tongue as he tapped me with a dried bundle of tobacco leaves. I leaned down and fell into a kind of stupor for what seemed like quite a while until I felt a "pop." Suddenly I sat up, full of energy. I saw a brilliant bluish white orb hovering in front of me. I pointed to the glowing ball and some of the others turned to see what I was pointing at.

Julio came to help me stand up. My visual center was normal again, but I felt unstable on my feet as he escorted me outside to a pallet of banana leaves that was laid out under the canopy of stars.

I sat down cross-legged and took a few deep breaths, trying to orient myself. I noticed that my breathing didn't seem entirely under my control. It felt as if some force inside me but outside my normal functioning was directing my respiration. Before I had a chance to panic, I found myself suddenly surrounded by a council of elder indigenous women. They held up their hands and in unison made hand gestures. I realized they were showing me how to breathe. So I followed the hand signals;

they pointed their hands up for the inhalation and slowly pointed them down for the exhalation. Guided by their signals, I took control of my respiration again. Each breath was longer and contained more volume. I didn't know it was possible to breathe so deeply. This continued for some time as my body and energy field seemed to expand with the rhythmic breath.

I sensed a great presence filling me; a sinuous movement began at the base of my spine and flowed up through my chest. It was very sensual. I welcomed the ecstatic sensation and experienced what I can only describe as a complete body high. And I knew it was the spirit of the medicine coming alive in me. The energy felt old, wise, feminine; it was undeniably the energy of the Grandmother. My eyes opened, and I felt her presence looking out through my eyes. How was this possible? I wondered. With her vision I was able to take in details that I couldn't normally see. When I looked at something or someone, I knew about them. It was like a kind of X-ray vision, but I saw their essence rather than their bones. Then I noticed that my hearing had also increased in sensitivity. I could hear rustling in the rainforest hundreds of yards away.

This is incredible, I thought. I have some kind of bionic super-senses! I heard laughter as if in response to my thoughts. I shook my head. This was all so much more than I had expected. The presence of the Grandmother was operating from inside me. Then I heard her voice in my right ear. She said she was so pleased to be here; she was grateful that I had been open to the medicine and allowed her to come inside me. She told me that her only stipulation was that I surrender totally, because only in surrendering the mind can the medicine really be integrated throughout the body. Grandmother told me that if I found my mind wandering or feeling fearful, I should just think "surrender" and let go.

I could hear the shaman nearby chanting in his native language. I turned toward the longhouse and saw someone lying on the ground in front of Raphael as he took big puffs of tobacco and blew it over the person. Julio sat next to him rolling tobacco in papers and giving it to Raphael to keep up with the demand. Suddenly I wanted to smoke, but Grandmother said "no." She told me if I smoked or lay down, I would be sick, but if I stayed sitting with my legs crossed, I would be fine. As if on cue, whoever was on the banana leaf pallet next to me turned and wretched.

So I closed my eyes and relaxed back into the process. That's when I saw the snakes. I couldn't feel them but I could see them. Large snakes slithered down from the crown of my head, moved down my body and arms to the ground, and then slinked away. I knew I was experiencing a healing, the release of old energies. But it was very uncomfortable and I wanted the snakes to leave, so I followed Grandmother's instruction; I stayed calm and detached and just thought, "let go." For the rest of the night, if I started to worry or grow anxious, a snake would appear and writhe its way up my arm or wrap around my head. If I immediately thought "surrender," it would slither down my body and leave.

Grandmother showed me visions of my future and told me about my mate and the love I would experience. I saw a man a little older than me walking through a row of grapes in a vineyard. She gave me advice about my work. She told me to stop apologizing for myself and to stop hiding under a bushel. She talked to me about living much more abundantly and instructed me to release what she called my "misplaced sense of modesty." She showed me the vastness and richness of life and how it was all around us but most people don't see it.

For hours, Grandmother instructed me. She showed me how to lift my energy field and expand it when I felt trapped or overwhelmed in the presence of others, which was a common sensation for me—spiritual claustrophobia. She also taught me how to clarify an intention. She said

that when there is enough life force—in other words, thought and feeling—put toward an intention, energy is drawn to it. The energy con-
geals and becomes matter and the intention manifests. This was something I had heard, but not fully understood; Grandmother showed me
precisely how the mechanism worked. She explained that there was no
need to be attached to the how or when of things, but to just trust and
observe instead.

When the moon began to set over the trees, I could feel Grandmother
waning, but I didn't want her to go. I knew that she had raised my consciousness and held it high during the entire vision. I had experienced a
kind of life force grounded in pure sensuality in a way I never knew possible. I felt infused with the power of love and wisdom; I didn't want to
return to normal consciousness. I felt I'd communed with the Goddess
herself!

"Yes," Grandmother said, "I am the Soul of the World, the Holy Spirit,
the divine feminine, Lilith and Eve are united in me—the feminine nature of God. Nature, Mother Earth, and Pachamama are manifestations
of me. You have let me experience myself through you. You have experienced yourself through me. You have lifted the lower to the higher, and
the higher has filled the lower."

When I told Grandmother that I didn't want to forget anything, didn't
want to lose the magic and return to normal consciousness again, she
laughed and said I couldn't forget her. There are only four words you
need to remember, she said: "Our souls are fused." I would recall everything else she had taught me when I needed the information. She said
she was with me from the inside out.

But her arrival had a catch; it also meant that I wouldn't be able to go
against my spirit anymore because my spirit was fused with hers. My
will and my fears wouldn't be able to override my soul's path. If I did

go against my spirit, the distress would be much more acute. As she explained this, a chill went through me.

As her presence faded, I felt suddenly exhausted and went to the longhouse. I found an empty pallet to sleep on, but after only a couple of hours I awoke full of energy. I was buzzing with excitement. What had happened? I wanted to share the awesomeness of my experience with someone. We had been instructed to keep our experiences to ourselves and not share too much with one another, but I found this idea very difficult, as I was overflowing with energy. I finally got up and took a walk around the village to burn off some of the restlessness.

Later that morning at breakfast, as I looked around the table, I could still see and sense others' energy. My senses were still heightened, including being able to pick up on subtle emotional cues. I soon began to grow uncomfortable. I needed to sort out my own feelings about the experience, but instead I felt overwhelmed by everyone else's. I began to feel claustrophobic and a little paranoid.

Then I remembered Grandmother's instructions from the night before. I went outside and took a couple of deep breaths and imagined sending my energy about a hundred feet above me. It worked! I spread my energy out horizontally. It was like a satellite photo of a hurricane, with clouds spiraling outward. I breathed more easily. I relaxed as my energy field found room to move, and I quickly felt calm and balanced and could return to the group.

Later that morning, we all gathered back at the longhouse and prepared for a meeting with Raphael. He invited those who wished to share an experience that we had with the medicine to do so. He would then give us his interpretation. I chose to relay my experience with the star transmissions.

I explained how Grandmother had guided me to look at certain stars. She said they sent encoded light transmissions that would be stored in the endocrine system. Then when I needed the information, it would be released into my body and mind. I felt a little self-conscious relaying this experience, but I figured that as a shaman, Raphael had heard it all!

It turned out that he was quite pleased. Apparently, this wasn't an uncommon idea in their tribe. Raphael said that when the Achuar people wanted to send a message to someone far away, they would fix their sights on the Pleiades constellation and give the message to the stars. The Pleiades would then transmit the message to the other person when they gazed at the same constellation. He explained that all the stars and planets transmit information and that it is important to understand our relationship to them so they can guide us.

CHAPTER ELEVEN

"Whoa, Ariel," Katie said. "All that really happened?"

Ariel nodded. "Yup, and that's the truncated version."

"What do you mean?" Katie asked. "More happened on the medicine?" Katie stretched across the sofa.

"More happened after I got back," Ariel said. "You know, the Ecuador trip was so extraordinary in so many ways—the people and places were full of mystery and magic. But I thought I was leaving all that behind once I got back to Tucson. That turned out not to be the case."

"You kept your bionic senses?" Katie asked.

Ariel laughed. "Actually, I did for a few days. And there was a series of uncanny coincidences. I began to suspect that the Grandmother was working quietly behind the scenes, leading me forward."

"What kind of coincidences?" Katie asked.

"Well, after the medicine ceremony we learned that Raphael's daughter was gravely ill. Before leaving the Achuar village, some of us wanted to do what we could to show support for Raphael and his family. Sue and others in the group pooled together supplies to leave for her comfort. I gave Raphael a copper medallion of the Virgin de Guadalupe, the same one that Ed had noticed some months before.

"Shortly after returning to Tucson, I got a package in the mail. I wasn't expecting anything so was truly shocked to find a medal of the Virgin Mary inside. It was from an organization I'd never heard of, in France of all places!

"A couple of days after that, I was at a cocktail party," Ariel continued, "and chatting with this doctor, an internist, who had spent several weeks in the Amazon with a neighboring tribe of the Achuar. He asked me if I had drank ayahuasca with them. When I told him I had, he shook his head, clearly alarmed. Then he told me that the effects of the medicine were permanent and proceeded to describe how the medicine hyper-activates the areas of the brain where cognitive reasoning takes place, creating new connections. He was worried about it, but I took it as good news!"

Ariel and Katie laughed.

Katie thought about what Ariel had told her. "Do you think the only way to have this kind of spiritual experience is by taking ayahuasca?"

"No, I don't," Ariel said. "Many people have profound mystical experiences through meditation, visiting sacred sites, through ecstatic dance or chanting. I do believe the medicine is a very powerful way in which someone can experience heightened states of consciousness though, whatever that may mean for them."

Katie nodded. "I get that. But the thing I don't quite understand is how the ayahuasca is related to the spirit of the feminine—the Grandmother."

"I don't know, really...but it is. I felt it. Look, the indigenous people have been working with these native plants for thousands of years," Ariel said. "And they believe the medicine is from Pachamama, the Earth, given to them to be guided by the Grandmother. From what I've discovered, not everyone has a direct experience of the divine feminine on the medicine. It's more common to have a physical or psychological experience, dealing with personal issues. But those who meet her often call her the Grandmother, which aligns directly with my experience."

"Can you find ayahuasca in the US?" Katie asked.

"You can," Ariel said. "But it should only be used in a sacred manner and not as a recreational drug."

"Ariel, I'd like to do the medicine," Katie said. "There's something about this that's calling me."

"I would highly recommend it. Don't worry, if you're feeling the call, it will find you." Ariel smiled. "Just please don't tell your mother I told you any of this!"

"Don't worry," Katie said. "But I doubt everybody has an experience like yours."

"That's true. But I think everybody has the experience they need," Ariel said.

Katie nodded.

"For me, meeting the Grandmother through ayahuasca was just the beginning. I began to understand what she meant when she said, "Our souls are fused." She gave me a strength and protection I'd not known before. My intuition increased, and I was able to go beyond myself and my own story to understand collective forces, life at play on a much larger scale. And she continued to guide me in surprising ways."

"Really?" Katie said, raising her eyebrows.

"Another time," Ariel said, waving her hand.

Katie nodded. "But you did say that Grandmother strengthened and protected you," Katie said. "So you never felt as afraid after the medicine?"

Ariel laughed. "Oh, no. After the Grandmother experience, the scale changed. I realized that there was a whole lot more to be afraid of! But I was able to handle much more; I could look at scary stuff directly whereas before I hid my head under the pillow."

"Oh," Katie said, raising her eyebrows. "I don't know if I want to find out what would scare you!"

Ariel laughed. She poured herself a little more whiskey.

"Maybe I will have a little," Katie said, nodding toward the Jameson's bottle.

Ariel reached across the coffee table and poured some whiskey into Katie's empty teacup.

"Thanks," Katie said. She took a sip. "Did you ever figure out what Raphael meant when he warned you about being bitten by a bad shaman?"

Ariel sat back into the stuffed chair, resting her feet on the edge of the coffee table. "Yeah, it did turn out to be kind of literal. There was a man who was trying to use 'black magic' on me."

Katie coughed and sprayed a little whiskey. She wiped her mouth with the back of her hand.

"Seriously?" she asked.

Ariel laughed. "My girl, there is so much crazy shit out there." She waved her arms open. "The Kabbalists say that if we knew how much negativity is bombarding us continually, we would die of fright!"

"Okay Ariel," Katie said, nervously. "You are actually starting to creep me out."

"Well, I'll tell you something, I really didn't believe this kind of thing existed before either. But this bad shaman situation got me to understand something about a much larger opponent—the patriarchy!" Ariel said, taking a big sip of whiskey.

Katie suspected her aunt was getting a little tipsy.

Ariel looked at her pointedly, "And it wasn't until I got a handle on this patriarchal world culture bullshit that I could even deal with a real partnership with a man!"

This caught Katie's attention. "What do you mean? How so?" she asked.

"Because, even though I considered myself an independent woman, I was always hooked into some man. It was as if something was faulty in my wiring and I didn't feel totally whole and complete within myself."

"You complete me," Katie said, smiling.

"Exactly!" Ariel said, laughing at the reference to the film *Jerry Maguire*. "This felt so disempowering, like something was missing inside that could only be filled by a relationship. After my first experience with the Grandmother, I began to suspect something was up. My own search for 'true love' took an interesting turn. I still believed the right one was out there—as prophesied first by Thundercloud, then the Chiricahua medicine man and then by Don Estaban. But I began to really observe my women friends and clients who were trying to get into relationships with men who weren't really interested, or were staying in relationships where they felt unseen, unappreciated, and not valued.

"I started to see that this wasn't just my issue, and that many women spent too much time and energy trying to be loved by a man. I wondered why we didn't love and value ourselves more. I sensed that there may be a more fundamental issue stirring in the depths of the feminine psyche. It seemed as though our wiring *was* faulty. We weren't getting all the current we needed and consequently we sought to wire ourselves through men. Or maybe on some deep level we thought we had to, and we called that love."

"Okay," Katie said. "But what does that have to do with bad shamans and the patriarchy?"

Ariel held up her glass of whiskey. "I'll tell you," she said.

CHAPTER TWELVE

ARIEL

After I returned from Ecuador, I got a call from Trudi, the woman who lived on Ed's compound. Trudi asked if she could see me for a tarot reading. She was coming into Tucson to work and hoped to see me after her shift. I was suspicious, thinking that perhaps Ed was sending her to look in on me. So I was a bit reserved when Trudi arrived at my doorstep. But her smile was genuine and when she reached out to give me a hug, I felt her relief.

We sat down to have a cup of tea before her reading. Trudi nervously told me she really needed the reading to be confidential. I assured her it was. I understood her apprehension when she asked me questions about my involvement with Ed. I let her know that I'd visited the compound only once and had not been in contact with Ed since.

I began Trudi's reading. Using clairvoyant sight and the tarot, I saw change, a geographical move, and opportunities opening in the next year or so. But I also sensed a rather sinister force around her. It looked like a gray cloud, thick and amorphous, hovering around her right shoulder. I sat with this for a few moments, trying to ascertain what I was witnessing. Its essence was cool, controlling, and authoritarian.

Observing the mass of energy, I realized that it was a dark force, a coagulation of negative thinking, judgment, and condemnation that could stick to things and people. Why was I seeing this energy attached to Trudi? I wondered. She was a rather warm, sweet person. Then I got my answer: precisely because of her light, the mass of negative energy was feeding off it. I realized it had a foothold in her consciousness and was creating a lot of self-doubt and making her feel disempowered and insecure. It was slowly draining her natural exuberance and positivity. This was scary stuff!

I did some energy clearing. I surrounded her in spiritual light and then lit some sage and smudged her. After asking her permission, I did a laying-on of hands to boost her energy field. I stood behind her with my hands on her shoulders and after praying for protection, I used my previous training as a massage therapist to run light into her energy field.

I explained to Trudi what I had seen. I told her I felt that she was in an environment that was really draining her energy. I saw others' negativity surrounding her and having a deleterious effect. The aspect that concerned me the most was the insidious nature of the negativity. It resulted in her feeling bad about *herself*, thinking that the problems were inside her when, more accurately, the negative energy was actually *attached* to her. I didn't want to scare her, but I said that she needed to take her situation seriously.

Trudi studied my face for a moment and then asked if she could share a recent dream she'd had. The dream, she told me, was the reason she'd called me for a reading. Of course, I agreed to hear it.

Trudi was sleeping in the roundhouse with Shirley and Ed. Something woke her and she found herself getting out of bed and going outside. She walked to the fence at the edge of the property and was surprised to find me standing on the other side of the fence. She asked what I was doing there in the desert in the middle of the night. I replied, I've come to take you out of here.

Whoa, I thought as I sat back in my chair. Trudi then revealed more about Ed and the compound. It was as I suspected: they were all lovers, or more accurately, "sister wives." He'd boasted to the group that I was "the next one." Trudi said Shirley, the "first wife" was there to make me feel comfortable so I would relax and trust Ed. Her job was to lure the women in. It was chilling to hear what Trudi said because I knew it was true. And I then knew I had grossly underestimated him.

I then realized *Ed* was the bad shaman. How could I have not thought of that? At first, I'd been somewhat taken in by his pedigree and his stories; I'd been flattered by his attention. In the end I'd just found him creepy, but not dangerous.

I told Trudi about my experience with the snake dream and Ed's guidance to let the snake bite me. Then I relayed the Achuar shaman's warning that I should be very careful. Suddenly I remembered the eagle feather Ed had given me. I jumped up and searched through my bookcase. It wasn't there. Where had I put it? I looked around a bit before finding it beneath the altar in my bedroom, lying under the Andean knit cap from Ecuador along with the talisman that Shirley had given me.

I brought the eagle feather and the talisman out and showed Trudi. She nodded as she recognized the talisman. It was called a "binding" and the intent was to attract someone to you. I was shocked. I found all of this really unnerving and I couldn't understand how Trudi could be so cool about it. I urged her not to return to the compound, but she insisted. She felt she could handle Ed and assured me that she would start making plans to leave. She offered to bury the binding talisman and the feather on the compound so Ed's energy would stay there. In the end, I let her go; it was all deeply disturbing, but I couldn't tell her what to do. I could only offer my support.

After Trudi left, I smudged myself and my whole apartment with sage. But I couldn't shake the nefarious sensation of the gray energy stuck to Trudi. And the more I thought about what Trudi told me, the angrier I became. Ed had inherited beautiful teachings from his grandmother that he was meant to pass on with integrity. He knew that his standing as a red fire priest attracted women to him. It was a gross betrayal of his spiritual lineage and I knew at least one woman, Trudi, who was being harmed by it. I wondered how many others he'd drawn in.It took me a while to calm down, but finally I went to bed. And that night I had a very disturbing dream.

I found myself in the middle of an argument with a man I couldn't see, but I knew he was there.

"I'm not here to carry some man," I yelled. "I'm here to follow my own path!"

The man's fist came out of nowhere and hit me square in the jaw.

I howled, holding the right side of my face.

I woke up from the dream gasping. My jaw throbbed painfully. I could almost feel the impression of thick knuckles on my skin. The heat of the man's anger permeated my bedroom. I jumped up and turned on the overhead light. How could a dream produce such intense physical sensations? Then I recalled my snake bite dream a few months earlier. It too had produced some physical sensations. But the pain of this "punch" didn't subside. After a day of ice packs and Advil, my jaw continued to ache and my teeth felt sore.

Finally, I called my dentist. He examined my mouth and said my teeth were fine. But he was surprised to see that I had severe TMD, or temporomandibular disorder, in the joint on the right side of my jaw. He asked if I'd fallen or hit the side of my head. I certainly couldn't tell my dentist that I'd been injured by a bad shaman who had slugged me in my dream. So I shrugged my shoulders and just shook my head. My jaw took three months to completely return to normal.

In Ecuador, Sue had told me that the Grandmother heightened intuition and protected those who worked with her. Yet I hadn't exactly felt protected from Ed's attack. In fact, the blurring of the line between dream and reality was frighteningly thin. However, thankfully, I didn't have any other interaction with Ed again, neither in the dreamtime nor waking life.

Trudi and I did stay in touch. Over the course of the next year, she came for a few more sessions. Her readings were always the same: encouraging her to believe in herself and to take the steps to leave. But she couldn't seem to break free. The longer she stayed, the more drained she became. Despite all the evidence to the contrary, Trudi didn't feel she could make it on her own anymore. So in the end she stayed at the compound with Ed, convinced she needed him to survive.

I began seeing what I termed the "gray force" in sessions with other clients. I observed this dark, authoritarian energy hovering around some people; it felt distinctly masculine—not a healthy masculine, but rather a cruel, judgmental, and punitive version. I sought to understand it better, sensing it was an energy that had been around a long time even though I'd just begun to see it. I called Sue to set a time to meet. Since the Ecuador trip we'd stayed in touch and I figured she'd be able to understand.

Sue and I met downtown to walk the trail around Randolph Park. As Chico trotted along, sniffing, I described Ed, the punch-in-the-jaw dream and the gray force—how it seemed so starkly masculine and authoritarian and that it was controlling and sucking the energy out of people it attached to.

"Everything you're describing," Sue said, "makes sense to me. And I've also seen what you call 'the gray force' on a psychological level, especially with women clients. I would say that this is classic patriarchy. A subject I've been reading about a lot lately."

Of course I'd heard of the patriarchy, at least from the standpoint of the three patriarchal religions descended from Abraham—Judaism, Christianity and Islam. But as Sue went on to describe some of what she'd been studying and observing, I realized it was much more insidious than I'd thought.

"So you know most of our institutions have been built on the hierarchical patriarchal model. Leader at the top, levels of management underneath to control the majority at the bottom. We've been living in this paradigm for thousands of years," Sue said.

"Like the Catholic church," I said.

"Exactly. Most corporations, governments, banking systems, basically all large organizations are also built on this model. And though it has some benefits, it's very unbalanced. It's a model of control and authoritarianism."

"Papa knows best," I said.

"Right. This has been going on for five thousand years or so. And has created a lot of problems: women became second class citizens, matrilineal cultures were destroyed, and now we find our planet, Mother Earth, in jeopardy.

"You know, the rainforest journeys started because the Achuar tribe saw the need for people outside their tribe to understand we were going down. They knew that the Grandmother could help turn the tide. It is part of the return of the feminine nature to all of us, both psychologically and in how we move forward as a society. It's time for us to move to fair, egalitarian systems that benefit everyone, and they thought the spirit medicine from the Earth could help show that."

Something about what Sue said struck me. The idea that Grandmother was entering people's consciousness to restore balance in each individual's psyche, which in turn would lead to building a better society, fascinated me. One by one, the Grandmother was waking people up.

"Wow, Sue," I said. "I never thought of the medicine that way. But it makes perfect sense."

Sue nodded, smiling. "And you had such a powerful experience, I think Grandmother wants you to be a voice for the feminine spirit."

I smiled, feeling flattered but unable to imagine how I'd go about this.

"It's really interesting that since you did the medicine you've had such a direct visceral experience with the patriarchy."

I laughed. "Yeah, first shaking off a bad shaman, and now I see the gray force everywhere! Not pleasant."

Sue laughed. We went on to discuss the insidious ways in which the collective patriarchal belief systems had affected our own thinking and self-perception. Sue said her number one priority was the empowerment of her women clients. She stressed that the ideas of what it meant to be a woman were passed down by society, history, men, and other women.

"And through the ages, women have allowed themselves to be dominated. We've played into the weakness so we could be taken care of, so we didn't have to be responsible for ourselves and own our true power as autonomous beings and live to our full potential.

"Women need to realize that we have everything we need within us. We've become dependent emotionally and financially, as if wiring ourselves through others will give us what we need. For so long women have been building their identities around men and their children, doing everyone a disservice. *En masse*, women need to realize their true nature, which is power. If we think femininity is always being nice and helpful and tidying up after others and trying to make everything work, we're really missing our purpose."

"Amen, sister!" I said.

"And Ariel, it isn't just women who've been so negatively affected by the patriarchy. Even though the patriarchy is an authoritarian belief system that has been largely perpetuated by men, men have been damaged too—they are afraid to embrace their sensitive, caring, more feminine side because it has been thought of as 'weak.' They've been trampled by the domination model too. Even this guy Ed; if he weren't so imbalanced by the system, he wouldn't be preying on women."

I cocked my head trying to look at Ed from a more compassionate angle. It wasn't easy, but I got Sue's point. We finished our walk and were back at the parking lot. We both felt inspired to meet up again and continue the discussion. Sue recommended a couple good books on the subject of the patriarchy and we set up a time to get together the following week.

That's how Sue and I began our greater conversation around spirituality and, I guess, classic feminism, which was coming through in topics like the Grandmother and the gray force. Soon thereafter, I drove to Sue's place in midtown. She had a studio attached to her house that she used as an office and consultation room. She was trained as a Jungian analyst but also used archetypal astrology to understand her clients. After settling in with a cup of tea we discussed how we wanted to explore the energetic framework of the patriarchy so we could understand more deeply the nature of the imbalance between the masculine and feminine and how it had been perpetuated for so long. We each had theories based on our individual work and experiences and took turns sharing some of our background.

Sue had gone into her career as an analyst to understand the patterns in her own psyche as well as that of others. She had long fought a deeply embedded belief that she needed a protector. Her father had always been the one to protect her from her unstable mother and from his own abusive father. She had also married someone who she felt was a protector—"I married my father," as she put it.

Sue pointed out that archetypes have the full spectrum of dark and light. The masculine father is the protector and provider and cared for the family, but the masculine, when unchecked, becomes authoritarian, controlling, and abusive. We talked about the anthropomorphizing of God as the judgmental father in western theology. Five thousand years of predominantly patriarchal conditioning had definitely produced an imbalance in the collective consciousness.

Sue then went on to explain how the current astrological cycles presented a mythology of the solar feminine. Even though I was also an astrologer, I'd never heard of the concept.

"Solar feminine?" I said. "That's not something I'm familiar with."

Sue smiled. "That's funny because, being a double Aries woman, you are the classic solar feminine archetype." She explained the concept further. "The solar feminine is the powerful warrior goddess, the independent woman leading a cause. This is a very different aspect of the

Red Spirit Woman

feminine than the predominant one of the last few thousand years. The focus of the feminine has been on the lunar aspect—the emotional, nurturing, passive qualities. Archetypes have a full spectrum. The power of the feminine has been driven underground while the masculine has assumed all the roles of empowerment. And conversely, the softer, caring, supportive qualities of the masculine have been hidden under the hardness of force. So both the feminine and masculine archetypes have been fractured."

It was a fascinating perspective, one I hadn't considered before. But it gave me a whole new framework for understanding. After our meeting discussing the patriarchy, I couldn't help feeling that all this information and insight were leading somewhere. Was Grandmother trying to tell me something? I wanted to somehow help correct this imbalance, to be a voice for the divine feminine. But I didn't really know how.

Since returning from the Ecuador trip, a new energy was surging through me. I was working a lot at Rancho Encantada and had added a weekly workshop to my schedule. I camped and hiked and got out of town when I could. I took Chico on our favorite walks and spent leisurely Sunday mornings at the local café. It was a good life, but I was restless. I felt there was something more I needed to be doing, but I didn't know what. So my mind went back to the same old questions and complaints.

Where was my love? Where was the home that I would love as prophesied by Don Esteban? Didn't he say that a good man was coming soon? That was months ago!

I thought about Julio. He'd told me that after he experienced the medicine, his life took on new meaning. His actions became centered on service to Pachamama. Julio was different from any man I'd ever met. He was masculine but also soft and open. He seemed anchored in both the physical and spiritual worlds.

I decided to reach out to Julio and tell him about some of the recent experiences I'd had since returning. Just writing things out in an email made me feel better. I didn't know if he would respond or even remember me because he guided and worked as a translator for hundreds of people every year. But I did get a response—a very thoughtful one.

This began a correspondence that went on for months. We shared meditations, websites, and documentaries available on the web about the medicine. We joked and relived some of our experiences on the rainforest journey together. I began to really look forward to his emails and wondered if they were leading to something more than shared experiences with Grandmother.

My longing was soon answered by a very vivid dream, or so I thought.

I lived in a large city, in a big warehouse apartment full of books and antique furniture. I answered a knock at my door and was surprised to find Sue standing in the hallway with Julio and our Achuar guide, Ronaldo.

"I'm here to talk to you," Sue said. "But we don't have a lot of time."

Sue asked me if I was taking care of myself, eating clean foods, meditating, and clearing away toxic thoughts. She asked how my finances were. I felt like I was being interviewed for something.

Sue explained that she was going back to Ecuador to bring more people to the medicine. She said that Ronaldo and Julio would be working with her as guides, but she needed another person to help the participants through their process. She had thought of me with my intuitive gifts and background in healing. I could help the participants understand the messages given by Grandmother. Sue said Grandmother and I had an affinity. She had been sent to observe me in person to make sure I was ready for the job.

"Do you want the job?" Sue asked.

I couldn't imagine anything else I wanted more. "Yes!" I said.

Sue looked at her watch. "It's time to go. Our car will be downstairs shortly."

I led them down the back stairs to the alley behind the building. The alley faced a large open market where vendors had their wares stored in crates. While Sue and Ronaldo stood at the corner waiting for their car and driver, Julio and I sat down on a couple of wooden crates.

"What are you doing here?" I asked, leaning close to be heard. "I didn't think you ever came to the States."

He smiled. "I come twice a year," he said. Julio's eyes glowed with rich amber light. A few yards away a black town car with tinted windows pulled up, and Sue and Ronaldo got in.

I didn't want Julio to go. I was so happy to see him and there was so much to talk about. He stood up and leaned down over me, his handsome face just inches from mine. I thought for a moment that he was going to kiss me. But instead he took a deep breath and put his lips to my forehead and exhaled. A warm blast of air permeated my skin, my skull, my brain. Pure bliss filled my body, my mind, my consciousness.

Sue called me the very next morning to tell me that the medicine was coming to Tucson. She invited me to experience the Grandmother once again. She explained that two shamans were bringing the medicine from the Amazon. It was all very clandestine. We were to meet at a secret location, held on private property at a large residence. I immediately signed on. We were each given a strict diet to follow for a week prior to the ceremony to clean out the body and prepare the mind. No alcohol, meat, sugar, or gluten. I followed it, and on the appointed day, I drove to the meeting point.

I was nervous, afraid that my first experience may have been a fluke. I hadn't vomited or had terrifying visions. This time could be different. It could be my night of reckoning. The group of sixteen gathered in the main room, and we were each guided to write our intention for the medicine on a little piece of paper. I wished to understand more deeply what my mission was, to gain more clarity about my future and my soul-mate—wherever the hell he was!

Each person rose one at a time to drink the small cupful of medicine. As I waited for my turn, I filled the room with light and surrounded myself with a column of light and prayed for guidance and protection. I got up and drank the cupful of medicine and then went into a very deep, quiet stillness. After a while I became cognizant of groans of pain. Then I heard the sounds of retching and vomiting around me.

I started to squirm. I didn't want to get sick. And I didn't like being confined in a room with so much suffering. I wanted to get up and leave for a while, but the leaders had asked us not to move from our spot unless we really needed to so we wouldn't interfere with the process. I took a couple of deep breaths and tried to stay calm. Suddenly, Grandmother's voice came into my right ear again. She told me to look up and as I did a brilliant golden light descended around me. Then I found myself surrounded by a large trunk and the limbs and leaves of a great tree.

Grandmother instructed me to bring the golden light down through the leaves and branches and send it into the roots of the tree. As I did this, I realized I *was* the tree. As I brought the golden light through me, it traveled through the root system that then spread across the room, connecting everyone in the group. As I did, I noticed a shift in the room. The groans lightened. There wasn't as much writhing and discomfort. It worked! I thought. Of course it works, Grandmother said.

Grandmother explained that I was witnessing the Tree of Life. It was symbolic of the transmission of energy from the heavens to earth. The Earth is the ground, the negative polarity, the circuit of Light cannot be complete without ground. Otherwise it is pure energy, the positive polarity, without manifestation. Drawing down the Light activates the feminine energy, completing the circuit.

Each person was like a tree and could take in the sunlight of spirit, channel it through the trunk and into the root system, which then fed the earth and those around us with spiritual light. Grandmother told me I could do this anytime. I could draw light from the source and send it into the collective matrix.

Grandmother asked me to go back into meditation. She told me the shamans were going to offer the group more medicine and I should take one more cupful. I stiffened, I didn't want to take more and be sick. But there was no response; it seemed Grandmother had left. A few minutes later the shamans did offer the participants more medicine. I reluctantly raised my hand and the female shaman came toward me with a small cup. I noticed she was walking deliberately, not in a straight line. Then I realized she could see the roots of the Tree of Life and was picking her steps around them!

I drank the second cup of medicine and took a couple of deep breaths to settle into meditation when I heard a great gust of air. I looked up and the ceiling of the room was gone. I sat under the open sky as a rush of spirits filled the room. The whoosh of movement was so loud that I looked at the other participants to see their reaction. A man seated across from me seemed to notice the great rush of energy too. Beings of wispy white light, much like ghosts in the movies, flooded the large room. They circled and danced, rejoicing in the space as if it were a ballroom. I watched in awe as more beings came in, indigenous South American spirits with great costumes of jewel colors. I heard music, chanting, drumming, even waltzes. It was a spirit party. I felt myself swept up in the gaiety. These spirits were having some fun!

After a while the spirits quieted and dispersed to the periphery of the room. The darkened room transformed and I found myself in a clearing in the rainforest. An old woman emerged from the shadows of the trees and stood in the clearing. She was small and slightly hunched over, and her long silver hair was pulled back in a bun. Her face was brown and ancient. I couldn't really look directly into her eyes. They were a kaleidoscopic dance of light. She flashed a high-wattage smile. The spirits laughed gaily.

"Grandmother?" I asked. The spirits around us tittered.

The woman nodded. "I've brought someone here for you to meet," she said. A man emerged from the edge of the forest and stood next to Grandmother. He was tall and handsome with brown hair and piercing blue eyes. My whole body tingled.

He smiled and approached me. The spirits giggled. I couldn't believe what I was seeing. I started to shake. My throat tightened and I had to work to swallow. I could feel my heart rate speed up.

"Breathe!" Grandmother said.

The beautiful man sat down next to me.

"You didn't think I would deliver," Grandmother said. "But here he is." She threw her hands up in the air in an exaggerated gesture. Then she began to do a funny little jig. Some of the spirits got up and danced with her.

I turned and looked at the man. We embraced as if we'd known each other for a long time. His hands gently held my head as we put our foreheads together. I'm coming, he whispered. I'll be there soon. Stop worrying. It's taking me a while but I'm almost there.

Suddenly I felt incredibly tired and slipped into a strange state of sleep.

"Chop, chop," Grandmother said, clapping loudly as she leaned over me. I woke up and looked around, but the man was gone. Before I could respond, she said, "The show's not over. You've got some work to do."

Grandmother pointed upward, and my consciousness flew right out of the room. Within seconds I found myself flying over a mountainous landscape. I heard Grandmother's voice in my right ear instructing me. I was not scared or uncomfortable, as if flying out of my body and around the globe happened every day. I stopped and hovered over a place I recognized. It was the giant sundial in Ecuador. Built right on the equator in the Andean mountains, it was a celestial marker. Our tour group had visited the sundial on the way to the rainforest. At noon we had stood in the large circular stone plaza with no shadow cast from the sun.

Now it was nighttime as I hovered over the plaza lit with moonlight. The marker of the sundial, a narrow stone tower, stood in the center of the great circle.

"Now bring in the light," Grandmother said.

I imagined a huge beam of white light descending into the tower. It appeared, and I strengthened it.

"Good," Grandmother said.

From my vantage point hovering hundreds of feet above the sundial, I focused on a continuous beam of light. It descended from the heavens and went straight down the tower, then dispersed along the compass points of the stone plaza. The light was going into the earth via the tower like a lightning rod. I kept sending the light. I sensed something was breaking open that had been trapped under the structure. I felt the calcification of the stuck energy but didn't really know what it was. It seemed stuck for thousands of years. Then I saw it. There was a deep pool of beautiful cobalt blue light located under the sundial. It was cool and nourishing and *masculine.*

"That's right, sacred masculine," Grandmother said. "Keep sending the light."

I started to understand the nature of the trapped energy. It was located in pockets all over the Earth. It had been covered and trapped by overlaying structures. This whole thing is far bigger than I am, I thought. I can't do this.

"Keep sending the light!" Grandmother yelled. "You're almost there."

I refocused and increased the volume of light into the tower. I was becoming very tired and didn't think I could keep hovering and sending the light much longer. Then I heard a loud crack. I looked down and saw buckling in the stone plaza. The ground started to rise and ripple. The earth shook and broke apart the cement and stone blocks. Cracks erupted along the lines of the sundial from the tower outward to the periphery of the circle. I watched in amazement as the whole structure crumbled and disintegrated. In its place, an enormous pool of cobalt liquid light filled the circle. The energy was free. It began to flow out in rivulets through the forest and down the mountains. As my vantage point grew higher, I could see the rivers of cobalt blue feeding the landscape below.

"Good job," Grandmother said. "You just helped free some of the stuck collective sacred masculine."

I found myself back in the darkened room. The spirits were gone and the people around me slept. I was exhausted. Grandmother whispered that I was done. The medicine was now complete in me.

"Now it is time for you to move forward," she said. "A lot is going to happen over the next couple of years. You're going to discover something, a forgotten aspect of the feminine. In the process you're going to integrate parts of yourself that were lost too. She can help you and you can help her."

I just wanted to sleep; I didn't have the concentration to understand Grandmother's cryptic words. "Help who?" I murmured.

"The red woman will come to you again," Grandmother said. "Walk the trail of the Magdalene and she'll find you."

CHAPTER THIRTEEN

"Ariel, I think this is like *The Godfather*—part two is even better than part one!"

"Hah!" Ariel laughed.

"So who was that man Grandmother brought to you?" Katie asked. "Was he the sacred masculine or your soul mate?"

Ariel cocked her head. "Probably all of the above!"

Katie continued. "I want to know what happened with Julio. I mean, it seems like you guys had a real connection."

"We did have a connection. We were certainly connected through our experiences with the Grandmother. And—"

Katie straightened up in her chair and leaned toward Ariel. "And?"

"I did reach out to him right before I did the medicine in Tucson. That dream had really gotten to me—and I had to find out if there was more between us," Ariel said. "I fantasized about going back to Ecuador, what it would be like to be together. To work with the Grandmother together. He seemed like a kindred spirit."

"So what happened?" Katie asked.

"Well, I wrote him and told him about my dream," Ariel said. "I was nervous but the energy was so juicy. But it wasn't the same for him. He wrote me a very sweet email saying he too felt the connection between us, but he'd recently met someone special and felt she was the one for him. He felt Grandmother had been working through him to bring me further on my journey. He said he'd always remember me fondly but for him the extent of our personal relationship was the Grandmother connection."

"Ouch! That must have hurt a little," Katie said.

Ariel nodded. "It did. But deep inside I knew he was right. Close but no cigar, as they say. And so it really helped when the man showed up with the Grandmother, then I *knew* I would meet my mate soon."

Katie nodded. "Do you think Julio was right, that Grandmother was the juicy energy somehow coming through him?"

Ariel nodded. "I do. I think it's exactly right. Grandmother love is juicy—sensual and exciting and in those early days with her, communicating via Julio was a way to reach me."

Ariel seemed lost in thought for a few moments. She turned back to Katie. "And the experience with the sacred masculine with the medicine—freeing what was stuck made me much more aware of the dynamics in the collective consciousness. It wasn't just the sacred or divine feminine that was suppressed. The masculine was too. And people have suffered, are suffering, for it."

"So, are you saying what the Grandmother had you do with the medicine somehow helped bring the sacred masculine out of the shadows?" Katie asked.

"I think so," Ariel said. "And the shaman that came to Tucson later told us that she'd heard experiences from participants in other ceremonies that were similar to mine. She felt there was an opening of the sacred masculine occurring at the same time that the power of the feminine was rising. For me, that's when it all started coming home."

"The Grandmother told you that you were done, that the medicine was complete," Katie said. "Does that mean you never did ayahuasca again?"

"I haven't done the medicine again," Ariel said. "I felt like I'd gotten what I needed from it. The rest was up to me."

Katie nodded. She pulled her legs up and curled into the back of the sofa. She let her chin drop to her knees. Her eyes were puffy from lack of sleep.

"You look like you're ready to drop," Ariel said. She got up and stretched her back. "And I need to hit the sack."

Katie nodded. "This was an amazing day, Ariel," she said. She felt almost too tired to get up off the comfy sofa and go to bed.

"It was indeed. Tomorrow if you wake up before me, help yourself to the coffee and some breakfast" Ariel gave her a warm smile, then made her way to the stairs of the master suite.

Katie turned in the bed and reached out for her cell phone on the nightstand. She felt around until her hand landed on the familiar flat sleek shape. She lifted it up and opened one eye.

"No way," she said aloud. It can't be two o'clock in the afternoon! She unhooked the phone from the charger and brought it closer to her face. Yep, 2:04 PM. Wow, she'd slept almost twelve hours. Her head was fuzzy and her mouth dry. She rolled out of bed and drank the whole glass of water on her nightstand, then shuffled to the bathroom. When she came out, she saw Ariel's office door open. She could hear her aunt typing on the keyboard. Not wanting to interrupt her, Katie decided to get some coffee and try to clear her head. She threw on some jeans and went downstairs.

In the kitchen Ariel had set out the French press with coffee grounds and a plate with a croissant. As always, the croissant looked perfect and the grounds smelled delicious. Katie put the kettle on and leaned against the counter waiting for it to boil. When the coffee was ready, she got some milk and sat down at the kitchen table. She ate the croissant and by the second cup she was starting to feel somewhat normal. She wondered what was on the agenda for the day—or the rest of the day. She poured the last of the coffee into her cup and went back upstairs.

Katie approached the doorway of Ariel's office. Her aunt was really focused on whatever was on the computer screen.

Ariel turned in her seat. "Hey, you're up," she said.

Katie nodded. "I can't believe I slept so long," she said and took a sip of coffee. "Thank you for breakfast."

"I figured you needed the rest and could help yourself when you got up," Ariel said, smiling.

"I'll never get tired of the croissants here," Katie said, smiling. "What are you working on?"

"I'm supposed to be writing a proposal to submit to a conference," Ariel said, grimacing. "Talking about the medicine experience last night made me think about the Tree of Life in a new way. So I'm reading my notes about Mary Magdalene and her writings and how they described the Tree of Life," Ariel said.

"You mentioned seeing a giant tree last night," Katie said. "But honestly, I've heard of the Tree of Life but don't really know what it is." She leaned against the door jamb.

"The Tree of Life is a motif in many spiritual traditions, but I'm referring to it in the esoteric Jewish sense, in Kabbalism. Well, their Tree of Life is a diagram with ten spheres called *sephirot* that make the shape of a geometric tree. As you look from top to bottom, you see the process that pure energy goes through as it becomes matter. With each *sephirot* being a distinct energy transducer, if you will. So then, you can also look at it from bottom to top—from matter back to energetic form. In that way, it's essentially a map illustrating the path to enlightenment by going where we are—on the ground and back up the tree to spirit, consciously."

"*Okay,*" Katie said, trying to take in what Ariel was saying. "And how is this connected to Mary Magdalene?"

Ariel turned her office chair around to face Katie. "Basically, from my research I discovered that Jesus was a master Kabbalist, one of several of the greatest Kabbalah teachers of that time. He grew up and studied in the Galilee, the center then and now of Kabbalism. He passed on some of these teachings to Magdalene, specifically about the Tree of Life, which she wrote about in her gospel. This was very radical on two fronts: Jesus shared teachings that had always been kept secret *and* he shared them with a woman."

"Women weren't supposed to have access to these spiritual teachings?" Katie asked.

"Hah! Women didn't have access to the esoteric teachings of Kabbalah until the 1970s!" Ariel said. "When a guy named Rav Berg brought Kabbalah from his teacher in Israel to the States. His wife or maybe even girlfriend at the time, Karen, wanted to learn too. So he started teaching people, anyone that wanted to learn, in the basement of his house. Then he and Karen opened the first center in New York to everyone—men, women, Jews, non-Jews. This was very radical. For nearly four thousand years, since Abraham, these teachings were kept secret. Only certain men from certain lineages could study. And for a long time, the teachings were only oral. So the fact that Jesus broke the rules and was teaching basic Kabbalah concepts to people was really radical."

Katie raised her eyebrows. This Magdalene seemed to get more and more impressive, at least in her aunt's eyes. She tried to follow Ariel's train of thought. "Okay, so you're saying that Jesus taught this esoteric stuff to Magdalene and she brought it to France?"

"Exactly," Ariel said. "And then I read her gospels. There are three fragments that were all found in Egypt in the late 1800s. In them, I thought I recognized the Tree of Life, a concept I was only vaguely familiar with. So I studied Kabbalah to see if this was the case, and sure enough, it was."

"So, I'm not trying to be difficult, but why is that a big deal?" Katie asked.

"Because as far as anyone knows, she is the only one that received these teachings from Jesus and wrote them down. Now, Jesus had a contemporary, Rav Akiva, also a master Kabbalist. He was also tortured and killed by the Romans. Akiva's top student, Rav ben Yochai and his son hid in a cave in the Galilee and spent thirteen years writing down all the oral teachings that had been passed down for thousands of years. All the Kabbalists at that time were being persecuted by the Romans and they were afraid if they didn't write the teachings down, they would be lost forever.

"The writings are called *The Zohar*. They were hidden under the ruins of the Temple of Solomon and didn't emerge until the 12th century in southern France. So the traditional lineage via Rav Akiva was preserved in *The Zohar*, and what I call the 'Christian lineage' was passed down from Jesus to Magdalene. And they both ended up in southern France. Quite the coincidence!"

"Okay," Katie said. "This is interesting, but how can you back it up? How do you know there *was* a 'Christian lineage'?"

"When I connected the dots between Magdalene's writings, which are authenticated, and Kabbalistic teachings, I contacted the head of the Kabbalah Center to present my ideas. It was common knowledge to them, meaning a part of their religious history, that Jesus was a master Kabbalist. He was from the line of David and Levi and was part of the familial lineage that was taught these deeper, more spiritual concepts. His contemporary Akiva was from the line of Joseph. They were well known as the two most elevated teachers of their respective lineages, fulfilling Jewish prophecy from way back.

"I had numerous discussions with the inner circle of the Kabbalah Center and they confirmed this. They knew Jesus had tried to bring the philosophy out to the masses, but it was prophesied that the concepts wouldn't be widely accepted until the Age of Aquarius—which is now. He tried, but he was two thousand years too early!

"Now, they didn't know about the whole Magdalene piece. But in their history of *The Zohar* in France, they knew about the Knights Templar-Cathar-Zohar connection and they kept seeing Magdalene as somehow part of it. But until I showed up with her history, they hadn't connected the dots."

"Jesus Christ!" Katie said.

"Here's the *piece de resistance*," Ariel said. "*The Zohar* was known to the Kabbalists as the Holy Grail. The Holy Grail legends were written in the 12th century, the same time frame, by Christian de Troyes and a German guy, Wolfram de Eschenbach. Wolfram said he was told the story by a Jewish man called Kyot, whom he met in Provence.

"Like I told you the other night, Magdalene is almost always portrayed with a jar, so my big theory is the jar represents the Holy Grail, because she carried the sacred teachings directly from Jesus."

Katie said. "Yeah, you said that you thought the jar represented the teachings or that she was carrying sacred teachings."

Ariel nodded. "This is where I diverge from Margaret Starbird. I believe *sang graal* is a reference to the Holy Grail. She and others believe it is holy blood, referencing Magdalene carrying the holy lineage of Jesus in her womb, a baby."

"I remember that idea from *The Da Vinci Code*," Katie said. "Do *you* think they were married?"

"I don't pretend to know! There's circumstantial evidence to say they were. And I suspect they were partners. But I stay neutral on the topic because I honestly *don't* know, and plus, I want her to be known for more than just being a wife and mother. So I say both things could be true," Ariel said. "I mean, Starbird and the rest *do* make a compelling case. Because the jar was also a symbol of the womb in the ancient cultures. And of course, the womb is the source of life. And a women's power center because she alone can carry life."

Katie's head was starting to swim.

"This is really pussy power," Ariel said, grinning.

Katie laughed.

"This is *la femme rouge*!" Ariel said.

"Okay, now I'm totally lost, what is *la femme rouge*?" Katie asked.

Ariel put up her hand. "Sorry," she said. "I'm jumping all over the place. After the medicine experiences with Grandmother, I started reading everything I could about Magdalene. This was the beginning of really following the trail of the Magdalene. The seeds had been planted years before by my experience in India, but it was the Grandmother who guided me to pick up the trail again and follow it.

"The name *la femme rouge* came to me one day in Tucson at that time. I was sitting out on my little patio with Chico and I had this vision. I saw this beautiful column of red sparkling energy. It surrounded me and somehow I knew it was the essence of the Magdalene, not in terms of her personality, not like a ghost, but a distinct kind of archetypal energy. Then I heard in my head, '*la femme rouge.*' It's funny that it came to me in French, because this was well before I came to France the first time."

"You know I like it, *la femme rouge*," Katie said. "It's kind of sexy and strong,"

"*Exactement!*" Ariel replied.

"In English, it would be 'red lady'?" Katie asked.

"Red woman," Ariel said. "But a more accurate translation to capture the intent is: red spirit woman. But regardless of the language, it kind of represents the blood, the womb, the jar, the teachings, and the independence and strength to carry the sacred knowledge and share it," Ariel said. "Anyway, all these ideas were inspired by Mary Magdalene, who by the way is often portrayed wearing red." She sat back in her desk chair and put her fingertips together, thinking for a moment. Then Ariel turned and looked at Katie.

"Henri likes to joke and say I could talk about her all day long. And he sometimes feels the need to remind me not everyone thinks this stuff is particularly interesting or relevant. Most people don't think what happened two thousand years ago has any bearing on today."

Katie nodded. She pretty much agreed with Henri—in her experience, religion was a societal concept designed to keep people in line—but she didn't want to admit that to Ariel. "It's an interesting story, but maybe most people wouldn't really understand it, unless they were religious or historians," Katie said.

"I realize that," Ariel said. "Often when you mention something connected with Jesus, secular people automatically think you're religious and they glaze over. And devout Christians often become defensive about anything that differs from the doctrine they've been taught. But I see it differently. I see who she was, what she did as vitally important. She was a pioneer on numerous fronts: an independent woman at that time, an enlightened person, and someone that actually made a huge contribution, even though it's been largely obliterated by the Church. To me, she is one of the founding women in what I see as spiritual feminism. She was a principle person who discovered a pathway toward greater happiness—for us individually, and also for the world—and offered it, or tried to offer it, to everyone."

Ariel looked at Katie, but her gaze seemed somewhere much farther away. "And she did it almost single handedly. With just the support of a handful of people who were driven into exile. Put on a boat and pushed out to sea. And they landed here, in a country that was open to women as teachers. A place in which the worship of the Goddess in her many forms was commonplace. She found fertile ground for what was given to her by Jesus and she planted the seeds. And they flourished and they were driven underground, then they flourished again, driven underground again. Like a tiny flower that miraculously grows in the crack of cement in the sidewalk. Stomped on, then coming back. Her story growing up through the hard, mean cement, to flower again. She is a flower, a wild crimson poppy, somehow managing to thrive in a tough, patriarchal, unnatural environment."

Katie stood staring at her aunt, her eyes misting. She was surprised that what Ariel had said got to her, but it did.

Ariel smiled and laughed a little self-consciously. "Hey, sorry, I didn't mean to deliver a sermon there. Something kind of came over me."

Katie wiped her eyes. "Well hell Ariel, you had me at 'spiritual feminism'!" Katie said.

They both laughed.

Katie took the last sip of her coffee and stared out the window. The hillside of green trees swayed in the afternoon breeze. She was finally starting to feel awake.

"You know, you don't have to stand in the doorway," Ariel said, smiling. "You can come in."

"Well, I didn't mean to keep you from your work," Katie said.

"Don't worry," Ariel replied. "I'm keeping me from my work."

Katie stepped into the office. There was a stack of papers on the chair next to Ariel's desk. Katie picked them up so she could sit down. She glanced down at a diagram on the top page.

"Is this part of your research?" Katie asked.

Ariel looked at the diagram and nodded.

"Can I look at these?" Katie asked.

"Sure," Ariel said. "I was hoping to expand on these to present at the conference, if I'm able to get my proposal in on time."

As Ariel explained the diagrams, Katie leafed through the pages and laid them side by side on the floor in front of her.

"The first diagram is a direct illustration of the Tree Mary describes with the eight branches and their corresponding names. The objective on the left side and the way to overcome on the right side."

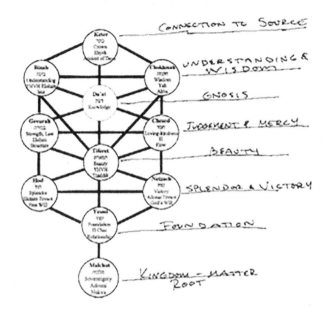

"From the description in the gospel, I drew out the great tree first. Jesus described an eight-branch tree. Then I printed out some Tree of Life diagrams from the Kabbalah tradition and drew lines as 'branches' extrapolating from the ten *sephirot*, or energy centers. The Tree of Life is diagrammatically more complex, as you can see because there are also pathways connecting the ten *sephirot*. When you look at the tree part, though, which is only these lines, the ten energy centers make eight branches. Going up the branches from the root to the crown is the process of enlightenment in both versions."

Katie looked over the diagrams. Ariel looked out the window a moment, then closed her computer.

"You know what, I think I need to get some air," Ariel said. "Usually, when I have a block, going for a walk helps. Then I'll come back and see if I can get some work done."

Katie looked up and nodded. She wanted to give Ariel some space to think, she paused a moment then said, "You know, I'd really like to finish that book you loaned me. I think I'll sit under the big oak tree in the garden. Do you mind?" Katie asked. "Seems like a nice way to spend the rest of the afternoon."

"Not at all," Ariel said as she stood. "We can each take some time and rendezvous for dinner."

"It's a date," Katie said grinning.

CHAPTER FOURTEEN

That evening Ariel prepared a dinner of salad and duck confit. Katie watched as her aunt opened a large metal container and pulled two cooked duck legs out of a sea of fat. She browned them in a sauté pan and drained the cooked fat back into the can. Katie had never heard of duck confit before, let alone eaten it. It was delicious and easy and very French, she thought as she got up to clear the table and put the dishes in the dishwasher. Ariel started the kettle and put the teapot, two cups, and a little bowl of chocolate-covered blueberries on a tray. She went to a cabinet and took out a tin of loose tea and put two pinches in the teapot. "This is a special brew," Ariel said. "Made by a certain herb-collecting, serpent-talking feminist I know."

Katie smiled thinly at the reference to the "Lilith" drama her aunt had performed the day before. In truth, the whole Lilith concept had gotten under her skin. It was stupid; they were just talking about archetypes or myths, but she was rattled by the mention of Lilith. Seeking to steer the conversation in a new direction, Katie asked, "Oh, who's that?"

"My friend Maureen. She's American but has been living in the Languedoc, near Rennes le Château for several years. I love this woman, she's a real character," Ariel said, smiling.

Katie nodded. "How did you meet her?"

"She was in the group I traveled with the first time I came to France to see the Mary Magdalene sites. We became friends and stayed in touch. She also helped me investigate a theory I had about Rennes le Château."

"Ah," Katie said, her tone somewhat distracted.

Ariel looked at her with a penetrating gaze that made Katie uncomfortable. She knew her aunt was "reading" her.

"Let's go outside," Ariel said suddenly. "We can sit down by the pool and watch the night."

Ariel picked up the tea tray and waited for Katie to open the door to the patio. The dogs ran out ahead of them down the grassy hill to the pool. Ariel set the tray down on a low patio table between two chaise lounge chairs. She lit a large candle lantern at the edge of the sitting area and it cast a pale glow around them as they sat and sipped their tea, each leaning back in their chairs, taking in the night.

After a few moments, Ariel turned toward Katie.

"Katie, what's going on?" She asked. "I saw this heaviness hanging in your aura when you first arrived and then again just now in the kitchen." Ariel paused. When Katie didn't respond, she said, "You know, whatever it is, you're not going to get any judgment from me."

Katie wanted to open up to her aunt. But in her family, they didn't really talk about things. For as long as she could remember, they were taught to be stoic, to keep their feelings in check. Katie could not remember a single time when her mother asked her how she felt or encouraged her to be vulnerable. It was not part of her mother's creed; even when her dad died, they were expected to soldier on, and they certainly knew not to burden their mother with their needs. So the idea of Ariel really wanting her to share was so foreign she needed a few moments to collect herself.

Katie held the warm cup in both hands and sipped her tea. She was so used to editing and shaping what she said, it felt strange to just tell the truth. But she knew she could with Ariel. Even though she didn't totally subscribe to Ariel's esoteric views, she knew she could trust her. She sat up, turning on the lounge chair to face Ariel and took a deep breath.

"It's just when you were talking about Lilith—I didn't say anything earlier, but when I went to the lower part of the cavern I realized the dream I had took place down there, and that is where the shrine to the lost innocents is," Katie said, and then stopped mid-sentence. She set the tea-cup down and looked at Ariel. "I didn't tell you the whole story earlier, about my manager Tom."

Ariel nodded. "The black Irish guy."

"Yeah," Katie said. "Well, I got pregnant. I couldn't believe it. I was with my ex for five years and we never even had a scare. Then one weekend with Tom and bam." Katie's voice started to shake. "The worst part is I really liked him. I thought we were starting something. I mean I was shocked to find out I was pregnant, but I may have felt differently about it if he hadn't dumped me."

Katie felt herself start to crack. She rubbed her forehead, resting her head in her hand. She knew tears were coming. "It was kind of a nightmare. Allen and I had just divorced, I'd quit the editing job and was barely getting by on my waitressing income." Katie stopped talking for a moment, sobs making her voice shaky. "I had to have an abortion. He didn't want to have anything to do with the situation. I went to the clinic by myself. It was terrible." That was it, she'd said it, Katie thought as tears streamed down her face. She wiped at them with the bottom of her t-shirt.

Ariel got up and sat next to Katie and put her arm around her niece's shoulders. Katie cried harder. She covered her face with her hands and let out a long, low moan.

"I really thought it was the best thing to do," Katie said, her voice choked with sobs. "I'm alone, don't know where my career's going, have no money...."

"Shh," Ariel whispered. "It's okay, Katie. You don't have to justify yourself."

Katie buried her face in her hands again as she leaned into Ariel's shoulder. She cried until she felt a release. Katie didn't realize how tense she'd been the last few weeks. She'd been holding it all in. She'd had to face Tom every day at work and try to act as though she was fine handling the whole situation herself. He'd completely distanced himself, had gone back to his ex and basically acted as if they'd never even been together. So she pretended to be okay, even to herself. As the tears subsided, Katie grew quiet. A feeling of emptiness, not quite peace but a sense of spaciousness, came over her.

Ariel patted Katie's arm. "I'll be right back," Ariel said, then she got up and went to the kitchen, returning with a box of tissues and a glass of water. Katie sat up and blew her nose and took a long drink of water.

"A little better?" Ariel asked.

Katie nodded.

When Ariel sat back down, she asked. "This just happened didn't it?"

Katie looked up at her, "A month ago."

"I'm the first person you told?"

Katie nodded.

Ariel reached out and held Katie's forearm. "I'm so sorry you had to go through this. Abortion is never easy, but to go through it alone is doubly hard. But you're not alone anymore. You've got me. And the solidarity of all of us women who've been through this," Ariel said.

Katie really appreciated Ariel's support; it did make a difference. She honestly felt better. Not only because she finally talked about it; she could also feel Ariel genuinely understood and cared.

"You've been through this too?" Katie asked, tentatively.

Ariel nodded. "I have, when I was eighteen. It was a similar situation to yours and it was really difficult."

She watched as a shadow flickered across Ariel's face. Then Ariel looked intently at Katie.

"I'd like to share something with you, something I've never told anyone, if that's okay," Ariel said.

"Yeah," Katie said, nodding.

"When I was eighteen, I made the mistake so many young women make: grasping at love. It was my first time and I didn't protect myself. I was so lost and naïve, I just fell into this guy's spell. And sure enough, my first and only time having sex, and I was pregnant! Back then there wasn't the morning after pill so I had a full procedure—a D&C—and it took a couple weeks before the bleeding and cramping stopped. Of course, I was thankful that it was safe and an option, but there was definitely a big physical as well as a psychological toll.

"But I want to tell you about what happened years later. It wasn't long after Dermot and I split up and I went to Tucson. There was a man

I met while hiking with Chico one day in the mountains. We became friends, not close, but the kind to have a coffee or go for a hike together. I knew he wanted more, but I just wanted some companionship. I'd just moved, didn't know anyone, was scared and lonely, starting over. Well, one night I made the mistake of going to his place for margaritas and... neither one of us had protection, but he swore he'd had a vasectomy.

"Sure enough, three weeks later I realize I'm pregnant. It felt surreal after twenty-two years of being careful to find myself pregnant. I really couldn't believe it. And of course, the timing was terrible. What was I thinking to sleep with this guy? Let alone without protection. What was wrong with me? I asked myself the same questions over and over."

"But Ariel, you were just lonely, looking for some love," Katie said.

Ariel smiled at her niece's kind words. "That's true, Katie. But it wasn't so smart."

"But you said he told you he'd had a vasectomy, so you didn't think pregnancy was even a possibility," Katie said.

"Also true," Ariel said. "After a few days of torturing myself, I realized that the situation wasn't going to change just because I was whipping myself in contrition. I had to calm down and think with a clear head. I knew I needed to make a decision about my life. Because of my age, I knew there was a good chance that it could be my last window to have a child."

"What did you do?" Katie asked as she leaned close to her aunt.

"I prayed," Ariel said. "I looked inside and asked my heart what it wanted.

"After the margarita night, this guy called several times claiming he was in love with me. But I did not want to be with him. And I knew in my deepest truth, that I didn't have what it took to raise a child on my own. I was barely taking care of myself. And I didn't really trust this guy; he'd been trying to get me into bed since we met. I also thought it was possible that he'd lied about the vasectomy."

"Oh my God, Ariel," Katie said.

Ariel shook her head. "So I made an appointment at a clinic to terminate the pregnancy. I was really nervous. I'd had a tough time before and honestly didn't want to go through it again. But I didn't think I had any other choice, I felt it was the right decision, but I was really nervous about it.

"That night I had a dream. Elder tribe women gathered around a cook fire. Herbs were picked and made into teas. I witnessed a time when women were in sync with the natural rhythms of the moon and healing properties of the Earth, when we controlled our fertility easily and naturally. When I woke up, it seemed as if this ancient knowledge had merged into my consciousness. It awakened my intuition and I knew what to do.

"I went to the local herb store and bought a tincture of the herb Vitex. It's good for bringing on a period and regulating a woman's cycle, especially if she is perimenopausal. I took the tincture three times a day and continued to pray. Every time my mind would panic, I would say, 'Thank you for my healing.'

"After several days of prayer and taking the herbal medicine, a friend of mine called—one whom I hadn't heard from in quite a while. She was a clinical acupuncturist and someone I trusted, so I told her my situation and asked her if there was something natural that could be done. At first, she was very reluctant to answer. However, when I explained I already had an appointment at a clinic for the following week, she agreed to work with me.

"She came over that night to do a treatment. She said she'd never done anything like this before but knew how to use a combination of acupuncture points to stimulate the uterus. If it was possible, the treatment would assist the body to miscarry naturally. Afterwards, she told me to rest and she would come back in two days to boost the treatment and see how my body was responding.

"As she packed up her gear to leave, I lay on my bed and fell into a deep sleep. I awoke several hours later; I remember it was around three in the morning. I felt flushed, and waves of heat coursed through my body. I had some abdominal cramping, which intensified, and an hour later my body released the three-week embryo. It was very simple, just a small clot like sometimes happens during a period. I did a ceremony and sent the spirit back to the light. I felt a deep calm and went back to bed, sleeping late into the morning.

"I called my friend the next day and told her what happened. She was surprised how quickly the treatment worked. And for the first time in her career, she wondered about using acupuncture to help women with unwanted pregnancies. But she was really uneasy about the whole process. 'Why?' I asked her. 'Probably nearly every woman we know has had to for one reason or another have an abortion. What if there were less intrusive, more natural ways of terminating a pregnancy?'

"I told my friend about my dream of the ancient women. They were at peace with their bodies and choices about reproduction. Most women I knew were at war with their bodies on some level. Of course, science had helped us! And we were thankful for birth control and our power to choose safe, legal abortions. But what I was speaking of was different. After that I did some research on various indigenous cultures and found out that in fact, natural procedures had been the way women decided about their own bodies and controlled their fertility for thousands of years. The 'ancient ways' had been lost—in our culture anyway."

Ariel stopped talking.

"So you never had to go for the procedure?" Katie asked. "That was it? Some herbs and acupuncture?"

"Yeah," Ariel said, nodding as she looked at Katie with a solemn expression in her eyes. "And maybe this sounds awful, but it was very empowering. Like I told my friend all those years ago, the ancient women completely controlled their own fertility both through understanding their natural rhythms of fertility and also through ending unwanted pregnancies very early. It was sacred women's business. Men had no part in it. Now look at what we have in the US, after such a hard won right to choose, the old patriarchal backlash stripping away women's access to birth control and abortion."

Katie nodded; it was true. Over the last couple of years access to abortion or even reproductive health was getting harder for many women. She was fortunate to live in a state that was progressive. But many women in the South and Midwest had fewer and fewer options. And of course, the most vulnerable women were the young and the poor. Women of color and those with less education were also falling through the cracks, having less opportunity to choose what was truly right for them.

Katie looked at Ariel closely in the soft light of the candle lantern.

"Ariel," Katie whispered. "What you just told me is pretty fucking revolutionary. And you never told anyone else about this?"

Ariel shook her head.

"Wow," Katie said, thinking about the implications of what Ariel had done. If alternatives like Ariel's were available, it gave women even more control. They could try acupuncture or herbal medicine in conjunction with the other options. They didn't necessarily have to go through procedures in a sterile clinic room. Thinking back to Ariel's story, Katie asked, "What happened with this guy? Did you ever tell him?"

Ariel took a deep breath. "Well," she said. "I debated about telling him. I really didn't want to have any more to do with him, yet I wanted him to understand the situation. It could be that his vasectomy had reversed. I didn't want another woman to suffer needlessly. So finally, I called him and asked him straight out about his vasectomy.

"And here it gets awful. He kind of giggled, like a little boy caught doing something bad. And I knew my intuition was right. I couldn't speak; this intense, icy anger came over me. What kind of man had no regard for women? He'd just wanted what he'd wanted. And unfortunately, he wasn't alone. There were far too many stupid narcissistic boy-men who play with women's lives and bodies as if it were their right.

"When I was silent for several moments, he stopped giggling. A strange composure descended over me, and I calmly told him about the pregnancy and the intentional miscarriage.

"He gasped and railed at me. 'How could you do such a horrible thing?' he cried. 'What kind of evil woman are you?'"

"'Don't *ever* lie to a woman again,'" I said. And I hung up. That's how it ended."

"Fuck," Katie said, drawing the word out for emphasis.

"Yup," Ariel agreed.

"What's wrong with these guys?" Katie asked.

"And what's wrong with us women?" Ariel said. "To have carried all the responsibility, shame and pain and have thought that was normal?"

Katie stared at her aunt. For a flicker of a moment, she thought she saw an ancient woman's face, fierce and wise, looking back at her. Katie blinked and it was gone. For a second she felt an intense crackling presence.

"Ariel," Katie whispered as she leaned toward her aunt. "I think I just *saw* something."

Ariel didn't say anything; she had a faraway look in her eyes as they sat together in the pale glow of the candle lantern. The pool water was still and dark. The night enclosed their little circle of light with warm whispers of breeze and the chattering of frogs and cicadas. Ariel looked over at the forested hill just visible at the back edge of the property.

"You know, there's a healing chapel on top of that hill over there," she said, pointing up over the forest. "There's a local legend: the chapel was built in the fourteenth century to honor Mother Mary. The villager believed she saved them from the plague that was making its way up north from Marseille. Since then, people began making the pilgrimage from the village below up the hill to visit the chapel and pray. It became a local custom to walk the trail in prayer for someone, asking for help, not for oneself but for someone else. When reaching the top of the hill, they pull the cord and ring the bell, releasing the prayer. There were many reports of miracles happening after these prayer requests were made."

It was a nice legend, Katie thought. But she didn't see how it related to their conversation.

"And we need to forgive," Ariel said. "Ourselves, the people who hurt us, and those we've hurt. One way to forgive is to pray for someone, to send them light. And I think it's the perfect time to do that."

"You mean you want to go up there *now*?" Katie asked. "How about tomorrow? It's dark, what if we get lost?"

"I've done that trail hundreds of times," Ariel stood up and pointed. "There's a shortcut through the woods behind our property, we can cut across and pick up the trail at the base of the hill. And the moon should be rising soon and will help light our way through the forest. I'll get a couple flashlights. Get your hiking shoes."

Katie sighed heavily but got up and followed her aunt to the house to change her shoes. After the talk they'd just had, she would have preferred to have a drink and then call it a night. But she could see Ariel wasn't going to back down. And she didn't have the energy to fight her headstrong aunt. So, hiking through the forest in the dark of night it was!

Ariel handed Katie a flashlight. They walked back down the grassy slope, past the swimming pool, then entered the edge of the forest. After a few minutes of navigating through the brush, they arrived at a clearly defined path. "Okay, "Ariel said. "Let's walk the trail in silence, so we can be in a prayerful state. The most powerful thing we can do is pray—send light to those who have hurt us. Because if they were more aware, they wouldn't have hurt us. So let's send them light, ask that they be blessed, healed, whatever you feel."

"Okay," Katie said, nodding. It was a stretch for her, but she liked the idea. It made her feel more powerful in a good way, not so much of a victim.

She followed close behind Ariel. A light breeze shook the leaves overhead. In the beam of the flashlight Katie could only see the back of Ariel and the ground right in front of her. She was nervous; she was a city girl, after all. Were there venomous snakes? Wild animals? Ariel had left the dogs inside the house, so they were alone in the dark.

The trail started to climb and Katie focused on her footing. Her breathing became more labored. But soon she found her rhythm and remembered the purpose of the trail. It was a pilgrimage, so she started with the only official prayer she knew—the Lord's Prayer, something she hadn't said for many years but could still recall. When she got to the part about forgiving those who trespass against us, she really understood it for the first time.

They walked in silence, each with their own thoughts. After about twenty minutes they approached the top of the hill. Ariel led them to the back of the chapel; she stopped and pointed her flashlight at the bell tower and the long cord hanging down. Ariel gestured for Katie to step forward and ring the bell, but Katie wasn't ready yet and shook her head. She gestured to Ariel, who nodded and went to the cord. Katie watched as her aunt bowed her head in prayer. She stood for a few moments under the bell tower and then reached up and pulled the cord.

The bell rang, echoing across the hilltop. Katie felt a chill. She sensed a ripple in the air. Ariel stepped back. Katie walked up under the bell tower, took a breath, and closed her eyes, concentrating. Then she pulled on the cord and released the prayers. As the bell rang, she felt something shift inside her. Maybe it was just the mystique of the ritual, but she had to admit she actually felt lighter.

Katie followed a path around the small chapel and saw her aunt sitting at a picnic table at the edge of a little clearing. She went to join her. Without speaking, Ariel pointed with her flashlight over the closed wooden door of the chapel. Katie followed the light and saw Mother Mary standing on a tower above them, glowing white and blue with her beatific smile.

Katie shuddered and felt another ripple pass through her. "She's awesome, Ariel," Katie whispered. "This place is magical."

Ariel nodded. Katie sat down across from her. Ariel had brought a small knapsack, and she set it on the table and pulled out two water bottles. She handed one to Katie, who took a long drink. Ariel then took out a little pouch of loose tobacco from the front pocket of the knapsack.

"An offering," Ariel said. "To the spirits of this place." Ariel took a pinch of tobacco, walked to the chapel, and placed it on the ground by the front step. She bowed her head and said a few words under her breath.

Katie wanted to leave an offering, too. "Can I?" Katie asked.

"Of course," Ariel said.

Katie took a pinch of tobacco and put it on the ground next to her aunt's. Ariel must be rubbing off on me, she thought. Yet for those few minutes, she could almost believe in the power of prayer and forgiveness.

As Katie walked back to the picnic table, Ariel pointed toward the roof of the chapel. "Look, Katie," she said.

A large, nearly full moon was just coming up over the treetops.

"Hello, Grandmother Moon!" Ariel called out, waving with both hands at the moon.

Katie smiled. They both sat watching as the moon rose, illuminating the chapel and then the clearing where they sat. Katie looked at her aunt, who seemed to be calculating something with her fingertips.

"Perfect," Ariel said. "The moon is in Scorpio—a time of prophecy and deep healing!"

"Really?" Katie said. She didn't really know exactly what that meant, but it felt right.

"At a time like this, you can really tune in to your intuition and receive some deep insight and guidance," Ariel said.

"Good," Katie said, laughing. "As you know, I can use all the guidance I can get!"

"Well, Grandmother Moon is helping you out," Ariel said. She took a drink of water and pointed at Katie. "I really think the divine feminine is courting you, Katie."

Katie smiled. Maybe Ariel was right. First Lilith, then Mother Mary, now Grandmother Moon. Though Katie still didn't think being courted by Lilith was such a good thing.

"Ariel?" Katie asked.

"Hmm," Ariel said.

"Do you think that woman in my dream was really Lilith?"

Ariel nodded. "I do. I think that you needed to look into what you've believed you've done wrong—your 'dark side'—to begin to understand who you are."

"In the book you loaned me, the author said something about Lilith and Eve coming together in Mary Magdalene. You know, making her whole," Katie said.

"Yeah, that's the idea. Bringing Lilith back from exile returns the feminine consciousness to wholeness," Ariel said. "She is the vilified one— unruly, independent, will take care of herself first. She is about power not nurturing. As women, we've been taught those characteristics are bad. We won't be loved if we aren't always caring for others first, putting their needs ahead of our own. If we don't, we're selfish."

Katie was quiet as she thought about what Ariel was saying.

"You know, when I first came across Lilith, I just saw her as lonely, angry, and living in the darkness because some man—Adam, no less—rejected her for being too independent. But the more I tuned into her, the more I could understand her. I also used to think that I could be loved only if I was subservient to others' wishes and ideas. I then felt a lot of compassion for Lilith. She is powerful and uncompromising in a way I find rather admirable."

"I get that," Katie said. "But this baby killer thing is disturbing."

"Katie!" Ariel said. "Who do you think labeled her that?"

"Patriarchy?" Katie ventured.

"*Exactement*," Ariel said. "Who do you think labeled the Magdalene as a whore to denigrate her?"

"Patriarchy," Katie said. "But in that book I read, they said she was sold into prostitution."

"Well, if that story is true, she climbed her way out of a terrible situation and became first independent and then Jesus' right-hand woman. The label of 'prostitute' wasn't put on her until the 6th century by Pope Gregory and it stuck. Even though in 1969, the Vatican officially removed the label and apologized for the mistake."

"Seriously?" Katie said. "They revoked it? How come nobody knows about this?"

Ariel cocked her head in mock frustration.

"According to the Church, Magdalene's claim to fame is being a repentant sinner," Ariel said. "But obviously Jesus didn't see her that way, and

I would trust his perceptions over the patriarchal world cultures."

"For sure!" Katie said, giving Ariel a high five. "You know, I think I get it. Magdalene faced and integrated her dark side, her Lilith, it gave her the strength to go on and liberate herself."

"Yes!" Ariel said.

Katie continued with her train of thought. "And she lived her truth, wore red, was beautiful, but claimed these things for herself. It was her nature to be a solar feminine, *a la femme rouge*."

"Yes, yes, yes!" Ariel said. "This was completely outside the few roles society had available for women. At least when she got to France, she found acceptance. They don't have so many issues with beautiful, strong women—or even prostitutes for that matter!"

Katie held up her water bottle. "*Vive la France*!" she said.

Ariel toasted with her water bottle, "*Absolutement*!"

Just then a barn owl flew only a few feet above them. Katie felt a swoosh over her head. "Oh my God," Katie yelped, instinctively covering her head with her arms. "What was that?" she asked as the owl disappeared into the forest.

"Whoa!" Ariel said. "That is owl medicine." She shook her head in disbelief. "Lilith's totem!"

Ariel raised both her arms over her head and called out. "Woo hoo!"

Katie felt the skin on the back of her neck prickle. She looked at her aunt, standing now and looking toward the forest where the owl had flown. Katie sat at the table, wearing a nervous grin.

Ariel saw her expression and laughed.

"Katie," she said. "What are you so worried about? You're witnessing some serious divine feminine magic in action!"

Katie smiled sheepishly. She wasn't used to magic flying right over her head in the middle of the night.

"C'mon, let's head back down," Ariel said, grinning broadly. "The trail will be lit up by now."

They left the chapel, now fully illuminated, and made their way to the trail and began the descent. It was much easier to see the path in the moonlight, so Katie relaxed quickly into a comfortable pace.

"You know, Katie," Ariel said. "Lilith is an important aspect of the collective unconscious that needs to be brought back into the light, to be loved and integrated. For women, she is the powerhouse. Lilith is a vital part of the divine feminine; she needs to be restored to her original glory."

"Okay...I get it, conceptually. But how can someone actually integrate Lilith?" Katie asked.

"Good question," Ariel said over her shoulder. "The simple answer is to be willing to look at what scares you about yourself. What part of you is wild and doesn't want to be tamed. What part is hiding in the shadows because you don't want to deal with it because, if you do, it's going to shake up your life or other people might not like it."

"Those are big questions," Katie said.

"They are indeed," Ariel said. "But I have found a shortcut. A way for each woman to integrate Lilith consciously."

Katie laughed. "You're just telling me that now?"

"Hey, you needed space to have your own process. Look at all the links you've made!" Ariel said excitedly. Then she stopped suddenly in the trail and turned and looked at Katie, her expression full of admiration. "Katie, you are figuring out some serious shit. You should feel proud of yourself."

Katie smiled awkwardly, feeling shy under her aunt's intense gaze.

Ariel turned to head back down the trail. "When we get home, I'll show you the shortcut—it's in your astrological chart."

CHAPTER FIFTEEN

When they entered the yard, the dogs ran out and greeted them. Chico barked until Ariel picked him up and held him.

"Who let you guys out, huh?" Ariel said.

Katie leaned down and petted Beau's back, which was wet from what appeared to be a recent romp in the swimming pool. Chico, on the other hand, was bone dry.

Ariel opened the door to the kitchen and they all went in. There were some dirty plates and glasses on the counter by the sink.

"The guys must have had a snack and are back at it," Ariel said. "Obviously too busy to clean up after themselves," Ariel winked. "Let's go upstairs and look at your chart."

Katie sat next to Ariel at her desk. She typed in a few commands and brought up Katie's

astrological chart. Katie recognized the wheel with all kinds of glyphs and crisscrossing lines.

"Okay, see this?" Ariel said. She pointed to a symbol that looked like a black crescent moon with a plus sign under it. "That's the black moon

Lilith glyph."

Katie leaned in closer to the computer screen. "And what is that exactly?" She asked.

"It's an astronomical point in space that the software calculates for each individual chart."

Ariel turned and grabbed a piece of paper from the printer. She drew a long elliptical circle and wrote "the moon's orbit." She then drew the Earth inside the circle and put the moon at the closest point of the orbit and put the Black Moon Lilith at the farthest point of the elliptical circle.

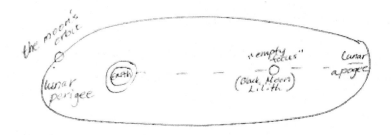

"The focal point close to the earth is the lunar perigee, and the furthest point is the apogee, that's where we find Black Moon Lilith," Ariel said.

"So, these are two focal points of the elliptical orbit of the moon?" Katie asked.

"Yes," Ariel said. "It's interesting because the Lilith point is the furthest point of the moon's orbit from the Earth. She's another aspect of the moon's journey, but not the one nearest the Earth, the Garden of Eden. Black Moon Lilith always resides out in the darkness, the shadow feminine."

"That is cool," Katie said. "So some astronomer named this Lilith intentionally?"

"Yeah," Ariel said. "It's funny how these old myths pop up from the collective unconscious."

"How did you find out about this?" Katie asked.

"From Sue. After I kept coming across Lilith in my research, I brought her up in one of our conversations. That's when Sue told me about the Black Moon Lilith point. It wasn't that well known in classical astrology then so I'd never heard of it. But that night after I got home from our meeting, I found the Black Moon Lilith point in my astrology software so I was able to include it in birth chart calculations.

"I brought up my own birth chart with the Black Moon Lilith point calculated in to see where she sat. It was rather telling, so I continued the investigation. I looked at other charts I'd done for friends and colleagues and noted the Black Moon Lilith point in each of them. I quickly saw a pattern. Because I knew everyone whose chart I had done, I had a sense of what their issues were.

"In every case, including mine, it was the same. Each one of our Lilith points showed where and how the exiled part of us was trying to return. It was the place of reconciliation.

"So I came to the hypothesis that Black Moon Lilith in astrological charts represents where and how the exiled feminine can be integrated. I really feel that the aspect of our psyche pushed to the shadows can be understood through the medium of astrology. And Lilith could be integrated—the powerful, wild aspect of the psyche brought back consciously."

179

"Okay, so each person has Lilith at a specific place, right?" Katie asked.

"Yes, in the birth chart, which is a snapshot of our solar system from the day, place and time we're born. It details where the planets, moon, and sun, and Black Moon Lilith were in relation to us, giving us a map to follow throughout our lifetime."

Ariel pointed to Katie's chart, showing her where the various planets were located on the big wheel.

"Black moon Lilith is in Gemini in your chart, in the third house. Remember that Lilith represents the exiled part of you, the aspect you need to bring in for wholeness and empowerment."

Katie nodded.

"Basically, that means your Lilith needs to be expressed through some form of communication, probably involved with writing, or digital media, through the internet or some other vehicle of communication." Ariel continued. "It's a double message about being a messenger because Gemini is ruled by Mercury, the messenger, and it's located in the house of Gemini."

"So I need to be a messenger?" Katie asked.

Ariel nodded. "Yes, there's information you are meant to communicate, and based on the other elements in your birth chart, I think you have chosen a great career path."

"So digital storytelling? You know my real love is filmmaking." Katie asked. "I just ended up editing to make some money."

Katie stared at her chart, her mind lost in thought. Then she looked up at her aunt. "Ariel, all this is incredible." Her tone was more serious now. "Everything seems so obvious looking at it like this," Katie said. She spoke slowly as the thoughts came to her. "I'm going to email my resume to the film production companies in New Mexico. I don't know if I'll get a job right away, but I'm going to go. If I need to, I can get a serving job there until I can break into the industry. It's time to move forward and follow my own path. I'm not sure how I'm going to fund this, but I know that the cost of living is so much cheaper in New Mexico than New York, so just making the change will improve my financial situation. And at least I'd be going in the right direction; doing something I've been wanting to do but was too scared to before."

"Well, you're not on your own," Ariel smiled. "You've got me in your corner, and..."Ariel turned to Katie, pausing.

Katie laughed. "And Lilith!"

Ariel snapped her fingers and pointed to Katie.

"I know how you can fund your move!" Ariel said suddenly. "I told your mother you were here to make a short documentary of the vineyard that we can use as a promo," Ariel said. "So, why don't you? You have your video camera."

Katie smiled. "I thought you were just saying that to cover my ass," Katie said. "But, yeah, I have my camera."

"Okay, I want to officially hire you to make a promo," Ariel said.

"But Ariel, I don't want you to offer just because you're trying to help me," Katie said, looking at Ariel intently.

Ariel snorted. "This isn't charity! Henri's been wanting to make a promo film to attach to the website. Believe me, he's looked into it. He found a guy in Avignon, but the estimate was really high so he put it on the back burner."

"Ariel, I don't know…" Katie said, feeling conflicted. She appreciated what her aunt was trying to do but it didn't seem fair somehow.

"Well, do you want the job or don't you?" Ariel asked, her eyes twinkling.

"Of course, I want the job!" Katie exclaimed.

"Great. But we can't start until next week because the cave is a mess. They're doing the expansion at the same time they're finishing the assemblage and there's shit everywhere," Ariel said. "But I can tell you, Henri would be very happy to make this film."

"That's no problem Ariel. For, say, a three-minute promo of finished work, I only need three or four days to film," Katie said. "Then I can edit and do the finishing touches when I get back to New York. No problem."

"So you're taking the job without even asking what the pay is." Ariel grinned mischievously. She pretended to be running numbers in her head. Then finally she said, "I figure with a family discount, five thousand should cover it."

"Oh my God, Ariel," Katie said as she jumped up and gave her aunt a hug. Katie smiled and shook her head in disbelief. "This is incredible, Ariel. This job will totally fund my move to New Mexico, easy."

"Good," Ariel said, wiping her hands together. "Done, you have a good plan."

Katie paused a minute as she sat back down. "You know, Ariel, I was going to offer to do it for free," she said.

"Shush!" Ariel said, smiling. "This is a job. Do you think *I* need *your* charity?"

Katie laughed.

Ariel chuckled. "Okay, I think our work here is done. It's late. Why don't we call it a night?"

But Katie was wide awake with renewed enthusiasm for her life. She wanted to keep talking but she could see lines of fatigue around her aunt's eyes. She also realized she'd only been awake for a few hours so her body clock was really askew.

"Okay," Katie said, trying to keep the reluctance out of her voice. Then she looked down at the folder on the corner of Ariel's desk. She knew it contained the papers with Ariel's diagrams.

"Ariel, do you mind if I take a look at your notes?" Katie asked. "I find this Tree of Life stuff interesting."

Ariel shrugged. "Sure, *ma chérie*, have at it." She reached down and picked up the folder and handed it to Katie.

Katie took the folder. "Thanks, Ariel. I'm kind of wired and need something to dig into."

Ariel stood up and stretched. Katie followed her out of the office.

"Can you get the light?" Ariel asked as she started down the hall.

"Sure," Katie followed, stopping by her bedroom door.

"Sleep well," Ariel said. "Let's rendezvous in the morning."

"Sounds good, Ariel," Katie said. "Sleep well."

Ariel went downstairs, her footsteps fading as she reached the kitchen.

Katie switched on the light by her bed and fluffed the pillows up against the headboard. She wasn't sure why, but she was inspired to look at Ariel's ideas. Maybe it was because Ariel had seemed so despondent earlier. Her aunt hadn't said much but Katie could tell she was really frustrated about her work. Katie gathered that she was having a hard time getting interest in it from a publisher. Or figuring out how to present the ideas in a manner that people would accept.

She sat crossed legged on the bed and opened the folder, spreading out the diagrams in front of her. She looked at the symmetrical Tree of Life with its ten *sephirot* and the numerous lines connecting them. The more she looked at it, the more she saw. There were rectangles and squares and an equilateral triangle within the overall structure. Katie set the pages aside and pulled a stack of loose typing paper out of the folder. Ariel apparently liked to write free hand with a blue pen on the loose sheets. There were pages of notes with scrolls and stars drawn on the borders.

Katie began to read through the notes. She'd heard enough of Ariel's ideas to follow most of the information. Within the loose pages, she saw how her aunt traced the link between the ancient mystical teachings of Kabbalah given to Magdalene by Jesus and later described in her gospel. She noted the resurgence of Magdalene's story in 13th century France at the same time the written version of the Kabbalah, *The Zohar*, appeared and was studied by Jewish scholars.

Katie was careful to lay the sheets she'd read face down in the same order in which she had found them. She removed the paper clip from another set of papers. On the front page, Ariel had written, *check out with Maureen—Rennes le Château*. Below was a photo copied diagram in red ink of the Tree of Life overlaid on what looked like a map. Katie brought the paper closer to the bedside lamp. It was definitely a map of a village with different buildings labeled that corresponded to the ten *sephirot*. *Rennes le Château* was written at the bottom of the map.

Katie recalled the name from an earlier conversation with Ariel. She got out her phone, looked up the village and saw that it was in the region called Languedoc. When she typed in the location to get directions, she saw it was four and a half hours west. She didn't know why exactly, but she sensed they needed to go there. Katie put all the papers back in the folder and set it on the desk. She went back to her phone and began reading the voluminous entries under Rennes le Château.

Eventually Katie's eyes grew heavy and she fell asleep, her head swimming with tales of a priest suddenly coming into great wealth after discovering a cache of books and treasure beneath the village church. She fell asleep and dreamed she was walking through the village and found herself standing on a precipice next to a weird-looking stone tower. Suddenly she jumped off the ledge, the sensation of falling woke her up. Whoa, she thought, her heart pounding.

Katie woke up early. She hadn't slept more than six hours, but she felt energized. And she had an idea. She got up, put on her cut-off Levis and a long-sleeved shirt, and went downstairs to make some coffee. There was a paper sack full of croissants and *pain au chocolate* with a sticky note from Henri. "*Bonjour,* ladies," it said, with a valentine heart drawn underneath. I could definitely get used to this, Katie thought as she took a big bite of the pastry with dark chocolate inside. She took it and a cup of coffee out to the patio to enjoy the morning sun.

Ariel came into the kitchen. She spotted Katie out on the patio.

"Good morning, early bird," Ariel said groggily. She poured herself some of the strong coffee and came to sit next to Katie. Katie smiled at her aunt in her short, striped cotton bathrobe, her thick hair wild and unkempt. Ariel took a couple of long sips of her coffee.

"You look ready for action," Ariel said.

185

"You know, I feel really good," Katie said. She gave her aunt a few moments to drink her coffee.

Ariel ran her hands through her hair then sat back in her chair, crossing her tanned legs.

"Ariel, I read through that file last night," Katie said.

Ariel groaned a little but looked at Katie.

"And honestly, your research is really interesting. I mean you make a lot of links. I don't understand it all but there are some fascinating ideas there," Katie said.

Ariel bobbed her head back and forth, not seeming entirely convinced herself.

"So I have a couple questions," Katie paused, waiting to see if Ariel was up for talking about her ideas.

"And..." Ariel said.

"Well, first of all," Katie said. "How come nobody knows about this?"

"I don't know," Ariel said, sighing as she sat back into her chair. "It's probably because all these traditions are separate. The Kabbalah is from the Jewish line. The gnostic tradition came from the early teachings of Christ and has its own Christian lineage. The scholars studying the gnostic gospels don't know the Kabbalah. The academic research on the fragments found of the Gospel of Mary that describe the esoteric teachings from Jesus are focused on the early Christian movement. They don't look to the Jewish tradition, *et cetera*."

"But you seemed to have pulled it all together," Katie said. She studied the expression of frustration on her aunt's face.

Ariel nodded. "It's probably because I'm *not* a scholar and have studied various traditions and esoteric practices, so I was able to make connections that others wouldn't think to link together. I'm not really aligned with any particular faith or point of view. I don't need to protect one particular way as *the* way."

"But that's the brilliant part, Ariel," Katie said. "You linked it all together, and that is huge. I mean, if I follow your ideas, it seems like you basically found the Holy Grail!" Katie grinned broadly.

Ariel smiled at her niece. She seemed genuinely moved by Katie's enthusiasm. "But here's the problem: the last year or so I've been stalled. There was some initial interest in my ideas and I was able to get an agent based on my first proposal, but in the end she couldn't find a publisher willing to take us on because I'm not a scholar. I've had no academic training in religion or theology; I have no letters after my name. So ironically, the thing that helped me make all the connections—my background as an astrologer and numerologist, being intuitive, good at pattern recognition—is the very thing that prevented my ideas from being taken seriously."

"But didn't you say yesterday that your agent wanted you to put together a new proposal to submit to a conference?" Katie asked.

"Yeah, the idea is if I can find a clear angle and present it in front of the academics at the Gnostic Conference, maybe one of them will work with me to get this research corroborated and, eventually, published," Ariel said. "But frankly, it's a long shot and I have less than two weeks to put something together." She yawned loudly, kind of turning the sound into a lion's roar. Then she looked at Katie. "Didn't you say you had a question about something?" Ariel asked as she took a long drink, finishing her coffee.

"Um," Katie scrambled to collect her thoughts from the previous night. "You said your American friend Maureen lives near this place, Rennes le Château. What is the deal with this village? There's a ton of stuff on the internet about it!"

"Ah ha," Ariel said, smirking. "Rennes le Château is a kind of Harry Potteresque village that attracts a lot of crazy people with crazy theories, myself being one of them."

"But what is that map with the Kabbalah diagram superimposed on it?" Katie asked.

"That's some information that was given to me, the theory being the priest who received a large sum of money from the Catholic Church for keeping his mouth shut about the treasure trove he found under his church couldn't talk about what he found but he built some strange buildings and had some strange things in his church, most of which are connected to Mary Magdalene and her legacy. But nobody has been able to crack the code. Last fall Maureen helped me look at this theory that the buildings form the diagram of the Tree of Life."

"And?" Katie asked.

"And, it didn't really come to anything, it was incomplete, too many stretches to make the theory work. I finally gave up. I didn't want to be another nutter poking around the village with a wild hare." Ariel said, feigning a British accent.

"I think we should go there," Katie said. "I think we'll find something that will help your research."

"What?" Ariel replied, shaking her head. "Believe me, I've exhausted that lead."

"I just have a feeling there is something there," Katie said, smiling mischievously. "Call it an intuition."

"Oh for God's sake," Ariel said, but Katie saw the light in her eye. "It's not next door, you know. It's a five-hour drive from here."

"Four and a half," Katie said. "I checked on Google maps."

"So we'd have to do an overnighter," Ariel said.

"Sounds great!" Katie replied.

"You're serious?" Ariel asked.

"Totally. Look, you said last night I can't start any filming until next week and honestly I have a feeling about this, so why not?" Katie said rapidly, hoping to get in the last persuasive argument for the trip.

Ariel groaned as she went into the kitchen and poured herself some more coffee. "I'll call Maureen and see if she's in the mood for guests," Ariel called to Katie.

When Ariel came back into the kitchen, Katie heard snippets of the conversation. "My niece... harebrained idea.... it would be great to see you... not too much trouble?" Then quiet. Katie waited for her aunt to come back out.

Ariel stepped into the open doorway. "Okay Miss Katie, get your shit packed, we're going on a road trip!"

"Yeah!" Katie said, clapping her hands together.

"I'll go to the cave and tell Henri what's happening. He's so busy, it's a good time to go. Can you be ready in a half hour?" Ariel said. "If we hurry, we can meet Maureen at her favorite restaurant for lunch."

"Sure," Katie said, smiling. She collected the breakfast dishes and came into the kitchen. Before Ariel left the room, Katie said again, "Ariel, I just have a feeling about this."

Ariel smiled as she turned to go and pack.

CHAPTER SIXTEEN

Katie cleaned up and quickly packed her bag. Then she went downstairs to wait for Ariel by her Peugeot. Ariel came out the front door, followed by her two dogs.

"Hey, over here," she called to Katie, "We're taking Henri's Porsche for the road trip."

"Cool!" Katie said as she picked up her bag and went to the silver Porsche Macan. "This is stylin'."

"Henri wants us to be extra comfortable and safe," Ariel said, winking at Katie. She opened the back and they put their gear inside. "Okay, you guys, be good. Don't let Henri feed you too much." Ariel leaned down and picked up Chico, giving the aged Chihuahua a kiss. She rubbed Beau's back affectionately. "We'll be back soon," she said as she got into the driver's seat and adjusted the seat and mirrors.

Katie got in the passenger side and closed the door gingerly. "I've never ridden in a Porsche before," she said.

"Oh, c'mon," Ariel chided her, "it's just a car."

They backed up as close as they could get to the cave and Ariel honked the horn. A few moments later Henri came out and waved. Ariel lowered her window, "Bye, darling, *a bientot*!" Katie smiled and waved excitedly. Henri blew them kisses then turned to go back inside the building.

As they drove across the foothills and turned onto the main road, Katie was beginning to recognize the surrounding countryside. Mount Ventoux was now behind them as they crossed the valley of vineyards and made their way to the freeway. But this time instead of heading east they went west. They didn't speak much. The radio played a mix of French and American pop songs. Katie was content to watch the Provence scenery go by. Ariel seemed content too; she had a slight smile on her lips. Katie wondered what she was thinking about.

After a couple hours of a good time, they stopped at a rest area for a bathroom break. Katie was amazed at the service centers in France. There was everything; coffee, pastries, baguette sandwiches, books, clothes, toys for kids. And they had a really good chocolate selection. Katie stopped to buy a bar of dark chocolate with hazelnuts and a couple of bottles of water while Ariel fueled the car. She fumbled a bit when she tried to pay. She couldn't get used to one- and two-euro coins, but the woman behind the counter picked the right amount from the palm of Katie's hand and nodded politely.

Katie found Ariel standing next to the Porsche stretching her arms and neck. The weather was a little cooler, the sky was overcast and Katie actually welcomed the break from the sun.

"Ready?" Ariel asked as Katie approached the car.

"Yep," Katie said. "I bought us a few provisions." Katie handed Ariel a bottle of Evian water. She held up the chocolate bar. "And they had my favorite chocolate!"

"Good, *ma cherie*," Ariel said, smiling. "That will get us there."

Not long after they got back on the freeway, Ariel pointed to a sign announcing "Les Routes du Pays Cathare."

"We're in Cathar country, *Pays Cathare*, now" Ariel said. "We're not far from Bezier, the site of one of the worst massacres in the crusade against the Cathars. It happened on July 22 1209, Magdalene's feast day." Ariel looked over at Katie with an expression of sadness mixed with exasperation. "It was the first big military offense and twenty thousand people died. They just went in and killed everyone."

"You think they were trying to make a statement by attacking on that particular day?" Katie asked.

"For sure," Ariel said. "Beginning a crusade against a peaceful people who practiced a simple but powerful kind of Christianity that came from Mary Magdalene's teachings on her feast day. Not a coincidence. There were people hiding in the main cathedral, Catholics, Cathars, and who knows who else. They blocked the doors and burned it down with everyone in it. When the leader of the crusade was asked by a soldier how they'd know who Cathar was, he replied, 'kill them all and let God sort it out.' It was a cathedral dedicated to Mary Magdalene."

Katie felt a chill. "No, that's not a coincidence," she said quietly. She looked out the window but they couldn't see much of the town from the freeway. "So is this the Languedoc?" Katie asked.

"Yeah, basically since Montpellier, we've been in the Languedoc," Ariel said.

"And you said that the Cathars were all here, in this region, right?" Katie asked.

"Yep, all this area, including where we're going—surrounding Rennes le Château is Pays Cathare."

Katie thought about the history she'd read in Ariel's notes as well as what Ariel had told her. "So you believe that Magdalene was walking and teaching throughout this area?" Katie asked.

"Yeah, I do. And the main reason is because the Cathar people had a gospel, this was the 'sacred book' I kept reading about in my research. A few years ago, a woman from their community published it. It's the first time it's been available outside the Cathar community: the complete gospel of Mary Magdalene." Ariel said. "Called the *Gospel of the Beloved Companion*."

Katie waited for Ariel to continue, but she pointed out the window.

"Hey, let's stop up there. There's a lookout with an amazing view of Carcassonne."

Ariel pulled the car over at an overlook and opened her door. Katie followed her, grabbing her camera case from the back seat. She looked out over the landscape. Fields of vineyards and farmhouses gave way to a village that looked like something from Disneyland. Katie got her camera and photographed the medieval city. It was completely surrounded by walls with stone turrets. A castle sat inside with stone houses densely built inside the fortifications.

"Wow," Katie said, as she shot some pictures.

"Yeah," Ariel nodded. "Maybe we can stop there on the way home. It really is something to see."

Katie looked over at her.

"Hey, Ariel," Katie said. "We're on a mission. I'm sure there are a million incredible places to visit, but we need to focus." Katie gave her aunt a kind of school matron look.

Ariel laughed. "Yes ma'am!" she said. "At the very least, we need to get to Maureen before the restaurant closes."

They got back in the car. Katie looked in the viewfinder at the photos she just took. She'd gotten some nice shots. As she put her camera back in the case and settled into her seat, she looked over at Ariel.

"So what were you saying? Something about the lost gospel?" Katie asked.

Ariel got back on the freeway and up to speed. Then she turned to Katie. "I was just thinking how, when I look back, everything happened at once. I never really thought about it before—probably because I was just living through the experiences. But my first trip to France to visit the Magdalene sites, the Gospel of the Beloved Companion had just been published, and meeting Henri, it all happened within a few months."

"Ariel," Katie said. "You know I've been patiently waiting to hear the story about how you and Henri got together." She gave her aunt an impish grin.

Ariel chuckled. "Forget rewriting biblical history, we all just want the love story," she said. "The happily ever after."

"Yeah, we do!" Katie said, smiling.

CHAPTER SEVENTEEN

ARIEL

After my experiences with Grandmother and her cryptic message about the red woman and Mary Magdalene, I read everything I could find related to her history. I also came across a trilogy of historical fiction based on the author's research on Magdalene's life and her own mystical experiences. I really enjoyed her work and signed up for the author's newsletter. One morning not long after, there was an email from the author. I could hardly believe the content as I read through it. The author and her husband had been exploring the mysteries of France since 1995. After receiving many requests from fans, they decided to run a tour. They would be following in the footsteps of Mary Magdalene after she arrived on the shores of France. It was not so much a tour, but more of a spiritual and historical journey. A shiver ran through me. I knew I would go. I recalled the promise I made to myself years before in India that I would one day visit Magdalene's cavern.

"They are doing a tour!" I said to Chico. "This is my big chance!" I got up and did a little happy dance. Chico looked at me from his spot on the love seat and cocked his head.

Not long after I'd signed up for the France trip, I woke up one morning in an especially good mood, so I dressed with some flair. A bit flashy in an olivine satin blouse and animal print blazer, I hurried to the main dining room at Rancho Encantada, arriving at the captain's table a few minutes late. Part of my job was to host a lunch table once a month. I sat down next to a man whose face was hidden behind a lunch menu.

He glanced up when I said hello. I stared for a moment. Surrounding him was an aura of white light. He looked at me through piercing blue eyes and then went back to his menu, only to look up again—the double take is always a good sign. I introduced myself, and we shook hands. He told me he was in a hurry, so I motioned for him to return to his menu. He explained that he was doing the ropes course next and was a little nervous because he was afraid of heights. I told him I loved heights and used to be a hang-glider pilot.

We started talking. I asked him about his French accent, and he explained that he was from Quebec and lived in Montreal. I said that my great-grandmother was from Montreal. He softened. I told him I was going to study French to prepare for my upcoming trip to southern France. He asked me what region I was traveling to. I told him Provence and the Languedoc. He sat up straighter and asked me what I'd be doing in the region. I told him I would be traveling with a small group led by two authors to trace the steps of Mary Magdalene across southern France. I also mentioned that I was planning to take a couple days to visit some vineyards and enjoy the countryside after the tour.

His company happened to own a large working vineyard in the Languedoc, he said. He offered to arrange a private tour for me. By the end of the lunch, he'd given me his contact information and told me to email him when I had my itinerary set. It was possible that we would both be in France at the same time. We couldn't stop grinning at each other.

I managed to walk back to my office without my feet touching the ground. I looked up at the sky and said, "Now I understand what you've been trying to tell me!" I had the sensation of a door opening to another dimension of my life. As I thought about the lunch, I realized that Henri had asked me more about myself in fifty minutes than my ex-husband had during our entire relationship! I got to the door of my office and saw my colleague sitting outside waiting for her next client. "What happened to you?" she asked. "You're glowing." "I think I just met him," I said. "Him, him?" "Him, him."

When I got home, I checked the website of Henri's vineyard in France. I couldn't read most of the French, but I saw pictures of vine-covered rolling hills and the pastoral countryside. After locating it on the Google map, I realized it was only a couple-hours drive from Lourdes. I could visit the vineyard during the last weekend of my trip.

I wrote Henri a short email to let him know I would be in the area and would love a tour of the vineyard in May. I also let him know that I was on my days off so unfortunately, I wouldn't see him around Rancho Encantada. I added that I was sorry we didn't have more time to talk about the region. That was subtle enough, I thought. If he was feeling the same, I figured he would pick up on the hint about having more time to talk. If not, it was a friendly email, not too assertive. Employees weren't supposed to reach out to guests privately. However, I'd had the strong sense to contact him while he was still in Tucson.

The next morning, I received an email from Henri inviting me to join him for breakfast the following day. Wow!

Over breakfast, we talked for two and a half hours about the Languedoc region of France and Cathar history. He asked me about my work. We talked about metaphysics and his experiences with intuition in his own life. We laughed a lot. When the dining room closed, we sat in the lobby and talked for another half hour.

"I think I would like to try this number thing," he said.

At first I wasn't sure what he meant. "Oh, you mean you want to do a numerology session?" I asked.

"Yes, do you have time tomorrow to do that?" he asked.

"How about ten o'clock?" I said. I was off the next day and my colleague had the office, but I'd make it work.

"Great." Henri was smiling. "I'll see you then."

"What's your birth date?" I thought to ask as I stood up to leave.

When Henri told me, my breath caught. He looked at me, then reached out and squeezed my hand. "Bye for now," he said. I walked away in a bit of a daze.

The next morning Henri was early, so I quickly drew up his numerology chart as he sat in the office with me. I went through each of his core numbers and described different aspects of his nature. Then I focused on his upcoming year. I described what I saw based on the number patterns. When I was through with my analysis, I asked if he had any questions.

"How do you know all this about me?" he asked.

"Because of the numbers," I said.

"You figured all this out from these numbers?" he said. "You didn't Google me?"

I laughed. "We are not in the habit of Googling guests," I said. "The number patterns form a language that I understand. It's as though the numbers speak to me."

"Wow," Henri said. "I didn't know it could be so precise."

I smiled. I was flattered. He seemed genuinely impressed.

"You really see me having this 'second act'?" Henri asked.

"Yes," I said. "In the next couple of years, there will be some profound changes. That will lead to a positive new beginning in pretty much every area of your life."

"It's been a difficult few years, so that is good news. A little hard to believe, but hopeful," he said.

We talked for a while longer, and the hour session turned into two. I knew that my colleague was coming soon and I needed to vacate the room. We stalled outside the office, standing under the portal as a heavy rain fell. Finally, Henri leaned in and gave me a kiss on each cheek. I wanted another excuse to see him during his stay but it seemed awkward, so I just smiled and we said goodbye.

As I left Rancho Encantada, I thought about Henri's numbers. They had revealed a lot about him and his life. I could see that he'd been going through a turbulent time in both his family life and professional life. I also knew that he was on the cusp of a much happier time. In fact, his birth chart showed that his "second act" would be his lightest and brightest.

While calculating his chart, I had also discovered more that I didn't share in the reading. Interestingly, Henri and I had the same time cycles. We would always be in the same numerological year and transiting cycles at the same time and this particular year was an auspicious one for love and relationship for us both. Of course, I didn't share this information with him.

I felt restless when I got back to my apartment, alternating between anxiety and elation, so I took Chico out for a walk. The rain had stopped and the afternoon had turned clear and sunny. While we walked, I called my friend Devra and told her the story of the last few days. She felt optimistic and thought I would be hearing from Henri soon.

I wanted to believe her, and believe in the numbers, but as the afternoon wore on, I became increasingly unsure. However, I did check my email that evening and was pleasantly surprised.

Bonsoir Ariel,

I just want to tell you how happy I am to have met you. I must say your numerology session was a profound experience for me and very helpful. I don't know what the future holds, but I feel strongly that one day soon we will be smiling over a glass of wine together.

Best to you,

Henri

During the next few months, I focused on my preparations for the France trip and continued to read about the Cathar people of the Languedoc region. In all my studies about Mary Magdalene in France, and the Cathar people, I found references to a lost book. The prevalent theory was that a book, which was the central guide and text of the Cathar people, was smuggled out and hidden during the siege of Montsegur in 1244, the last holdout of the Cathar people against the Pope and the King of France.

And I found such a book in Tucson. Just when I thought I'd pretty much read everything connected to Magdalene—the good, the bad, and the kind of crazy—Devra called me to ask if I'd heard about some new complete gospel of Mary Magdalene. I told her the only book on the

Gospel of Mary I'd found was the definitive scholarly work of Karen L. King, a Harvard Divinity School professor. She'd studied the three fragments found in Egypt, all which happen to contain parts of the mystical passages from Jesus. So I assumed whatever Devra had stumbled across was probably in the crazy category.

Devra knew about the research I'd been doing. She told me she went online to check out some of the books I told her about and ended up getting sucked into the search engine vortex. We both laughed and I didn't think anymore about it—until a couple of days later, when I received a package from Amazon. It was a *bon voyage* gift from Devra.

I opened the packaging to find *The Gospel of the Beloved Companion: The Complete Gospel of Mary Magdalene*. It was the first time I'd seen it, or even heard of the title. A chill ran through me. I opened to the first pages to find more information and saw that the book had just been published. In my research of Mary Magdalene, this was the first book I'd come across actually written by someone from the Cathar community.

That night, to get in the spirit of the upcoming trip, I sat on my patio and had a light supper of baguette, cheese, sausage, and red wine. I opened the book and read the lengthy introduction. The author laid out the history of the Cathar people. It dovetailed with what I'd discovered from other sources. She claimed they'd had the gospel in their community since the first century. If what the author said was true, this gospel could prove to be a missing link in the chain, connecting the history of Magdalene in Provence and the legacy of her teachings in Languedoc.

I set it down and took a long sip of wine. Could this be real? I wondered. It was almost too much to believe. I set aside my questions and read the actual gospel. Much of the basic narrative was familiar. However, there were the incredibly mystical teachings of Jesus in their entirety. Up until then, I'd only read fragments of these teachings in the three gospel pieces that had been authenticated by Harvard professor Karen L. King.

I poured another glass of wine and thought about the book. It seemed very plausible that Mary Magdalene had either brought her gospel, the account of her time with Jesus—as his beloved companion—to southern France with her or written it there. It was written in Greek, the predominant language of the literate at that time. As she taught and spread Jesus's message, she would have shared the gospel stories. After her death, the gospel would have become the founding document upon which Catharism was built. The word Cathar meant "pure one" in Greek.

This would be the basis of the Cathar version of Christ's message: a message of love that brought the light and power of the spirit to the Earth for each person to experience directly. It was a book and a faith that the early church fathers in the Council of Nicaea and later the Albigensian Crusade would try to obliterate—along with the memory of Mary Magdalene, apostle and beloved companion of Jesus Christ.

As the departure date for the France trip approached, I kept myself busy with work and preparations. But I couldn't hide the fact that I was disappointed I hadn't heard from Henri in months. Had he changed his mind about meeting me in Languedoc? Had he forgotten? Did something else come up? Why didn't he get back to me? There was no way of knowing, and I wasn't going to contact him again. The ball was decisively in his court. So I did what I'd (reluctantly) learned to do when it came to men: I let it go. Let go, let God.

Devra drove me to the airport. I was nervous and fidgety and kept checking my purse to make sure I had my passport and all the papers with the itinerary. As I gave Devra a hug goodbye, she told me to just be open to the magic and not worry about what may or may not happen. I nodded and then made my way inside the airport.

I arrived in Marseille a couple days before our group was convening, and spent time walking around the harbor and visiting some of the landmarks. I liked it there, being alongside the Mediterranean Sea. The sandstone architecture was inviting, and I found the people very warm and helpful. When it was time to meet the tour group, I was somewhat acclimated and ready for whatever the pilgrimage had in store. I was so excited to finally be seeing, firsthand, the sites I had been reading about in the fictional and nonfictional accounts of Mary Magdalene's life. And it turned out that first trip laid the groundwork for so much of what came later, both in researching Magdalene and also in my personal life.

From Marseille we traveled the short distance to Saint-Maximin-la-Sainte Baume. As you can imagine, that first time at Magdalene's crypt was very powerful for me. As I looked at the skull resting on a cushion inside that strange ornate glass case, it was hard to wrap my mind around the idea that it could actually be her skull and that I was standing over the place where her skeleton had been found. I took a moment trying to absorb the fact that I was where I was. And that's when I thought to say a prayer to the woman who had become my heroine, mentor, and muse. I lit a candle for her and for all those who had been healed and inspired by her presence and her life. Then I asked her for a favor.

Dear Magdalene,

I appreciate your huge contribution to the emergence of the divine feminine. And that is really important to me. But honestly, I really need to ask a personal favor: anything you could do to help move things along in my love life would be greatly appreciated!

Thank you.

After the morning in the basilica, we traveled the short distance to La Baume. I'll never forget that first visit to the cavern. As I reached the final rock outcropping, I felt completely overwhelmed by a palpable mix of grief and heightened awareness. I sat down at the mouth of the cavern; the mist formed a shimmering curtain. I could feel *her*. In my pursuits of the spiritual, I have been to many sacred sites. But I had never experienced such a poignant spiritual energy. It was as if time stood still and I was back two thousand years ago. I felt like I had entered a room that she had just left.

A black-robed Dominican monk patrolled the area, shushing the visitors quiet. I walked back into the shadows, sat down on a damp rock, and closed my eyes to meditate. I felt myself dissolving into the energy, a sparkling effervescence. Eventually I came back to myself. I stood up, walked around the cavern, and lit candles at the altar.

I studied the series of stained glass windows at the entrance and was transfixed by the one of Mary Magdalene anointing Jesus. I noticed the strange red pyramid situated above her with seven serpents descending from it. Was this referencing the seven demons Jesus released? It reminded me of my experience in Ecuador with Grandmother. When I released fears and worries, the snakes slithered away from me. I also took photos of the stained glass windows, each one depicting a part of her story.

When we returned from the cavern, I went back to the hotel to take a nap. I was tired from the power and emotion of the day. But as I came through the lobby, I saw that the hotel's one computer was free. I wanted to check and see if there was any news from Devra, who was watching Chico. I scrolled down quickly through my emails, but stopped the cursor at the one from Henri.

Bonjour Ariel,

I apologize for the delay. I just finalized my agenda. I will be in the Languedoc the last weekend of May. If you're still available, I would be delighted to show you the region. I can take you to some interesting vineyards, as well as on a tour of my own.

Henri

I sat staring at the screen. I checked the date; he had sent the email that afternoon. What timing.

"Thank you, Magdalene," I whispered. "That was impressively fast work!"

When I got to my room, Maureen was resting. We had just met. At the time, I didn't know that being assigned roommates for that week was the beginning of a long and lively friendship. I was so wired I kept pacing back and forth to the bathroom.

"What happened to you?" Maureen asked. "Looks like your pants are on fire!"

I told her the Henri story. And was finally able to sit down on my bed.

"But now I don't know what to do," I said. "I had kind of given up on him, and here at the last second he writes me."

Maureen fixed me with a steely gaze behind her round glasses. "Hmmf," she said. "It's not a marriage proposal. Do you want to meet up with him for a weekend or not?"

"Well, when you put it like that," I said, smiling, "it seems pretty simple."

"It is simple!" Maureen said. "And heck, you just had a Magdalene miracle. You gonna throw that away?"

So I went back downstairs and wrote Henri, that yes, I could still meet him. And over the next couple days we were able to organize a meeting place near Henri's vineyard.

The next morning our group boarded the coach and left Saint-Maximin. The sun shone brightly, and after three days of rain, the villages and forests we drove through looked sparkling clean. As we headed south toward the Camargue region, the landscape flattened into fields of grasses dotted with red poppies. I immediately thought of *la femme rouge*. This *is* her terrain, I thought, smiling to myself.

We pulled into the crowded village of Saintes-Maries-de-la-Mer, a coastal town on the Mediterranean. It was the weekend of May 24, the annual Saint Sarah festival. Every year the Gitanes (Gypsies) re-enact the arrival of Mary Magdalene, Mary Jacobe, Mary Salome, Martha, Lazarus, and Sarah by boat to the sandy beaches of present-day Saintes-Maries-de-la-Mer. The town is named for the two Marys—Salome and Jacobe—who stayed in the village with the young girl, Sarah, for many years.

We stepped inside the crowded church and were pressed against one another as people pushed to exit. I was sandwiched in the crowd as we entered the crypt. Inside were hundreds of lighted candles, which produced an incredible wave of heat as we stepped down to see the beautiful black Madonna Sarah, patron saint of the Gitanes, glowing mahogany in the candlelight and adorned with garlands of real and silk flowers. It was the first black Madonna I had ever seen, and I quickly understood the veneration. She had a palpable mystical energy, and her expression was enigmatic. She is referred to as Sarah "the Egyptian" or "the dark queen." The name *Sarah* itself means princess in Hebrew.

After dinner at our hotel, our guides led lively discussions about their personal experiences in southern France. There was plenty of evidence of Mary Magdalene's legacy, as well as that of Martha, Lazarus, the Marys, and Sarah. We all had our own versions of what their particular stories might be, which probably reflected each of our own personal stories. Like many, I felt that it was possible that Sarah could be Mary Magdalene's daughter, maybe even Jesus' too. I speculated that Mary Magdalene may have left her daughter with the other Marys in Saintes-Maries-de-la-Mer and then went on to teach the gospel, traveling across Languedoc and Provence. This may be the reason why Sarah is buried in the village with the two Marys but Mary Magdalene is not.

Many people believe that upon the group's arrival on the shores of Saint-es-Maries-de-la-Mer, they claimed that Sarah was an Egyptian servant girl to conceal her identity as Jesus's daughter. She was twelve years old when they arrived, so she would have spent most of her childhood in Egypt before crossing the Mediterranean in 42 AD. My guess was that the local people suspected who she was but protected her identity. Margaret Starbird and other researchers believed she needed to be protected from the Romans because she was Jesus' only offspring. But it could also be that she needed to be protected from the Jews. Roman Gaul—that's what France was called at this time—was also home to the largest Jewish population outside of Judea. And the Jewish religious leaders were not happy about the growing movement around the man who stood against them to bring the teachings to anyone who wished to receive them. It was the religious leaders, after all, who insisted Rome crucify him.

So Sarah became a "black Madonna," revered but hidden in the shadows. The fact that the Gitane people adopted Sarah as their patron saint suggested that she wasn't a mere servant girl. I'm not sure who she was, but she was somebody.

The black Madonna part is interesting, too. Black Madonnas were nearly always portrayed as Semitic or Caucasian and were either painted black or made from dark wood. Black in this case referring to the mystery, to staying in the shadows. Just like Lilith, the Black Moon, hidden from view until women were able to bring her back into the collective consciousness. And her story could finally be told.

The next day we made our way to the Languedoc region. After getting settled into a fabulous fifteenth-century castle-turned-hotel in the village of Couiza, we drove a few miles to the infamous Rennes le Château. This small village on top of a large rocky hill that has attracted an assortment of people: treasure hunters, grail seekers, energy workers, and people like us, interested in how the village was linked with Mary Magdalene. Since the book *The Holy Blood, The Holy Grail* was published in 1982, lots of people have been coming to the village searching for answers to the mystery of the parish priest who found a treasure trove of information and left clues as to the meaning of his discoveries that people were still trying to figure out.

We toured the Church of Mary Magdalene first. The unusual imagery throughout the church added to the mystery around Rennes le Château. Holding up the holy water stoup there's a devilish-looking character called Rex Mundi (king of the world). An inscription read *Par ce signet, tu le vaincras*—"by that sign you shall overcome him." It was creepy and a strange thing to find in a church.

One of our guides, Pierre, handed out little maps to our group of the village. He was developing a theory that all the structures the priest had built were linked to the Tree of Life in Kabbalah. Maureen and I just looked at each other and rolled our eyes. I didn't know anything about Kabbalah, but I knew people tried to link all kinds of theories to this place, and this one was new to me. We wandered around the village and stopped at a small grotto dedicated to Magdalene made of rocks that had a stone bench inside.

The authors of *The Holy Blood, The Holy Grail* believed this bench was one of the most important clues that the priest had left. But nobody could figure out what it meant. Embedded across the bench were the letters KXS LX. Immediately I added the numerological value of the letters up and got 18/9. It was a habit for me to add numbers or letters to figure out the numerological meaning. I do it with license plates, addresses, names. This particular sequence was interesting as it was *chai* in Hebrew or "new life." Considered the most sacred and auspicious number of all. But that's as far as I got and it didn't seem to crack any codes.

The guided tour with the authors ended the next day at the Toulouse airport; we said our goodbyes. And I gave Maureen a big hug. I'd grown quite fond of my rather short, round, sixties-era radical, acerbic roomie; I think you will too, when you meet her. Anyway, I picked up my rental car and headed back east to find my B&B and the next morning drove to the small village in the Pyrenees that was rich with Cathar history.

I parked my car at the foot of Montsegur and began the vigorous climb up the mountain. Once reaching the peak, I was surprised to find the energy of the fortress ruins really peaceful and light. In fact, the whole mountain had a really strong positive energy. This was the site of the last holdout of these unusual people and the place from which a sacred book and other treasures of the community were smuggled out before they surrendered to the French troops below and were burned alive. As I sat on the mountaintop, I felt again that the book could be *The Gospel of the Beloved Companion*. The Cathars had a prophecy that the truth and the teachings would resurface again seven hundred years after their demise. The woman that published the gospel was supported by most of her community to bring their history and the lost gospel out from the shadows.

That evening I sat out with the owners of the B&B in their garden sharing a bottle of local wine. They asked me about the places I had visited. They knew the Cathar sites of the Languedoc but they didn't know the Magdalene connection or about her tomb and cavern in Provence. Then

I remembered I had some photos of the places I was trying to describe. I went up to my room to get my digital camera and they brought out their laptop and another bottle of wine.

We plugged the USB cable into my camera and connected it to the laptop to have a better view. I showed them the crypt under the basilica and Mary Magdalene's cavern at La Baume. They were surprised how big it was and that it was an official pilgrimage site of the Catholic Church. I brought up a photo of a stained glass panel from the front of the cavern. On the laptop screen I saw much more detail than I'd seen in person.

This was when I noticed there was writing embedded in the imagery. It was the picture of Mary Magdalene sitting in candlelight, with the large book in front of her. We enlarged the part of the photo with the writing. That level of French was beyond me then. It said, "*jusqu'a la fin des temps, on dira ce qu'elle a fait.*" As they translated "until the end of time, we will tell what she did," a shiver went through me. We searched the photo for other clues like the artist's mark, and found the artist's name, Tourangeau, *le disciple de la lumière*. Even I understood "disciple of the light." Who was this person? I wondered. We Googled his name and found that Tourangeau was his Compagnon name.

The artist's real name was Pierre Petit; he was a master glassmaker, one of the Compagnon trades. That is when I discovered the Compagnons were a French guild of trades passed down from master to apprentice since the Gothic period. They were the builders—masons—of the Gothic cathedrals, which sprang up all over France in the 1200s. It was the Knights Templar who funded them and created the organization. When I learned that Mary Magdalene was the patron saint of the Compagnons, and annual pilgrimages to her cavern were part of their spiritual tradition even to this day, well, that was when I first suspected that Magdalene's legacy and the Templars were connected.

The artist made sure that the clues to her larger story were embedded in his stained glass designs. As far as the Dominican monk who'd commissioned him, he must have chosen a Compagnon purposefully. I had mixed feelings about the Dominicans charged with protecting her cavern. Yes, they had kept it from falling into obscurity and ruin, but they also kept the story cloistered. Protected but also controlled—how very patriarchal! To add to the paradox, the founder of the Dominican order, Dominico de Guzman, was one of the most ardent persecutors of the Cathar people at the beginning of the Albigensian crusade, the very order instated in 1279 to guard Magdalene's legacy.

On my last day in the region, I drove around the enigmatic Mount Bugarach along single-lane roads to the Gorge de Galamus, where there was an ancient hermitage dedicated to Magdalene. By the time I parked in the lot next to a small gift shop, my head was spinning—partly from the narrow, curvy gorge drive and partly from the energy of the place. But I found the trailhead and hiked down the steep wooded trail to the hermitage, which was built into the side of the gorge. I stepped up into the large mouth of the cavern and sat in one of the wooden pews. Grateful to be alone in the grotto, I closed my eyes. As I meditated, I sensed Magdalene's presence.

I thought about her legacy: meeting Jesus Christ, being healed, being able to transcend the past and awaken as a fully realized woman. I firmly believed that she was his beloved companion, there at all the critical moments in the last years of his life. She is called the apostle to the apostles because she was the first to see him after the resurrection. But after reporting the resurrection to the other disciples, her story in the holy land fades.

Maybe she was Jesus's wife and maybe she wasn't. Maybe she did have a child with him and carried on the bloodline. But being someone's wife or mother wasn't what made her special, even if it was Jesus! She was special for so many reasons. She had received advanced teachings and went on to write of these teachings and she carried her gospel to southern France. The other disciples had taken their gospels out into the world, and so did she!

I imagined how she would have walked from place to place, teaching in small villages across southern France, speaking and counseling as she went. Traveling on foot and staying in hermitages like this cavern—caverns that were dedicated to Artemis, Cybele, Diana, and Isis in earlier times. These "Mary grottos" were ubiquitous across the region, honoring both Magdalene and Mother Mary. But I also wondered about the larger symbolism of the divine feminine and the Earth. The powerful places where women had connected to Earth energies to fuel their ascent in consciousness, unifying matter and spirit.

Suddenly the sun streamed into the cavern, bathing the pew where I sat. I felt a shimmer of pure magic, a fleeting moment of communion with the muse. Finally, I got up and walked past the stone altar to the back of the grotto to leave an offering. I swept some leaves to create a clearing and then took out a pinch of tobacco, put it on the rock floor, and thanked the land and the people of the region for preserving Magdalene's legacy, for accepting her as an emissary of the divine feminine and seeing the light and the wisdom in her words and deeds.

The next day, I hit the freeway and headed west to visit the last place on my divine feminine tour. As I entered Lourdes, the bustling village teeming with tourists, my GPS went haywire and I found myself going in circles trying to find my hotel. Finally, I parked the car and tuned into the other GPS, Goddess positioning system and found the place I'd be staying. After I checked in, I wandered down the cobblestone streets past hotels and cafes and shops selling religious souvenirs. Then found the line of pilgrims waiting to go into the most famous grotto in the world. This was a place where the Virgin Mary appeared to a young girl many times. And like the other grottos I'd visited, it contained a spring. This particular grotto was replicated all over the world as the Lourdes shrine.

Lourdes represented the ordinary person's ability to connect with the divine feminine. And even though thousands of people came through a day and the village was commercial, as I walked in the long line into the grotto and touched the rock, the palpable reverence for the Holy Mother was truly humbling. Lourdes grotto is very powerful, a veritable anchoring of feminine Light.

Later that night I lay in the narrow bed under the window opened to the moonlight, I thought of the thousands, maybe millions of women who had found refuge in the Virgin Mary. And the structure of the Catholic Church had at least created another alternative for women, the sisterhood. Living in a convent, devoting one's life to a spiritual path, had given women a safe way to participate in the mystery when there had been so few options. Not to mention the millions of lay women who found solace, grace, and connection to a feminine archetype.

And in the south of France, the honored memory of Mary Magdalene remained. Her legacy could be found across the Languedoc and Provence like the beautiful red poppies that grow in the fields. Following in her footsteps had filled me with a sense of empowerment. Understanding her story had helped me understand my own. Loving her helped me love myself more. And it had brought me to my passion. That was when I truly sensed what *la femme rouge* was doing, leading me to a greater expression of myself and purpose in the world. I realized that walking the ground of the sacred feminine across southern France had activated something inside me that, until that first trip, had been dormant. Now

I was ready for more.

"Thank you, *la femme rouge*," I said to the night. I thought I heard the soft rumble of Grandmother's laughter as I drifted off into a dreamless sleep.

The next morning after a croissant and coffee, I checked out of the hotel, put my overnight bag in the car, and walked back through the village. I needed to visit the grotto again to collect some of the healing water. There was a row of stainless steel spigots open to the pilgrims so I filled a jug to take and then splashed some of the cold running water over my head.

On my way out of the sanctuary, I walked by the stunning gilded mosaics on the façade of the basilica. One of them depicted what I assumed was the wedding of Cana. I stopped to take a closer look. It was an unusual portrayal of Jesus and, supposedly, his mother, Mary. This mosaic showed them both the same age—and more like partners than mother and son. They were youthful and happy, like it was their marriage. It struck me that the mosaic could be depicting the wedding of Cana as the marriage of Jesus and Magdalene, a theory I'd heard before but never seen represented. This seemed to me an illustration of the sacred marriage. I smiled. That's a good sign, I thought.

I walked back to my rental car and found the highway heading north. It was a warm, sunny day so I drove with the windows down and enjoyed the French countryside. I reached the bed and breakfast faster than I'd expected and had time to settle into my room. Then I went out to sit on the patio and sip a glass of wine. Soon I heard a car pull to a stop on the gravel driveway and French voices as the proprietor greeted a guest.

"Ariel?" a man called.

I got up and looked over the railing. Henri stood below, smiling up at me.

CHAPTER EIGHTEEN

"Okay, almost there!" Ariel announced. "We need to come back to the present."

They turned sharply left and began a steep climb up a narrow road. Katie caught a glimpse of the small village perched on top of the mountain.

"But Ariel," Katie said, as she braced herself against the dashboard. "You just got to the good part!"

Ariel smiled, driving rather quickly up the narrow, winding road. "I need to concentrate on driving. Maureen will be pissed if we miss lunch," Ariel said. "We can finish the love story some other time."

"Okay," Katie said. Her aunt had a knack for cinematic timing.

The view opened up to a panorama of the surrounding countryside, small villages set along the river valley. As they rounded the final bend, a dramatic mountain range came into view.

"Wow! What are those mountains?" Katie asked.

"The Pyrenees," Ariel said. She glanced quickly out the window. "When it's really clear, you can see all the way to Spain."

Ariel pulled into a parking lot. They both got out of the car, happy to stretch their legs. Katie reached into the back seat and grabbed her camera bag. They climbed a long set of wooden steps that led from the parking area to a narrow street, then entered the small village. Maybe it was because of what Ariel had told her, but as they passed shops selling new age books and trinkets and an old château with a flag of a dragon, Katie felt there was something odd about the town. It was kind of Harry Potteresque.

"We'll visit all the key sites after we eat," Ariel said as she ushered Katie along. They stepped through an open gate into a garden courtyard dotted with tables.

Ariel looked around, then approached an older woman with short gray hair and round wire glasses sitting under a large tree.

"There she is!" Ariel said.

The woman looked up and smiled. She pushed her generous form out of the chair and stood, giving Ariel a warm embrace.

"Good to see you, *mon amie*," the woman said.

"This is my niece, and the instigator of this probably misguided adventure, Katie," Ariel stepped back. "Katie, Maureen, one of the coolest women I know."

Katie approached Maureen and shook her hand. Maureen sized her up.

"She's kind of skinny; aren't you feeding her?" Maureen said.

Ariel sat down next to Maureen. "Well, we are probably doing more drinking than eating," Ariel smiled.

"Well, let's order before we get talking, you know how that goes," Maureen said.

Katie picked up her menu but it was all in French. After Ariel translated, she chose fish with vegetables. She was hungry, she realized. A nice looking waiter arrived. After they ordered and he learned Katie only spoke English, he asked her in a charming accent,

"Where are you from mademoiselle?"

Katie smiled, "New York City."

"Oh, I want to go there!" he said.

"All right Romeo," Maureen cut in, "You've got a couple hungry, middle-aged women here—okay, maybe one middle-aged and one just aged—needing to be fed."

The waiter smiled at Maureen and raised his eyebrows. "She always likes to...how do you say, tease me."

Katie smiled even wider, tilting her head up at him.

He winked at her. "Wine for you?"

"Oh, if you twist my arm," Maureen said, "Yes, bring us a carafe of blanc,"

"Bon," he said and left with their menus, turning briefly to give Katie another look.

"I like this place!" Katie said. She reached up to adjust her bangs in their bobby pin. She couldn't remember the last time she flirted.

"Your aunt and I have had many memorable lunches here," Maureen said.

Katie looked at Maureen with a curious expression.

"Maureen, Katie doesn't need to know the details," Ariel said, shaking her head.

"Okay," Maureen said, smiling. "So if you're not here for debauchery, what *is* the plan?"

Ariel waved her hand dismissively. "Well, we want to check Pierre's theory again, I'm hoping that I can find a new angle somehow. Georgia wants me to submit a new proposal to try and get some attention at the next Gnostic Conference. But I haven't come up with anything yet and the clock is ticking. It was Katie's idea to come here and get inspired."

The waiter came back with the wine and a bottle of water. Katie poured them all a glass of each. She reached inside her knapsack and pulled out the file of Ariel's papers she'd read the night before.

"Well, I think it would help if I could learn more about the history of this place. I want to see these strange buildings the priest built with the Vatican hush money," Katie said.

"This niece is all business!" Maureen said as she took a big sip of wine.

Ariel shrugged innocently. "It looks like she caught the bug," she said.

"And I want to know more about this map of the Tree of Life overlaying the position of the buildings," Katie continued, ignoring the two women's comments.

Their meal arrived and each woman focused on their food. Katie wolfed down her fish, potato and ratatouille, then mopped up the sauce with a couple pieces of baguette. She sat back in her chair feeling very satisfied. Ariel and Maureen took their time, stopping for sips of wine between bites.

The waiter came by to check on them.

"*C'est bon?*" he asked.

"*Oui, tres bon,*" Maureen said. "Everyone want coffee?"

"*Oui,*" Ariel said.

"*Oui,*" Katie said, smiling up at the waiter.

"*Trois noisettes,* Marc" Maureen said. "And why don't you bring that chocolate ganache for us to share."

"*A toute suite,*" Marc said, lingering a moment before turning toward the kitchen.

After they had their coffee and enjoyed the chocolate cake with fresh cream, they resumed their conversation.

"So, your aunt already told you about this Kabbalah connection she's been working on, and what it points to—that the priest found Kabbalistic writings and built the structures according to the Tree of Life diagram?" Maureen asked Katie.

Katie nodded.

"I told her I was here last fall stomping around the village with you, trying to find any truth to the theory, but we were unable to confirm it," Ariel said.

Maureen shrugged. "I still think there is something to Pierre's theory, Ariel. You just haven't uncovered it yet. And I believe he would want someone to carry on his work."

Katie wasn't sure what Maureen was talking about. "Who's work? I'm not sure I'm following you," Katie said.

Maureen looked at her, peering down through her wire-rim glasses. Then she looked at Ariel.

"I gather you haven't told Katie how you came by this theory," Maureen said with a slight smile on her lips.

Ariel put both her hands on the table and stood up. "I'm going inside to pee and pay the bill; why don't you fill Katie in."

Maureen leaned toward Katie, lowering her voice as if to discuss top secret information.

"Pierre was one of the authors who'd led our group on that first trip to France that your aunt and I went on. When we arrived at Rennes le Château he handed us all papers with the map of the village and the Tree of Life diagram. We thought it was another crazy Rennes idea and dismissed it."

"Okay," Katie said. She recalled this part from Ariel's story.

"Tragically, he died several months later. We were all shocked and it kind of spooked your aunt. She's superstitious, that one, and she's convinced that anyone who gets deeply involved in the Magdalene story is tested in some way. Starbird had a breakdown, Pierre died so young, another researcher lost all his money in a lawsuit. But I don't think there's some kind of curse, I link it to the depths of the suppression of Magdalene's history by the misogynist Church!"

Katie tried to keep up with Maureen's narrative. "But you said you guys dismissed his theories—Pierre's theories," Katie said. "Right?"

"Yeah, we did at first. It must have been three or four years later when Ariel called me to say she'd followed a hunch that Magdalene's gospel contained Tree of Life teachings from Kabbalah, and discovered the hunch was right," Maureen said. "So she starts telling me all the links she made, and you know how that woman can talk."

Katie smiled.

"Well, suddenly we both remember our first trip here and Pierre's Kabbalah map in Rennes le Château!" Maureen said, grinning at the memory.

Ariel returned and stood between them. "That was wild," Ariel said, grinning. "I still believe he was guiding us from the other side."

Maureen shook her head.

"That's when I suspected he must have come upon the link between Magdalene and the Tree of Life from all his research at Rennes. I came upon the information from a completely different angle: I was using her gospel, pieced together from the authenticated fragments and the *Beloved Companion* book. He'd probably never even read; it was published not long before his death," Ariel said. "It just so happened that I was on his tour—Maureen, too. Otherwise, we would have never made the connection to Rennes. Or maybe we would have, but it would have taken longer."

Maureen looked at Katie. "I have to say one thing I've learned after hanging around with your aunt: that in some way, on some level, this cosmic synchronicity shit's real."

"Thank you for that glowing endorsement, Maureen," Ariel said.

"Not long after that, your aunt's theory of the Tree of Life teachings was confirmed by the Kabbalah people, and you know the Jews don't mess around with their history. And we found that Pierre had published some articles laying out his theory, so we were able to get the map again."

Maureen picked up one of the papers that Katie had laid on the table. "That's the very same diagram he handed out to the group."

"So, you guys checked it out, what did you find?" Katie asked.

"Well, we found that there may be some merit to it, but it's not complete," Ariel said. "We've found some of the *sephirot* but need them all to present the theory. Just a few points is too weak of a connection. For this to get any serious scholarship, we need it to align exactly."

Maureen stood up, a bit wobbly in her chair. That's when Katie realized she had a cane to help her walk. "Well, let's stop gabbing and show her what we found."

"Kid, you carry the map and we'll walk you through it," Maureen said.

Katie gathered the papers and grabbed her bag.

They walked slowly so Maureen could keep pace navigating the uneven ground of the garden. When they got to the road they turned right, passing the church, then stopped in front of a small, man made grotto with a stone bench set at the back.

"There used to be a statue of Magdalene in here, but some ass stole it," Maureen said.

"When Maureen and I met with one of the authors of Holy Blood, Holy Grail, he told us the most important thing in all these mysterious structures was this stone bench," Ariel said.

Katie looked down at the large letters carved into the stone, covering the bench. KXS LX.

"You told me about this earlier, in the car..." Katie said, looking to Ariel to remind her.

"The only thing I could come up with is in numerology, these letters make 18/9 or *chai*, a sacred number in Judaism, meaning new life," Ariel said. "Maybe that's part of what the priest was trying to say when he built this. I found out only recently from a Kabbalah teacher that the word *chai* also means Tree of Life in Hebrew."

"Well that seems important, Ariel," Katie said.

Maureen nodded. "I think so too," she said. "Ariel is the first person that ever cracked the code of the bench."

"Is this grotto also part of the Tree of Life on the map?" Katie asked.

"This is the bottom of the tree, *malchut*, the vessel, the tenth *sephirot*," Ariel said. "And I should say the Christian Kabbalists, also descendants of Magdalene's spiritual lineage, associate Magdalene with *malchut*."

Katie found *malchut* and the grotto on the map. "Okay, I see it. What about the rest?"

"Hey ladies, I'm going to sit in here while you map it out," Maureen said as she settled herself on the stone bench.

"Okay," Ariel said, as she brought Katie into the center of a small courtyard adjacent to the grotto. She pointed to a raised mound with a large Jesus on the cross. "This is the Calvary. It corresponds with the ninth *sephirot, yesod*. As you can see, it's in exact alignment with the central pillar." Ariel pointed to the *sephirot* running down the center of the tree of life diagram. "Then you've got *hod* here to the left and *netzach* to the right, the eighth and seventh, respectively."

Katie paced out the alignment, easy to do because a paved path conformed perfectly to the diagrammatic structure on the map.

"Now it gets trickier because *tiferet*, number six, is inside the church over the altar. But we've rudimentarily measured it out and it's in proportion to the rest."

Katie followed on her map as they walked to a closed gate.

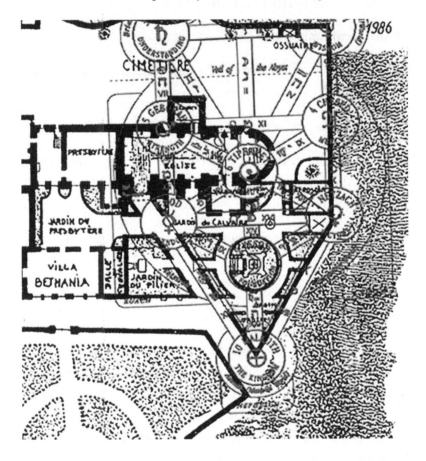

"This is the cemetery," Ariel said. She pointed through the wrought iron to a long stone wall. "Along this wall, there is number four, *chesed*, and number two, *chokmah*, but even though the wall diagrammatically aligns with these two points, there's nothing specific to mark them."

Ariel shook the gate but it was locked. "This cemetery is closed to everyone except family members of the deceased buried here."

Ariel turned and smiled mischievously at Katie. "But last fall, we happened to be here on All Souls Day, November 1, and the gate was open, so Maureen and I were able to map out number five and three, *gevorah* and *binah*, in the cemetery. *Gevorah* corresponds to a stained glass window at the back of the church and *binah* roughly along the back wall, but not to any specific monument as far as we could see."

"Okay," Katie said, checking the map. "And what about the top of the tree?"

"*Keter* is the top, number one, but it's not on the map, nor does it correspond with a building or wall or architectural feature. It kind of hangs out in space on the other side of that retaining wall." Ariel pointed to the wall at the very back of the cemetery. "So the connection really is incomplete."

"Hmm," Katie said. "But did Pierre think it was incomplete?" She realized she really wanted it all to match up, to solve the mystery of this strange place.

"No, he felt it was fitting that *keter*, which represents the Godhead, would be vast and not marked by a structure. That its placement was intentional," Ariel said. "And that could be the case—it's not illogical—but I need something more. Something stronger—for myself and for this proposal. Somehow, I need to take Pierre's theory and go further if I'm going to hope to get an academic to work with me on this."

Katie nodded, sensing Ariel's frustration begin to rise again.

Ariel looked at her watch. "If you want, we can go to the museum before they close, so we can get inside the courtyard and see the Tour Magdala."

Ariel said. "It's pretty wild."

"Yeah, let's do that," Katie said. She wanted to keep her aunt moving.

They walked back to the grotto to get Maureen. But she said she'd wait for them in the church. So Ariel led the way down the little street to a museum next to the church.

Ariel paid the fee and she and Katie moved rather quickly through the exhibits, which led to a large center courtyard.

As they stood in the courtyard, Ariel pointed to the far wall, built on the edge of a large rock outcropping. "That tower to the left is called Tour Magdala. The priest referred to it as the 'black tower'."

Katie looked up at the medieval style stone tower. "Oh my God!" Katie said. She turned to Ariel, eyes wide. "I dreamt about that tower last night!"

"Really?" Ariel asked. "Maybe you saw pictures of it somewhere."

Katie shook her head. "I've never seen that strange looking tower before," she said. Katie walked across the courtyard to the edge of the rock wall. The tower was built to stand out over the ledge. She turned back to Ariel. "I dreamt I was standing on this ledge and then I jumped off." She pointed to the steep drop that descended down for several hundred feet to a meadow below.

Ariel stood next to Katie. "That's pretty wild," she said. "Did you fly or wake up before you fell?"

Katie thought about the dream. "I launched like I was going to fly but then I woke up."

Ariel nodded. "Okay, that might be a message. I'm not exactly sure what it means but it's interesting."

Katie nodded. "It's a little weird, Ariel. I just dreamt I was here, and now I'm here. And the other night I had that creepy dream about Lilith in a damp cave and the next day I found that altar in the lower part of Magdalene's cavern."

Ariel smiled. "Well, they say this stuff runs in families, you know. Maybe spending time with me is awakening your natural intuitive abilities." She winked at Katie.

Katie had a chill. "Look I've got chicken skin," she said.

"That, my dear, is always a sign truth's been spoken," Ariel said grinning. "Or there's a ghost around. And the priest did die in the tower."

"Okay, Ariel, you're freaking me out a little," Katie said. She left the ledge and headed back to the courtyard.

"Like I said, this is called the black tower and is dedicated to Magdalene," Ariel said following Katie back to the center of the courtyard. "The building over there he called the 'white tower,' it was the orangery, that's why it's made of glass. That whole raised area connecting the two towers is perfectly centered and has 11 steps on either side. There are 22 steps in the Tour Magdala. Both 11 and 22 are master numbers in numerology. 11 is a number of the spirit and inspiration, 22 is the master builder of form, as in the 22 letters of the Hebrew alphabet. So there's a message here about spirit and matter. Most people don't know numerology but still feel there is meaning to all this symmetry."

Finally, they left the museum grounds and went to the church. It was the strangest church Katie had ever been in. A devil-looking creature was at the door, holding up the water stoop. It was dark, not unusual for an old church, but instead of having a comforting feeling, it felt unsettling to be there. They found Maureen sitting in the front pew and went to join her. Ariel pointed out the many references to Magdalene, including a stone relief of her in her cavern at the base of the altar. Then she gestured to the wall behind the altar. There was a cross painted on one side and a jar painted on the other. Katie understood the reference, both symbols representing Jesus and Magdalene, respectively.

Maureen leaned closer to Katie, pointing her cane at the stone floor near the altar.

"That's where the priest found the crypt full of documents and treasure," she whispered.

Katie felt kind of light-headed; maybe it was the wine with lunch or the last couple hours of sleuthing through the strange village, but she would need to lie down soon.

The church bell rang and Maureen looked at her watch.

"Time to go," Maureen said. "They'll be closing up soon."

"Okay, good," Katie said, feeling relieved.

Maureen got up and found her balance then slid out to the narrow aisle, Katie and Ariel followed. Katie snapped some shots of the church as they left and was happy to step outside into the daylight. The weather had changed. A strong wind had kicked up while they were inside and clouds started to gather above them.

Maureen was parked in the small upper lot, so she had a short walk to her car. Katie and Ariel made their way back through the village and to the lower parking lot. They were going to meet Maureen at her house a few kilometers away in Couiza. The sun hung low and was partially hidden by the changing sky as they drove down the windy, narrow road.

Soon they pulled into a gravel drive surrounded by a thicket of trees. Ariel parked to the side of a car port and they both sat for a moment. Katie took in the rustic stone cottage, partially covered by ivy and with lilac colored shutters. There were several large terracotta sculptures of voluptuous nude women in the somewhat unkempt garden of wildflowers.

"Those sculptures are cool," Katie said, nodding toward the garden.

"Maureen makes those herself," Ariel said. "Now that she's retired, she draws and does sculpture. She belongs to an art cooperative in Limoux."

"They're quite sensual," Katie said. "The women look very free in their bodies."

Ariel smiled and nodded. Just then Maureen pulled into the drive and rolled to a stop in the carport. She got out, then opened the backseat door and retrieved her cane and a couple of baguettes wrapped in brown paper.

"C'mon in, ladies," Maureen said, waving them toward the front door.

"Katie finds your sculptures very sensual," Ariel called out.

"Ha!" Maureen said. "Those are modeled after my last two girlfriends."

Katie smiled, raising her eyebrows, but not totally surprised by Maureen's comment.

Ariel and Katie got their bags out from the back. They followed Maureen to the front door and waited as she fumbled for the keys. As soon as she opened the door, a very large orange tabby cat stepped out.

"Hello, Charo," Maureen called as the tabby rubbed against her leg. They stepped into a small foyer and Maureen turned on the light. "I only have one guest room Katie, so you're on the couch. But it's very comfy, I sleep there half the time myself."

Ariel went to a room on the right side of the hall as Katie followed Maureen into a large living room. There was a big sectional couch and coffee table piled with books in front of a fireplace. Behind the couch was a rustic farmhouse style dining table also piled with art books and sketch pads.

"Just throw your stuff anywhere, Katie," Maureen said, gesturing to a stuffed chair next to the couch. "Bathroom is the second door on the right past the guest room."

Katie set her duffle and camera bag down next to the sofa and sat down, sinking into the numerous earth-toned pillows. She looked around. The place was homey with a kind of paisley, sixties/seventies feel. She liked it. Maureen went to the kitchen and puttered around. Ariel came in the living room and winked at Katie as she went by to join Maureen in the kitchen. Katie leaned back into the cushions and thought she would just close her eyes for a few minutes.

Katie dreamed she was floating in a warm sea, her limbs heavy and soft. She rested in a deep state of relaxation then realized she was lying in a sea of cushions. She opened her eyes and felt a blanket on her that someone must have provided after she fell asleep. It was dark in the living room but there was a glow of light from behind the sofa. She heard Ariel's voice.

"I don't know exactly what it is, but there's something special about France. As you know, Maureen, before Magdalene and her entourage got here, goddess worship had been in full swing for a long time. The Romans adopted goddesses from all over the empire: Egyptian Isis, Greek Artemis and Roman Diana. Sacred groves and standing stones of the ancient Druids from the Celtic past were where the Roman altars were built. Then churches were erected on the same locations by the Christians. It seems as though France has been divine feminine central for a long time!"

"*Vive la France*," Maureen said. "She appreciates women in all her forms!"

"Then we've got the Knights Templar carrying this devotion to the Divine Feminine forward by funding the building of the Gothic cathedrals in the thirteenth century. All devoted to Notre Dame, our lady, keeping the feminine spirit alive right under the auspices of the Catholic Church."

Katie smiled as she listened to her aunt. She was so animated—and also sounded a little inebriated.

"It seems to me," Maureen said. "That the Knights Templar did this on purpose, building the Gothics to save the feminine from the patriarchal stranglehold of the church."

"I think that's right," Ariel said. "But I sense there's more to it than that. The Gothic cathedrals were built in a completely new architectural style that most historians believe was discovered by the Templars under the ruins of the Temple of Solomon in Jerusalem and brought back to France."

"Well, and they built most of the Gothic cathedrals within a hundred years all over France—quite a feat," Maureen said. "But I don't see how that can be connected with Mary Magdalene."

Ariel sighed. "I just feel somehow it is, through the Tree of Life teachings in Kabbalah. So many pieces of the puzzle fit around her. Now the Kabbalah folks confirmed it was the Knights Templar who brought the *Zohar*—the written Kabbalah back from the ruins under the Temple of Solomon," Ariel said. "That was their main mission, to recover these sacred texts that had been hidden since the fall of the Temple in 70AD. We know Bernard de Clairvaux, a big player, leader of the Cistercian monks, sent these original nine knights—all from France and Belgium, mind you—down there. He was working with Rabbi Abraham ben David, the premier Jewish scholar of all of Europe who happened to live in Provence." Ariel stopped a moment. "Can you imagine if people knew that? That the Jews and Catholic monks—well at least the Cistercians— were all working together to bring back ancient texts?"

"Okay, wait. You're losing me here," Maureen said. "I thought you told me Mary Magdalene wrote about Kabbalistic concepts."

"She only wrote specifically about the Tree of Life teachings she got from Jesus," Ariel said. "And the Kabbalists I talked to had all come across her in their history. But they didn't know who she was and what she actually did. But let me back this up a little: we know the spread of the Kabbalah happened in France at roughly the same time as the Gothic cathedrals were being built, funded by Templars. We know their—the Templars'— veneration of the divine feminine. We know the resurgence of the cult of Mary Magdalene happened at the same time. And somehow this is all related. Magdalene had something to do with this, and was central to the history of Kabbalah in France.

"But when I told several of the teachers and the head of the Kabbalah center she'd actually written about the Tree of Life in her gospel and brought it over with her to France 1200 years earlier, they didn't seem to see the importance of this outside of their own narrative. Huh, it's still a boy's club."

"You're preaching to the choir, Missy," Maureen said. Katie heard two glasses clink.

"There's a missing link between Magdalene's history and the Tree of Life-like teachings, then both the discovery of the *Zohar* and the push to build Gothic buildings in the 1200s. And it seems that Pierre's theory that the priest left a message about the importance of Magdalene and the Tree of Life in Rennes le Château is pointing to that link."

"Ariel, I really hope you're close to something here," Maureen said, her voice slurring a bit.

"Ahh," Ariel moaned. "I feel like something is right under my nose, but I can't see it. I need some more wine."

Katie lifted her head above the back of the sofa. "Hey, what time is it?" she asked groggily.

"Oh, it's sleeping beauty," Maureen said.

Ariel looked at her cell phone. "It's almost 10:00 PM."

"Oh, my God, I slept three hours!" Katie said. She was famished. "And missed dinner, didn't I?" she asked with an exaggerated frown.

"Nobody goes hungry in this house missy," Maureen said. "There's some *cassoulet* on the stove."

Katie wasn't sure what that was but it sounded good. She stood up and stretched then went over to the dining table. There was a place setting at one end with a clean bowl and utensils and a basket of sliced baguette. Ariel and Maureen had abandoned their dirty dishes and were sitting at the other end of the table with a pile of books and papers spread out. Katie went to the stove and helped herself, filling the bowl with *cassoulet* then returned to sit down. She reached for the bottle of wine in the center of the table but it was empty.

Maureen reached across the table and handed Katie another opened bottle of wine. She poured the remains into a glass. "Wow, you two are having some fun," she said as she ate a spoonful of the white bean stew. "Hmm, this is good!"

"Well, you know how your aunt is when she gets going," Maureen said, winking at Katie.

Katie raised her eyebrows, not willing to put down the spoon to comment. She finished the bowl and mopped up the sauce with a couple of pieces of bread. *God, they have good bread in France!* She thought.

The women continued talking while Katie ate.

"Ariel, let's think back on what Pierre believed about the connections," Maureen said. "It seems to me he thought that the priest at Rennes wasn't just leaving a message about what he'd found, but that he'd built this three dimensional Tree of Life because it was sacred geometry. Thinking that if people walked through it, it could help them elevate their consciousness."

"Yeah, that was Pierre's theory," Ariel said.

Maureen sat back in her chair, thinking for a moment before she spoke. "You know, that's the same thing that people say about labyrinths."

"What do you mean?" Ariel asked.

"That to walk a labyrinth, a very ancient sacred practice, was a meditation that could elevate a person's consciousness," Maureen said.

"Yeah, that and all the red wine you two are drinking," Katie said, smiling.

"Oh ho, the kid has some chops!" Maureen said. "Hey, we need to ease the frustration and get the creative juices flowing."

"That's right," Ariel said as she raised her glass.

"And you know several of the most prominent Gothic cathedrals in France have labyrinths," Maureen said. "Chartres cathedral is the most famous—not only is it the largest Gothic cathedral, it was home to the first university studying mathematics, astronomy, sacred geometry..." Maureen paused, deep in thought. "I think we need to think about Chartres," she said.

"I'm not following you, Maureen," Ariel said.

"Katie, do an old drunk lady a favor and get a book for me," Maureen pointed to a large bookcase next to the fireplace. "It's called *The Mysteries of Chartres Cathedral.*"

Katie got up and went to the bookcase. She turned on a lamp next to the reading chair so she could see the titles.

"It's black with gold or white letters," Maureen called out.

"Oh, I think I see where you may be going with this," Ariel said, watching her friend intently.

"Yep, Chartres, ground zero of Gothic cathedrals, sacred geometry, labyrinth, built on the holiest site of the Druids," Maureen said. "Has incredible energy that I personally had a hand in recording," Maureen smiled mischievously.

Katie found the book and brought it back to the table, handing it to Maureen. Maureen thumbed through it, searching for something. Katie looked over her shoulder.

"Ariel, did you ever read this?" Maureen showed Ariel the cover.

Ariel nodded. "Sure, years ago. It's fascinating. And the author, is it Louis Charpentier? I remember thinking he was interesting, too."

Maureen began paging through the book, looking for something. "Ahh!" she said in frustration.

"Can I take a look?" Katie asked.

"Sure kid, I swear he put a picture of the labyrinth in that book," Maureen said. "Maybe you can find it."

She looked over at Ariel. "What do you say we take a time out and go out for a smoke?"

"Sounds good," Ariel said and went to get her pouch of tobacco. "My brain needs a break."

Maureen poured herself and Ariel some more wine, then both women went out the sliding glass doors to the patio.

Katie looked through the pictures in the book about Chartres. It didn't take her long to find a picture of the labyrinth. In the center of the large Cathedral floor, a remarkable stone inlay created a circular design with a single path that twisted back and forth, filling the circle to the edges. Intently, she traced the pathway to the center of the labyrinth, where there was a six-petaled flower, and back out again. It *was* sacred geometry. She didn't know whether walking the path would elevate one's consciousness, but it would probably do *something*.

But then another image caught her eye: one showing not only the labyrinth, but the floor plan of the entire cathedral. She then thumbed through Ariel's notes searching for the diagram of the Tree of Life.

238

"Did you find something Katie? You seem very engrossed," Ariel asked when she and Maureen came back inside.

Katie felt a rush of excitement. She picked up the Chartres book. "This floor plan caught my eye," Katie held up the page so Maureen and Ariel could see. "And maybe it's because I've been looking at that map all day of the Tree of Life diagram, but don't they kind of look similar?"

"Let me see that," Ariel said. She took the book and pressed the page flat so she could get a good look. She looked back and forth from the simple drawing of the diagrammatic Tree of Life and the floor plan of Chartres cathedral. "It's possible," she said quietly.

"Hey, hand me the book and I'll make a copy of the floor plan, then we can superimpose the Tree of Life on it," Maureen said. Maureen went to her printer and made a copy then found a red pencil in the desk drawer and sketched the Tree of Life diagram over the floor plan. Ariel and Katie gathered around her.

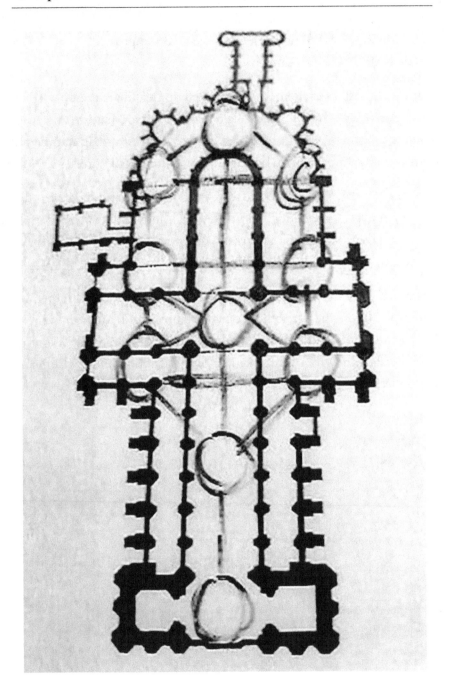

"But there are these two extra buildings," Ariel said, her voice dropping.

Maureen looked closely. "They didn't add those two side structures until much later. The original floor plan fits the diagram exactly!"

Maureen looked at Ariel wide eyed. Ariel stared at the sketch another moment, shaking her head. Katie continued to study the book, flipping the pages to find more information.

"Wait, look at this," Katie said suddenly, reading from a page. "Here, the author says he thinks the whole Cathedral was built according to sacred geometry, not just the labyrinth. He writes that he thinks the architectural information was retrieved from under the ruins of...oh my goodness!... *the Temple of Solomon*." Her voice trembled on the last few words.

"Are you serious? And he wrote this in the 70's!" Maureen said. "How did we never make this connection before?"

"Holy Mother of God," Ariel whispered.

Katie watched Ariel.

"Jesus, Katie, what an eye you have!" Ariel exclaimed. "It looks like the Templars may have actually built the Gothic cathedral as a three-dimensional Tree of Life!" Ariel kept staring at the sketch, shaking her head. "I can't believe it."

"So maybe what Pierre surmised was true," Maureen said. "The priest organized the structures in Rennes le Château to be a living Tree of Life to leave a clue. So maybe the priest knew the Templars, whose treasures and documents were thought to be buried under his church, had done the very same thing with the Gothic Cathedrals. And Charpentier knew somehow the proportions of Chartres were according to some sort of sacred geometry, he just didn't know it was the Tree of Life because he probably had never seen it before."

Ariel looked up at Maureen. "They each had a piece of the puzzle. Pierre figured out the Kabbalah-slash-Rennes le Château link. Charpentier knew there was the Temple of Solomon-slash-sacred geometry building link to the floor plan. But just maybe we figured out the connection between the two: that Mary Magdalene brought the Kabbalah, the Holy Grail, to France," Ariel said.

"That she was teaching the Tree of Life," Maureen said slowly. For a moment, all three women were silent.

"Is it possible?" Ariel asked suddenly, looking almost spooked. "That the common denominator to it all was Magdalene and the priest knew it. *Tour Magdala*, he built as a symbol. You know, *magdaleder*, the Hebrew of *magdala*, means 'watch tower.' It was the nickname Jesus gave her. And that tower was where the priest died. And Katie here had a dream about it last night."

"Okay, you're losing me, Ariel," Maureen said. "Let's just focus on proving the Gothics, Chartres being the premier Gothic cathedral, were built as a living temple of enlightenment. We can look at other stuff later. You need something big to present in your proposal? That is a big fucking theory."

"You're right. But Maureen, all the Gothic cathedrals are dedicated to *Notre Dame*, our lady. Coincidence? If Tree of Life sacred geometry, the clues at Rennes le Château, and the floor plans of the Gothics are all linked, maybe somehow *Notre Dame* is also referring to Mary Magdalene!"

242

"Well, Holy Mother of God, wouldn't that be something," Maureen said. "The most vanquished woman in the Bible ruling over the Gothic cathedrals. Gotta love that!"

Suddenly everyone was quiet. The air around them felt electrified. Ariel kept staring at the floor plan with Maureen's Tree of Life sketch. Maureen stared at Ariel, seemingly transfixed. Katie looked back and forth between the two women, waiting to see what would happen next.

Maureen struck her cane on the floor. "We need to go to Chartres, ladies," she said.

"How long is the drive from here, Maureen?" Ariel asked.

"Hmm, we can do it in eight hours," Maureen said. "What day is it?" she asked.

"Ah, it's still Thursday—but barely, it's after 11:00 PM," Ariel said, checking her cell phone.

"Yes, yes, yes," Maureen said, excitedly. "The labyrinth is only open on Fridays. It's the only day when they take the chairs away, so we'll get a better look at things. And frankly I think the labyrinth, which is why so many people come to Chartres, is connected to the whole floor-plan-sacred-geometry idea, too."

"Okay, Maureen. But I need to concentrate on one theory at a time!" Ariel said.

Maureen cocked her head haughtily. "Fair enough," she said. "But come on, if we drive all night, we can be there when they open, first thing. Then, we can see the whole show, and you may be able to get enough information to hook some academics or a publisher or whoever you need to hook."

"You're right," Ariel said. "Let's go, GPS is guiding us tonight!"

"Damn straight!" Maureen said as she reached up and gave Ariel a high five. "I love that Great Pussy in the Sky."

Ariel laughed.

"You mean go now?" Katie asked. "You want to drive all night—tonight?" She didn't think she wanted to get in a car with either one of them behind the wheel, let alone spend all night driving. "Where is this place?" Katie asked.

"Near Paris," Maureen said, looking at Katie with a funny grin.

"Can't we wait until tomorrow and take a train or wait until you two sober up?" Katie asked.

"We don't need to sober up," Maureen said. "We have you to drive us!"

Katie felt a rush of fear, "What?" she said, "Oh no, I live in New York City, I rarely drive, and I definitely can't in France. I don't even understand the road signs."

"Don't worry about that, kid. We'll tell you where to go! Where's your spunk? We have a chance to check out one hell of a theory that you helped put together! Of course we're going," Maureen said.

Katie looked wide eyed at Ariel, sending her a telepathic message to stop this insanity. But Ariel just smiled. "C'mon Katie, you wanted a road trip. Let's go! And the Porsche can practically drive itself."

"Oh my God, I can't drive Henri's Porsche!" Katie said, feeling doubly horrified.

But Maureen and Ariel ignored her and went about collecting their purses and grabbing water bottles and snacks from the kitchen. Katie wished she hadn't opened Pandora's Box. But she did also want to see Ariel find the information she needed to move her work forward. And her aunt was running out of time. They needed to act fast.

"Okay," Katie finally said, to no one in particular. The other two were already on their way out the door.

She grabbed her camera bag and followed suit.

Katie nervously backed the Porsche out of the dark driveway and then proceeded slowly down the narrow road that led to the village. Ariel sat in the passenger seat and gave her directions. The benefit of driving so late at night was there were few people on the road. Maureen was draped across the backseat, her head buried in a pillow she had brought from home. Once Ariel got Katie onto the freeway, she put her seat back and fell asleep, too. Ariel had put Chartres in the car's GPS but it was all in French. She just told Katie to wake her up in a few hours when she saw the signs for the A20.

Katie stayed in the right lane and tried to remember to think in kilometers per hour. She felt a little abandoned by the two women but once she became more comfortable it gave her time to think. She realized in the last few days she hadn't thought about herself in the same way. She'd been letting stuff go, she could tell, because when she thought about Tom or the life she'd left in New York, it seemed so distant. She had a plan now; she knew this time, she'd be able to leave and find her way. *I Did It My Way* played in her mind as she smiled.

My God, how much had happened since she'd arrived in France! And now she found herself driving her aunt and her eccentric friend to Chartres Cathedral to check on some wild theories that she herself had helped put together. She could barely get her head around it. Somehow the Tree of Life teachings that Magdalene had received from Jesus and brought with her to France were part of something very big. Some kind of sacred geometry that the most famous cathedrals were built on—cathedrals that were possibly dedicated to her, Mary Magdalene, and not Mary the Mother. Talk about going from whore to Madonna! This stuff was interesting, she thought. And she was part of it. Part of an idea that could put an extraordinary woman back at the top where she belonged.

Oh, my God, Katie thought to herself, I'm actually having fun! For sure the last few days had pushed her beyond her old comfort zone, challenging some of her belief systems and ways of looking at the world, but it had been exciting to be with Ariel and be part of whatever was going to happen next.

Katie squirmed in her seat, realizing she really needed to pee. It had been a while since they'd passed a service area. She was considering just pulling over to the side of the road when she saw a sign with a picture of a gas pump, fork and knife, and the ubiquitous sign of a man and a woman together only ten kilometers ahead. When she turned off to exit the freeway, she glanced at the gas gauge and saw it was getting low. Katie pulled into the service area and ran in to use the bathroom before getting fuel. When she came back out, Ariel was just opening the passenger side door.

"Looks like you've got everything under control," Ariel said groggily as she stepped out.

"Yep, we need some gas but I'm not sure what kind to put in," Katie said.

"It's diesel, but they call it *gazole*, the yellow one," Ariel said, handing Katie her Visa. "I'm going to pee and get some coffee. You want one?"

"Yeah, sounds good. Thank you," Katie said as she reached for the fuel pump marked *gazole*. When Ariel returned to the car with two cups of coffee, Maureen was still asleep in the backseat.

"You good to keep driving?" Ariel asked.

"Yeah, I'm actually enjoying myself," Katie said. "I never thought I'd find myself driving a Porsche all night through the French countryside!"

"Alrighty then," Ariel said as she slipped back into the passenger side. She put the two coffees in the cup holder and adjusted her seat to come up a bit.

Once they got back on the freeway, Katie turned to Ariel. "Ariel, you know, you told me how you met Henri and about your first trip to France, complete with the Hollywood ending of seeing him from your balcony. But obviously there's much more."

Ariel took a sip of coffee. "Well, sure there's more, but we'd arrived at the road to Rennes le Château. And I thought it was nice to stop at the happily ever after point."

Katie chuckled. "Fair enough, but I'd like to know how you navigated it all, moving to Montreal then ending up in France...."

"So you want the real story?" Ariel asked. "You know, it's not all tulips and roses."

"Yes!" Katie said, her voice a little too loud. She glanced behind her to see Maureen snoring softly. "I want the real story."

CHAPTER NINETEEN

ARIEL

Henri and I spent a couple of days wandering through vineyards in France tasting wines and having long, luxurious meals in charming cafes. Henri played guitar and sang French love songs on the patio of the bed and breakfast. We talked into the late hours about all aspects of our lives. We both felt that something special was happening. But his situation at home was complex; he'd been separated for quite a while but was wrestling with the whole process of divorce. He didn't know what he could offer me. So we avoided talking about the future and relished the idyllic present.

Afterward, we kept in touch by phone and email, just keeping it light, talking about our lives. It was not an easy practice for me to stay in my own lane and not collapse into his saga. I felt that there was a powerful connection between us, but our lives, locations and backgrounds were so different. And I wondered how it could all possibly come together. A part of me wanted to believe in the fairy tale and the other part demanded I keep the cold, hard facts of the situation in mind.

A few months after returning from France, Henri made another visit to Rancho Encantada. This time I moved into his room for his stay and we enjoyed the undeniable sensuality and ease between us. Our relationship went to the next level as a greater intimacy developed and we relished the time together.

The low-calorie, healthy meals we shared at the spa became sacraments and walks in the desert together became expressions of happiness. Henri asked me a lot of questions about my life. He wanted to know about my fears and worries, my past. He asked about my dreams for the future. We talked constantly. I pretty much relayed my life story over the course of his six-day stay. Henri believed I'd already accomplished many of the goals I had set for myself. He sensed that I was still insecure because of my past. He encouraged me to see where I was, to look around at the foundation I had already built up doing what I wanted.

On the last night of his stay at Rancho Encantada, Henri and I went to the lounge for "mocktails"— no alcohol served at the spa—and we joked that it was the first time together without the influence of wine. Then the conversation turned more serious.

"You've done well here," Henri said.

I nodded; it was true. In many ways, Tucson and Rancho Encantada had redeemed me, brought me back on course.

"I think this is a good place for you. You have your freedom, your work, nature, and the things you love to do. You're happy here."

Even though what he said was true, I felt as if an invisible hand were pressing against my chest, as though someone was trying to push me down.

"I have done well here, and I'm very grateful for that, believe me. But I feel like I'm capable of more," I said. "I feel this force inside compelling me to keep seeking greater expressions of who I am."

"Are you speaking of ambition?" Henri asked.

I laughed. "I've been woefully lacking ambition in the career sense for most of my life. No, it's deeper than that. It's a knowing that I can do more, and need to do more. It's as if over the last year or so my inner self is just waking up—from a long slumber."

While I was talking to Henri, I realized that the waking-up sensation I'd just spoken of corresponded to my experience with the medicine—and to Grandmother. Since the medicine, I'd sensed more was possible and had really begun to see the magic shining through the firmament of everyday life.

Henri extended his visit by a couple of days, staying with me in my apartment.

"You like the magic," Henri said over dinner one night.

"Yep, I like the magic," I said, holding up my glass of wine.

"You're just interested in the magic," Henri said then, his tone sounding suspiciously close to a pout.

Where was he going with this? I wondered and looked at him questioningly.

"That's what you said," Henri continued. "You just want the magic."

Aha! Now I understood his meaning. "I didn't say I was *only* interested in the magic."

"Oh, so you're interested in something more?" Henri asked.

I shook my head and chose my words carefully.

"What I mean is there's magic between us, and this doesn't come along very often, so I believe we should explore it without worrying about the future."

Henri nodded in agreement. "So you may be interested in something more than just the magic?"

"Yes," I said, smiling. "I'm interested in something more than *just* the magic. I'm interested in being in something real and lasting, too."

Then Henri told me he was in the process of legal divorce. It would be a long process, possibly two years until everything was final. He'd built a large business importing wine, as well as owning vineyards in France and Spain with his business partners. It was the first inkling I had of how wealthy he was. Rancho Encantada was very expensive, and I'd worked with many successful people there, but as Henri was explaining the complexity of navigating the financial aspects of his life, I realized much more about the world he lived in.

We agreed to keep the options open and continue to stay in contact. But we didn't make a plan to see each other next. He felt he needed to take care of his life as cleanly as possible and didn't want to commit to anything until he'd sorted through his own process. I didn't sleep well that night. It felt like the fairytale might be over.

Over the next few weeks I grew restless. My work at Rancho Encantada was feeling more tedious than inspired. The conversation with Henri about wanting more haunted me. Because I could only think of wanting more with him and how that was not possible at this time and maybe never would be.

I decided to drive to San Diego for a long weekend. There was a little motel I'd stay at only a few blocks from the beach. Every day I'd go with my chair and book and spend the afternoon. Chico was older by then, but he was like a puppy at the beach; he liked to dig holes in the sand and chase the foam of the waves. There is something about the sea and sand that always cleanses my soul. After the weekend as I drove back east across the open expanse of desert, and I witnessed an extraordinary moment in nature. The top of the Jeep was down so I had an unobstructed view as an enormous full moon rose over the horizon. It looked like the long highway rolled right up to it. At the same time the big red sun was setting directly behind me.

With the rearview mirror I could see both at the same time. And for several minutes they seemed perfectly balanced in the sky, reflecting each other. Witnessing such a beautiful sight, I experienced a palpable sense that there was enough room for everything, and all in its right timing. One aspect could be setting as another was rising. I realized I had enough room inside myself to hold the space for Henri *and* myself. I could allow the magic to unfold between us in its own time *and* to continue to engage fully in my own life. Both were within my own control. This may sound obvious, but for me it was a revelation.

When I returned, I felt inspired to write down my experiences with Grandmother. I needed a new project and it was something that I'd been thinking about since I'd returned from Ecuador. So I bought a stack of legal pads and began writing. The whole experience came back with crystal clarity. I recalled the shaman telling us about the Achuar sending messages via the stars. That night under the clear Arizona sky, I looked up at the Pleiades and sent a message of love to Henri. I imagined him wherever he was in the world looking up at the sky and somehow receiving the star transmission.

The "Grandmother project" gave me a lift. And my writing continued to chronicle the experiences following the history of Magdalene. I began to see more and more links between what Grandmother had told me in Ecuador and what had transpired over the last year. I then began to shape the notes into a book proposal. Sue was very encouraging; she felt that Grandmother was working through me and the story should find a wider audience.

For months I worked on the proposal, worked at Rancho Encantada, but had less and less contact with Henri. There was the occasional call and text, but we still hadn't made any plans to see each other. I again felt an increasing tension between the desire for change and expansion in my work and life and the need for comfort and security. I wanted an easy opening, not the same deep dive off a cliff which had always been my *modus operandi*.

There were several other Rancho Encantada properties around the country, and it occurred to me I could take a look on the website for job postings. Perhaps I could find a new location and bring some change into my life without losing my security. So I spent some time online looking at the other Rancho Encantada properties. I found that the facility near Rhinebeck, in upstate New York, was the only other property with a metaphysical department. I visited the employment page but didn't see anything listed. Even though positions in my work opened rarely, I still felt hopeful. I also went to the local Chamber of Commerce website. I found photographs of Rhinebeck, an idyllic village nestled in the rolling forested hills. I enlarged the map of the region and saw that it was near the border of Massachusetts and Connecticut. I still had a lot of extended family in the area, which was only a few hours' drive from Rhinebeck. Then I moved the cursor to expand the view of New York State and southern Canada. Rhinebeck was only about 250 miles due south of Montreal.

As many things have happened in my life, when things move, they move quickly. The following weekend at Rancho Encantada, I went online to check the Rhinebeck facility employment site. I scrolled down the listings and stopped on "Metaphysical practitioner wanted." I read it through three times. Within the week I had a phone interview, a background check, and a release from my Tucson manager. I made arrangements to fly to New York to meet the managers in person to see if it was a fit. If I got the new position, I would be doing all metaphysical services: numerology, astrology, tarot, and clairvoyance. It was a big jump to be able to practice everything; I was excited about the chance to expand my practice.

I flew to New York and spent two days there touring the facility, doing sessions for management. I was offered the position. The next day, I found housing, got a post office box, and put in the paperwork for a transfer effective in four weeks. After that, it was a whirlwind last month in Tucson: saying goodbye to Rancho Encantada friends and colleagues and then packing the contents of my apartment and cleaning it. The wonderful women I'd met in my years there gathered around and made the work light.

It was strange to be heading back to the Northeast where I grew up. Rhinebeck was a new location for me, and I felt this change was heralding all kinds of new possibilities. But I also felt the tremors of the past under my wheels as I drove across some old terrain. Ironically, my truck-driving training came in handy as I navigated the 2,500 miles in a sixteen-foot moving van towing a trailer carrying my car. However, my deep-seated fear of backing up with a trailer ran deep, and I managed to drive the whole distance to Rhinebeck without ever having to go in reverse!

Feeling nervous but optimistic, I arrived at the little farmhouse I had rented the month before and immediately faced a series of problems. There was a propane leak in the kitchen, the staircase was too narrow to get my queen bed up the stairs, there was no phone service or internet even though I had set it up from Tucson, and the road out front was much busier than I expected and was difficult to enter and exit. I remember being on the phone with your mother describing the days of constant troubleshooting. She listened to the list of problems and said, "I hope you didn't make a big mistake, Ariel."

I had been wondering the same thing. But hearing the words spoken out loud brought my fears to a head. Had I stretched myself too thin? Was a new house, a new job, a new state, and a completely new environment all at the same time too much? It was odd I even questioned this move. Compared to my other daring changes, like going to Australia and making a living reading tarot cards in a café, or moving to Hawaii on a shoestring and living in the jungle, it was strange that I would be nervous now. I had plenty of money in the bank, I was working for the same company, and I was in fairly familiar terrain. That's when it hit me: it was the old Little Match Girl fears. Afraid that somehow I'd dared to want too much, and that this would bring me to lose everything and end up out in the cold alone.

I sat back on my mattress on the floor surrounded by boxes. The weather was damp and cool; it had been raining on and off for two days. I searched my bag for a sweater. If it's this cold in summer, I thought, I'm going to freeze come winter. Laying back I covered my face with my folded arms. What had I done? I'd given up all my hard-won security for some notion of expanding my life. I had taken a new and more exciting position and suddenly it felt like a big gamble. I'd moved to a place with a significantly higher cost of living. I groaned, turned onto my stomach, and pulled the pillow over my head. Survival fears run long and deep. And when there is a crack in the façade of daily life, the fears seep their poisonous contents. Memories of making mistakes and being alone and scared oozed out.

It took a few weeks to get the house and my home office set up. After six years of living in a small apartment surrounded by hundreds of other people in their small apartments, I was now struggling with a quiet, remote location and big spaces with not enough furniture to fill them. My two-bedroom house sat at the edge of a large farm with only two distant neighbors. At night I often went to bed after dinner with my laptop and watched a Netflix movie for company.

My new position at Rancho Encantada did not get off to a good start. On my first evening I was shown to my office in the basement with no windows and awful fluorescent lighting. I was told it was temporary; they were setting up new offices upstairs for the metaphysical practitioners. The computer didn't have internet access, and I didn't have cell phone service, so I felt completely cut off from the outside world.

My first client was an employee. I was relieved; employees got big discounts for services and were generally more easy going. He wanted a fifty-minute clairvoyant session, which was a service offered in my new position. Clairvoyance is the process of seeing what to most people is invisible. It requires extreme concentration to get into the meditative space then hold that concentration as colors, images, guidance quickly comes across the mind's eye.

Before, I did this for ten minutes and then used one of my other tools such as tarot for the rest of the session. Whatever I didn't pick up in the beginning, my cards would fill in the blanks to provide a comprehensive reading of the client and their situation. So I was a little nervous when I started my process; it was my first full length clairvoyant session. However, once I got going, I felt quite pleased at the clarity of what I saw and was able to relay to him.

But when I looked up after I came out of the meditative state and asked if he had any questions, I was just met with a bored expression. He told me that the only reason he'd booked with me was to find out how he could win the lottery. I thought he was joking! Unfortunately, he wasn't. These skills took a lot of focus and energy and I was accustomed to people coming for serious guidance in Tucson, so the fact that he was my very first client in Rhinebeck didn't bode well.

On my shift the next morning, I had no clients. I tried to keep myself busy by walking around the grounds to familiarize myself with the new property. I stopped to introduce myself to the staff at the front desk. Then I went to the spa and consoled myself with the fact that I had access to excellent facilities. I returned to my basement office and rehearsed my new talk. Part of my job was to give a weekly presentation. I'd done many lectures and workshops on numerology in Tucson and generally enjoyed public speaking, so I wasn't too concerned about it.

For my new position, I wrote a new lecture called "Exploring Metaphysics," which described how each process worked. The guests would thereby become more familiar with metaphysical services and hopefully would book a private session. I began my talk by telling the group a bit about my background and making a few jokes to lighten the atmosphere. I followed the outline I'd written for the lecture and then wrapped it up, almost on time. I thought it had gone pretty well. Several of the women asked questions and seemed genuinely interested in the topic. I gathered my supplies and headed back down to my office to see if any of the attendees had booked, like they so often had when I was in Tucson.

But no one had, and to make matters worse, my manager called me to ask if the lecture had gone okay. I told her it had—I felt good about the new material. I'd worked diligently preparing the lecture and getting my new services up to speed. Yet it hadn't gone that well after all. A woman had come to the front desk directly after my lecture and let it be known that she was not happy. In all my years at Rancho Encantada Tucson, I'd never once had a formal complaint. My lectures were really well received and resulted in a very high booking rate. Now, in my first two days at the Rhinebeck facility, I had both a formal complaint from a guest and a disgruntled employee.

I went to bed that night with frayed nerves, tossing and turning as the fan circulated the humid night air. I had been trying not to slip into the oh-shit-what-have-I-done mode, but I really questioned whether I had made the right choice to leave Tucson. I tried to calm my mind, telling myself I could always go back there. My manager had taken me aside on my last day and told me that if I ever wanted to return, she would find a place for me. But I didn't spend thousands of dollars moving and setting up, not to mention countless hours struggling with services and bureaucracy, to turn around and leave.

I felt trapped. I didn't want to go back, yet I was terrified of failing. Could I have been wrong to think I could do more? I had felt so sure; the guidance had been so clear. But did I make a mistake, some misstep along the way? Was I guilty of a kind of hubris, thinking I could have more in my life? I was so exhausted from the move and all the necessary troubleshooting that I couldn't answer my own questions. Whatever objectivity I'd had was gone as my anxiety grew. So I prayed. I asked my angels, guides, and any beings of light to come help me. I felt frightened and alone and worried that I had truly overextended myself. I prayed for guidance over and over until I fell into a fitful sleep.

Sometime in the early-morning hours, I sensed a presence near me. I slowly rolled over and saw a woman sitting in bed next to me. It was Grandmother, wearing a disguise I'd seen before in dreams. I'd coined it her "red lady" outfit: a short red-haired wig styled with big curls, a long red skirt and blouse, and her signature pair of oversized sunglasses. She was comfortably lounged against a pillow with her legs outstretched and loosely crossed at the ankles. Groggy, I took a moment to realize I wasn't dreaming.

"Oh my God!" I whispered. It was the first time I'd *seen* Grandmother since my last experience with the medicine two years earlier.

"I was wondering when you were going to call on me," Grandmother said. She held up a hand as if she were examining her manicure. I smiled, feeling immediately better. Grandmother's here, I thought with relief. Her presence was reassuring. I wasn't under the effects of the medicine, and I was *seeing* her. Other than a whiskey before bed, I was very sober.

As Grandmother spoke, I found myself going into an altered state—part meditation and part dream. She continued to sit on my bed and talk to me for hours. She guided me on how to proceed with my work. She told me how to access the higher states of consciousness with more confidence. She talked to me about money, assuring me that I had everything I needed to live comfortably. She showed me a vision of the near future with Henri; he and I were laughing as we spun around a dance floor. She reassured me that I was on the right path and would soon be feeling much more secure.

I got up just after dawn, as if floating on a warm current of well-being. I opened the curtains in the bedroom, sat back against the pillows, and watched as a misty red sun rose over the hills. I felt a magical spaciousness inside. I hadn't felt that peaceful in a long time. I was surprised and grateful that my fervent prayers for help and guidance were answered.

And it happened that over the next several months I followed Grandmother's advice and saw things shift in my life. I began to communicate with her much more frequently as I recalled her words, "Our souls are fused." I became more at ease with the clairvoyant work when I realized I could ask for Grandmother's assistance and she would guide me directly in the sessions. I was able to detach more as her guidance increased my strength and capacity to access greater intuition. I felt more centered in my personal life, as well. I didn't feel quite as affected by the energy of others. With Grandmother's heightened presence, I experienced a stronger sense of self. My client base grew both privately by word of mouth and at Rancho Encantada. Feeling steadier, I began to relax, and it was around this time that Henri and I made plans to see each other.

We spent a few days on his boat on Martha's Vineyard and had a fun time making a nest for ourselves in the V-berth. I enjoyed the break from work and relished being totally taken care of. Henri called a lot, at the same time protesting that he didn't like the telephone. He said he didn't want to make any commitments, but then he suggested plans to meet one after another. I just rolled with it. After a few months of Henri coming down to stay with me, or meeting in New York City, I drove up to Montreal and met Henri's sisters and his assistant and colleagues.

Days and weeks went by. I was enjoying my little farmhouse immensely. I'd made the second bedroom my home office, which I loved with the steeply sloped ceilings and windows facing the trees at the back of the property. I finally had the space to hang all the folk art and spiritual trinkets I'd collected from my various travels. I had a cow skull that I had painted in an indigenous ceremony hanging above the window in front of me.

Feeling inspired, I began working on the book proposal for "The Grandmother Project." I bought a how-to-write-a-successful-book-proposal book and followed the recommendations. It was a lot of work to not only write a synopsis of each chapter but also put together a platform. However, the project also invigorated me, and by Thanksgiving I'd completed it to the best of my ability. In keeping with the advice of the recommendations, I wrote up a query letter and sent it to agents that represented my genre.

One morning a few weeks later, I was really surprised to see a response from one of the literary agents. She wanted to see my proposal! I got up and did a little dance around my office. I picked up a small brass statue of Ganesh—the Hindu god with the head of an elephant; he's the remover of obstacles and patron of writers—and gave him a kiss. An agent was interested! Then I sat back down. I didn't want to get my hopes up too high. It was just the first step. But I swear there was a crackling energy as I sent the agent an email reply with my proposal attached.

As I went downstairs to pour another cup of coffee before getting ready for work, I realized I was having a very full life! It had seemed for years that I had been striving to fill a void. I'd been searching for more: more work or more money or more community, and certainly more of a love life. I realized how much had happened in the last several months since I'd moved to Rhinebeck. Every area of my life had grown considerably.

CHAPTER TWENTY

To use a garden metaphor—once everything had blossomed, it didn't take long for the garden of my life to become overgrown. I was ill equipped to manage the situation, which unearthed an old belief: either follow my own path for success but remain alone, or subjugate my life to devote time and energy to another's wants and needs to have a relationship. This became apparent during the first winter in Rhinebeck.

I received an email from the agent, Georgia. She really liked the ideas in the proposal and wanted to sign me on. She felt she had a good chance of selling to one of the spiritual/new age publishers. I was overjoyed and sat at my computer feeling one of those rare moments of deep satisfaction. I had spent countless hours working on that forty-page proposal—essentially a mini-book—and I'd experienced a sense of purpose just reliving the stories and ideas for myself. But it wasn't until that moment of signing with an agent that the real possibility of the story finding an audience hit me.

That moment of satisfaction passed quickly, though, when I realized I had a lot more work in front of me. Georgia said she would be sending the proposal back with editorial comments. It apparently needed a lot of revising to make it more professional before she could shop it to publishers. And she would be sending her contract for me to look over and sign. Suddenly, it dawned on me that I wasn't on my own time schedule anymore. And I had a day job! I tried not to panic. I got up and paced around the house, got a glass of water, then went back and sent an email letting Georgia know I was good to go.

I was so busy that whole day that I hadn't taken time to email Henri and tell him the good news. He was in Europe on vineyard business. For the last couple of weeks, we had been only emailing or texting. So I was surprised when he called me from Spain late that day. He was excited to tell me that he was organizing a trip to Southeast Asia and wanted me to join him. I was happy to be invited, but the timing was terrible. I had a full work schedule and now the upcoming revision and contract with Georgia. For some reason, I didn't tell Henri about the agent. I just told him I was feeling overwhelmed at the moment and would need some time to consider my schedule.

I could hear the disappointment in his voice. It was the first time I had even hesitated to join him. Until then, I had always made the space to be together, even when it meant I was exhausted from fitting in my private readings between social functions and trading shifts at Rancho Encantada so I could travel.

When Henri returned from Europe a few days later, he called me on Skype. I'd been avoiding him and the topic of the Asia trip. I brought the laptop into bed and propped myself against my pillows. It had been a good three weeks since we had seen each other. I was happy to see him on Skype, but I felt an underlying strain. He had been sending me emails and texts to tell me how much he missed me and how he hated to be alone and how much it meant to him that I traveled with him. In his previous relationship, he was always alone on his excursions.

Henri smiled nervously on my laptop screen.

"I won't keep you up too late," he said. "But I've been thinking about what you said the other night. How important it is for you to do your work and take care of yourself. And I think I understand why you feel tense right now. You've been alone a long time, really alone. I think even when you were married before, you were alone. You thought you had to do everything yourself because you never had a safety net."

Henri looked at me earnestly.

"I want you to know that you're not alone anymore. You have me. I hope our relationship continues to grow and we'll be together for a very long time. But even if that isn't the case, you will always have me as your friend and ally. And that means if you ever need help, money, advice, or support, you'll get it. And I want to help you now. Let me take you on this Asia trip. Take a couple weeks off and relax. Enjoy a little vacation."

I couldn't respond. No one had ever said such things to me before. I tried to take in the generosity and thoughtfulness of his words. But I also felt pressured and mistrustful. If I let him take care of things, and me, he might then expect me to always go along with his agenda. I didn't want to forfeit my sovereignty. I wanted someone who understood me and supported me in achieving my own dreams, not just going along with theirs. But I also deeply wanted the relationship to evolve. I didn't know what to tell him, so I just smiled and nodded.

That night I had a peculiar dream with a very clear message.

I sat in a dimly lit waiting room of an elegant office building. A woman, an executive assistant, rose from her desk, called my name, and then escorted me to a door. She opened it and gestured for me to enter an office suite. Behind a large wooden desk sat my maternal grandmother. She looked similar to how I remembered her but somehow more powerful, with thick white hair and an air of authority.

"I'm going to tell you something important," she said. Her tone was all business. Her gaze held me in its directness. "All issues come from childhood. That is true for everyone. Everything you are wrestling with comes from your past. You don't need to look anywhere else. Understand your childhood issues and you will be free."

I woke up startled, thinking about what my grandmother had said. I knew I had some trust issues stemming from my childhood. Henri was right when he said I'd been on my own for a very long time. Why didn't I trust him when he was saying he cared deeply for my welfare? Was I taking that as a threat to my independence? Was this because I had trusted before, only to be left fending for myself in the end?

I still hadn't told Henri that I had signed on with an agent. I didn't really know why, except that I felt protective of my project, like it was my child. I didn't want someone pressuring me to give it up. I didn't even realize how strange that idea, that someone would pressure me to give it up, was; I just instinctively became more self-protective. I felt increasingly wary that Henri's life and luxurious lifestyle were taking up more and more space. I was afraid I would be swallowed up by it and lose myself and my own identity. Yet I wanted to be together: I had long been searching for such a dynamic relationship. It seemed that different parts of my psyche were poised for battle. The aspect that just wanted time and space for my own projects seemed at odds with the aspect that desired a loving relationship.

The next morning, I received an email from Georgia saying she was in the middle of several deals at once and it would take her a few weeks to get the proposal back to me to work on. In the meantime, I didn't need to do anything more until I received her notes. Our contract was signed.

We were also past the holidays and going into the slow season at Rancho Encantada, so I had no more excuses regarding the Asia trip. I reasoned that maybe it would be good to get out of the New England winter for a couple of weeks.

I was a seasoned traveler. I had been to Asia numerous times when I lived in Australia, and for the most part I enjoyed it. But during this trip, I struggled with illness and exhaustion. The level of poverty in Cambodia was heartbreaking, even more so when contrasted with luxury travel, something I wasn't used to. I had always traveled as a backpacker on a budget.

I tried to be in "vacation mode" but found it difficult. I wasn't sleeping well. My unease grew during a weeklong cruise down the Mekong River. The riverboat docked near an impoverished village for yet another tour of another cottage industry. I lagged behind the other passengers as they disembarked. Our Cambodian guide, Wala, pointed to a row of ramshackle huts that served as the market and said if I wanted to buy some school supplies, the local school would appreciate any donations. I brightened immediately and left the group to gather supplies.

The elementary school was right in the center of the village. I approached the classroom and a young teacher met me at the door. She didn't speak English, so I pointed to the supplies and then to the classroom. She welcomed me inside and said a few words to the children in Khmer, and the room erupted in song. The students sang and jumped up and down and clapped and yelled as the bags were passed around. I stood at the front of the room trying not to tear up.

For the first time since we'd been in Asia, I felt happy. I waved goodbye to the class and walked back to the boat, eager to find Henri and tell him about my adventure. But when I found him on the upper deck, drinking a gin and tonic, he was in a foul mood. Attempting to ignore his sulking behavior, I relayed the story of the schoolchildren and their beautiful, welcoming song. He shrugged nonchalantly, not meeting my eyes.

"What's wrong with you?" I asked.

He finally looked at me. "I've been trying to give you a great vacation. And you haven't felt well, don't have any energy. Then Wala tells you about the school and suddenly you're fine and you run off and become Mother Teresa."

Oh my God! I thought. Anger shot up from my gut. He's actually jealous of the time I spent with those kids! I went downstairs and unlocked our tiny stateroom. I sat on the bed feeling sick to my stomach. I looked at my suitcase wedged against the foot of the bed. I've had enough, I thought. I don't like being trapped on this cruise, and I'm pretty damned sick of spoiled rich people! I started planning my escape. I could find my way to the border, cross into Vietnam, and make my way to Saigon. I had a plane ticket out of Saigon to Shanghai, China, and then to New York. That felt a lot easier than staying on the boat and trying to deal with Henri's behavior.

Henri opened the door and sat on the bed next to me. He held his head in his hands.

"No matter what I do, you're happier when you're on your own." His voice cracked. He lay back down on the bed and covered his face with his hands. Then he talked softly. He thought if he could just do enough for me and give me enough, he would be loved. But it felt like no matter what he did, I didn't seem happy.

My anger started to evaporate. I sat back on the bed next to him. I began to understand something about our dynamic and the tension we'd been feeling. I craved more space and time for my own endeavors. He craved more time together. The problem wasn't that we didn't love each other, but we had very different needs and ways of being in the world, which that trip clearly revealed.

After the Asia trip, I realized that if Henri were indeed the "right one" and the soul mate that all the seers had predicted, then finding him was not the end of the story. It was just the beginning of a whole new level of growth. I had a sense I'd been searching for a mountain for as long as I could remember only to arrive at its base and realize now I had to climb it! And I realized I wasn't really equipped for that part of the journey. I did finally summon the courage to tell Henri about my contract with the agent. Instead of being hurt or angry, which I'd feared, he seemed genuinely happy for me. He knew it meant that I would be busier now that I had someone actively working with me to get the proposal sold to a publisher, but he seemed to take it in stride.

That summer, Henri and I began to talk about taking the next step. We wanted to be together and that meant I would be the one to relocate. He was firmly entrenched in Montreal, and although he traveled a great deal, he couldn't move his base. Being the gypsy I was, I was open to moving. But I was very reluctant to give up my job at Rancho Encanta-da. It had been my lifeline, and I did not want to lose my autonomy. I thought perhaps I could split my shifts with a colleague and commute down every other weekend. I did the numbers over and over in my head and realized that if I let go of my rental house and stayed at a colleagues' extra room for a nominal rate, I could make it work. And I would still have my private clients over the phone and on Skype.

However, I didn't think I'd be ready to make the move until at least the end of the year. I was finally feeling settled and was enjoying my farm-house in Rhinebeck, and I couldn't face another round of upheaval. Also, I was working on the revision of the proposal for Georgia; we were hopeful about a publisher picking it up quickly, which meant next I'd need to actually write the book. And I wanted to do that while I still had time and space to myself.

As fall came around and the time to move grew closer, I became even more apprehensive. Henri kept insisting that living with him in Montreal would cost me nothing, that I would be freer to do what I wanted and write my book, and that my life could expand in all kinds of good ways. Although I agreed with this theoretically, I didn't trust it. I was scared to be in a vulnerable position: moving into *his* apartment, sharing *his* life, in *his* country.

To sweeten the deal, Henri offered me an insurance policy. He said since I was the one making the lion's share of the big changes—letting go of my house and a lot of my stuff (because there wasn't room in his apartment), as well as changing location and countries—if I really didn't like living in Montreal, or our relationship didn't work out, he would set me up wherever I wanted to go. He would pay for a complete relocation. I could buy all new stuff. He promised to make sure I had everything I needed to succeed somewhere else. He even offered to help with a down payment to buy something instead of renting.

I told my friend Devra about this offer. She said, "Get it in writing!"

I liked the guarantee and thought it was fair, but I was still apprehensive. I didn't want to relocate again to be left high and dry emotionally. I was wary of both feeling lost and alone in a new city and also of feeling smothered by Henri's rather big and luxurious life. It was hard for me to comprehend losing my autonomy.

Since his separation, Henri had been seeing a therapist in Montreal. And he told me he took it to heart when his therapist told him in the first session that if he didn't address the root causes of the problems in his previous relationship, he was doomed to repeat them. The therapist warned about the mistaken belief that many people have: love would magically evaporate any insecurity or fear and solve all hurts and wounds, when in fact being in a relationship opened up the possibility for much deeper

270

growth and healing.

I realized I needed to find my own counsel. Though I'd been to healers, psychics and seers my whole life, I'd actually never been in any kind of therapy and wasn't sure where to look. As luck would have it, I found out the next day when I visited my chiropractor. The woman in the adjacent office to his was a well-regarded therapist. I picked up her business card and called the number when I got home. I liked Patty immediately. She explained she was a licensed therapist but also used alternative techniques such as hypnosis and shamanic journeying. I made an appointment for the following week.

A tall, slim woman with steely gray hair and an air of authority opened the door. As Patty and I sat in her spacious office, I told her what was going on in my life: Henri, the upcoming move north, my fears about losing my autonomy, and the exhaustion I'd been experiencing over the last several months. Patty had already received the six pages of intake forms I had filled out about my general health and well-being.

Patty sat back in her chair and looked directly at me for a few moments. She said she thought the best place to start would be to do some journeying. She led me to the massage table at the back of her office. I stretched out and she put a light blanket over me. She led me in some deep breathing exercises, and soon I was quite relaxed. Journeying was similar to hypnosis. The client is brought into a deep meditative state to access information from the subconscious.

I found myself going down into a dark cellar. A shaft of light from the open door at the top of a stairwell shone down, framing a little girl. She sat on the damp floor with her head in her arms. I ran down the stairs, picked up the little girl, and carried her back up and through the open door. We found ourselves in a large well-furnished living room with wood floors and lots of sunlight streaming through the windows. There were several people

waiting in the living room to help. The scene reminded me of a crime dra-
ma on TV. There were police and nurses and a therapist on hand to assist
me after the rescue.

I described the scene to Patty. She guided me to sit with the child, hold
her close, and reassure her. The little girl looked up at me with terrified
big round eyes. I told her she was safe, but frankly I had no idea what to
do! When I told Patty about my apprehension, that I didn't really know
how to help this little girl, she replied that the fact that I saw the others in
my vision ready to assist was a good sign. Help was at hand. Patty helped
me sit up and I went back to the chair. There was a pitcher of water on
the table between us; she poured me a glass. I felt shaky—I knew that
what I'd seen was only a vision from somewhere in my psyche, but it had
really unnerved me.

Patty leaned forward in her chair. "There are three main survival strategies that children adopt when they feel unsafe in their place of origin
or when some kind of trauma has occurred," Patty said. "There is the
'caretaker'—children who learn to help or care for those around them as
a means of ensuring their own well-being. They often become a parent
to their own parent. But they never learn how to get their own needs
met. The next one is the 'rebel'—children who feel they need to fight
for themselves. They project their own fear and pain onto those around
them, expressing anger and rage. Then there is the 'lost child'—children
who feel they don't fit in. They don't know how to be in their situation,
so they disappear somehow, either by hiding inside themselves or by always moving from one place to the next. When they feel unsafe, they
run. They can be very independent but have a hard time forming lasting
bonds."

Patty continued. "I believe what happened is at some point in childhood you needed to protect yourself, so you disappeared, became the

'lost child.' That's the part of you that stayed hidden from the world. As you got older, you developed a coping mechanism, let's call her the 'uber-independent girl.' That's the part of you that moved from place to place and got along with everyone but was wary of relationships and was often alone. Uber-independent girl learned that the only thing she could really count on was herself."

She felt I was able to access the little girl in my vision because I was ready to integrate the 'lost child' fully into my personality. The little girl had been hiding in the basement of my psyche since childhood, waiting for the day when I was ready and able to reclaim her.

The way Patty explained it, the whole pattern seemed so obvious. I was astounded that she figured all that out in the first session! I now understood why I was so afraid to give up any autonomy. I knew I could trust myself and my work and my capabilities to survive on my own. But I didn't know how to stop being alone, how to stop being uber-independent in a relationship.

I also was able to see how my brother had become a 'caretaker.' He was always the one trying to manage our unpredictable mother. And it was his nature to be diplomatic and try to smooth things out for everyone around him. It probably made him a great dad to you, Katie, but his ability to still relate to the family made me feel even more alienated.

"Uber-independent girl has been running the show for a while now. But as with all survival strategies, there comes a time to dismantle the need to always use them. It has been your primary way of being in the world and it has really served you. Uber-independent girl has kept you safe and functioning. You want to praise her. But she needs to know that there is more that your spirit wishes you to experience," Patty explained.

I told Patty about my recent dream with my maternal grandmother. How she'd said all the answers were in childhood, and that understanding those dynamics would free me.

Patty nodded. "And today, in this journey, without hesitating, you went down into the bottom of your psyche and brought back the lost part of you. This little girl just wants to be loved and accepted. She wants to feel safe and welcomed and surrounded by those who really care for her.

"So now you have a man who truly loves you. He promises to help you and take care of you. And you know he's trustworthy because he cares for those around him. Your little girl is thrilled; she wants to feel safe. She wants emotional and material security. But uber-independent girl is on high alert because she knows that moving forward in the relationship means that you're going to lose some of your autonomy. Hence the inner tension you feel."

Patty explained that I needed uber-independent girl to step back a bit and let the little girl have some of what she needed. Patty gave me some homework: spend time listening and acknowledging the little girl, and find ways to trust and honor her so she can find her rightful place in my psyche.

Over the following months as Patty and I continued to work together, I realized that I needed to integrate the lost child. She was the magical, joyful part of me looking to be seen and loved. I realized that this was true of most people. Most of us have some version of feeling unloved or unseen, and in some cases outright abuse and neglect, resulting in the child going "underground."

I was grateful to uber-independent girl, who I thought sounded a bit like Lilith. She was tough and wily. The more I grew to love the child who had been found, the more I could appreciate the uber-independent girl.

All this work with Patty helped me to reframe my relationship with Henri in a way I was comfortable with. I saw it as a part of my spiritual journey—an opportunity to grow past childhood needs. A relationship became the ground for each partner to grow and thrive, the garden of possibility in which the man and woman could become conscious and equal partners. This was not the patriarchal paradigm of leader and follower, of parent and child, of one with the power over the other. It was a paradigm of king and queen, each a sovereign in their own right. It was, in short, time to bring the idea of the sacred marriage into my own relationship.

I told Patty about my realization. I wanted to live a microcosmic version of the sacred marriage. As above, so below. I'd learned through astrology that this was the time of the sacred marriage, the union of divine masculine and feminine. We needed to bring back the disparate parts of ourselves that had gone underground or were cast into the shadows. The divine feminine was emerging in her fullness—solar and lunar aspect, Queen of Heaven and Earth.

Patty smiled.

"You did it," Patty said. "You found your lost child, a treasure that's been waiting to be found. Now your uber-independent girl will have a chance to evolve into her best self. She can go from warrior to queen."

"How about warrior queen?" I asked Patty. I was holding on to all I had discovered about the solar feminine, the warrior, Lilith.

Patty laughed as she got up from her chair and went to a cabinet in the corner of the office. She reached in and pulled out a plastic silver tiara studded with rhinestones. She placed it on my head. I laughed as I adjusted the tiara; it was a toy from a costume shop, but I felt rather regal. Like a shiny queen.

Patty told me she had so many women in her practice looking for love, and they all wanted a king; someone strong, successful, and powerful. Most wanted to be rescued on some level, as in fairy tales. She said the most important factor wasn't so much the search for the king. It was whether you believed you were a queen. Inevitably she would ask each woman: Do you believe you're a queen? If you don't, then it's time to take care of your own domain.

CHAPTER TWENTY ONE

"So, you figured it out," Katie said. "You became queen of your domain."

"Well yes, eventually," Ariel said.

Katie's thoughts then turned to what Ariel had said about her dad. He'd always been kind, gentle and soft spoken. Katie could see how he could be a "caretaker." She never knew much about his mother; she'd lived somewhere in the Midwest and had died when Katie was a toddler. But after hearing what Ariel said, she wondered about her dad's childhood, something she'd really never thought about before.

"Ariel," Katie said. "Do you think my dad married someone like my mom because he was a 'caretaker'?"

Ariel looked over at her niece; they hadn't spoken much about her brother, Katie's father.

She nodded. "I think so," Ariel said softly. "He chose someone that wanted to be taken care of, that was demanding and, sorry to say, manipulative."

Ariel watched Katie. But Katie just nodded in agreement, she certainly knew what Ariel said was true. She'd experienced her mother's behavior her whole life.

"You know, I always thought my dad was just a softie, I never really knew about his childhood—your childhood," Katie said. She suddenly felt a sadness welling up in her chest.

Ariel reached over and squeezed Katie's shoulder. "Your dad was naturally a really kind person. He did a great job providing for you, your brother and mother. He loved you guys and was happy to take care of you. Don't ever question that, okay?" Ariel said.

Katie nodded, smiling a little. "Thanks Ariel," she said. "I still miss him, you know."

"Of course you do," Ariel said. "I miss him too."

Both women fell silent for a few moments.

"Hey ladies, where are we?" Maureen asked groggily from the back seat.

"We're not far from Orleans," Ariel said. She looked over her shoulder. "Looks like you got some sleep."

Maureen yawned loudly. "I did. But I was fading in and out, so I heard some of your Henri story. You never told me about that Asia trip, Jesus," Maureen said as she sat up. "Henri wasn't exactly Mister Philanthropic." She rummaged for her water bottle and took a big swig. "Did I miss the good part—when you finally took a stand against his patriarchal bullshit?"

Katie shot Ariel a questioning look.

Ariel groaned. "Maureen, I was going to leave it at moving up to Montreal and happily ever after!"

"You've got to be kidding," Maureen said, nodding toward Katie. "You're going to perpetuate the fantasy and do your niece here a great disservice."

"Yeah," Katie said, nodding at Ariel. She really didn't know what Maureen was talking about but wanted Ariel to continue.

Ariel looked out the passenger window.

"She needs some guidance, Ariel," Maureen said. "So she doesn't fall into the trap of losing herself to some man!"

Ariel turned and smirked at Maureen. "Oh for God's sake, Maureen, I thought *I* was dramatic! And Katie's heard enough of my stories, and certainly enough about the patriarchy."

"Hah! It's up to us crones to pass on some of our wisdom to the maidens," Maureen said.

"Hey, speak for yourself!" Ariel said. "I'm not a crone yet."

"Okay, a..." Maureen prompted.

Ariel thought for a moment. "Well, maybe a demi-crone."

"Sounds like a French dessert," Maureen said.

"Something you take with tea," Ariel said and both women laughed.

"Are you two still drunk?" Katie said, looking sidelong at Ariel and Maureen.

"Whoa ho!" Maureen said. And they laughed even harder.

"When you two are done cackling, *I'd* like to hear the rest of the story," Katie said. "And the real version, not the sugar-coated."

"That's my girl," Maureen said. She fumbled in her bag then pulled out a small tin. "Hey, it's time for my medicine, I hope you ladies don't mind."

Ariel turned and saw Maureen pull a joint out of the tin.

"Maureen, you can't smoke a joint in Henri's Porsche!" Ariel said.

"Oh, c'mon, I'll blow it out the window," Maureen said. "And it's for medical purposes, pain relief. I'm sure even Henri would understand that!" She lit the joint then opened her window part way down and blew the smoke out.

"All right, then give me a toke," Ariel said, as she turned and reached behind her for the joint.

Katie shook her head.

"I don't think the maiden approves," Maureen said.

"Well, you are a bad influence Maureen, let's face it," Ariel said, taking a big drag, holding it then blowing the smoke out her window. Then she turned to face Maureen and patted her arm. "But you've always been a great friend."

"Thank you, my dear," Maureen said. Then she leaned toward Katie, "Your aunt is a very special person. If she played for my team, I'd actually consider love again."

"You flatter me," Ariel said, winking at her friend.

"Ahem," Katie cleared her throat. She figured these two could go on all day, and according to the GPS they were only an hour from Chartres.

"Okay," Ariel said, in an exaggerated tone. "Let's finish the story. But now I can't remember where I left off."

"Have you talked about that time in Paris, yet? When we met up at St. Severin, and Henri was being such a dickhead?" Maureen asked. She took another puff of the joint. "As I recall, your ol' buddy Maureen helped set you straight!"

"Hah!" Ariel said, cocking her head to Katie. "Well she's kind of right about that actually."

"You told me it was after that you decided to go back to Tucson," Maureen said.

"Well, that's basically what happened," Ariel said. She turned toward Maureen. "But Maureen, you need to let me tell the story as I remember it—*sans interruption.*"Maureen made an exaggerated motion of zipping her mouth closed.

"You left Henri and went back to Tucson?" Katie said, looking at Ariel incredulously.

Ariel didn't answer right away. Then she smiled to herself. "Yeah, I did," she said.

CHAPTER TWENTY TWO

ARIEL

As planned, I moved up to Montreal at the beginning of the year. I sold most of my stuff in a garage sale, donated the rest and drove up with a small U-Haul. After eight years of living alone since my divorce, and many years single before that, I was moving into someone else's home. I converted the downstairs guest bedroom into an office, and though I decorated it with furniture and artwork I'd brought for "my" room I couldn't shake the feeling of being in someone else's domain. Even though Henri wanted me to feel it was my place too, it was essentially his apartment. He paid for everything, managed everything and had all the control. I felt like a kid moving back home after being out on my own for a while. And it made me anxious, bringing back old feelings of vulnerability and powerlessness.

Of course, it was a big adjustment all the way around: a foreign country, the French culture and language, a much more affluent lifestyle. I struggled with balancing everything. For the first year I commuted down to Rhinebeck every other weekend to work. But the cost of the commute, the room I was renting, and not being at Rancho Encantada regularly to build clientele was a losing proposition. Most months I barely broke even, so my income was half what it used to be. And this contributed to my feeling of powerlessness and exhaustion. On one hand, I was very fortunate; I had no expenses and a forced two-year hiatus before I could apply for a work permit and eventual residency in Canada. But until then I had to rely on Henri. He was happy to take care of everything; that is what he'd always done.

On the outside it looked like a fairy tale. I was Cinderella, the glass slipper fit, I went to live in the castle. My friends and family were amazed at our whirlwind lifestyle: private jet, a boat moored at Martha's Vineyard, five-star hotels, Henri's vineyards in Europe, diamond jewelry.

But my inner world was being neglected; most of my energy was spent keeping up with the constant changes in my outer world. I've always needed downtime and quiet space to think, meditate, and read. Henri never took downtime. His schedule was always full with his work and friends. I tried to adjust to his schedule, but I couldn't keep up with it. And I couldn't seem to assert my own needs, no matter how hard I tried.

Some part of me, the inner child, wanted so badly to be loved and cherished that she tried everything to be the "good girl." This created a lot of internal stress because of course I couldn't do it all. I needed my own time and space, but since moving up to Montreal, I didn't feel I had a right to claim it. The patterns from my own childhood were deeply ingrained and I fell right into them. I had a string of illnesses: strep throat, sinus infections, bronchitis, colds, flu, then a lingering digestive disorder. My body was trying to show me that there was a problem, but I kept trying to override my inner needs and just make it work. I visited doctors. Henri thought that being perimenopausal must be the source of all my issues. Every woman has probably heard that our hormones are the cause of any distress!

Finally, I decided to take unpaid leave from Rancho Encantada. Trying to hang onto my old life and establish a new life had taken their toll physically. I decided to let go of commuting to the States and settle more into life in Montreal, hoping that incorporating more of a sane schedule would ease the exhaustion. But it didn't change the fundamental tension I felt.

Georgia encouraged me to get the first draft of the Grandmother project started even though we still didn't have a publisher. She insisted there was a lot of interest in the proposal and felt something would happen soon so it would be prudent to start work on the manuscript. And I wanted to work on it, too—to keep the momentum going and stay focused on my own agenda.

When I returned from my last scheduled shifts at Rancho Encantada, ready to settle into my new writing schedule, Henri surprised me with a trip to Paris. I told myself it was only one week, and I could travel *and* write. I could bring my laptop, and when Henri had meetings I could work. Wasn't this a dream life? I thought. My mind could agree, but my gut rebelled. We arrived at the hotel and I set up my computer on the hotel room desk so I could look through the proposal and begin outlining the draft. But when I sat down in front of the laptop, my head was fuzzy from jet lag and the greeting glass of champagne from the hotel.

I had just gotten up to make a coffee from the machine on the service bar when my cell phone rang. It was Henri. He was at a meeting with some associates and they were putting on a dinner that night. Henri had thought it was just for the team, but at the meeting he realized that the wives were included. I hesitated. I thought I'd have a free evening and really wanted to get started.

"Can't you come tonight?" he asked. "You have the next three days free to work while I'm in meetings."

I took a deep breath. Maybe he was right, I thought. I rarely went to his dinners with associates, and I'd been hearing him complain about this more and more lately. I acquiesced. I closed the laptop and went to shower and get ready. I spent an evening smiling and nodding, trying to keep up with the conversations in French. Dinner was a long, slow production with one course of rich food after another passing in front of me, all paired with wine. My recent digestive issues prevented me from enjoying much of it. Henri drank too much and became quite surly when we returned to the hotel. I tried to ignore his mood and went to make a cup of mint tea before turning on my laptop.

"How is it that I bring you on this romantic trip to Paris and you just want to work?" Henri asked.

I did not want to get into it. This was a sensitive topic. I really wanted him to be supportive or at the very least not be an obstacle and create disharmony. Otherwise it was difficult for me to get into the headspace I needed to concentrate. I shrugged but stayed quiet as I changed into a hotel robe.

"You know, Francois offered us his tickets to the French Open. He knows how much I like tennis, and the men's final is tomorrow. I can reschedule my meetings so we can go."

My gut tightened and gurgled. I grimaced at the sensation. It felt like I had cement in my belly.

"What is that face?" Henri asked.

"It's my stomach again," I said.

"I don't know why you won't take a Zantac," Henri said.

I shook my head. "You know I don't like pharmaceuticals, and besides, the doctor said it's my colon, not actually my stomach," I said. I sat down at the desk and took a sip of tea and began reading through the proposal.

"Ariel don't you have anything to say about the tennis?" Henri said. He sat on the bed with his arms folded across his chest.

I shook my head. "Henri, I told you I need to work. Then I'm going to visit St. Severin Church with Maureen. She came up especially to meet me; she's got some big evidence of Magdalene's story."

"Oh, that's right, another Mary Magdalene site," Henri said. "I know for you that a church is *much* more interesting than tennis."

There is always a moment when we hit the wall and know we have to change course. Or "get off the truck," as I had experienced in my brief truck driving career. I'd taken so many trips with Henri to visit his friends or his family and go along with his program. I rarely asserted what I wanted because I felt he was offering the trips and paying for them, so I should keep him company doing what he wanted. Of course, now I realize how unbalanced that was, but I had become very adept at fitting myself around the corners and edges, not taking up too much space for my own needs. There, sitting at the desk in the hotel, I had a moment of lucidity. I had slowly whittled away my own life, and I couldn't do it anymore.

"Henri, tomorrow is the only day Maureen and I can meet. She came up from the Languedoc so we could spend the day together," I said with as much neutrality as I could muster.

"And there is only one men's final," Henri said.

"Why don't you just go with Francois?" I said.

"He wants to give the tickets to *us*. He thinks you would be thrilled to go to the French Open because, Ariel, most people would be. Most people are interested in *this* world—not your spirit world."

I looked at Henri and wondered, *who is this person?* Since the day he met me at the captain's table at Rancho Encantada, I've let him know who I was and what mattered to me. Why was I now being attacked? A sickening feeling came over me. I felt tired and overwhelmed. My heart started to pound. It felt like it was accelerating. I took a deep breath, but it caught in my throat. I felt a terrible pressure in my chest. I kept trying to breathe deeply, but it made the symptoms worse.

"Ariel, what is wrong with you?" Henri asked from the bed.

"I don't know," I whispered. I stood up. "I can't breathe."

Suddenly I thought to get in the shower. I went to the bathroom and turned on the hot water, stepped into the shower, and let the water run over me. The steam helped. Soon I could breathe better if I took slow careful breaths. Henri came into the bathroom.

"Do you need me to call the hotel doctor?" he asked.

"No, I'm okay," I said between breaths.

I felt scared, lonely, and as if I couldn't trust anyone. Henri was supposed to be my partner, the one who cared about my welfare. On one level, I knew he did. But the hard truth was that his care and support seemed more and more conditional. It was predicated on my behavior conforming to his paradigm. *It wasn't always like this, was it?* I asked myself. In the early days of our relationship, he'd been so supportive of my work and had encouraged me to follow my dreams, but lately he seemed more sullen and demanding.

I finally went to bed but stayed curled on my side and didn't sleep well. Henri and I were coldly polite at breakfast and I left early to take some time and write before I met Maureen. I found a quiet café but I couldn't concentrate on the proposal. So I just sat and let myself think about my situation. In my effort to be a supportive, loving partner, I had voluntarily relinquished too many of my own needs. I thought that was my spiritual work; I thought it was what I was supposed to do to be in a relationship. I had been searching for love for so long, and thought I'd met the right mate. When I found him, I was so eager to be in a relationship that I took on the whole thing like a quest. But this relationship wasn't the conscious equal partnership I had dreamed of, no matter how I tried to spin it. It wasn't a sacred marriage. Not only that, I was definitely behaving like the lesser partner.

Wasn't my life—spirituality, my work, my project—worth just as much as Henri's? *Is it about money?* I wondered. Obviously, my work didn't pay as well as Henri's; I could never compete with his wealth. But didn't my work and ideas have value too? Was trying to be in Henri's life taking me out of alignment, so I actually couldn't succeed with my own work and my own path? I suddenly felt overwhelmed by these questions and the uncertainty of my future.

This is how I remember that day, Maureen: We met in front of St. Severin church. Katie, I was so happy to see her! I remember that we hugged, but I avoided too much eye contact. I felt raw and vulnerable. It seemed like I had done so many of the things I'd been determined not to do, like lose my life to a man. And I didn't want Maureen to see my fear and shame. I could barely handle my own self-criticism and couldn't take being judged by her.

Maureen sensed something though. She looked at me as she cocked her head and leaned on her cane. "How about we get a drink first?"

"It's only 11:00 AM," I said.

"So what, we're in Paris," Maureen turned and headed to a café next to the church.

We each ordered a glass of rosé.

"Santé," we toasted, clinking glasses.

"Trouble in paradise?" Maureen asked.

I nodded, my eyes welling with tears.

"C'mon, spill it," Maureen said.

I couldn't hold it in so I told Maureen what had been happening. How much I'd been struggling to keep my own life going in the midst of Henri's. My exhaustion and string of illnesses, my failure to get going on the book. I talked for a long time and Maureen just listened. Finally, I stopped and took a big sip of wine.

Maureen then asked me, "What is it *you* want for yourself, in this relationship?"

I said I needed Henri to understand, to be supportive so I could move forward, but he wasn't. He said he was, but his actions demonstrated otherwise.

"Okay, I get that," Maureen said. "Now tell me what you need for yourself exactly. Time, space to work on the manuscript?"

I nodded. "Well, yeah," I said.

"Then take it. Stop waiting for him to give you permission. I've known you through this whole relationship. And I know you love Henri and he loves you. But you need to be at the center of your own life. If you need time and space, take it," Maureen said.

"But, I'm afraid," I said.

"What? That he'll find someone else to replace you? A Barbie who looks up to him, thinks he's Jesus Christ?" Maureen said, making exaggerated prayer gestures.

I laughed a little. "Well, yeah, maybe," I said.

"Ah, Ariel!" Maureen said. "There's no one like you, and Henri knows it. He's had many years to find a Barbie and he didn't. You offer him something—soul and honesty and magic. Enough of this. You need to take care of yourself, write your god-damned book, and get your strength back. Henri can fucking wait. As far as I can see it, you were the one to take all the risks and make all the sacrifices. It's time for him to adjust to you and your needs. Don't fall into some kind of bullshit patriarchal model of relationship that makes him and his life more important than yours. Both people need to have their needs met."

I put my head in my hands and took a deep breath, trying to calm my nerves and then looked up at Maureen.

"Maureen, feel free to be direct," I said, smiling a little.

"I am direct, because I care about you and you just don't know how god-damned lovable you are. And I want you to know it and live it. His money and his fancy lifestyle aren't more important than you and what you need," Maureen said. "And from my vantage point Henri needs to figure some shit out about what's really important in life. If he doesn't, I'm going to go over there and kick his ass." She signaled the waiter for the bill.

"What, you're going to beat him with your cane?" I asked.

"*Absolument*," Maureen said. "Now let's go to St. Severin. There's an entire wall of stained glass telling the story of Magdalene in France—calling her the Apostle of Provence. Let's get some inspiration from the lady in red!"

The air between Henri and me was frosty for the rest of our stay in Paris. But I took Maureen's words to heart and made a commitment in my mind to my own schedule once I got home. It would include daily writing, walks with Chico and time for meditation and yoga. I knew what I needed to do to be well; I just had to stick to it and not be swayed, to control my space. On the flight home I told Henri about my plans.

"It doesn't sound like you've included any time for boating this summer," was Henri's response.

My gut tightened. I had told Henri I wanted a summer without travel. The point of my sabbatical from Rancho Encantada was to have space and time to work on my project. I looked forward to staying in Montreal, when the weather was warm and I could sit in the garden and write. But Henri didn't like spending summers in Montreal. He had bought a new boat, which he kept docked in Martha's Vineyard. The boat was bigger than his previous one, equipped for long stays, with a full head and stateroom and plenty of seating in the cockpit. I didn't agree with the new purchase for several reasons, one being I didn't want to commit to a boating life. Spending endless days bobbing around doing nothing wasn't what I envisioned for my future. But it was Henri's money and his decision, and I didn't want to get in the way of what he wanted. Now I realized he hoped I would change my mind.

"Henri, I've been traveling almost nonstop for two years. I need a break. I need to write this book," I said. "Georgia is on the cusp of getting us a publishing contract and I have so much work to do."

"You can take it with you on the boat. I even had an extra table built into the cockpit so you can sit and write," Henri said.

A wave of exhaustion washed over me. "Let me think about it," I said. I finished my drink and handed the glass to the flight attendant. I reached down and took my wrap from my purse and put the seat back to take a nap. We hadn't even returned to Montreal and my resolve was already being tested. I closed my eyes, letting the drone of the engines lull me to sleep.

I found myself in the high desert mountains with a small group of hikers. We were being guided by two naturalists. It was a beautiful clear sunny day and we were enjoying the view from a high vantage point when I heard a loud rustle in a tall pine tree nearby. I walked closer and saw a large hawk flapping around awkwardly; watching it, I realized it had a broken wing.

Then I heard rustling lower in the tree. I backed up and looked under the skirt of branches. There was a baby hawk on the ground, stumbling around, making distressed chirping sounds. The mother hawk began flapping her good wing frantically. I backed away from the tree and went back to the group and told them about the hawks.

The naturalists, both men, looked at me with an air of condescension. We can't do anything about it anyway, one of them said. Besides, a snake will have that chick for dinner by nightfall.

Disturbed by their lack of interest, I went back to the tree and realized the mother hawk was becoming increasingly desperate as she flapped her good wing, futilely trying to position herself on the branch to look after her chick. The fear and powerlessness of the hawk were palpable; I really felt something must be done. Once, years before, I'd rescued an injured owl and it was able to be rehabilitated and released back into the wild. But I didn't think I could do it myself without the help of the naturalists.

Then, a woman approached me from the group. I didn't recall seeing her before; her bearing emanated power and status. She had spiky red hair and an impossibly bright white T-shirt. She stood in front of me with tears silently streaming from her eyes. In my mind I heard, "I have no power here to help the hawk, but you do."

When we got home, I busied myself unpacking then went to my office to sort through my mail. I was trying to avoid Henri until I felt clearer and stronger. But after a couple of hours he came to my office door.

"You're not going to talk to me now?" Henri asked.

"I want to talk, Henri," I said. "But I'm trying to sort out my schedule."

"So you can come on the boat?" He said, leaning against the door jamb.

I inhaled deeply, taking a moment to choose my words carefully. "Henri, it's not that I don't want to spend time with you, but. . ." I stumbled with my words.

"But, what?" Henri said, now with a sarcastic edge.

"But it's very difficult for me to concentrate and write around you," I said.

"That's why I bought the bigger boat, and installed the extra table, so you could do your work," Henri said.

I leaned into my desk chair feeling a mess of conflict inside me. Was Henri being supportive and I just didn't get it? I asked myself. I had told him I didn't want to spend a lot of time on the boat. I'd told him I really needed the summer to complete the first draft of the manuscript. But was I being selfish? Too much uber-independent girl? These were only thoughts in my head; I didn't really expect an answer. But I got one, as clear as day. There, sitting in my office, I heard Grandmother's voice in my right ear say an emphatic, "No!"

I felt shaky. My stomach was in knots, and the pressure on my chest was accompanied by fluttering sensations in my heart. On the outside it was a trivial situation: my boyfriend wanted me to join him on a boat for the summer. I'm sure that many people would gladly take this "problem." Beneath the surface, however, it felt like a fight for my life. I felt like the baby hawk in my dream, flapping around on the ground, in danger of being eaten by a snake unless someone intervened. And there, in the context of my dream, I saw the choice: do the easier thing, the one that made sense to those around me, or use my wits and find a way to help the struggling, fledgling part of me.

"I need to stay and work, Henri," I said. "You know what will happen if I go. You'll be unhappy because I'm not really doing the stuff you want to do."

Henri looked indignant. "Because what I want is bad?" he said.

Here we go again, I thought. "It's what *you* want. It's not what I want. You said it yourself, you want to play and enjoy your new boat for the rest of the summer."

Henri grimaced. "You know what I think?" he said. "I think you don't really want to be in this relationship. You seem only interested in your own agenda. You don't really care about me. It's obvious I'm not your priority."

I put my head in my hands. I couldn't keep trying to negotiate with Henri about my right to work on my own projects; to have my own needs met. I was tired of trying to make it all work—to find a balance between his needs and mine. More and more, I was fighting for my right to exist.

And he was relentless. If I tried to stay in Montreal to work, he would keep hounding me. And I felt weaker there; it was, after all, his territory. I had a hard time staying true to what I needed. Suddenly I remembered something Grandmother had told me during the medicine ceremony in Ecuador. She had warned that if I wasn't totally authentic, if I went against my spirit for any reason, it would be really painful.

There was a pressure on my chest. I realized it was fear. In that moment I was totally honest with myself about my feelings even though just feeling them was frightening. A ripple of deep survival fear moved through me. I couldn't deny it. It was familiar, and it was old. It was a sensation that I had first experienced in my childhood. A pressure on my chest and then a feeling of metallic liquid fear opening at the base of my throat and spilling into my body. I took some shallow breaths.

Henri left the room and spent the rest of the afternoon running errands then had dinner with colleagues. I stayed in my office and stared out the window for a long time. Then I went out to the garden, filled the bird feeder with birdseed, and sat in a patio chair. There was a large pine tree on the other side of the garden barrier. I looked up at it. "Grandmother, what do I do?" I whispered. The songbirds swooped down from the branches of the tree and alit around the bird feeder.

Fly, I heard in my mind. *Go somewhere that feeds you.* Where could I go? I thought about Rhinebeck, but I didn't have a house anymore and hadn't been there long enough to make friends. I was either working, traveling, or with Henri. Then I thought, what about Tucson? I had good friends there, and colleagues I'd kept in touch with. Then I thought about Sue. She had two vacation rentals that she managed herself.

I called Sue and told her I was thinking of coming to Tucson. She was thrilled with the idea.

"Both rentals are empty," Sue said. "It's the off season here. You can have the little cottage; it's quiet with a covered patio that would be great for writing. You can stay the whole summer if you want. I don't usually start getting bookings until the middle or end of September."

"Wow, that's really generous, Sue," I said. That was three months of accommodation.

"It would be great to see you. We've missed you," Sue said. "And I'm sure that your clients here would love sessions if you wanted to work, too."

Then I called Devra to let her know I was coming. She was surprised but understood my need to take some space. I also told her about the hawk dream.

"Wow, that's really interesting," she said. "I can see the parallel of you rescuing the little hawk, a part of yourself that needs help. But I wonder about the mother hawk with the broken wing. Was your mother broken in some way?"

"Hah! I don't have the time or the energy to go there. I've got enough to sort through with my relationship with Henri," I said.

"I hear you, but your dream is suggesting they are directly related. Also, I find this woman with the red hair interesting. Seems like a spirit guide. Usually, when the clothes are bright white, it indicates a helper in the spirit world," Devra said.

"Grandmother?" I wondered.

"Ah yes! I remember you said she always has red hair in your dreams and visions," Devra said. "How interesting that she told you she couldn't intervene directly, but you could."

298

CHAPTER TWENTY THREE

Henri was hurt and angry when I told him about my plan to go to Tucson for the summer. He railed against it, told me that I was running away, that I was selfish—didn't know how to share my life, that my work was more important than he was, et cetera. I nodded, didn't say much, and packed my laptop, and the tools of my trade: tarot cards, numerology paperwork, the ephemeris for astrology sessions. I knew what I needed to do for myself, and I knew he needed time, too. No matter what I said, he could not seem to understand the need for my own self-actualization. I pointed out that I supported him in his work, time with his family, the actualization of his dreams; I was certainly not threatened by them. I only wanted the same respect and latitude. But he could not see this. And I had exhausted all my ways of trying to explain this to him. It was like trying to tell a fish about water: they're so immersed in what they have, they can't understand what it would be like to not have it.

Once I made the decision to go, I felt the power of the divine feminine with me. I had a renewed sense of clarity and mission. Henri and I both left a couple of days later. He went to Martha's Vineyard. I drove across the border into New York State. On my drive west I gained more objectivity. It seemed as if every state I drove through, every turn of the odometer, afforded me more insight and clarity on our relationship.

Somewhere on the highway, I recognized I had slipped into an old paradigm. It was the patriarchal paradigm of relationship. I had given over more and more of my autonomy for the "benefit" of the union and unwittingly had slid into a support role. Henri had fallen into the old model of provide and control, the only way he knew how to be in a relationship. But both of these roles were undermining who we were and the kind of relationship we wanted.

There was no question that I had been struggling with some issues from my past that weren't resolved yet. I thought about what Patty had said during our sessions. About how rescuing the lost child was essential before becoming the queen of my domain.

I thought a lot about my past as I drove across the corn fields of southern Illinois. My mother, your grandmother, lived the last years of her life with her husband on a large horse farm in the nearby state of Kentucky. I don't know if Dan talked about her much, but she and I really struggled, especially at the end. For the twenty-five years since her death, I'd been avoiding the entire state whenever I crossed the country, even if I had to drive far out of my way. But I knew I had an opportunity to change that story, so I stopped at the next rest area and pulled up the region on Google maps.

I needed to break my vow to never return to that state and pay respects to a very special woman. So I took the three-hour detour off my route west and drove south to the small town in Kentucky where they lived. I wasn't sure where to start my search, so I parked on the main street in front of the courthouse. I figured they'd have some records. I went to the front desk and told the nice woman in the lobby I was trying to find my friend Elizabeth's gravesite. She instructed me to go to the historical society, where I was able to find what I was looking for. In friendly southern style, the two women located the grave site, drew me a map, and gave me the local gossip.

It was only a twenty-minute drive to find Elizabeth's grave. I don't think I've told you about her yet. She was buried next to her first husband, Bill. He had lived through service in World War II, only to die in a car accident a month after returning home. He was the love of Elizabeth's life, and even though she eventually remarried, she wanted her final resting place next to him. I'd heard the whole story at the historical society because this was considered rather scandalous. The ladies were surprised I knew about Bill. But Elizabeth and I had shared so much of our lives with each other. She had even given me his black army locker from the war. It sat in my office in Montreal.

It was drizzling and chilly for summertime. I found Elizabeth's grave and crouched down. I thanked her for being such a good friend. Twenty-five years earlier, I had thought of her as my godmother. As I sat by her grave, our time together came back with astonishing clarity. And I found myself reliving the whole story.

I was twenty years old when I moved to Hawaii. I'd trained to crew on large sailboats back in New England and had also apprenticed and worked for a woman, boat detailing and refinishing. When I had enough money and experience to go out on my own, I did. During this time, your grandfather died rather suddenly of a heart attack. My brother and I planned his funeral in Connecticut. My father's wishes were to be cremated and to have his ashes sprinkled in the ocean off the Big Island of Hawaii, a place that we'd spent family vacations when I was young. I volunteered to do it because your dad was in graduate school. It was when I was there, carrying out your grandfather's wishes, that I decided to pick up shop and move myself to Hawaii, a dream I'd had since those childhood vacations.

I quickly got a job on a tourist catamaran, the first woman they had ever hired. And I set up my own side business detailing boats at the local marina. I lived in a rustic cabin surrounded by coffee and fruit trees. The toilet was an outhouse under a banana tree, and the old claw-foot bath-tub sat under a portable water heater outside the back door.

This was my first real experience of following my spirit. But I was plagued by uncertainty and fear. Of course, back then, I didn't realize it was inside *me*. I thought it was caused by outer circumstances. I had always been caught between two polarities: one side was the desperate need to feel safe and supported, and the other side was a great need for adventure and freedom. Moving to Hawaii was my first real taste of free-dom. I was seeing my desires manifesting for the first time, but that had the paradoxical effect of making me nervous. I had a strange underlying irrational belief—a superstition that I would have to pay for daring to be happy and successful following my own path.

And romance soon followed. There was a nice guy, part of the crew on the catamaran, that I preferred working with. He also helped with some of my big jobs at the marina, often followed by an after-work beer. We enjoyed each other's company, but it took me by surprise when he asked me out for dinner. I'd only seen him as a buddy and politely declined. He took it in stride and we continued to be work friends, until one night when I found myself stalling to stay with him in the car on a commute back from the marina.

"What took you so long?" Bill asked as I leaned into the first kiss. It was fireworks! I'll never forget the smell of his skin. What they say about pheromones is true. So we continued to work together, play together, be friends, be lovers. Maybe it is true for everyone, but there's nothing like the first love. But it didn't take long for me to become anxious.

One part of me longed to open up and let myself be seen—and I knew that Bill could really see me—but the other, stronger part battened down the hatches, to use a boating metaphor. So I began telling myself stories and making up excuses about why I didn't want to pursue our relationship. I needed to seek out a more secure future. I needed to take my life in a better direction: go back to college, get a real degree, and focus on leading a normal life rather than spending my time sailing and playing in the sun.

I decided to return to the mainland and pursue a degree, much to the delight of my mother, who even offered to help me. It occurred to me that I could let myself be more open to Bill if I had a departure date. I had three months to love and live, to really enjoy paradise. I figured that nothing could go really wrong because I had an end date, so it felt safe. I didn't have to really be vulnerable because I was moving on. Of course, this is a strange convoluted logic, but it was how I thought at the time.

As the departure date neared, though, I began to suspect that I was making a huge mistake by leaving Hawaii. Bill was upset that I was leaving, but he said he wanted what was best for me. And by then I was so far into the scheme of returning to the mainland—some notion of family security, getting a degree, and finally "getting it right"—that I felt I couldn't back out.

So I continued to dismantle my life. I moved out of my coffee shack in the tropical forest, left my crewing job on a tourist catamaran, and closed up my side business of detailing boats. I said goodbye to a man I really loved. It wasn't until I completely undid my life that I actually realized how much I'd had.

On departure day I stood crying in front of a pay phone in the Honolulu airport. I remember being desperate for advice as I waited for my flight to the mainland. So I called a close friend and sobbed into the pay phone that I thought I was making a huge mistake. I didn't want to get on the flight. My friend told me to keep going because I had already made all the arrangements. He assured me that I was making the right choice to leave, that it was the reasonable thing to do. I hung up the phone and felt an unmistakable presence surrounding me.

A deep voice said, "Turn around and go back to Kona!"

I jumped and looked around me. But I was the only person at the line of pay phones. I'd never experienced such a thing before—these events became more common later in my life but back then this was mind-blowing. For a few fleeting moments, my heart leapt at the idea of turning around. In that brief instant I felt free and brave, a romantic heroine in my own story. But then my rational mind took over. What about the plane ticket? What about the boxes of stuff traveling through the mail? Could I get my job back? I'd have to find a new place to live. Could I stay with Bill? What if I turned around and he didn't want me anymore? I got on the plane to the mainland. And suffered the consequences.

Back on the mainland, I found myself lost in an alien environment. I didn't fit in at all. I was living with my mom and stepfather on the farm. I couldn't find a good job and ended up working at a bar. After years of living independently, suddenly everything I did was questioned. Why was I writing that guy Bill in Hawaii? He wasn't right for me; he was just a guy who worked on boats. Why didn't I consider dating a local man? The dentist and the district attorney were both single. Why was I working at the local bar? Why was I sad all the time?

As quickly as I could, I moved out of my mother's house and into a neighbor's empty farmhouse that needed fixing up in exchange for rent. I didn't know the neighbor, Elizabeth, well, but we became fast friends. She was a retired professor and a pioneer in the field of early childhood development. I was a lost, lonely young woman but we clicked immediately. And soon I began working as her assistant as well. She needed someone to organize a huge amount of correspondence she had with former students and colleagues.

So a few mornings a week, I went to her house to work. We took a lot of coffee breaks. She showed me her vast antique collection and told fabulous stories about her life. One afternoon over coffee and little chocolate cookies shaped like bears, Elizabeth told me about her first love and that his name was Bill.

The color must have drained from my face. Elizabeth got up and made some fresh coffee. She announced that we were done with work for the day. She wanted to hear my story. Elizabeth knew I had moved there from Hawaii. After she poured me a fresh cup of coffee, she sat back down, patted my hand and asked me to tell her about Hawaii.

I brightened as I began telling Elizabeth about the catamaran I crewed on and my private business detailing boats in the harbor. I described the coffee shack in the jungle, the fruit trees, and the outdoor bathtub. Then I told her about my Bill and how I'd never experienced a love like that. By the time I got to the booming voice in the Honolulu airport telling me to turn around and go back to Kona, I was in tears.

Elizabeth pushed the plate of little chocolate bear cookies toward me.

"Why did you leave a man and a place you loved so much?" Elizabeth asked.

"I don't know," I said, still choked up. "I was scared that something bad would happen. Almost like I didn't have a right to be happy. And I was afraid I would get my heart broken. So I left when everything was good. So I'd at least have the memories."

Elizabeth nodded. "And why did you move here?" she asked.

I looked up at her. She had a definite style, with her dyed red hair coiffed into big curls and her oversized glasses.

"I was looking for security, a sense of home and family. I thought maybe if I did everything I was supposed to do, I would finally have that," I said. "But I know better. I don't know what I was thinking. This has happened before. In fact, I seem to keep repeating the same mistake, like I'm stuck in a loop. I keep chasing after the idea of home, only to have to start over on my own." I looked up at Elizabeth. "Pretty dumb, huh? To keep doing the same thing yet hoping for a different result?" I laughed awkwardly. "Clearly, I'm really not very bright."

Elizabeth looked at me with understanding in her eyes.

"Honey, were you abandoned in some way when you were young?" Elizabeth asked, tentatively.

I nodded my head. Our mother left us when I was twelve. It was something I hadn't talked about for a long time, but once I got started, I poured out my history to Elizabeth. My father became our primary caregiver but was away a great deal of the time due to work, so he hired the rather eccentric lady next door to take care of me and my brother. I found in her a kindred spirit and after months of fear and grief I began to feel more stable.

Even at that young age I understood my mother had been miserable. Being a homemaker and full-time mom was not really in her genes. She'd always been looking for ways to express herself and live a freer life. Even though our household had become more peaceful after she left, I couldn't seem to let her go. It was as if there was an invisible cord that kept pulling me toward her, though it wasn't in my best interest.

I began to act out with my Dad and distanced myself from our caregiver. And eventually I packed up and moved in with my mother, only to discover that she didn't have as much time for me as I'd hoped. She was busy setting up a new career and had been dating someone for a while. When I realized my situation, I tried to go back. But my father had already let our caregiver go and he and Dan found their own rhythm. This time, it seemed that the household was much more peaceful without *me*. He didn't want me going back and forth, repeating the disruptions.

This began a push-pull relationship between my mother and me. Even though I wanted to be close, it wasn't really possible. I would leave, start to do well on my own, and then this invisible cord would pull me back, each time hoping the dynamic would be different. But it never was and it was having an increasingly deleterious effect on me. I had to cut the cord. Later, I would come to understand that I'd internalized the dynamic with my mother and was repeatedly abandoning myself. The lost child didn't know how to get back home.

Elizabeth pushed back her chair and stood up in her bright orange housecoat and motioned for me to get up too. She steered me to an antique mirror in the dining room.

"I want you to look into that mirror," Elizabeth said. "Go ahead, right now. Look into your pretty eyes."

I looked into the mirror.

"Now I want to hear you say, 'I am a smart girl, and I deserve love.'"

I turned and looked at Elizabeth with an exaggerated smirk.

"Now!" she said, pointing to the mirror.

I looked into the mirror and repeated her words.

"Good," she said. "Now we need to work on getting you back to Hawaii where you belong."

Elizabeth gave me even more employment. I painted the exterior of her house, cleaned, and helped her with her son's wedding. I spent nearly every day with her. Elizabeth co-signed on my first credit card. I managed to save enough for a one-way ticket and some money to start over in Hawaii. My mother and I never spoke again. And I never returned to Kentucky. Elizabeth understood. She visited me in Hawaii and we stayed in touch right up until her passing.

I did put my life back together in Hawaii and eventually put myself through school. I studied massage therapy, which opened up the whole next chapter of my work and life, financial stability, and spiritual studies. But even after I'd returned, I could not open up to Bill. I just wasn't able to be vulnerable, I would show up on his doorstep just to disappear again. Eventually, understandably, he closed the door on us for good.

For years this haunted me. I vowed if I ever got another chance, no matter how afraid I was, I would face my fears and be vulnerable—I would choose love. I always remembered Bill's birthday. When I met Henri twenty years later at Rancho Encantada and did his numerology chart, I discovered they were born on the exact same date.

This time, I left Kentucky with a heart full of gratitude instead of pain. I had worked through so many of the issues with my mother and our very troubled relationship over the years. I understood that she did the best she could and that she had inherited wounds from her early life. Still, when I thought back on key moments in my past, I'd always focused on the hurt and not on the blessings. When I looked back now, I saw that someone *had* stepped in with kindness and support and understanding. I had gained a very dear friend in Elizabeth. And that is what I remembered when I got back on the road and crossed through Missouri and

Oklahoma on my way back to Arizona.

When I arrived in Tucson, it was the end of June. Illuminated sheets of heat lightning lit up the surrounding mountains. Soon it would be the monsoon season. The desert would be green and fresh; cacti would blossom pink, red, and magenta wonders; and rainbows would once again arc across the landscape, transforming it into paradise.

It was early evening when I drove up to Sue's house. As I got out of the air-conditioned car, I took a deep breath. I had forgotten the delicious smell of creosote in the desert air and the way the warmth could wrap itself around you. Sue greeted me with a margarita and we sat on her back patio. But I was eager to get settled after the long drive, so I didn't stay long. Sue gave me directions and the keys to the cottage.

I loved the little one-bedroom cottage. It sat on a half-acre of natural desert in a quiet neighborhood. The ceilings were high and the terracotta floor felt good under my feet. Chico ran out to the fenced yard and marked his territory. He was out for a while when I heard him growling at something.

"What is it, little guy?" I asked, stepping out back. I followed his gaze and spotted a hawk on an upper branch of the mesquite tree. "Okay, bud," I said and scooped Chico up and went back inside. I closed the door but looked out the window at the hawk. That was a good sign

CHAPTER TWENTY FOUR

I quickly settled into a nice schedule in Tucson. As Georgia suggested, I outlined each chapter of the proposal. I wrote the key ideas on index cards so I could work on each section without getting overwhelmed. Just writing the forty-page proposal was the most I'd ever written, so it was daunting to even think about writing a draft of hundreds of pages. But the index cards helped me to focus just on the section at hand instead of becoming overwhelmed.

Every morning after meditation, with a French press full of coffee, I'd work on a section. I found once I got going the words would just pour out of me. I had wanted a chance to write the full story for so long and I finally had the space and time.

I also entertained a stream of clients and continued my Kabbalah studies online. One afternoon I stumbled across something that really caught my attention. I learned about the history behind an age-old symbol: the Star of David.

As it turns out, the Star of David isn't just a symbol of the Jewish state. Symbolically it represented the unification of the upper and lower *shekinah*, or feminine nature of God. The downward-pointing triangle is the lower *shekinah*—the daughter, also called *malchut*, or the vessel, in the

Tree of Life. And the upward-pointing triangle represents the mother, or *binah*, the upper *shekinah*. In other words, the Star of David refers to the daughter who seeks to unite with the mother spirit, and the mother spirit who wishes to be received by the daughter.

Later that evening, after the temperatures cooled down, Sue and I met for a walk. I was explaining the Kabbalistic concept of the upper and lower *shekinah* to her, when I had an "aha" moment, gaining another level of insight about the power of unifying all aspects of the feminine. Mother spirit/daughter spirit = *binah/malchut* = uniting the upper and lower feminine. In Kabbalah, this unification is considered a fast track to enlightenment.

Sue stopped me on the path and looked at me pointedly. "This sounds awfully similar to that hawk dream you told me about."

I thought back to the recent dream, trying to make the connection to the Kabbalah. I looked at Sue. "Okay, I can see the baby hawk as the lower feminine, daughter, and the mother hawk as the upper feminine. But in my dream the mother was injured. How could the upper feminine be broken?" I asked.

Sue stared out at the darkening sky. "Maybe Mother Spirit can be broken," she said. "Maybe that was why the Grandmother in your dream was crying and told you she couldn't do anything, but you could. Maybe we affect spirit just as much as spirit affects us."

That seemed a strange concept to me. How could Mother Spirit be broken? I'd always thought of the spiritual realm as unbreakable. Then I thought about the mythology of Eve and Lilith. They were archetypal spiritual energies, and unless a person consciously retrieved Lilith from exile and integrated her, the dark feminine power, with the nurturing aspect of Eve, she'd remain out in space. There was another example of

312

the "broken" feminine right there.

"You know," Sue said, turning back toward me. "The mysteries need us as much as we need the mysteries."

I got the chills. A gust of wind blew across the park, lifting leaves and debris in its wake. I sensed these concepts were really important, especially for women. Uniting the light and dark feminine, the upper and lower *shekinah* was essential for our own healing. Sue seemed to read my mind.

"Ariel, maybe the work you've been doing to find healing and peace in your own life is helping to heal the Mother Spirit," Sue said. "And that is something we all need to do. But not everyone will go there; not everyone will find what needs to be healed and integrated. It can be really frightening terrain. Ultimately, I believe that is what we're here to do. Grandmother's work is to help us heal so we can restore balance in our world."

"Oh my God!" I shouted, stopping in my tracks.

"What is it?" Sue asked, clearly alarmed.

"Grandmother is the upper feminine! Or at least a way we can open to Mother Spirit. Holy Mother!" In my excitement, the air felt electric.

Sue laughed. "Jesus, Ariel, you scared me," she said. "I thought you saw a snake or something."

I laughed. "Oh no. No snake, just Mother God!"

Suddenly a serious gust of wind blew through the park, followed by rolling thunder. I picked up Chico as Sue and I ran for our cars. We made it to the parking lot just as the sky seemed to crack open. The monsoon season had officially started.

Henri and I hadn't talked since I left for Tucson and, frankly, I was relieved. We did exchange a few emails, though. At first we were polite and cautious with each other. I believe he was shocked that I came out West for the summer instead of going to Martha's Vineyard. In the weeks I'd been gone, I felt something I hadn't felt for a while: self-respect. I'd done what I needed to do even though it wasn't popular, and I was thriving. It was so good to be among friends and colleagues. I realized how isolated I'd become in Montreal, where I didn't have work, friends, or any kind of community of my own. After a couple of years, it had taken its toll.

In our emails, Henri began sharing his feelings about our relationship. The distance was helping him get clearer about himself. He said he loved me and wanted us to be together. He recognized that he'd fallen into some old unconscious behaviors that he needed to work on. He was hurt that I left. But he still didn't seem to understand I *needed* to leave because he wouldn't give me space and time for my own life. He thought I needed to leave to figure out what I wanted in life, meaning whether or not I wanted to be with him. I knew he was trying, but Henri still thought it was all about him.

I had Sue's vacation rental until the end of September. It was early August and I was finished with the first draft of the manuscript. Unfortunately, Georgia hadn't had success selling the proposal to a publisher. She still felt optimistic that we'd find the right home for the book, but it was taking longer than we'd expected. She told me she would do an overall edit on the manuscript and get back to me in the next couple of months.

The big tidal wave of clients I'd had since returning to Tucson had also died down. I had some time on my hands and knew that I needed to really figure out whether I wanted to be with Henri. Henri was right when he said I was conflicted. A part of me questioned whether I could deal with a relationship at all; the cost to my personal well-being seemed so high.

And I couldn't stay in hiatus in Tucson forever. I needed to make decisions about my future. So I prayed for guidance, remembering a Kabbalah technique of calling on an *ibur*, a spiritual master, to help me lift my consciousness so I could find a solution. Usually I called on Mother Mary, Mary Magdalene, or Jesus Christ. But this time I thought of Moses. I had a mental image of him from the movies standing in front of the Red Sea, hair and beard wild in the wind, planting his staff on the ground as he commanded the sea to part.

The only friend I hadn't connected with since returning to Tucson was Devra. She'd been in Australia on "walkabout." We met for dinner at a local Thai restaurant to catch up. Devra described her adventures in Australia, and I told her in more detail about the dynamic with Henri. I explained how I'd seen more and more behaviors in him that reminded me of my past. This made me nervous and insecure, which seemed to only make his behavior worse.

"This sounds like participation mystique," Devra said.

"What the hell is that?" I asked, taking a sip of Singha beer.

"It's a really interesting concept that Jung adopted. When a person has a very strong narrative about reality from their past that they haven't let go of, often they project that narrative onto others. That's projection. Participation mystique is when the *other* person gets drawn into that projection, almost against their will. And they start acting out from the projection—doing and saying things they normally wouldn't."

I took a couple bites of Bathing Rama and tried to take in what Devra was saying. "Okay, so if I understand correctly, it's as if we are looking at another through the lens of the past and projecting that past outward, and if it's strong enough, the other person gets sucked into the projection?"

"Yeah, pretty much," Devra said. "We're somehow mysteriously pulled into participating in the other's drama, even when it isn't how we want to behave. Now of course, the person drawn in must have similar issues on some level. But seriously, other people's dramas can be really magnetic. Look at mob mentality."

I stopped eating and set down my fork. I saw it.

"Oh my God, Devra," I said. "I can see what you're saying. I feel like I'm in a vicious circle, my fear of abandonment is clouding my perspective and I'm scared, so I haven't been listening to myself and taking care of my own needs. I feel like a kid and he's my parent instead of my partner. Seeing things through the lens of my past, I get how his behaviors are triggering my childhood fears and vice versa!"

"What exactly is being triggered?" Devra asked, slipping into therapist mode.

"I'm afraid to really relax and trust Henri. So I can't fully let my guard down."

"What do you think would happen if you let your guard down?" Devra asked.

"He'd tried to manipulate me because he sees caring about my needs in competition with caring about his own," I said, realizing the truth of my words as I spoke them. "I'm afraid he wants me around only conditionally, if I'm catering to him and don't have any needs of my own." I took a breath and a big swig of beer. "I'm afraid if I express my needs, he's going to turn on me, and frankly it's been happening." Wow, there it is, I thought.

"Is that what happened with your mother?" Devra asked.

I nodded.

Devra sat back in her chair and seemed to be deep in thought. I took another bite of my meal but could hardly taste the peanut sauce.

"Have you ever heard of EMDR?" Devra asked.

I shook my head.

"It stands for eye movement desensitization and reprocessing," Devra said. "We use a light bar that you follow with your eyes as it moves back and forth—bilateral stimulation of the brain. When activating the bilateral stimulation people are able to process past traumas—whether they're physical, mental, or emotional—very quickly. EMDR kind of rewires the brain, and then we program in new positive cognitions. It's very effective. I use it with almost all my clients now."

I nodded as I listened to Devra.

"So, do you want to try it?" Devra asked.

"Well, sure," I said. *Why not?* I thought.

"You're here for another few weeks, right?"

"Yeah," I said.

"So if you're game, we have time to fit in the ten sessions."

"Ten sessions!" I said, suddenly not as keen.

"This is a comprehensive process, and frankly I think you need it," Devra said. "And it's on the house."

"My God, Devra, that's too much," I said.

Devra shook her head. "No, it's not. I want to see you in a healthy relationship. You deserve it."

I was incredibly moved and grateful. "This is really generous, Devra," I said. "Are you sure?"

"I'm quite sure," she said. "I feel really strongly about offering this to you."

I looked at Devra. "You really think it will help me release the old patterns?"

"I know it will," Devra said. "You'll be able to see Henri as just Henri, in real time. He has no power over you in real time so you won't be so fearful. Then you'll be able to make choices that are good for you in the present. And believe me, when one person changes, the other changes or the relationship dissolves naturally—not because of the past or because of fear, but because you released the root causes of the fear. So one way or another, you will find yourself in a much healthier situation."

I nodded. What Devra was saying made sense. I thought of my recent prayer to the *ibur* to lift up my consciousness. I told Devra about my call to Moses for help.

She laughed and raised her glass of beer. "*Mazel tov!*"

I sat in the stuffed chair in Devra's darkened office and stared at the light bar as green dots moved back and forth across my field of vision. I wore full-sized headphones, which emitted a soft beep in sync with the movements of the green light. In my palms were two buzzers, which also vibrated in sync with the lights. Devra and I had already spent two sessions compiling the intake, which was a recapitulation of the traumatic moments in my life. The treatment plan was then to take each incident as an entry to the EMDR processing. Via the bilateral stimulation of the brain—through the three senses of eye movement, hearing, and touch vibration—I was drawn into a heightened awareness state. This facilitated the brain to release the traumatic memory and the negative cognition associated with each event and replace it with a positive cognition.

Devra had been over the process thoroughly with me, so I thought I knew what to expect. But as the bilateral stimulation started, I found myself quickly drawn into a state of awareness not unlike the medicine. As Devra took me back to the first memory, I saw it clearly. It was an experience I had when I was three or four years old. The whole picture came back: I was hiding in a dark bathroom, crouched between the toilet and the vanity. My mother was having one of her episodes, screaming and throwing things, and I was hurt and scared. It was the first time and I didn't understand what I'd done to make her so angry. I now remembered the incident clearly, including the feelings and the cognition, much more than I'd been able to recall during our intake.

I reported this to Devra.

As I continued to observe the scene, even though the bathroom was nearly pitch black, I could see the faint outline of a presence in the bathroom with me.

"Oh my God!" I whispered.

"What are you noticing now?" Devra asked, steadily.

"Someone is with me that I don't remember seeing then," I whispered. I was astounded by what I was seeing: someone was standing right next to me.

"You're seeing someone who you didn't see in the original incident?"

Devra asked.

"Correct," I said, continuing to watch the light bar.

I began to see the spirit clearer. She looked like a Disney-like fairy god-mother, with a long red skirt belted over a red blouse. She had red hair, cut short with big curls, and she wore oversized eyeglasses.

"Oh my God! It looks like Grandmother in her red lady disguise," I cried.

"Stay calm, continue to observe," Devra said.

I watched as the red lady Grandmother told my three-year-old self that what was happening was not my fault. She assured me that I would be okay. She stayed with me, her reddish-orange energy enveloping me with its warm, vibrant love. I could tell my three-year-old self felt more at ease; she'd stopped crying and her breathing calmed.

The red lady Grandmother appeared in two more childhood memories as I revisited them in the EMDR sessions, guiding, consoling, and sur-rounding me with her warm embrace. In all cases, I was not cognizant of her presence at the time.

During the following sessions, I realized that she wasn't just a vision; the line between spirit and material reality had really been crossed. As I relived later memories, I recounted three different women at three differ-ent times in my life that had been so helpful to me. I'd never put together how similar they'd all been. But after reviewing so many memories in such a short period of time, it was evident. Each of these flesh and blood angels all had red curly hair, wore big round glasses and had rather flam-boyant personalities. And they'd all acted as fairy godmothers.

The first was the woman my father had hired to take care of me and my brother after my mother left. She'd pick me up from school when I felt sick, and she shared the love of theater and musicals with me, was always ready with a kind word and encouragement. The next was Elizabeth. She came to my aid by hiring me as her assistant so I could get on my feet and return to Hawaii. She'd gone on to be a source of love and encouragement for twenty-five years. During the last memory I recalled the third—a woman who lived in the apartment below when I first arrived in Tucson. She was there only six months, but during that time her door was always open. She took care of Chico when I went on the truck and celebrated with me when I landed my job at Rancho Encantada.

I discovered in the EMDR work that the spirit of the red lady had always been with me. And after the medicine in Ecuador, often the Grandmother presented herself in the guise of the red lady. During this work with Devra, I was able to relive and release some very painful memories around abandonment. But at the same time, I was able to see that when I really needed my fairy godmother, she appeared, either in the form of a loving mother figure or in the form of a spiritual guide. In one form or another, the red lady was always with me.

CHAPTER TWENTY FIVE

"So you see Katie, it is Mother Spirit who saves the day!" Maureen said. "Not some prince on a horse carrying the banner of a patriarchal God."

"Maureen, men have suffered under the patriarchy too,' Ariel said, shaking her head. "They lost Mother God, too."

"Yeah, yeah, yeah... poor men," Maureen said. "I'm a little cranky without my morning coffee."

"We see that," Ariel said.

Katie ignored Maureen. She turned to Ariel. "So in a way, the red lady who helped you when you were young was like a guardian angel but also a real lady—three different women actually. And the same as how Grandmother comes to you. But somehow this red lady energy is also the same energy as Mary Magdalene, right? She came to you as *la femme rouge*. I'm not sure how all this works."

"I'm not sure how it all works either. It's a mystery, but somehow they're all manifestations of *la femme rouge*." Ariel said. "And they've all helped me love myself, and see that I have the red spirit energy too." She took a big drink of water. She saw the sign for the Chartres turn-off up ahead.

"We need to exit there."

"Okay," Katie said. "But what happened at the end of the summer with Henri? Did you go back to Montreal?" Katie asked.

Ariel thought back over the sequence of events.

"I don't think I can take another example of how hard women work to sort out relationships with men." Maureen said. "So please tell us what miracle caused ol' Henri to wake the fuck up!"

Ariel chuckled. "You know what, Maureen? Now that I look back, I think somehow it was GPS that got through to Henri and re-routed him."

CHAPTER TWENTY SIX

ARIEL

The end of summer approached. Henri and I had been emailing sporadically but hadn't talked. So I was surprised to find a rather panicked voicemail from him one evening after returning from a walk.

His older brother Jean's wife had died in an accident. Her car skidded and swerved off the road, hitting an embankment, and she was killed instantly. Henri was flying up to his hometown in Quebec for the funeral. He sounded really shaken. I'd only met Jean and his wife a couple of times. Neither spoke English, and my French was limited, so we hadn't really connected. But of course, I was sorry for Jean's loss and for the family. I called Henri back but he didn't pick up so I left a message with my condolences.

He didn't respond. I called again to check in on him but the phone went straight to voicemail. A few days later he sent me a text asking if he could come see me in Tucson. He had some important things to talk about and didn't want to do it over the phone.

This made me anxious. After the amazing EMDR with Devra and the joy and ease of being the center of my own life again, I didn't know how

I'd feel seeing Henri. But I wasn't ready to end the relationship either. I truly didn't know what he was going to say, but I realized it was time he and I talked. So I said yes, he should come to Tucson.

A few days later, I picked him up at the airport. We held each other so long at the arrivals area that security had to ask us to move on or risk a ticket. His face looked different—more open somehow. We had reservations at Hacienda del Sol, my favorite place to eat, for lunch. As we sat in the garden courtyard, he told me what had transpired over the last week.

Henri closed up the boat and flew up north to his hometown in Quebec for the funeral. When he arrived at Jean's house, he was shocked. His older, rather rigid, stoic brother was a wreck, and the house was in shambles. Clearly Jean had been on a drinking binge; the kitchen table was covered in photo albums, pictures of his wife and their kids were taken out and strewn across the table. Henri set his bag down and made some coffee.

Henri asked what he could do to help, thinking about getting ready for the funeral, but his brother erupted in grief. Jean looked at him with watery eyes and said, "Don't do what I did! Anne was a modest woman. She didn't have a lot of dreams... she spent her life taking care of me and the kids—so we could have our dreams."

Jean pushed an open scrap book toward Henri. "Look at this," he said.

Henri thumbed through a few pages: there were magazine cutouts of the Eiffel tower, the Arc de Triomphe, and other Paris monuments. There were notes in flowery handwriting about restaurants and museums and stores to visit on the Champs Elysees.

Jean slapped the table with his hand. "Her big dream was to visit Paris. She wanted to rent an apartment and stay a month to experience what it was like to live there. She'd been putting this scrapbook together for God knows how long—I kept delaying, telling her we'd go after all the kids were out of the house, after I retired, etc. And now she's dead. Killed twenty kilometers from where she spent her whole life."

Jean's face collapsed, he put his head in his hands and just sobbed.

Henri was uncomfortable. He didn't know what to say. Finally, he managed, "It's not your fault Jean."

Jean looked up at Henri. "Yes, it is. Every summer for the last ten years, I said, 'next year.' Because *I* didn't want to go to Paris; I wanted to stay here and fish and stay up in the family camp in the woods with the boys. I couldn't even give her one month of something she wanted."

Henri didn't say anything. Jean got up and said he was going to lie down for a while. The funeral wasn't until late afternoon. Their older sister had done all the organizing and was hosting a meal after the service. Henri got up and put some of the dishes in the sink. The trash stank so he took it outside to put in the bin. He looked across the village where he'd grown up. He took in the bay and the tall, wooded mountains.

It was a warm fall day, and he didn't want to go back inside. Jean's sadness and remorse hung in the air, heavy and dark. Henri decided to take a walk along the bay. He was going to go back to the house, but he said something pulled him to the graveyard behind the village church. He hadn't visited his mother's grave since she'd passed.

As he stood looking at the headstone, something struck him that he'd never thought about before. Except for her name and dates of birth and death, the only thing it said about her was, "loving wife and mother." These words, carved into stone, caught him. Henri thought about what Jean had just said. He hadn't ever made the time to do something that was for his wife—one of her dreams. She'd spent thirty years taking care of Jean and the boys, and he couldn't give her a month.

Henri stared at his mother's grave. She was a dynamic woman in so many ways. She'd done so much for the community, the church, did the book keeping for his father's business, and raised seven kids, most of whom went on to have advanced degrees and successful lives. But the only thing it said was, "loving wife and mother." Henri had complex feelings regarding his mother but for the first time he truly understood that she'd given everything for them. He had no idea what her dreams might have been. And nobody even thought to ask. They never considered that the women in their lives wouldn't be fulfilled simply by being with them.

We'd finished our lunch and most of a bottle of Sauvignon Blanc. Henri was crying softly, and I reached out and held his hand. We didn't say anything for a few minutes. Then he looked up at me and smiled.

He told me he could see how much better I was doing away from him and his lifestyle. And he couldn't fault me for wanting to take care of myself and succeed in my own right. After all, that's what he had done his whole life. It took the events of the last weeks for him to truly realize how important my dream was to me. And that if pushed, I would choose it over him. He hadn't fully grasped the way he had subtly, and sometimes not so subtly, been undermining me. He'd only known the paradigm of his mother and sisters—to forgo their own dreams for relationships.

Henri said he actually envied my sense of purpose and the tenacity to keep following it. It helped him to look at what he wanted more deeply. He'd all but forgotten what had brought him to working with wine in the first place. Then he told me he had an idea—a proposal.

Henri got up from his chair, took something out of his jacket pocket, and got down on one knee, his blue eyes lit with emotion. He pulled out a little blue box tied with white ribbon and handed it to me.

I untied the ribbon and opened the box; inside there was a folded piece of paper. I opened it.

This rare jewel symbolizes you. I give this to you as a token of my love and respect and promise to always support your dreams as if they were my own.

Pasted to the bottom of the paper was a magazine cut out of a Provencal style house set in an idyllic vineyard.

I looked up at Henri. I didn't completely understand. He took my hand and said, "We need a place that can hold both our dreams. How about southern France? Let's find a place right in the heart of Mary Magdalene territory. You can further your research, your exploration of the divine feminine, and write. And I'll get back to the land and work on creating a soulful, artisanal red wine. It will be our kingdom as conscious equal partners.

CHAPTER TWENTY SEVEN

"Well, needless to say, I accepted the proposal. A couple of months later we found the property, and that is how I came to live near the bones of my muse. And the rest, as they say, is history—and her-story," Ariel said.

"Took him long enough!" Maureen said.

Ariel ignored her comment.

"I love this ending, Ariel!" Katie said. "You are an inspiration."

Ariel smiled. "Looking back, I see we were building a new paradigm. It takes courage to look inside ourselves and be authentic in a relationship. We must face these fears and be spiritual warriors for ourselves. That is the only way we'll find the love we deserve."

"Oh, for God's sake," Maureen said, fanning her hand back and forth. "That's enough!"

Ariel pointed to the road. "Take a right here," she said.

Katie turned on the indicator, and then looked up ahead, catching a glimpse of the cathedral in the rosy morning light. She had to admit, it was majestic; maybe it was the lack of sleep or the all-night drive, but she felt a current of excitement as they approached.

"Maureen, where should we park?" Ariel asked, turning to Maureen in the back seat.

"Keep following this main road. We'll circle through town. I know a good place only a couple blocks from the Cathedral."

Katie nodded, following Maureen's directions, and parked in a small lot. They all got out of the car and stretched. The sun was still low on the horizon and the air was fresh. Katie fished through her camera bag and put the essential equipment into her knapsack. Ariel had the file with the drawings of the Tree of Life and the sketch of the Chartres cathedral floor plan.

They walked across the cobblestone lane, to the south side of the cathedral. Maureen pointed with her cane to a small café. "We have a few minutes until they open the south entrance. Let's get a coffee and make a game plan," Maureen said.

"Good idea," Ariel said. They sat at a table facing the cathedral.

"They open the side door at 8:30 AM, but most people don't start to arrive until nine or ten o'clock. I think you should go inside and while they're busy moving the chairs off the labyrinth, walk the points that would relate to the Tree of Life structure. Make sure you also show Katie the 'Blue Virgin.' It is some of the oldest stained glass in the cathedral. You'll see this image repeated: Mary on a throne with Jesus in her lap. But it's not a baby, it is a grown Jesus giving the blessing with his right hand and holding tablets in his left."

"What do you mean 'you'?" Katie asked. "You're not coming with us?"

"Well, I had a little issue with the cathedral a few years back, and…" Maureen said.

"And what?" Katie asked.

"When I first moved to France I'd come up to Paris and Chartres quite often. And a few times I brought people here to walk the labyrinth and experience the energy and the church didn't like it," Maureen said.

"The church doesn't like people to experience the energy of the place? I don't get it. You must have done something." Katie eyed Maureen suspiciously.

"As I recall, Maureen," Ariel said. "You got into some trouble because you and a friend were trying to measure the frequency of magnetic energy over the labyrinth without permission."

"Well, yeah," Maureen said. "And we did record the magnetic field of the earth at 18,000 megahertz right over the center, which is really high, but then they threw us out. And banned me from returning."

"I didn't know they banned you from returning," Ariel said.

Katie said. "How can they ban you from a place of God?"

"Well, my dearie, they can and they do! Have you not gleaned anything from your aunt's account of patriarchal bullshit?" Maureen said.

"Maureen, can we get back to the present?" Ariel said. "I didn't know you wouldn't be coming with us."

Maureen shook her head forlornly. "Look, I don't want to cause you any trouble. It's been a couple of years since the fiasco, but they would probably recognize me if I came in with you. My job was to get you here so you could find what you need for your proposal."

"It's okay," Ariel said. "Katie and I can manage."

"But I'm warning you, they don't want anyone discussing energy, ancient cultures, the zodiac, the power of the feminine archetypes, etc. Just regular old Catholicism, please! So when you and Katie go in, you can't discuss what we've been talking about openly. And don't stop anywhere too long. Look like normal tourists, take pictures but keep it moving."

"You're exaggerating, right?" Katie said, looking at Maureen.

"I am not!" Maureen said. "They are militant about anything not in their narrative." At this, Ariel nodded her agreement.

Maureen took a sip of her second café au lait. Ariel and Katie finished their coffees and Ariel checked the time.

"Okay," Ariel said. "We should go. So Katie, we are going to take a quick look around then walk the Kabbalah diagram. I've got the map. If you could photograph what structures or art are at each point, I can analyze it later."

"Got it," Katie said.

Ariel looked at Maureen. "We'll meet you back here soon—say, at 10:30?"

Maureen nodded and gave them a thumbs up.

Ariel and Katie crossed the street and walked up the massive stone steps which lead to the south door. The cathedral was nearly empty and their footsteps seemed to reverberate in the sanctified air. Ariel stopped in front of a large stained glass panel. Katie got her camera and focused on the incredibly vibrant Mary in luminous blue robes against a backdrop of ruby red. Just as Maureen described, the Jesus in Mary's lap was full grown. Ariel stood at her side looking at the panel. She leaned closer and whispered, "What do you think it means that he is full grown? Normally it's Mary with baby Jesus, right?" Katie asked.

Ariel nodded. "This design is what the Church calls 'the wisdom seat.' Mother Mary represents either the celestial mother, who holds the wisdom, or the structure of the Church, which allows Jesus' teachings to be presented."

A chill went through Katie.

"And there are a lot more of these 'wisdom seats' here. The mission of Bernard de Clairvaux, who organized the original nine Templars, was to build structures which he called, 'the Earthly palace of the Queen of Heaven,'" Ariel whispered. "They were establishing these Gothic cathedrals to honor Mother God. All are dedicated to Notre Dame, Our Lady—Mother God."

Katie looked at her aunt, she seemed to be in a kind of trance as she spoke.

"Maybe I'm just reaching to find connections, but it just occurred to me that Mother Mary is associated with *binah* in the Christian Kabbalah, and Magdalene with *malchut*. *Binah*, celestial Mother, Queen of Heaven, Mother Mary, all saying the same thing. And Magdalene, the daughter, the lower that seeks to unite with the upper. Both Marys represent vital aspects of the feminine. And this aligns with one of the esoteric meanings of the Star of David, uniting the upper and lower feminine, the *shekinah,* as well," Ariel said. Then she nodded her head to the left. "Okay let's keep moving, I want to show you a few things before we walk the Kabbalah points."

Katie followed Ariel, who stopped to point to a large window. Each panel was a sign of the zodiac. Katie photographed each. "Wow," she said. "I've never seen that in a church before."

335

They continued on, Ariel walking quickly with Katie trailing behind her. Katie looked around and tried to take in the immensity of the stone columns, the incredibly ornate rose windows. She felt overwhelmed by the magnitude of the cathedral but didn't want to stop and mess up Ariel's plan, so she kept walking, following Ariel around the cathedral until they were near the main entrance. Ariel stopped in front of a vertical stained glass panel of a tree. Ariel pointed and described each of the seven squares, one on top of the next.

"This is the Tree of Jesse. Jesse is King David's father. These are Jesus' ancestors: Jesse is the base of the tree, then David, Solomon, Roboam and Abia. Now look, the sixth square is Mother Mary, and above her at the top of the tree is Jesus," Ariel said.

Katie took photos of all the squares using her telephoto lens. When she had taken all the shots, she turned to Ariel.

"Ah, is this a coincidence?" Katie whispered. "It seems awfully similar to the Tree of Life—seven branches, but with Jesus on top."

Ariel turned to Katie, eyebrows raised as she nodded her head.

Suddenly, the bells rang. Katie jumped, then giggled nervously. A few more people were wandering around the cathedral and the church staff had almost finished removing the wooden chairs from the labyrinth.

Ariel whispered to Katie. "Okay let's try and map out the Tree of Life points." She pulled out the Kabbalah map she had superimposed on the cathedral's floor plan the night before and leaned close to Katie. "We'll start over here at *malchut*, the first point if we go from the root of the Tree up. Normally the *sephirot* are numbered from the first at the top to the tenth at the bottom, *malchut*. But the process of enlightenment from Jesus' teaching to Magdalene starts from the root and goes up, ultimately uniting with Mother God. And this is how it is laid out in the cathedral-*malchut* is the starting point here at the main entrance."

"*Pardon, madames,*" a voice said. Ariel and Katie turned. A petite elderly woman stood behind them. Ariel slipped the file under her arm and smiled politely at the woman.

"*Oui?*" Ariel said.

Katie held her breath.

"Oh, *français or anglais?*" the woman asked.

"*Anglais c'est plus facile pour nous,*" Ariel said.

"I noticed you ladies have been here since we opened. You seem captivated by our glorious cathedral," the woman said in nearly flawless English.

"Absolutely," Ariel said. "I've brought my niece; she and I are particularly intrigued by Mary and the wisdom seat."

The woman smiled the subtle catlike smile that French women seem to possess. "Ahh, yes. *Bon.* Did you notice the center of the labyrinth is aligned with the wisdom seat stained glass at the very front of the cathedral? The architects were really conveying a message, weren't they?"

Ariel smiled. "Yes, they seemed to be exalting the feminine," she said.

"Indeed. I've been a volunteer guide here for many years and I never tire of pointing out the importance of Mary on the Pillar as well," the woman said, looking pointedly at Ariel. "Spend some time contemplating her message, she has secrets to reveal."

Ariel nodded slowly, her gaze fixed on the enigmatic woman. "Thank you, we will," Ariel said. "I didn't catch your name," she added as the woman began to walk away.

337

"Marie-Claude. They call me the grandmother of Chartres," she said, smiling.

Katie shot Ariel a look.

"Pleased to meet you, Marie Claude," Ariel said.

She nodded then turned and walked away.

"Are you kidding me," Katie whispered. "Did you catch that? The *grandmother* of Chartres? You can't make this stuff up!"

Ariel chuckled. "Welcome to my world," she said, and Katie was reminded that just a few days before, she had thought her aunt's tendency to make meaning of things was sweet. "Okay, let's do this. We start here in front of the main door, this rectangular stone is different from the rest, I believe it is *malchut*, the root of the Tree.. The center of the labyrinth, *yesod*, the next *sephirot* going up the Tree. I'm going to cut across the labyrinth instead of walking it to avoid confusion. But you should walk the labyrinth; it's special, the oldest complete labyrinth in Europe. I'll wait for you on the other side of it and we'll continue on from there. I'm counting my steps to measure it out as best I can," Ariel said. "Let's make our way to the front of the cathedral then see what we've got. On the left side of the altar there's a small pillar with a sculpture of Mary on it; let's see if we can figure out what Marie-Claude was talking about."

"Okay," Katie whispered.

Ariel stepped on the large rectangular stone embedded in the floor at the center of the entrance of the cathedral. She then walked slowly to the entrance of the labyrinth. Katie walked close behind. Ariel stood at the opening and Katie saw her pull a pen from the sleeve of her shirt and write something on the palm of her left hand. She snapped a few shots around her, quickly. Then Ariel walked around the labyrinth and stood on the far side, gesturing to Katie.

Katie began the labyrinth walk. It was a strange sensation to take the turns and get very close to the center only to be led out to the periphery again. Then the opposite would happen; when she thought she'd keep circling the outer part, the path would quickly lead her to the center. Katie watched the steps in front of her and realized there was a pattern of moving in and out of four quadrants until the path led her to the flower pattern at the center of the labyrinth.

Katie stepped into each of the six petals of the flower shape before she stepped into the very center. She made a mental note to ask Ariel about the design later, as she'd found it curious ever since she first saw it in Charpentier's book.

Ariel turned and looked at Katie pointedly, then faced the back of the church looking up. Katie followed her gaze. Ariel turned around slowly and faced the altar. She looked up and stared at the stained glass at the very front of the cathedral. Katie used her telephoto lenses and clicked photos of another Mary as the wisdom seat, aligned with the center of the labyrinth just like Marie-Claude had said.

Then something caught her eye. Directly behind the altar was an immense white marble sculpture of Mary rising from the clouds surrounded by angels. She had a feeling this was important but didn't know why. Katie heard shuffling behind her. She turned and realized people had entered the labyrinth and begun the meditative walk. She stepped on the dark stones that led out of the top of the labyrinth, near the front of the cathedral, and joined Ariel; then they walked together, measuring out the other *sephirot*. Ariel stopped at each to write the number of steps she took on her palm. Each time they stopped, Katie took photos around the point so they could examine the details later.

When they had mapped out all ten points, Ariel whispered. "You know, everything seems to line up with the Tree of Life diagrammatically. Except, I expected the Assumption of Mary to be at the top and it isn't. It's where..." Ariel stopped talking. She studied the diagram. "Holy shit!" she exclaimed. Then she covered her mouth, her words echoing in the cathedral around them. A few people turned to look. "Sorry," she whispered sheepishly.

"What is it?" Katie whispered.

"It looks like the Assumption of Mary isn't the tenth point, as we thought. It's *da'at*," Ariel said. "The mysterious eleventh point."

Katie looked over Ariel's shoulder at the diagram on the paper. "I thought you said there were only ten points on the Tree," Katie said.

"There's an eleventh, but it flickers in and out. Most diagrams of Tree of Life don't include it but many descriptions allude to it: *da'at*. It is said *da'at* is the bridge between the lower world and the upper world. It sits between *tiferet* and *keter* on the central column. And it hasn't totally manifested yet, so the bridge isn't completely established. Now I'm wondering if this is related to bringing back an aspect of the feminine. Maybe it flickers in and out depending on the scholar, and none of them, as far as I know, have connected it to the revelation of the feminine."

Ariel walked to the area behind the altar to the Assumption of Mary sculpture, counting her steps. "If this is *da'at*, it indicates that Mary is the key to the manifestation of this energy center. Number 11 is a master number meaning divine inspiration, manifestation of spirit."

Katie tried to take in what Ariel was saying. Then she shared the feeling she'd had in the center of the labyrinth: that the sculpture of Mary was very important, somehow.

Ariel didn't take her eyes off the sculpture. "You know, there's a prophecy from a sixteenth century master Kabbalist called the Ari. When women elevate to the same status as men, spiritually and materially, this will be the final redemption, and usher in a golden age."

Katie grimaced. "That sounds really sexist," she said.

"It could, but I think it isn't. He was simply pointing out the situation at the time and still now to some degree. Until quite recently, women haven't had access to spiritual study. And for the most part they still don't have material equality. The prophecy was simply stating the facts. Don't forget, women couldn't openly study the Kabbalah until the 1970s! Before that, Jesus was the last person to share the concepts with women—and look what happened to him."

Katie nodded her head, connecting the dots. "I see what you're saying. It could represent all women, or maybe the Magdalene. Didn't you say that he gave her the name 'watch tower'?"

Ariel nodded, still deep in thought.

Katie snapped some more photos of the sculpture and points of reference from where they stood at the sculpture. Ariel reached into the pocket of her coat and took out her phone.

"I just got a text from Maureen," Ariel said. "She says they're opening the underground crypt for the 11AM mass. She wants us to meet her near the entrance and go in together."

"But I thought she couldn't go inside the cathedral?" Katie asked.

Ariel shrugged. "Well technically it's *under* the cathedral," she said, smirking. She looked at Katie. "Let's go see what she's up to."

CHAPTER TWENTY EIGHT

They left the cathedral from the main entrance and walked around the building, keeping an eye out for Maureen. Ariel pointed to the metal grate, now open, at the top of the stone stairwell leading to the crypt. Katie took a few photos of the gargoyles and stone sculptures surrounding the entrance. The bells rang; mass would start soon.

"Where's Maureen?" Katie asked. She felt a tap on her shoulder and jumped.

"It's me, kiddo!" Maureen whispered.

Katie turned to see a woman who looked like a peasant from another era, with a long purple skirt and a black veil wrapped loosely around her head and shoulders. Except this peasant wore a pair of oversized glasses.

"Oh my God, Maureen," Ariel whispered. "Where did you get that outfit?"

"At the souvenir shop in the village," Maureen said. "The glasses are mine. You know, I was sitting there enjoying my coffee when I got this strong feeling we should go to the underground chapel. How did it go with mapping out the Kabbalah points?"

"Good, but of all the alignments between any structures and the points, the surprising one was the huge Assumption of Mary sculpture behind the altar. I think it's on the point of *da'at*—which is really strange, because most Tree of Life diagrams don't even include *da'at*. They say it's the bridge between worlds and hasn't fully manifested yet. So that would mean this huge Assumption of Mary sculpture is on that point in the floor plan."

"It's a little ways behind the altar, right?" Maureen asked.

Ariel nodded. Then she told Maureen about the cryptic message that Marie-Claude gave them about Mary on the Pillar.

Maureen was uncharacteristically quiet for a minute. "So this woman told you there was something important about Mary on the Pillar?" she asked slowly. "You know, I think it may be connected to the placement of the sculpture."

"How so? There's a small virgin on the pillar to the left of the altar, but it's not connected to the points," Ariel said.

"I don't think that's what she was talking about," Maureen whispered. "It's not that pillar. There's another pillar, an enormous one, in the underground passage built on the original Druidic mound. Remember, there were chapels and, before that, Mother God temples built on this site through the ages. The pillar marks the exact center of those old sites, but since it's below the floor of the Gothic Cathedral, most people don't know it's there. For some reason, even though the public wouldn't see it, the Templars thought it was important to mark the site. And I think it may be directly under that big Assumption of Mary sculpture."

Ariel's eyes widened. "Can we get in to see it?"

"The underground is closed off except for the chapel at mass. You have to get permission ahead of time from the church to go down there, and only with one of their sanctified guides," Maureen said.

"How long would that take?" Ariel asked.

"Days, if not weeks," Maureen said.

"So that's not going to help us now," Ariel said, a tone of dejection in her voice.

The bells rang again.

"But Ariel, maybe we can put all this together with the floor plan in the Charpentier book. We can still try and map out this idea of Mary on the Pillar," Katie said, trying to give Ariel a lift.

"I've studied all the books and have never seen even a photograph of the ancient pillar," Maureen said. "I only know about it because I went on the tour."

"Ugh," Ariel moaned. "Well, Maureen's all dressed up for Mass, so let's at least go into the underground chapel."

Maureen led them down the stone steps, leaning on Ariel for support. Katie barely had a moment to take in the beautiful black Madonna as they descended underground. There were a number of parishioners filing into the long damp room. A young man with a broom and clanging keys hanging from his belt swept the back of the crypt chapel.

Before they reached the back row of wooden chairs, Maureen started to groan.

"What's wrong, Maureen?" Ariel asked.

"Hah, plenty!" Maureen whispered. She reached up and pulled Ariel down close to her. "Listen, I've got an idea. I'm going to try and distract

345

this guy before the priest comes down. You two can make a run for it. Just go around the screen behind the altar and keep following the underground passage. It should take you to the pillar."

"No way!" Ariel whispered. "We can't do that, they'll know we're back there."

Maureen groaned again, dropping to her knees. She let go of her cane and pulled Ariel and Katie close to her.

"No, they won't. Just stay back there until I give you the all clear. You need to go, Ariel. You need to see this, feel the energy. I didn't tell you this before, but when my friend and I were measuring the energy centers, the area at the back of the altar—where the Assumption of Mary is—was really high, too. I was focused on the labyrinth so didn't think that much about it. But that pillar is important; it sits on the sacred energy point of the Druids. These guys built the cathedral right on it for a reason, and for some reason, they built this giant pillar that no one would ever see. Go do your witchy stuff. Go feel the energy," Maureen whispered.

Katie nodded to Ariel. Ariel looked back and forth between Katie and Maureen. "C'mon, Ariel, let's go find this pillar," Katie whispered.

Maureen winked at Katie, letting out a louder groan as she doubled over again. The young man who was sweeping the back walked over towards them.

"*Qu'est-ce qui arrive?*" he asked.

"*Je ne sais pas!*" Ariel responded. She looked about frenetically. "*Ma tante, ma tante est très malade. s'il vous plait, trouvez aide!*"

The young man looked completely ill at ease. Ariel and Maureen amped up their game. Maureen bent forward and did a rather awkward collapse onto the stone floor.

"Oh, *ma tante!*" Ariel exclaimed.

The man looked down at the large hulk of purple and black on the floor with another distressed woman crouching over her and ran up the stairs to find help.

"Go!" Maureen whispered. "Find the pillar, then hide out until mass is over and people start leaving. I'll send you a text when it's safe to come back into the chapel."

Katie peeked around at the entrance to the chapel and saw the young man talking excitedly to a priest. "There's the priest, there's the priest!" Katie said out of the corner of her mouth.

"Go now!" Maureen said. Ariel stood up and glanced at Katie, then led the way straight up the aisle and slipped behind the screen at the back of the altar. Katie followed at her heels, willing them to be invisible, not daring to look back until they were behind the screen.

Maureen was now flailing her arms and legs, shrieking in a way that looked like part tantrum and part seizure. The young man and the priest were crouched around Maureen, trying to calm her. The smattering of parishioners all looked behind them, witnessing the spectacle at the back of the chapel.

"C'mon!" Ariel said. They ran until they got to the large, strange modern glass partition. It took up nearly the width of the underground passage. They squeezed sideways around the edge and kept running until they got to a metal gate. It was locked with a massive iron padlock. Ariel shook it with both hands. "Shit!" she exclaimed.

347

Katie pulled at the heavy metal gate to no avail. Then she looked at the ancient lock. *It can't be that sophisticated*, she thought. Sweeping her too-long bangs aside, she pulled the black bobby pin out of her hair, holding it up for Ariel to see.

"Is this cliché or what?" Katie smiled.

"Well, try it!" Ariel said excitedly.

Katie poked around with the bobby pin, trying to feel for some kind of trigger. She felt a raised part in the back of the lock, but the hair pin wasn't strong enough to press it. "We need something else, something stronger," Katie said.

Ariel reached in her bag and pulled out a Swiss army knife. She opened the little nail file and handed it to Katie.

"That might work," Katie said. She kept the bobby pin in and slid the file underneath to reinforce the pressure. Just as the lock clicked, they heard the echo of men's voices. "Shit!" they both whispered simultaneously. Ariel opened the lock. Both women pressed against the heavy metal door and it creaked open as they slid through. They pushed it back closed and Katie looked up at Ariel. "Should we put the lock back?"

Ariel looked at her niece. "Yeah, good idea! We can always open it again to get back out, but this way, nobody will think we made it past here."

Katie reached around and put the lock back facing out like nothing had happened. There wasn't any more lighting, so they both pulled out their cell phones to use the flashlight. They walked quickly until they got to a curve in the passage. Then, they both stopped. There was a raised platform, and upon it, a semi-circle of excavated stone, revealing the base of a large pillar.

"There it is," Ariel whispered.

Katie took shots of the large stone base and the walls and apses around them.

"Imagine: people gathered here since megalithic times for ceremony. This pillar was built at the apex," Ariel said. She counted out steps from the base to the outer wall, writing a number on her forearm. Katie took a few shots of her aunt against the backdrop of the ancient church wall. "If it does turn out that the Assumption of Mary is built right on top of this pillar, and it is aligned with *da'at* the eleventh *sephirot*," Ariel said. "I think we have something big here."

They heard men's voices again. Katie looked around and gestured to Ariel. There was a narrow passageway to the side of the platform with a wooden gate across the entrance. They climbed over it and walked a few steps into the dark passage, and then turned off their lights, feeling their way along the rough stone walls. They came to another turn and waited, crouching low and trying to still their breathing as they listened for footsteps.

After a few moments, Katie realized the men must have continued along the main passageway. They sat in silence for a few more minutes. Then Ariel whispered, "You know, the Black Madonna we passed by the altar is called, 'Our Lady Under the Earth.' It's a replica of one lost in the sixteenth century. This place has always been dedicated to the Virgin since Celtic times."

"It's like the builders were showing that the Goddess was here, under the earth, but would one day rise up, so they built a giant pillar to help lift her. Taking her out of the darkness and into the light," Katie said.

"You're really getting the hang of this ancient divine feminine stuff!"

Ariel said. "The Goddess rises from the earth, bridging the lower world with the upper. Reaching the heavens. Mary on the Pillar. Mary and Jesus at the top of the Jesse Tree. Magdalene, rising up through the Tree of Life. *malchut* to *binah*, the daughter to the mother. The vessel to the seat of Mother God. I think this is a big piece, Katie—maybe the central theme in my proposal. We not only have the Kabbalah Tree of Life diagrammatically laid out in the floor plan, but it turns out that the missing link, the bridge that is needed to activate the whole thing, is the elevation of the feminine with the eleventh *sephirot*!"

"Wow, it's amazing," Katie whispered excitedly. "This whole place is centered around the elevation of the feminine—literally!"

"I'd say we're somewhere behind the pillar right now. This passage was probably carved out to build it," Ariel said.

Ariel and Katie sat back against the stone, comfortable in the dark, and just tried to take it all in.

They both fell silent, each with their own thoughts.

Katie realized she'd never felt more alive. It was the first time she'd ever felt so passionate about something other than a man. For years, she'd felt weaker without a man, always longing to feel support. Maybe the only thing she needed all along was to be really seen, understood. And Ariel had given her that. Ariel had really seen her, encouraged her and trusted her. Maybe that was the key—we only need that one person who sees us and loves us so we can soar. Katie thought about Ariel's story of the women that had come into her life, just when she needed them. Ariel was like that for her; she'd pulled her up, lifted her, like Mary on the Pillar. Katie let out a sigh.

"You okay?" Ariel whispered.

"Yeah," Katie said. "I think I just understood the meaning of the elevation of the feminine."

"Did you just have a moment?" Ariel asked with a smile in her voice.

Katie nodded, and then realized Ariel couldn't see it. "Yeah, I did. I feel somehow—whole. I know that sounds weird, but, Ariel, you pulled me up. You're like my *binah*."

Ariel was quiet a moment. "Well I can't take too much credit," she said. "We *are* sitting on an ancient energy center, under one of the most powerful cathedrals in the world, so I'm not surprised by what you feel."

Katie nodded. "I feel, well, whole," she said.

"A woman whole unto herself," Ariel whispered. "That's actually what *virgin* means, you know, in the ancient definition," Ariel said.

"Not a person who hasn't had sex?" Katie said.

"No, that was misunderstood by the Catholic Church. Mother Mary as virgin, they made it about whether she'd had sex to conceive rather than understanding it as describing her stature. Of course she had sex; she was just whole, anyway. No man owned her, and partnership only added to her wholeness, instead of taking something away," Ariel said.

"Wow," Katie said. "Mary Magdalene known as repentant prostitute and Mother Mary as chaste. Always about women and sex with the patriarchy."

"That's right, sister," Ariel said. She pulled her cell phone out of her pocket to check the time. "Should only be another few minutes until mass is over."

"Should we start making our way back?" Katie said. "Seems like the passage is clear; I haven't heard voices for a while."

"Yeah, let's." Ariel leaned forward and stood up slowly. Then they followed the narrow passage back to the wooden gate, waiting to check for voices. But it was quiet. They climbed over the gate and stood by the pillar. Ariel said a prayer under her breath. Katie got a few more photos of the surroundings and then they made their way back toward the altar.

"Did I tell you about the star Spica in the Virgo constellation?" Ariel whispered.

Katie shook her head.

"Spica is the star associated with the divine feminine. According to the ancients, she's the brightest star in Virgo, the virgin," Ariel said. "Sue told me the Sumerians held annual rituals every year in August when Spica, and the whole Virgo constellation, went into the underworld, which means being so close to the sun as to be invisible to the observer. These rituals honoring the death and rebirth of the divine feminine were the predecessors of the feast day of the Assumption of the Virgin Mary, on August 15. When the Virgin died and was lifted into the heavens, that was an echo of the earlier ceremonies held for Virgo, the Virgin, going to the sun."

"Wow, that's really interesting," Katie said.

"Another example of how Virgo, the Goddess, was around long before the church's version of her."

Katie wanted to tell Ariel about an idea that came to her during the drive to Chartres. She was about to say something when she heard the ping of Ariel's phone.

"Mass is over and people are leaving the crypt chapel," Ariel said, reading the text from Maureen. They walked quickly back to the iron gate and Katie reached through the bars, turning the lock toward her. Then she used the bobby pin and nail file, fishing around until she heard the click. "Have tools, will travel," Katie said.

"Indeed!" Ariel said, smiling.

They stopped when they got to the modern glass partition to see if they heard anyone. They slipped by, this time stopping by the holy well. Katie took several photos as Ariel peeked out from the back of the altar. Nearly everyone was gone; only the young custodian remained, straightening out the rows of chairs. When he turned his back, Ariel and Katie came around the altar and made their way to the aisle. The young man looked at them quizzically as they passed by.

Ariel gave him a little wave. "*Bonne journée*," she said sweetly.

He just shook his head as they walked to the stairs and made their way out of the crypt. Katie held up her hand to shield her eyes from the sun.

"Maureen said she'd meet us at the café," she said.

They crossed the large plaza, walking on the far side of the street and made their way to the café. Maureen lounged, back in her regular clothes, taking in the warm sun.

"Maureen!" Katie said, rushing up to her and giving her a hug.

"Oh, what's this? It feels good, like appreciation," Maureen said, hugging Katie awkwardly with one arm.

Ariel pulled out a chair next to her friend and gave her shoulder a squeeze. "Maureen, you are a star! Who knew you could act like that?" Ariel sat down, smiling.

"It was impressive!" Katie said.

"So what happened after we got behind the altar?" Ariel asked.

"Oh, I flailed for a while, then I let them help me up and bring me upstairs. I told them both of you had left the crypt and gone looking for help. They weren't totally convinced and went looking for you. That's when I got out of Dodge and hung out in the park until mass was over. Then a very nice young *gendarme* helped me across the plaza back to our café."

They laughed at the absurdity of it.

"You two must have hidden well," Maureen said, looking between Ariel and Katie.

"We did. We managed to get past this big iron gate. Katie popped the lock with a bobby pin and nail file. Then we hid in a narrow tunnel behind the pillar. So I believe we were really in the heart of the most ancient part of the cathedral."

"And the pillar is amazing," Katie added. "Even I could... you know... *feel* it."

"Excellent! You got to absorb that ancient juju," Maureen said. "I think this all calls for a celebration." Maureen signaled the waiter and ordered a bottle of champagne.

While they waited Maureen turned to Ariel, "Did you get any inspiration down there?"

"I did," Ariel said, nodding. "I think I can present some compelling ideas: Magdalene carrying the Tree of Life to France, the clues at Rennes le Château demonstrate this. With the building of the Gothic cathedrals following the diagram and the *piece de resistance*, Mary on the Pillar, elevating the feminine as the missing link in the Tree of Life. If these ideas don't get the attention of the academics at the conference, I don't know what will!"

"Thank you, Maureen, for getting us down there. I certainly feel elevated, to say the least," Katie said, grinning widely.

The waiter came with a bottle of champagne and three flutes. He popped the cork and poured them each a glass. "What do you celebrate today?" he asked.

Maureen looked at Ariel and Katie. "We celebrate the god-damned feminine in all her glory!"

"Ohh," the waiter said, smiling with uncertainty.

They held up their glasses, and the sun streamed down, lighting up the little bubbles. Ariel looked at Maureen.

"To Mother God!" Ariel said, angling her head cockily.

"To the feminine in all her glory—dark, light and otherwise!" Katie said.

"To Mary Magdalene bringing forward the sacred knowledge!" Ariel said.

"To three unlikely women—who found the Holy Grail!" Maureen said, gleefully.

They clinked glasses and each took a drink.

"To the screenplay I think we should write about all this!" Katie said.

"Hey kid, that's not a bad idea," Maureen said, turning toward Katie. "You know what, it could be like *Da Vinci Code*—for women!"

"Exactly!" Katie exclaimed and they clinked glasses again.

They both looked at Ariel.

"Damn, Katie, that's not a half-bad idea," Ariel said.

They took another drink and were just about to start another round of toasts when Ariel's phone rang. She looked down at the caller ID. "Oh shit!" she said. "I better get this; I forgot to call Henri yesterday and let him know we arrived safely."

Maureen rolled her eyes. "Well, can you make it short? We're just getting going. Tell him we're about sacred women's business," she said, smiling.

They all set their glasses back down. Ariel picked up the phone, winking at Maureen.

"Sorry *darling*, I forgot to call. We ended up driving all night to Chartres," Ariel said. Then she stopped. "Oh yeah, what is it?"

Maureen and Katie watched her, listening intently. Ariel's eyes began to well up with tears. "Of course, that would be okay," she said, her voice cracking.

Maureen motioned impatiently for Ariel to tell them what was going on.

Ariel nodded excitedly. "*Darling*, I need to tell the ladies about this, I'll call you back later okay? Okay, bye-bye."

Ariel hung up the phone. Her eyes were full of tears.

"What's going on?" Maureen asked.

"They just finished the assemblage of the red wine. The one aged in clay jars; it's the first vintage aged this way. Henri says it's the best red yet," Ariel said.

356

"You're crying because of red wine?" Maureen asked, shaking her head.

"He says it has a very special soul. So he wants to call it *la femme rouge* in honor of Mary Magdalene and... me," Ariel said, wiping at her eyes.

Maureen scratched her head. "Well, well," she said.

"That's pretty cool, Ariel," Katie said.

The three women sat quiet a moment.

Then Katie raised her glass. "Well then, how about a toast to *la femme rouge*," she said.

Ariel and Maureen joined her. "To *la femme rouge!*"

THE END

EPILOGUE

Katie and Ariel took their time walking the wooded path. As they ascended the mountain, they discussed the "cavern scene." They had written it in the second act of the screenplay, staying true to the chronological events in Ariel's book.

When they arrived at the mouth of the cavern, some of the crew were taking a break; they'd hauled a lot of equipment up the steep path. It had been an epic fight to get the Dominican monks to allow them access for the filming. In the end, the French government had stepped in, proud of their patrimony and eager to share the Provencal legends with a greater audience.

"Okay, the lighting is ready. Let's get some shots of the stained glass," the director yelled from inside the cavern.

Katie and Ariel followed the crew, stepping carefully over electrical cords and equipment, finding a place along the back wall to stand.

As Ariel turned to look at the stained glass above the mouth of the cavern, her breath caught. It was brilliantly illuminated, beautifully capturing Magdalene writing her gospel, surrounded by the symbols associated with her history: the jar, the crown, the skull, the living cross. Ariel felt a chill run through her as she read the words, etched in the glass, translating them from French. "Until the end of time, we will tell what she did."

ABOUT THE AUTHOR

 Kathleen Medina is a professional intuitive and has been using tarot, numerology, and astrology to guide her clients for twenty-five years. She is the author of: *Tarot A to Z, The Intuitive Tarot Workbook* and *Angel Numbers Journal.* She loves traveling to sacred sites around the world and studying all things mystical. She currently resides in the Caribbean.

Learn more at redspiritwoman.com and follow her on Instagram @redspiritwoman.

Made in the USA
Las Vegas, NV
14 January 2025

16255176R10215